FREEDOM
OF
SCREECH

EDITED BY CRAIG SPECTOR

Old Mill was like a magnet for weird. The human brain, it seemed, had an incredible facility for ignoring the obvious in favor of the comfortable.

—From "The Tree," by David Niall Wilson

He finished by talking about the cross-pollination going on between horror and suspense, mystery, sci- and even teen romance and finally paraphrased King's famous line on Clive Barker. I have seen the future of horror, and it's all over the place. A little glib but what the hell.

Then he opened it up for questions. He got the usual. Where do you get your ideas? How long does it take you to write a novel? Why do you write the kinds of things you do?

That last one, from Eleanor Bradley, seated with Will Harris up front, seemed to have a slight edge to it.

He gathered Ms. Bradley didn't entirely approve. He smiled.

"I try to fight the good fight while I entertain you. So that I tend to start with what pisses me off," he said. "Child abuse, animal abuse, thrill-killers, the legal system."

"But you believe in your own work, right?" said beard-guy.

"Sure. I write cautionary tales, mostly. I hope in some way they're useful. Though a lot of it's just for fun."

"Fun?" It was one of the younger women he thought of as sisters. And she was scowling.

"I get it," he said. "There's a good bit of mayhem in my books, sure. So? You could say the same of any writer in the field."

"That doesn't make it right, though, does it? And we're not talking about any writer in the field. We're talking about you."

He was thinking, who the hell are these people?

From "Group of Thirty," by Jack Ketchum

DEDICATION

For Tess

OBSEQUIOUS AND OBLIGATORY TRIGGER WARNING

How does the old saying go: art should comfort the disturbed and disturb the comfortable?

The stories contained herein are freedom of speech-themed fiction for the dark of heart. It should go without saying, but in this tender and pedantic age I'll say it anyway:

These stories are entertaining and dangerous; they may disturb and challenge you; they might haunt and discomfort you; they may cause nightmares, daymares, and all mares in between; they may by turns shock or appall you, unsettle or distress you, cause you to question your preferred belief system, rattle your cages, or bundle your undies... if they've done their job right.

Side effects might include palpitations, jaw droppage, disrupted digestion, and anal leakage. Well, maybe not the last one, but just in case.

You have been warned.

xoxo,
Craig Spector
Editor, Freedom of Screech
Summer, 2019

ACKNOWLEDGEMENTS

This is my first foray into editorial in a very long time, some very big thanks are in order:

Thanks to David Niall Wilson and David Dodd of Crossroad Press, without whom this book would not exist;

Special thanks to all of my contributors, whose talent, imagination, and good will made this book what it is;

Ginormous and deeply appreciative thanks to MJ Sydney and my gofundme contributors for their generosity and support in getting this project off the ground;

A special thank you to Ashley Davis for her keen editorial assist, early on;

Thanks to my entertainment attorney L. Wayne Alexander of lo these many years, for always having my back when I need it;

Huge thanks to my medical team – Dr. Jody Boggs, Dr. Douglas Kelly, Dr. Mark Fleming, Dr. Wiley Zhu, Dr. Eric Lappinen -- and the Sentara Medical staff, for the excellent care and for working to keep me around a bit longer;

Mucho thanks to Chris Sliwoski of Change.org for helping navigate the ever-shifting bureaucracies;

To my family and friends, with special shout outs to only sister Kim, RC Matheson, Robert Montena and Cheryl Fratello, Kevin Kovelant, Craig Upton, Mercedes Murdock Yardley (miss you, girl), Trish Wilson, Elizabeth Massie, Matt Hayward, Lori Stark Treirweiller, the inimitable Dona Sadock, Georgia R. Buns, and Lacey the amazing rescue pup, for being there, online or IRL, or both.

To my readers, fans, and advocates of free speech everywhere – hoorah, and keep fighting the good fight. We need you more than ever.

And as ever, endless thanks and boundless love to my life partner, best friend, fearless advocate, and beloved wife, Maria Theresa 'Tess' Ugot, for absolutely everything, every day. Love you big time, bebe.

MEET THE EDITOR

Craig Spector is a bestselling author, editor, and screenwriter for feature film and television: his books have millions of copies in print and reprints in nine languages. His work has been published with Bantam Books, Tor/St. Martins, Crossroad Press, and other major and specialty publishers. His previous editorial work includes co-editing the award-winning fiction in *Book of the Dead* and *Still Dead: Book of the Dead 2*.

Spector's film and television work includes A NIGHTMARE ON ELM STREET 5: THE DREAM CHILD and projects for New Line Cinema, Anonymous Content, ABC, NBC, Fox TV, Wonderful World of Disney, and others.

Spector is also an accomplished musician and a graduate of the Berklee College of Music in Boston MA; he has three indie albums out – Resurrection Road (2017), Outposts (2018), and Kicking Cans (2019). He is at work on his fourth, Dangertown (2020). His music is available on amazon, iTunes, CD Baby, Spotify, and wherever fine digital downloads and old school CDs are sold online. You can hear more at www.craigspector-music.com.

Spector lives and works in Virginia Beach VA.

CONTENTS

SIPPING TEA IN TURBULENT TIMES

FOREWORD BY CRAIG SPECTOR

So there I was, sitting on my patio one fine day in the summer of 2017. I was drinking iced tea and reading Facebook posts on my iPhone, yet another political argument that had popped into my feed. That moment's topic *du jour* was freedom of speech.

Like pretty much all political posts on social media, it was rancorous, impassioned, borderline obnoxious, and more about people yelling at each other than anything resembling a dialogue.

After a few too many such entries, I commented to the thread host, a writer and editor known for specializing in controversial posts: *you should do an anthology about this.*

I went about my business, just enjoying the weather, and the day. Other people were commenting—more truculence, more hostile retorts. But no answer from the host. I posted again: *I'm serious, you should really do one.*

A few more minutes went by, still with no response. I thought about it a bit more, then posted: *Never mind, I'm going to do it.*

I private messaged the author, just to sink it in: *Seriously dude, I'm gonna do this. Wanna contribute a story?*

Now, in the time it took to do all this I had compiled a list of writers I would invite to contribute. I also messaged my favorite publisher, David Wilson at Crossroad Press, and asked if he would be interested. In fairly short order, I had initial commitments from some writers of note, and a publisher for the book. That left me time to contemplate exactly what I was getting myself into.

Freedom of Speech. One of our most vital and important Constitutional rights. Something generally considered to be part of the foundational fabric of our society. What does it mean in this modern age?

There is clearly a lot of debate on that these days. Some people are freedom of speech hardliners, believing that all speech should be protected, and that freedom of speech by its very nature is at the heart of what makes America "America." Even ugly speech, stupid speech, ignorant speech. All of it, protected. Because the freedom to speak is the freedom to think, and the freedom to dream. And in this of all times, dreams must be protected.

As an old school lifelong liberal progressive type, I tend toward this definition—like freedom of association and freedom of thought—I find it an essential component to a free society. I'm old enough to remember the struggles of the 60s, when free speech was a battle between the "counterculture" and the "establishment."

But flash forward fifty years, and the counterculture *is* the establishment. And at this juncture--the back half of the second decade of the 21st century--that makes me somewhat of an anachronism: my old school liberal progressivism has been pretty much entirely usurped by new improved versions of those concepts.

One in which only approved people, who say approved things, should be allowed to say anything at all.

Perhaps most surprising to me in this is that most of the resistance I see these days seems to come from the left edge of the sociopolitical spectrum, rather than the right. Don't get me wrong, the right is still the right, and their extreme is as boneheaded and backward as it ever was.

But the brave new thinkers of the radical left envision a world in which only certain types of speech are protected, and all others should be curtailed, squelched, silenced, punished, if not outright banned. If not by the state, then by easily manipulated and craven corporate entities, who readily trade their capitulation for increased control, and bulwarked by the ever-swarming outrage mobs of the internet, ready to click and dox and blame and shame.

Sometimes it seems as if an entire generation has transformed into tongue clucking hall monitors with torches and pitchforks, facing off against tiki-torch inbred wannabes yammering about blood and soil, or something. And absolutely everyone itching for a fight.

It's kind of scary to me. Or funny, in a grim way. Or both.

In particular, and with the advent of certain intersectionalist identitarian ideologues who are working hard to remake this bright new shiny world in their own image... which seems to feature a lot of talk of "smashing" this and "destroying" that... I hear a lot of people saying, with earnest intent: *"freedom of speech does not mean freedom from consequences."*

With rare exception, this caveat seems to be offered with a sense of relished threat, like, sure, go ahead and speak, sucker, see what happens.

That, to me, is even scarier.

In my humble estimation, the right taken to its extreme is, by its nature, authoritarian—it wants to control everything you say and do. Conversely and ironically, the left, taken to its illiberal extreme, is totalitarian—it wants to control everything you say and do and think and feel.

Ah well, said the old school liberal apostate heretic straight white guy in his 60s, with cancer. As another old white guy writer of some note once wrote, *so it goes.*

But as I sat on my porch that fine summer day in 2017, enjoying my semi-retired privilege bubble and tending to my stage four metastatic funfest, I thought, *all of this makes for a natural anthology of dark-hearted short fiction.*

And so, here we are.

The writers who responded represent a fine diversity of thought. Some have been around long enough to be considered living legends. One has sadly left us but his work lives on. Some are just at the outset of their own literary ascent. Some are established professionals, and for some this is their first time in print. Their visions span the socio-political divide and range from today to centuries old.

I am pleased and proud to present them to you, the reader. This is my first editorial jaunt since @1990, the world has changed much since then. But as the old French saying goes, *plus ça change, plus c'est la même chose.* The more things change, the more they stay the same.

Or as David Byrne of The Talking Heads once sang... *same as it ever was, same as it ever was, same as it ever was, same as it ever was....*

Craig Spector
Virginia Beach VA
Spring 2019

KEEPING THE PEACE

BY ELIZABETH MASSIE

"Stick out your tongue."

Alice shook her head.

Mama leaned over, so close eight-year-old Alice could see the tiny pimples on her chin. Mama was holding her embroidery needle between her thumb and forefinger. Around the table, the other children watched without a word as Papa gazed silently at the ceiling.

"Stick out your tongue."

Alice shook her head.

"Alice."

Alice drew her face down to her chest and shook her head.

Mama pinched Alice's leg under the table, the ragged fingernails digging into Alice's flesh, and she cried out. Mama, as quick with punishment as with sewing, jabbed the needle into Alice's tongue. Pain exploded in Alice's mouth and she flopped backward in her chair. "Mama!" she wailed.

"There," said Mama, putting the needle down beside her plate, picking up her fork, and spearing several green beans. Before she put them into her mouth, she gave Alice her no-nonsense stare. "Now, Alice, tell me the rule that you so thoughtlessly broke."

Alice dug tears from her eyes and ran her front teeth back and forth across her tongue, trying to scrape away the pain. "I said...something hurtful."

"That's right," said Mama. "You said something hurtful. You tattled. And what was that thing you said?"

Alice's eyes widened. "I don't wanna say it again!"

"Alice."

"If I say it again, you will stick me again!"

Mama put down her fork. It made a thumping sound that was much louder than it should have been. Around the table, the other children shifted in their seats, watching silently. Papa pulled at his beard. "I want to make sure you know what you did wrong, Alice. The only way I can be sure, is if you tell me."

"But I do know what I did wrong," said Alice.

"Alice."

"Mama, please."

"Alice."

Alice screwed up her face. "I said that Frances didn't shut his eyes when you said grace before supper."

Before Alice could snap her mouth shut, Mama grabbed the tongue and jabbed the needle into it again. Alice screamed and threw her arms around her head.

"You were telling tales, weren't you?" asked Mama.

Alice sobbed, her tongue feeling as if it were swelling twice the size.

"Alice, you were telling tales on your brother, weren't you? You were tattling?"

Alice nodded.

"You will never tell tales on others again, will you?"

Alice shook her head.

"Tell me."

Around her fattening tongue, Alice managed, "No, ma'am, I'll never tattle again."

Mama got up from her chair and took Alice in smothering hug. Through the soft, massive breasts Alice heard her mother's heart beating, and through her hair Alice heard her mother whisper, "I'm very sorry, my sweet. But we must watch our words. We must guard our tongues. It's not up to us to tell on others in order to seek judgment against them. We must keep God's peace."

Papa let a deep breath out through his nose; it whistled slightly, like an owl in the distance. Then the family focused once again on their supper.

Papa was the preacher at the Oak Grove Baptist Church in the tiny, forest-choked settlement of Oak Grove seated not far from the northern bank of the Ohio River. He had married Mama in Richmond, Virginia in 1822, and the voice of God had called the couple away from civilization and into the wilderness to save the souls of the lost and the far-flung.

The church was a simple but sturdy log structure, built by Papa and several devout men of the settlement. It featured a lovely peaked roof topped by a cross, and three rooms—a cloak-room at the front, a sanctuary with eighteen rows of backless pews, and the minister's office to the rear of church behind the pulpit. There were few church rules and they were posted inside the front door:

Wipe Your Feet.
No Cursing.
Keep the Peace.
No One Allowed in Minister's Office Without Permission.
Men Remove Your Hats.
Ladies Cover Your Heads.

Papa spent most of his days squirreled away in his church office, leaning over his desk in the light of the single, small window on sunny days or in lantern light on rainy days. There he wrote his sermons and letters, chose the weekly hymns and verses, read his Bible, and prayed. He was a quiet but stalwart man, so dedicated to his cause and to his flock that he was distant from his wife and his children. Alice longed to please Papa but was rarely able to even make eye contact. He was always looking past her, past his family, out to the flock or up to Heaven. Every so often Alice would go into the church and place some wildflowers or pretty river pebbles outside the closed door to Papa's forbidden office, hoping he'd come out and see her with her gift. But he never did, and he never knew.

Of the seventy-three settlers in Oak Grove, fifty-nine regularly attended Papa's services. The others were invalids or heathens. Mama and the children visited the invalids and took them fresh potatoes, dry land cress, and eggs. Mama and the children avoided the heathens, who consisted of fur traders and drunks, but never let her daughters and sons speak ill of them. "We are all God's creations," she would say, "and it is up to us to protect the feelings of others."

Yet just five days earlier, Alice hadn't been able to help herself and had told her thirteen-year-old sister Prudence that she'd watched Abraham Denner, Oak Grove's foulest drunk, unbutton his trousers and piss into the horse trough in front of the mercantile. Mama had found out about the tattling and had stuck Alice's tongue for it. "God knows what each of us do. It is up to Him to correct us or to leave us be," Mama had explained sadly yet firmly as Alice had cried. "Therefore, we do not carry tales. We do not share secrets nor tattle. Words can slay more violently than the lash. We must care for each other and protect each other in the name of Christian charity."

How the embroidery needle hurt! But oh, how difficult it was to follow that rule! Oh, to be free to speak! The other children in her family were right and good, of course. Prudence never told secrets. Fourteen-year-old Frances was admirable and always did as he should. Ten-year-old Thomas was obedient and shy. And yet there was so much going on in Oak Grove. Old Widdy Cheswick stole the ripest tomatoes from Mrs. Farley's garden. Derby Jones kissed young Martha Prescott behind the Prescott barn, even as Martha begged him not to. Little Aaron Pugh had broken a stoneware bowl in the mercantile then kicked the pieces behind the flour barrel. Alice knew these things, had witnessed these things, and yet was duty bound to keep the peace, for what happened in secret would be handled by God and God alone in His own time.

Alice feared she might never have control of her tongue.

Though if it would please Papa and have him notice her, she would tie a gag around her mouth and never utter another word again.

The runaways began showing up in early September. Bedraggled, damp from the river, taking silent refuge and rest in the forest near Oak Grove. There were never many at one time. Two or three usually, dark-skinned, tight-jawed, thin from running and hiding, wading and swimming. Papa met the first pair when he was down near the river, praying for rain. Papa put his arm around the two men as if they were his Christian brothers, and he led them into the settlement square. There, he promptly told the two he would have to lock them up until their rightful owners came for them.

"This is not a matter of tattling," Papa told the curious who had gathered around. "This is a matter of ownership. A matter of what the Bible tells us of masters and slaves. Who does not remember the blessed verse, the beloved Ephesians 6:5-9? 'Servants, be obedient to them that are *your* masters according to the flesh, with fear and trembling, in singleness of your heart, as unto Christ!'"

With that, Papa passed the slaves—who were too exhausted to fight back but whose eyes were round and hollow with dread—over to Amos Randall and Parker Scott, who in turn locked them in Amos' tool shed.

Alice had been with Mama, bringing baked bread through the village to old Widdy Cheswick when this had happened. Mama had stopped dead in her tracks to watch and listen. While the other settlers had nodded their heads and muttered "amen" following Papa's proclamation, Mama's brows had furrowed, and her hands tightened around the crusty loaf. I had never noticed such a thing before. Mama disagreeing with Papa, even if that disagreement was silent, unspoken, was shocking.

Later that night, when supper was done, prayers were said, and Papa was seated before the fire with his pipe, Mama tucked the children in their cots and kissed them, one by one. When Mama got to Alice, Alice whispered, "Mama, tell me about Richmond, where you used to live. When you were a little girl like me." Mama smiled a small smile and leaned close. But then the smile vanished and Mama sat up straight. "We need none of that, it is time to sleep. Goodnight, daughter." This was because Mama was smart. Mama knew she had told her children about her youth in Richmond, the daughter of a fairly wealthy lawyer who owned four slaves, even in the middle of the city. How Mama did not like the fact that her family owned other human beings and how she'd begged her father to set them free. Mama knew that Alice was trying to get her to admit she still felt the same way, that she disagreed with what Papa had done with the poor runaways. Mama would not be tricked. Alice flipped over onto her stomach and muttered into her pillow, "Good night, Mama," and hoped that Mama would not feel the need for punishment.

And Mama didn't. It seemed her thoughts were elsewhere.

In the weeks that followed, other runaways showed up in the woods surrounding Oak Grove. Most were captured, locked in the tool shed, and taken away by men on horses, back across the wide water to wherever it was they had been slaves. Alice always went to the town square when word came that slaves were in custody. She watched and nodded and listened as Papa gave his speech about God's will and slavery, and when he pivoted in her direction, she gave him a big smile. Maybe, she hoped, he would notice her. Maybe he would at last be pleased with his youngest child. But he didn't notice. He said a prayer with the gathering of town folks, a prayer that the hearts of the slaves would soften so they would accept their position in life. Then he retired to his private office in the church.

It was a late October evening. Red leaves had tumbled from the oaks and maples and covered the muddy road into Oak Grove like a blood-soaked blanket. Rabbits and groundhogs hid in their burrows and foxes barked at the setting sun. Families retired to their homes for suppers. Afterwards they washed dishes, read the Bible, cleaning harvesting tools, and mended socks as babies and the senile old cried in their beds.

Mama had gone out to take supper to Old Widdy Cheswick and was not yet home. Papa was smoking his pipe and staring into the red coals of the hearth. Frances was practicing his penmanship with Papa's pen, Prudence was hemming a skirt, and Thomas was snapping the last of the season's pole beans.

Alice was restless. She was supposed to be helping Thomas, but her mind wanted to be doing something else, anything else. Maybe now she could win a bit of Papa's attention.

"Papa," said Alice.

Papa rubbed his beard and watched the popping coals.

"Papa?" said Alice.

Papa turned toward Alice but she wasn't sure he was looking at her.

"Papa, would you read to me? Perhaps from your next sermon? I should like to hear that."

Papa's lip twitched as if he was going to say something, but then he looked back at the fire.

Alice sighed and crossed her arms. There was no pleasing the man. No getting him to see her or hear her.

So she said, "Papa. I want to go help Mama at Widdy Cheswick's."

Papa made a little grunting sound.

Alice took it as permission. At least outside in the night she could watch for skunks and chase raccoons. It was fun outside alone at night. She could tattle to the trees and carry tales to the moon and not a soul would care.

The night was heavily shadowed and filled with the chirring of late-season crickets. Alice strolled down the muddy, leaf-strewn road toward the center of town and Widdy Cheswick's house. She passed the several homes, the mercantile, the public storehouse, the church...

She slowed and stopped in front of the church. There was a pale glow to the rear of the building, pooling out on the grass. It was not moonlight; the moon was behind a thick cloud. Curious, Alice tiptoed around the church.

There was a light inside Papa's private office, shining through the small window. Alice was too short to peer inside, so she rolled a large stone over and climbed on top.

She lifted herself on her toes to have a look.

Mama was inside the office with a young black woman. The woman—clearly a runaway with her soaked, ragged skirt and scabby knuckles—was sitting in Papa's chair at Papa's desk. She was crying softly. Mama was kneeling beside her with her hand on the runaway's shoulder. A lard oil lamp glowed atop Papa's papers on Papa's desk.

Mama's voice was muffled but Alice could hear what she was saying.

"Stay here for the night. There is a blanket in the cabinet to keep you warm. I will return by five in the morning and wake you so you can be gone well before my husband comes to the church at seven. I will bring some food for you to take with you. Here is the key to the office. Keep the door locked and I will rap when I arrive so you can let me in."

The runaway nodded with effort and took the key from Mama's hand.

"Thank you, Ma'am," she said. "Thank you ever so much."

"No need to thank me," said Mama. "This is the least I can do."

At that moment, Alice lost her balance and her forehead bumped the windowpane. Mama gasped at the noise and jerked up, her hand knocking over the lamp, sending oil and fire across the papers. The runaway flinched and the key flew out of her hand. It dropped into a crack between the floorboards, out of reach.

Mama tried to slap out the fire on the desk but it leapt up Mama's sleeve. "Dear God!" she cried as she smacked the flame on her arm, which fanned it up higher.

The runaway shoved the burning papers off the desk and stomped on them, but the fire was determined and flaming sheets blew everywhere about the room.

Mama screamed as the fire rolled up her shoulder toward her face.

Then she looked at the window and saw Alice.

"Alice!" she screamed. "Get your Papa!"

Alice stood, watching. Mama had broken one of the church rules.

"Get your Papa!" wailed the runaway.

Alice stood on the rock on her tiptoes. To tell Papa that Mama had broken the rules and had gone into his office would be tattling.

The runaway knocked Mama down and jumped on her, shouting, "I'll put it out, hold still!"

But she couldn't put it out and Mama couldn't hold still. Her dress, covered with spattered fats from cooking meats, was a perfect fuel. The fire raced across her bodice and down her other arm and up into her face.

Alice had never heard anyone scream that way before. It was like the sound of a fox when a bear ripped its skin off.

The runaway jumped up and tried the door, but of course it was locked and the key deep in the floor. The runaway lifted her hands to the ceiling as if to pray. Mama burned like a torch on the floor.

Alice hopped off the rock and wandered home. She thought she heard the windowpane break and the runaway trying to squeeze through. She didn't think the woman would make it; it was such a tiny little window.

Alice wasn't going to carry tales about Mama. She wasn't going to tattle.

Papa was going to be so proud.

He might even give Alice a hug and a kiss for being such a good girl.

For keeping the peace.

BLANK

BY GEORGIA R. BUNS

I sit and wait for them to get him. As I sit and wait, I do not realize that I am being watched, stalked, plans are being put into motion. As I sit and wait for them to get him, little do I know that I will be their next target... make that their victim.

Every move that I make is noted; even when I do not make a move, it is still noted. Left, right, center, they are there: watching, stalking, crafting their plan.

His room seems darker, colder. The silence is deafening. No more monitors beeping, no breathing machine attached. I watch him in the dark, willing him to breathe, just one more time. A chill wind blows outside. A shiver runs down my spine.

I think about the last few days, and so do they. The last few hours, and so do they. The anger resonates in me. It resonates in them too. They have not gotten him yet, yet they have. My world has turned upside down. That cold, dark, quiet day. The orderlies are coming to take his body.

I sit and wait for them to get him.

First it was: ruin her name, ruin their relationship, make her pay for everything he had done. What exactly had he done? What exactly had she done? And why did she have to pay for his sins? What was it about her, and him, that they hated, that disgusted them, that made them obsess about her, and him?

They wanted to destroy her. They lived, breathed, wanted, needed this hate, this obsession. It became their life. Destroy, ruin, humiliate, conquer, devour her. Make her suffer. It became their motto, their screed. Torment the weak. Revel in their righteousness.

She was paralyzed with grief, and fear. She wanted to die. Moving, breathing, living became unrecognizable. She wandered through her life wondering when it would end, how would it end, would they ever stop?

She wanted the madness to stop.

She felt betrayed. No, she was betrayed. By his so-called friends. Smile to her face, accept every kindness she offered... then talk about her when she was gone. Comparing notes. Word by unkind word, brick by cold brick. Building on their chapel of ugliness.

They planned, hunted, executed. Carefully whispered slanders, ugly rumors, swirling in a fetid pool. All in the name of him. In the name of his body of work. They saw themselves as keepers of the legend in their mind, and his. He sought fame but died fameless. They thought themselves saviors of his tattered legacy, of all that was good in him, protecting him from the tramp that dared call herself his widow. They claimed amongst themselves that they were on the side of the angels.

But no, they pulled the trigger in the name of themselves. To make a name for themselves. To be in the inner circle. To gloat that it was their words that destroyed her, destroyed him, destroyed them.

In memory, and in the flesh.

Deception was the first hit that stung. Back in the ward, him tethered to machines that kept him alive. She let everyone in, to say their goodbyes. She thought they were there to help him, but she was wrong. They got to them: his family. They got them to do their work for them. The heat, the graze, being blindsided. Deception, manipulation...

The second hit awakened her, blindsiding her again. This time with a video call: a distant relative, far away. They continued to plot against her. Again, she thought she was getting help. Help protecting him. Instead it was a ruse, to see how she was not capable of protecting him. Taking care of him. They drew blood. In her most vulnerable moment, they came after her. Laughing, mocking, terrorizing her, with ugly words and thoughts and deeds. It was a nightmare she could not wake up from.

The third hit came full force. She saw it coming. Didn't hide from it but stared it down. It was then she realized what it was and what she had to do. Protect him, protect her, but most importantly: bury him, bury them.

She was served with papers on the day she buried him. It was not a surprise, but it cut deep. They did not wait. They sliced through her, trying to draw more blood. Trying to break her. She knelt by his graveside, as a cold breeze blew, crying, screaming, burying him deep in the earth.

She knew what they wanted, knew they were coming after her, coming after him. They wanted his words, and control of his work. But more, they wanted his remains: to strip her of even that, and leave her with nothing but her poisoned grief, and their scorn.

She didn't cower before them. She did not know how to cower. Nor did she know how to fight. Fight this obsession. Fight those who waged war on her, and him.

She did not want to engage in this battle, yet she had to. For him, and for her. So, she consumed their words, the way they consumed her. She became fascinated with them. Trying to find out everything about them. What they wanted, what was in it for them? Blood, ego, humiliation, decimation. They wanted to erase her in every conceivable way.

She let them think they could.

She had no other choice but to fight. She repeated to herself, protect him. Bury him. Bury them.

The memory of that cold, dark quiet day rushed back to her. She watched him take his last breath. Watch the rigor mortis set in. He was gone.

But he kept coming back.

Sometimes she sensed him. Felt him. Smelled him. The faint scent of cigarette smoke, cheap alcohol. Not just in dreams. Signs would appear randomly, and she knew: he was there. He lingered. Everywhere she turned, he was with her.

What do you want from me? She asked. Why are you doing this? Why are they?

He never answered. But she knew: his life was a series of boxes—compartmentalized, secrets built on secrets, a precarious house of cards, waiting for one stiff breeze, one stiff drink to bring it all tumbling down.

His death was no different. Secrets upon secrets, once hidden, now exposed. He had nothing but his work. Nothing but words, artful lies writ in story. Toxic drama and chaos. They wanted it, to claim as their own. To remake in their own image.

She let them think they could.

She dreamt of smoke and liquor and knew he was there. Where are you? she cried. Nothing at first. Then she turned and saw an urn. She went to it, hands trembling, and opened the lid. Inside, another urn: smaller. She opened that one, and inside, another, even smaller. Then another, and another, each smaller than the last, like a Russian doll. Smaller and smaller, until she could hold it in the palm of her hand.

Her fingers closed around it, making a fist. Where are you? She screamed.

And then, he appeared: a shadow man, made of funeral ash. He gazed at her with sunken eyes, full of sorrow. She had only ever loved him, accepted him for who and what he was. But now she told him: this was his mess she was cleaning up. His fight. And it was up to him to make it right.

And then she told him what to do.

You win, she told them. Come and get him.

They sent her papers, relinquishing her claim. She signed them. They did not know where he was buried. She told them. With every stroke, they erased her. Until it was as if she had never been, at all. She let them.

I sit and wait for them to get him. As I sit and wait, they do not realize that they are being watched. Every move that they make is noted; even when they do not make a move, it is still noted.

It is almost dark, and cold, at his grave. I sit on a headstone some distance away, and sip coffee, hot and black. As headlights appear on the cemetery drive, a shiver runs down my spine. Cold tears well in my eyes. Soon there will be no more tears. I am all cried out.

I think about the last few days, and so do they. The last few hours, and so do they. But the anger no longer resonates within me. They have not gotten him yet, yet they have.

My world turned upside down, that cold, dark, quiet day. But there are no more monitors beeping, no breathing machines or tubes. As they approach his headstone I watch, willing him to breathe, just one more time.

His grave is open, his urn sat upon the base of the stone, the lid ajar. The silence is deafening. As they come closer a stiff breeze blows. In the fading light I see grey ash, wafting up and up. And then twirling, dervish-like, into the shadow shape of a man.

They are coming to take his body.

I sit and wait for them to get him.

HEY NONNY DING DONG, ALANG ALANG ALANG...

BY MICHAEL PICCO

By the time you read this, I'll be dead. Or worse. You know... just *gone*. 'Maybe I'll just fade away and not have to face the facts...' Perhaps Mick and the boys had it right all along. Aw, hell—I figure if my brain tumor doesn't kill me, then the "authorities" will; or their corporate cronies; or these sons-of-bitchin' skinheads. Take your pick; but dead is dead no matter how you cut it. Besides, it's not about *how* you die that matters. It's about how many bad guys you took down with you.

At the moment, you could say that I am 'circling the drain.' That's how my old man would've described the state I'm in—you know—not quite dead, but well on my way. After being awake for as long as I have, I have to tell ya, I'm actually looking forward to the kind of rest and oblivion that death brings. Yeah, 'there'll be time enough to sleep when you're dead.' That's another one of my old man's favorites. If only he could see me now. All he wanted for me was to follow in his footsteps; get a decent education; and do something respectable with my life. But here I am.

The compound is quiet tonight, that is, except for the grand cricket chorale being performed in the weeds around me. Their eager songs reverberate from the stony hard pack that forms the parade grounds of this place. Between me and the compound, there's a tangle of single-strand barb wire, starting just beyond the tree line. It outlines an oddly denuded ten-foot clearing around the perimeter. I've no doubt that these terracotta-toothed imbeciles have rigged some improvised landmines around the

front of the compound ('I.E.D.s'—that's how we used to char-
acterize those in the Corp. I know about those friggin' things
all too well, and I have the scars to prove it). There aren't any
of those back here where I've set up my blind. Out here, there's
nothing but brush and bugs. Lots and lots of bugs.

I roll my shoulders and grind the amphetamine and Demerol
capsules between my teeth. Demerol for the migraines; amphet-
amines to keep the blackouts at bay. The amphetamine burns
dull and alkaline beneath my tongue, bringing the night into
manically sharp focus. For an instant, I can almost see the sap
moving through the trees around me. And that migraine that's
been tugging at my consciousness for the last couple of hours
finally starts to recede—the pain of it unclenching like a fist.
Putting the thing inside my head back to sleep... at least for a
while.

Long enough to get this done, I hope.

It took me a while to find the right combination and drug
dosages to manage this condition of mine. This particular combination being the only thing that quells the queer squirming
sensation behind my right ear without leaving me completely
loopy in the process. I tried opioids at first—you know, the
kinda shit that the doctors push on you for pain. But that stuff
didn't do fuck all for me except bind me up tighter than a nun's
cunt. Pot eased the headaches but killed my ambition and I'll be
damned if I'm going to go quietly into that good night.

Fuck that.

That bluegrass Reveille of theirs will start blasting outta
those two-bit loudspeakers here pretty soon, rousin' this merry
band of paramilitary fuck-o's. It's the only time that the whole
lot of 'em are all gathered all in one place. Otherwise, they're
like cockroaches, scattered over the compound. They think that
they're God's holy, white-bred Christian soldiers; but they're
really just piss poor excuses for human beings. They've got the
stars and bars flying under a bastardized Gadsden flag—some
kind of neo-Nazi standard with a swastika all wrapped up in
the coils of a cobra or viper. It's probably something they consider real badass.

I plan to burn both of those flags later. Along with the rest of this place. That is if I make it outta here without getting my ass shot off.

But, where was I? Oh yeah… my tumor. It's a real bitch this thing, lemme tell ya.

I never go to sleep, but I keep waking up. That's the crux of it, really. I have these strange blackouts. Most times, I dunno if I am dreaming or awake. I guess you could say that I'm sleepwalking, but I'm not *actually* asleep—you know, truly unconscious during my blackouts—but I'm not exactly *here* either. Part of me just goes away. To the outside world, I appear utterly conscious and aware, but the truth is, I'm just *gone*. By then, it's too late to say I'm sorry, not that I'd know—and why should I care? 'Please don't bother tryin' to find me—I'm not there!'

I know you're singing that in your head now. You're welcome.

The tumor has metastasized through my hypothalamus. That's the part of your brain that regulates your sleep/conscious cycles. Normally, it works like this: your hypothalamus tells your body when to sleep and when to wake up. But, due to the intrusion of the tumor, my hypothalamus is whatcha might call F.U.B.A.R. (although, most of the civilian doctors I've talked to don't seem to recognize that term). On the CT scan, the tumor looks like some kind of stringy black octopus all coiled up in the base of my skull.

The doctors tell me that I am "a unique specimen." They claim that they haven't seen something like this before. While they suspect that my blackouts are related to the tumor, they don't quite know why the symptoms manifest in the way that they do. They're at a loss to explain why I exhibit some strange form of waking narcolepsy. All I know is that I check out, but my body remains in motion. Newton's First Law of Motion takes on a whole new meaning. I like to think that when I black out, it means that a higher power is taking over. Maybe an angel is pushing my consciousness aside, shielding my mind from whatever it is that I'm doing, or from what it is that I am about to do. That would be convenient, wouldn't it? If only I believed in that sorta bullshit. Like I said, I have no memory of anything occurring while I am "out of it." Any recollection of those events just seems to be swallowed up by my brain tumor. Like I said: I'm just *gone*.

I'll tell you something: It's a damn odd thing, finding your-self in a strange place, holding a gun to someone's head and hav-ing no earthly idea how you got there. I keep telling myself that no sane person would do the things that I've done; but then, we live in an insane world, don't we? What was it that Shakespeare said? "Though this be madness, yet there is method in't." I dunno if I am sane or not, but it doesn't really matter. "Mad call I it; for, to define true madness. What is't but to be nothing else but mad?" I don't think that I'm insane, but maybe my tumor is. Aw, hell... why debate it? I'll be dead soon enough. I'll let the coroner figure that one out.

But I'm getting ahead of myself. You're wondering what brought me to this point—sitting out here in this foxhole with god-knows-what crawling all over me. I don't quite know where to start, really...

It didn't happen all at once, you know. That's the insidious nature of this kind of cancer—you don't know you got it until it's too late to treat it. But as it so happens, it was the insomnia that was the first symptom. It came on gradually, but it was pretty entrenched by the time I sought treatment for it. The doctors at the V.A. just told me that I needed to take some sleeping pills and get the hell over it. They had bigger fish to fry over there at the hospital: the amputees; the shell-shocked; all those poor bastards burned or shot all to hell. So, I didn't press them. And for a while, the pills seemed to work. Until they didn't. Within a couple of months, I was back to staring at the clock all night, waiting for the sun to rise. I put off seeing a real doctor as long as I could, telling myself that I was just being a pussy because I wasn't getting my beauty sleep. After all, I'm pretty enough!

When I was deployed in Afghanistan, I was used to get-ting around five hours sleep, tops. But, after I got discharged and settled stateside again, I started to lose sleep in a big way. I know what you're thinking: insomnia is a symptom of P.T.S.D. You'd be in good company in thinking that, too. That's exactly what the V.A. docs thought the first time I went to see them. By then I was lucky if I got three hours of sleep a night. In the months that followed my initial visit, I'd toss and turn until about 2 AM, then snap awake just before sunup. After a month or two, I found myself watching the night dissolve into dawn before sleep took me. These days I just lie in bed and stare at the television. Entranced by the endless news cycles; waiting for sleep that I know will never come. You can handle that sort of sleep deficit for a while, but the lack of shut eye begins to accumulate. It wears you down. It triggers other symptoms.

Yeah, first came the insomnia, then the hallucinations. "Sleep Deprivation Induced Hallucinations"— 'S.D.I.H.' in medical lingo. After you stop sleeping for as long as I have, you start *seeing* things. Some people with S.D.I.H. see phantoms; some people report seeing flashes of light; some report seeing Martians. Me? I started seeing peoples' 'auras' for fuck sakes. And, just like you are probably thinking right now, when I started seeing auras, I thought I was losing my damn mind. I didn't know what the hell was happening to me. I suppose you could say that's when I really started to crack. Or at least, that's when people began to notice. I'd see people turn their heads toward me, then quickly look away. I'd hear their hushed whispers about me behind my back. Like some distant radio broadcast, riddled with bursts of static and hiss. They'd murmur like that damn thing squirming behind my eyes does now—just loud enough to hear, and just quiet enough that you can't quite make out what they're saying. But I didn't need to hear them to know what they were saying. They all looked at me the same damn way: like I was *crazy*.

And, I'll admit it: it does sound crazy. I can't really say that I blame them. The herd gets troubled when one of theirs deviates from the norm. It's not their fault. It's their survival instinct culling out the weak. Or the sick. Or the terminal. Yeah: this condition is terminal: that's the one thing that *all* of the doctors agree on. I'm a walking, talking dead man. If having that kind of knowledge doesn't drive you crazy, then I don't know what will. The mad cow says: "Hey nonny ding dong, alang, alang, alang!" Yeah, life could be dream, sweetheart. Or it could be a never-ending nightmare. Take your pick.

I remember seeing my first aura like it was yesterday. I was coming out of the courthouse, and this guy brushed past me. No big deal, that. I must've flinched though. I remember him looking back at me, mumbling an apology. But I was too gob-smacked to even respond. You see, what I saw that day was not just some random asshole on his way home. What I saw was a man *on fire*. Yeah, you read that right. Slow motion, radiant tongues of flame lifted off the guy's big bald head as he pushed past me. And I'll be damned if they didn't form a perfect halo just above his brow! I swear I could've lit a cigarette off 'em! Even the air around the guy was warped and buckled, like heat waves radiating off a stove! It was the damnedest thing I'd ever seen. I thought someone had slipped me some acid at the DMV! I looked around, but nobody else was walking around with their head on fire that day.

Turns out, that guy I saw that day was the district attorney. He'd just convicted some dirt bag of killing a little girl. Said dirt bag was getting the death penalty and the D.A. was on the six-o'clock news that evening taking a victory lap. I barely recognized him without the halo of fire around his head. At first, I thought that auras don't translate to broadcast media. But then, they flashed a picture of the murderer. His face was wreathed in thick bands of greasy black smoke. I sat there in front of the television and just blinked.

Well, lemme tell ya: that night I went out and got good and shitfaced! If I was going around the bend to Loonyville, at least I would get there lit. All that night, I didn't see anything out of the ordinary. At least, not until I left the bar. Around closing time, I stumbled out to a taxicab, the world pitching and twirl-ing around me. I remember glancing at the driver through the plexiglass partition, wondering why there was so much mud on his face. Well, not mud exactly but some kind of chunky black ichor. I dimly recall asking him about that. He insisted that I was just seeing things, but as I watched him in the rear-view mirror, the slime poured outta his eyes like slow motion tears, clinging to him like tar. Before I got out, he asked me if I had any meth on me. His hands were starting to twitch, he explained, and his shift didn't end for another four hours.

As time went on, I began to see other things, different manifestations of these 'auras.' I began to get a feel for what they represented. You know, that feeling you get when there's something not entirely right about someone? Seeing auras is just like that—only in technicolor! Anytime that I saw someone smoldering, or covered in some kind of mist, I knew that they were bad news. Violence always seems to show up as smoke or mist. Lust presents itself as a thick shell, like someone had been dipped in shellac over and over again. Drug use always manifests itself as a kind of seeping rot, boiling out of peoples' eyes and mouths. Greed though, well... that is usually the hardest to see. The auras of the greedy seem to draw the light out of everything around them. Up close, you can see these strange black cilia growing off them—like the tentacles of a sea anemone.

That's indicative of the sorts of things that I see now. I won't tell you what I see when I look in the mirror—only that my eyes are as black as night and lusterless as coal. Like the sun blotted out from the sky. Sometimes I think I see the tumor thrashing behind them. It's during those times that I want to turn my own weapon on me. Just wrap my teeth around the barrel and enjoy a nice bracing hot lead salad.

Yeah, I know I *sound* crazy. But hell, why should you believe me? I hardly believe it myself! The doctors sure as hell didn't believe a word of it. My insomnia didn't get their attention but telling them about the auras sure did! That's when they found it: this fuckin' tumor. But, by then it was too late to do anything about it.

Thankfully, it isn't always bad things that I see. There are the good things in people, too. Some folks' auras are brilliant and radiant, like looking at the sun. They're bright shining avatars of light. Take Lynda, she's the dyke bartender at that bar I frequent: her aura is bright green. Like sunlight sparkling through an emerald. I saw a kid the other day, a little girl, whose aura was like seeing an ember trapped in a pool of amber. She burned with a glow that cast this honey-hued gleam over everyone around her. It was so beautiful; it would've made a lesser man weep. I remember she glanced my way and smiled at me. It was the kind of sweet warm smile that just scours away all the shit that's accumulated on your soul.

There are more things in heaven and hell than are dreamed of, huh? You don't have to answer me.

I watch a thick slow-moving centipede crawl across the scope of my Armalite AR-10 .308. Man... it's one big, nasty-looking fucker. Its carapace is all mottled red and black, except for its legs. Those are yellow-orange and just laden with venom. The thing is all business too, the way you think a successful alpha predator would be. By way of contrast, just inside the perimeter, there's that fat tub of shit waddling around the compound with a gun on his shoulder—an insect masquerading as a human being. For shits and grins, I line up the swastika tattooed large on the back of this dickhead's shiny bald skull as he takes another long drag off his menthol cigarette. He pulls his underwear out of his ass crack and leans his .22 rife against the fence. This fuck-o's aura barely registers in my sights. It hangs around his head and shoulders like a damp fog. I could drop this worthless piece of shit right now without even thinking twice; but, it's not him that I'm after.

No... my target priority is the head honcho of this so-called outfit: "Colonel" Frazier Cross. Do you recognize the name? You should—his story got wall-to-wall news coverage about ten years back. He was the ringleader behind that gang of skinheads that targeted all those synagogues and mosques in Kansas City. You know, the ones who shot all those poor bastards praying for peace and safety at that big rally downtown. One of the victims, Rory Machowicz, was only thirteen. He just had his bar mitzvah a week before. Rory was a skinny and homely little fella; he probably hadn't even gotten his first handjob. Nope, poor Rory didn't even have time to sin before Cross' men mowed him down.

Even though Cross was conspicuously absent during the shootings themselves, during his trial the prosecution demonstrated that he was the undisputed mastermind behind them. Cross was eventually convicted of three counts of conspiracy, six counts of aiding and abetting and two counts of accessory to those murders. That's why he got such a stiff sentence: twenty-five-years-to-life (well, that and the fact that he is clearly a worthless racist piece of shit). But he never served a day of that sentence. Cross was sprung by his "associates" following the trial. It was in all the papers. There was a nationwide manhunt, but Cross simply up and vanished. There were rumors that the K.K.K. spirited him outta the state. Others claimed it was some neo-Nazi group. And still others claim it was a bunch of crooked, racist cops who let him go. Whoever did it, Cross just up and disappeared—'like a fart in a windstorm' my old man would say. I understand the bastard even made the F.B.I.'s most wanted list for a while. But the Feds never found him.

But I did. It took me a long damn time, but good things come to those who wait. That's why I've been sitting out here in the boonies, biding my time here in my blind behind this hillbilly haven. Waiting for the sun to rise for the last time on The White Thunderbolt Compound.

One of Cross' acolytes, Douglas J. Sheets, built this shit-hole. Since his escape, Cross has been hiding out here under the name of Wilhelm Slade. Sheets owns the place and handles the day-to-day operations (you know, the business end of being a scumbag), but Cross is the black soul of the operation. He's the ideologue, the siren that brings all these human shipwrecks to one place. He's also the one behind all the shady shit that happens out here—and believe me when I say there's a lot of shady shit going down here: underage prostitution, meth manufacturing, gun running, you name it. There's even a rumor that a lynching took place out here just last month. Yeah... here we are in the bright and shiny twenty-first century and this kind of backwoods Klan bullshit is still going on.

Cross was well known for promoting anti-Semitism and his Aryan agendas. At his trial, his lawyers tried to make a case for his freedom of speech, in an attempt to muddy the waters around the murder charges, you see. They implied that he'd been set up, that he was just a convenient lightning rod for the murders. The defense argued that his racist rants and public tirades were merely him expressing his First Amendment rights. They claimed that Cross wasn't even connected to the murders. Problem was, one of the gang, (the driver), flipped on him and fingered Cross to keep himself from frying. He testified that Cross was not only his backer but also his mentor—that Cross was the one who actually taught him and the gang how to shoot. He shocked jurists when he stated that Cross had used pictures of Holocaust victims for target practice.

Yeah, what a real peach of a guy, huh?

Cross' free speech defense didn't do him a damn bit of good. In fact, it was Cross' history of anti-Semitism that ended up convicting him. His lawyers misjudged the jury *entirely*. When the judge made his statement before sentencing, he said famously: "Freedom of speech does not mean freedom from consequence. How many lives were destroyed by this man and his poison ideas? How many suffered because of his hatred?" On and on... The fact that Cross escaped justice enraged me. But, I'll tell you something: he won't escape me.

I am consequence. I am judgment incarnate.

My old man would probably be horrified about what I've been doing with my time. He was an academic, one of those liberals you see wearing pink hats and marching on the White House— protesting injustice but never really doing anything concrete about it. He thought he was a man of action, but in actuality, he was just a bitcher. I wish I could have explained that to him, you know, before he got run down by Cross' gang. The shooting victims got most of the coverage, but the old man's death garnered an eight-second spot on the evening news, before the news cycle rolled on to the next senseless tragedy. For all his talk of 'creating a dialog' or 'establishing a rapport' with the 'deplorables' of the world, all that his high-minded rhetoric got him was a tire tread across his back and a closed-casket funeral.

Anyway...

From what I've been able to ascertain, sitting here in this foxhole for the last three days, is that Cross only shows his face once a day: during the morning pep talk he gives to the mishmash of neo-Nazis and skinheads who find their way out here. That's when I plan to unleash hell on this place. Or die trying. I figure it's better to go out this way than dying in some hospital or in hospice. Like I said: nobody knows exactly when they'll go. The only assurance you have is when it's your time, it's your time. There's no avoiding it, no protesting it, no praying it away. You're born—you die. That's the deal. Only in my case, in between birth and death, there's this fucking tumor that ate my brain.

I wasn't always this way, you know. Before my deep green

sea turned a darker blue, I used to be such a nice guy. Until my dad got killed, I was well on my way to being just like him: educated, but naive where the rougher side of life was concerned. Back then, I didn't see auras or hear whispering in my head. I didn't have any desire to go out and murder people, either. Nope, back then, my aura was as clean and clear as day.

But after he was killed, something in me changed.

That shit-heel who ran him over that day outside the synagogue only got five years for his crime. Five lousy years, can you believe it? For his cooperation with the prosecution, his charges were reduced to vehicular manslaughter—ain't that a bitch? There's no justice in the world anymore. Well... at least, not until I got involved. After the trial, I quit school and joined the Marines, determined to make a difference in the world. I served most of my M.S.O. (that's "military service obligation" to all of you civilians out there) in Afghanistan. There, I got a real taste for all that was wrong in the world. In Afghanistan, you didn't pause to debate things. There, it was all about survival. Kill or be killed.

But, it didn't quite prepare me for how to cope with a brain tumor.

I went through the usual coping process when I got the diagnosis. Disbelief. Anger. Resentment. Fear and loathing... you know, the usual stuff you feel when you get your final notice. You might say that I've reached the "fuck it" stage now (although, I'm guessing old Kübler-Ross couldn't quite push that one through the review committee). The doctors told me that I only had about three months to live, but what the fuck do they *really* know? Life and death—it's a crapshoot. The only thing that the doctors really agree on is that removing the tumor will definitely kill me. And, for this form of cancer, radiation therapy is completely useless. They tell me that chemo may prolong my life... or it may not. Truth is, they just don't know.

Cancer: what a total damn shit show.

Just to spite them, I've lived seven whole months since I got my diagnosis... death sentence... whatever you want to call it. The way I figure it, I'm living on double borrowed time. Maybe God wants me to do a little housecleaning while I'm here. Maybe

He has granted me a special project extension, huh? Yeah, if you believe in that sorta thing, I guess. Despite having this slithering time bomb in my head, I consider myself lucky. Nobody knows for sure when they'll die, but at least I got a heads up. And lemme tell ya: it's motivated the shit out of me. After I got over my pity party, I sold my Dad's place and most of his things; cashed in my life insurance policy and pooled that with my pathetic combat pay, and hit the road, determined to take out as many scumbags as I could before taking my own long dirt nap.

Yeah... nobody knows when they'll die, or how they'll go, really. I could die in a hail of gunfire in the next few minutes or I could die protesting gun violence out in the street like my old man did. So, here I sit, putting my final days to good use.

The Marines taught me to be *efficient*, not *original*. I am just a grunt with an aptitude for violence... oh, and marksmanship too, I guess. One thing that I am determined to do with the time I have left is make a damn change in the world. Make a statement. Do something with the life I have left that *means* something. That's how I want to be remembered. Not by pussyfooting around, bitchin' or carrying a sign while the bastards continue to grind us down. No. My legacy is action. Protesting may work for you; but, ridding the world of scumbags works for me. What I do to these shitheels is no less than any of them deserve. Some people say karma's a bitch, but those people haven't met me. I guess history will tell which method changed things for the better.

Fat-boy's cigarette bobs in the darkness as he flips a switch. There's a crackle of static as the P.A. powers up and Reveille starts blaring through the speakers. I dry swallow another Demerol and ready my weapon. As if it can sense the tension, the centipede clears out—scuttling his black-and-red spotted ass clear outta sight. Floodlights pierce the darkness and a couple dozen 'men' (most of 'em just skinny tattooed boys) stumble out of the barracks around the compound. From my nest, I have a clear vantage of not only the parade grounds where they've gathered but a clean line of sight to the main stage. It's less than a hundred yards away. There's no breeze. I am hoping for a clean C.B.S. (that means "Catastrophic Brain Shot," kids).

Where Cross and the members of the Thunderbolt Compound are concerned, I'm not going for subtlety or for metaphor—what I am after today is body count, plain and simple. I figure I have a good ninety-second engagement period before these skinheads get their act together and start to return fire. That's what the semi-auto lying next to me is for. I've got eight-hundred rounds for that. And a couple of I.E.D.s of my own wired around the compound in case things get hairy.

When things get hairy. Not *if*.

A lot of shit can happen during a firefight. My drill sergeant used to say that 'a perfect tactical plan is like a unicorn. Even though everybody knows what one looks like, no one has ever actually seen one in real life.' If I can eliminate Cross, I will consider my mission here a success. If I get Sheets too, well, that would be a bonus. If I get them both and manage to take a slew of neo-Nazis down with 'em, well that would pretty much make my last mission on the planet a success!

And I won't lie: I relish the opportunity to finally avenge my old man.

Cross limps over to the bandstand: a beat-up flatbed wrapped with trailer siding. His aura is a churning miasma of thick writhing gray-green smoke. It twists and billows around him like he's standing atop a smokestack. Two heavily tattooed fucktards flank him on either side: one holding a Nazi flag with a thunderbolt across it, the other bearing the stars and bars. Each pole ends in a gilded spike—as though either of them could adequately defend themselves using pikes—especially against what I have in store for them. The thirty or so piles of shit assembled before them are largely unarmed. The worst thing most of 'em have are 9 mm Glocks (which shouldn't pose much of a threat unless someone manages to get close to me). Their drift lines should take them to either the "armory" adjacent to the parade grounds or directly to the Compound's exit. Both of which are well covered in my field of fire.

Cross is dressed in his usual paramilitary gear: black calf-high jackboots, freshly-pressed *Wehrmacht* uniform paired with a jaunty red beret. "Der Fuhrer würde nicht zustimmen..." I whisper under my breath. Cross' mirrored shades glint in the dawn light as his ragtag company assembles. Sheets calls the 'men' to order and makes a show of performing a cursory inspection. From my vantage, their ragged line and spacing would send any drill sergeant into apoplexy.

I dope the wind and adjust my scope while Sheets berates his raggedy-ass regiment.

Satisfied that he has sufficiently abused his conscripts, Sheets turns and salutes Cross. "Sieg Heil!" The men shout in unison. I doubt that most of them even know what that means. Cross mounts the platform and his head bobs into my reticle. The rising sun glints off his mirrored shades, giving his eyes the illusion of radiance; and for a fraction of a second, I am reminded of my first aura. I slow my breathing and line up the shot. I wrap my finger around the trigger.

It's just then that I feel something moving on my lap. Distracted, I glance down. Wouldn't you know it: it's that goddamn monster centipede that visited me earlier. There it is, all curled up nice and cozy, right next to my nut sack. Its legs click rhythmically on my camos, a hundred legs moving like a wave along its body—tapping and scratching at the denim.

Call me crazy but, it kinda sounds like purring. Yeah, you read that right: goddamn purring. You know, like a cat.

There's a moist tearing sound inside my head, like some vital partition of my skull has been breached, and the world is suddenly painted black. With that comes a sensation of becoming unmoored from reality. Passing through the opaque gossamer veils of this dimension, and into the in between spaces and worlds beyond our ken. Perhaps the tumor in my head has triggered some as yet unknown capacity of the human mind that unlocks the doorway to these worlds—dimensions closer than a hair's breadth, but as far removed from our perception as the dark side of the moon. Perhaps the tumor allows my mind, my consciousness, to slip the bonds of physics, space and time, allowing it to pass from one body to another. Where this world is merely someone else's dream. A dream of another place and time and circumstance. A Quantum Leap with no design or purpose other than for the amusement of some mad god. Or devil. Or whatever made this thing thrash and squirm inside my head.

Perhaps.

Perhaps I should heap this notion onto the same mental shit pile as angels and God and Heaven and Hell. After all, I don't believe in that sorta bullshit. There's no 'Champion Eternal' (hero or heroine) mystically unfettered from iron shackles of our petty existence. The notion smacks more of fantasy and wishful thinking than of a sound mind.

Still, I can't shake the sensation of plummeting, however briefly, across a vast expanse of space and time. A mote adrift on the seas of fate, a spark of conscious flotsam against the grand design of all creation. Against this backdrop, this immense and unfathomable mosaic of infinite dimensions, what influence do my actions have? What significance does my life have? Where in all the universe is my impact? Where have I left my mark on the walls of eternity? For all my high-brow notions of justice and expression, my voice is lost in the cacophony of the Music of the Spheres, the desperate, lonesome howl of a soul wrested from life and cast into the vast black void.

I wake with a start. Judging from the light coming in through my bay window, it's late afternoon. Jackson, my orange and black calico, lies curled up, purring on my lap. It seems that I've fallen asleep in front of the television again. The talking heads drone on about the attacks in Kansas City. Their guest *du jour* mentions that the noose is closing on the suspects and that it's only a matter of time before the killer (or killers) are apprehended. I fumble for the remote and turn off the idiot box before he can continue. The ensuing silence seems jarring. Disoriented and sweating, I fight down the nausea that comes from the chemo. Jackson stirs, and peers at me out of a half-closed eye. My stomach gurgles as I lift his fat ass off of me and onto the sofa. He meows in protest but doesn't seem too bothered by the change in venue.

The nausea builds as my quivering legs carry me to the bathroom. I stumble to the toilet just in time to vomit a torrent of stringy black bile into the basin. In the dim light, it looks as though I've puked up some bizarre species of black squid. Tendrils of darkness crowd the edges of my vision as I lean on the sink to steady myself. Dizzy, I wipe the drool from my mouth onto the sleeve of my bathrobe, not caring that it's still crusty from the last time I wiped the vomit and spit away there. I catch a glimpse of myself in the mirror. My sunken eyes look like holes in the dim light—black and featureless, like lumps of coal. The face I see staring back at me looks nothing like mine. It looks like its skin has been stretched unevenly over its bones.

I splash some lukewarm water onto my face, in an attempt to wash the weariness from my mind. I shuffle out into the hallway, cursing as I force my aching joints into motion. My attention is drawn to the clattering mail slot and the creak of doorframe as the wind brushes its muzzle against it. The pile of mail spilled underneath it bears the same old tidings: an endless stream of medical bills and another late notice from my mortgage company. The envelope is stamped "final notice." You know—it's just doesn't seem fair: I've made every payment for fifteen years, even paid a little extra, and now the bank is threatening to foreclose on me. I would like to think that they will seize my home over my dead body... which, given my prognosis, might be prophetic. I toss the letter onto the end table.

Fuck 'em. Greedy, rotten bastards.

The dreams I've been having lately have gotten worse; although, thankfully, I don't remember much of them long after I've awakened. This afternoon's nightmare, so vivid on waking, now is fragmented and elusive, dissipating like a morning fog. I rub my eyes trying to draw the dream back up from the deep well of my stupor. All that I seem to haul up from its depths are violent images that make my conscious mind shudder. The concepts and imagery from the dream are receding from my waking mind—consigned to the netherworld of sleep.

I vaguely recall dreaming that I was falling—plunging through some black eternal night. But of something else, too... I dreamed that I was some kind of soldier. A mercenary, maybe? Yeah... that sounds about right. I think that I was being buried... no, wait. Not buried, exactly but hiding underground. Hiding out in some kind of blind, I think. Hunting? No... I was a sniper. Yes! I was a sniper! Chuckle... the shit my unconscious mind conjures, these days! To think: I don't even own a gun! I guess that I need to stop reading all of those soldier of fortune rags!

I pour myself a cup of two-day-old coffee, choking it down, even though it tastes like battery acid—caustic, black, inky bile. I get so damn thirsty these days—cotton mouth from the marijuana, I'm betting. Still, the thirst is a minor irritation when compared to the aches and nausea. And, it helps with my lack of appetite. The pot doesn't make anything taste better, but, at least I feel hungry again.

Jackson meets me in the hallway, stretches languidly and saunters into the garage. I can hear him meow and paw at the outside door. I guess he wants out.

I shamble across the kitchen, not bothering to hit the lights until I step into the garage. I flick the switch and the overhead light stutters on. The florescent light buzzes and hums, casting long gray shadows deep into the rafters. Jackson meows impatiently at me and I open the back door. The fall breeze stirs around my slippers, chilling my exposed shins.

I glance up at the denuded trees wondering if the season's first snowfall is finally on its way. The leaves shuffle and scratch along the sidewalk as a gust of wind stirs them from their shallow graves. Jackson rubs against my ankles, breaking my reverie. He has something in his mouth. He drops his prize unceremoniously at my feet, no doubt expecting me to applaud him on his hunting prowess. Where does he find this shit anyway? I wince and clutch at my robe, bending down to pick it up. The blood rushes to my head, making me woozy all over again. I can hear my heartbeat pounding in my ears, like rough surf. Unsteady, I brace myself on the doorframe and wait for the dizziness to pass. I turn Jackson's offering over in my hand. I can't be entirely sure, but it looks like a beret, crusty and stained with old blood.

I AM THE HATE

BY JESSICA MCHUGH

I know what kind of girl you are.

Don't give me that "I'm a grown-ass woman" bullshit either. Until they're withered and frothing on their deathbeds, every female on the planet is a child despot stepping on the necks of innocents while whining about uncomfortable shoes.

You sit like a little girl too, sandals kicked off and legs crossed on the armchair behind the Modern Philosophy stacks at the Lake Jackson library. You're incapable of acting your age no matter where you are, but at least you're better here than you are in bars. When the lights are low, you brazenly chat up strangers and check your cleavage every few seconds—yes, it's still there, and yes, it'll still get you anything you want. But here, in the reflective quiet, there are glimmers of someone who used to love me.

As I meander the stacks and watch you, I think about all the precious things you stole with one retweet. In a moment unclickable, you mutilated my God-given freedoms beyond recognition. You turned my country against me and sold off every artistic identity I've cultivated...and why? You know I didn't help plan the assault on those alt-left rioters. I hardly knew it was happening until it was too late. What was I supposed to do? Sacrifice my life for people who don't have the good sense to jump out of the way?

No. I've got more to offer this country than blood.

Now with warrants issued and patriots unmasked, life is more dangerous for me than I've ever been to anyone else. I rarely leave the house—did you know that? Too many people recognize me, and too few remember that the US Constitution protects me too. But there are still places for me, online and off. Like here, with you.

I pull up my damp hood and peek around the shelves. You're curled up reading a book of Maya Angelou's poetry—for show, obviously. Like your barroom cleavage, it's your first and most audacious lie. It tells the casual observer that you're a beautiful person who supports art, diversity, equality, and the destruction of the human race as we know it. But get too close and anyone can see really quick how flimsy your convictions are. Hell, you couldn't get through three poems in my new poetry collection without asking if I needed to go back to therapy. That proves you don't know shit about art. Art is therapy, little girl. I could write a million poems about how much hotter women would be with their bellies split and organs scattered like the pickled cats in high school anatomy and never actually cut a bitch open. But you never tried to understand that—or me—and that's why none of my art's about you.

No amount of exploration could make you hot anyway, because I already know what's inside. I can name every organ—what they do, where they go. There's nothing your body can teach me that I don't already know. If I lowered myself to dive into you, it would only be to confirm the deformities in the thing you call a heart.

You hide yours better than most—though I suppose that's where cleavage comes into play. If it weren't for tits, and if we could actually see the unnatural thing spinning chaos in a feminazi's chest, there'd be a lot fewer cucks in this country, I can tell you that.

Girls like you dangle diseased and ice-hardened nipples in front of us with all the trickery and rage of a starving parasite. It's an apt metaphor, actually. Men's hearts are like fists squeezing out blood and ambition, but women have spiders in their chests: dry curled-up things that knit lusty webs long after death.

It's true that not all girls take pride in being frigid bitches who want to see white men eradicated from the country we built, but all girls do crave power. Christian Americans and godless libtards alike, it's an inexorable flaw in female genetics. No matter how docile they act, they're all born with cunning hungry spiders where their hearts should be.

I explore this phenomenon in my forthcoming poetry collection, which you'll probably one-star out of spite. You hated everything about it, the title especially, and I don't know why I expected any different from a creature with parasitic tits.

I'm crouched behind a stack of magazines, typing "parasitic tits" into my notepad when a shadow falls over me, followed by the sterile smell of dryer lint. It triggers both nausea and memory, and my legs quake as I stand. I've been pacing this library too long, that's all. Why are you making me pace this library for so long?

I haven't looked you in the eyes since the day after the rally. It was already done, and I didn't know it when you stood in my doorway and asked if I needed more OJ. You'd outed me as an alt-right white supremacist via retweet and then filled my glass with pulpless juice. One retweet, one picture, and five words was all it took to ruin my life, and worst of all, it was a lie.

I'm not racist or sexist. I don't even have a problem with gay people as long as they don't shove it in my face. I just want to preserve the history and culture that makes this country great, and I won't be shamed for it because identity politics are in fashion right now. It's like getting my first tattoo all over again. No matter how many times I've explained that swastikas weren't originally hate symbols, historical facts never quite align with your agenda. Loyalty either. Or commitment.

He warned me about this, you know. Years ago, he told me you wouldn't have my back, and he was right. He was right about a lot.

"You've been following me."

I stare out the window at the crowded parking lot. "It's a public library. And it's still a free country, right?"

You say, "For some," and I groan. You love incendiary shit like that. You want me to fly off the handle and fill this morgue with the truth it's sorely lacking, but I don't need to resort to those piss-slinging Antifa tactics. Daring to hold a different opinion is criminal enough for the "tolerant Left," so I do my best to keep my temper in check.

I finally face you, chin held high. The thing is, sweat's soaking through my shirt so bad my armpits are chafing, and I feel like I'm going to shit my pants. I clench my ass to keep the rage from leaking down my leg, but I've never been more uncomfortable in my life, and I don't fucking deserve it.

Why don't you feel like this?

Why aren't you crying?

Why can't you just admit how guilty you feel?

How lonely you are.

How utterly fucking wrong you are.

Why don't you say fucking anything?

Even if sorrow's clogging up your throat like mine, it doesn't show on your face. Not a hint of the fear that dimpled your chin when I tried out for football, not a tremble in the brow where you stored disappointment with my grades. I inspire no emotion in you, not even the paranoia you usually feel opposite good old boys like me.

Maybe you don't think I can't hurt you anymore. Maybe you never thought I could.

"Tony..."

I hate the way you say my name. I should make my new pen name official. Then you wouldn't be able to ignore the art in what I'm doing. Then you'd have to sink your teeth into a persona you loathe and cough up a sloppy chunk of self-respect when you want to address me. You'd have to acknowledge what we've both created and destroyed in each other.

That's a brilliant line.

I turn from you with a chuckle and type the words into my phone. I finish just as a pair of women jog by the window to get out of the oh so terrifying rain.

"Tony..."

I want to rip out your tongue and crush it under my boot. "Okay! Yes! I've been following you."

"I know you've been following me, Tony. You're shit at it."

Navy uniforms appear in my periphery. Between the stacks on both sides of me, rain-drenched policewomen advance, their right hands resting on their sidearms.

The smell of laundry increases when you float your hand out to meet me. "I'm sorry there's so much hate in you."

Mastering a disingenuous smile is one of the easiest routes to power, which is why I don't smile for you. I don't want to be this easy for either of us. Truth, like art, lifts violence to the light. It untethers us from shame, from the lies we once called liberty, and it gives us the goddamn balls to say, yes, there is hate in me, Mom. And yes, it usually squeezes and wrings humanity until the concept's a pruned-up useless thing, but today I crack humanity open like the pale dead spider in your breast. Today I look in your eyes and release a swarm of spindly architects to fix a world I can only ever destroy.

The five words you tweeted that morning were so right. I'm not your son anymore. I am the voice the world wants to blame. I am the hate the world needs to burn.

I wish Dad were here to watch his boy become a man. I wish we could raise a beer to what I've reclaimed for us, for this country, for mankind, and for the shriveling liberty in his ex-wife's tits.

I know you like to think he still loved you after you left, and that's why he followed you around, but you're wrong. Vanity has made you delusional, like the jocks who thought I actually wanted to be on their shitty team. Or teachers who worshiped political correctness over freedom of expression. Like two-faced girls who lock nice guys like me in the friendzone and spread their legs for everyone else.

Wake up, Mom. He didn't follow you for love. He followed you because he wanted you to watch him die.

Tears fill your eyes as I tell you this, and though your jaw clenches tighter in refusal, your spider heart blooms for me. The thin legs snap and weep as they unfurl, and I crawl inside its corpse, nestled safe in the fresh linen webbing of your love.

This is how it's supposed to feel. This is how you save your son.

Toss your guilt around me. Open your legs and feast.

I reach for my phone so I can remember this, and one of the twats pulls her Glock.

You scream for her to stop. I'm just getting my phone, you tell them. I'm a poet, you tell them.

When I realize it's the first time you've called me a poet, my legs wobble and I tilt onto my toes. I throw out my hands to catch myself, but I land wrong. My fingers look like that, too. Wrong. And the cavalier way you stare down at me, even when the bitches cuff my broken wrist. Wrong.

They pull me to my feet, and you pout the way you did all the times I threw up in your bed. Yellow nausea in your eyes, white resentment in your heart. Now you know for sure that I've always been weak. Maybe even weaker than Dad. All his useless warnings, all his anger and shame like genetic napalm in my guts. That's why you take my phone the way you do, like I'm a child who doesn't know the difference between skim milk and bleach. You don't want me to die as quick and cowardly as he did. You want to kill me yourself, slow, with censorship. You want to neuter me with identity politics and the notion that someone who hates with all their heart can't speak truth or beauty.

It hurts. Please, God, help me, it hurts.

I don't want to cry like this, but two bulldykes are crucifying me, and you're twisting the goddamn nails. You push up your right sleeve as you walk toward me, your face quiet and reflective as the library used to be, and you lift your arm until the greasy, semi-scabbed tattoo is centimeters from my nose.

"i am the hate the world needs" is deep-set in crimson courier on your forearm, but my "hate" is paler, nearly undetectable beneath your neon blue "love."

My words. On your skin. My poetry, my beautiful title. Wrong. On your skin.

You drop my phone on the floor and lift your foot.

Raw as I am, leaking rage and betrayal, I'm not afraid. There will always be places for me. There will always be places for hate to burn.

Your heel falls, the screen spiders, and nobody feasts.

The End

THE TREE

AN OLD MILL, NC STORY FEATURING CLETUS J. DIGGS

BY DAVID NIALL WILSON

It had been a long time since any services were held in the First Revival Church and Mission. Cletus J. Diggs had always considered it a place to leave rather than come back to. Until a dog was killed in the middle of the night. Until a family who wasn't even vaguely aware of the history of the abandoned building, they lived beside had grown afraid. Until that inevitable moment when Cletus' phone rang, and it became his problem.

There are only a few roads in and out of Old Mill, North Carolina. They all have state or county numbers associated with them. Most of them intersect, eventually, with US 17, which runs up and down the East Coast. Branching off from those main roads, though, are a thousand smaller ones, and those branch again, and again, some to dirt roads, others to odd loops around and through fields and farms. It's easy to get lost traveling the old ways—and it's not only travelers that go missing. Small communities, farms, places you might have once called a town—or the embryo of a town—have crumbled, been covered in vines and trees, rotted and rusted.

Occasionally you'll see a building half-collapsed with wood where the glass should be in the windows and graffiti on the walls, only to turn back as you pass and see a battered truck parked outside. You seldom see the people who own the trucks, or the houses, if they actually do own them, but you turn away and take a deep breath. If someone is with you, and they also notice, it's likely one or the other of you will comment on how grateful you are not to live like that. You'll drive on, without any real thought of helping whoever is inside. It's what people do. It's how they cope and survive. America is a country built on an innate ability to look the other way and move on, with a heart formed from the moments, days, and events where something snaps, and looking away is no longer possible.

Among the broken homes and dying vehicles are the churches. North Carolinians will make a church out of anything. An old shed might have a sign proclaiming it the "Shining Light Tabernacle of Starry Wisdom," and no matter how odd, uninviting, or outright disturbing the place might be, come Sunday... it will be filled with one or another flavor of the faithful. In some towns, particularly those that are very old, by American standards, if young by those of the world, there seem to be more churches than businesses. Many of them have their own private graveyards. Apparently, it's important to be certain, even after death, that mixed congregations, and races, families and bloodlines don't mix.

Another oddity about rural North Carolina can be found right next door to many of the ruined buildings, hovels, or plowed fields. Newly built homes with well-groomed yards, outbuildings, fountains and flowers often share real estate with rusted trailers and forgotten farm equipment. Without regard to property value, many North Carolina families simply pick a spot, and settle in. It can be disconcerting for an outsider to drive though the countryside, trying to figure out how the uneven, unpredictable layout of housing and business, farms and place of worship ever came to be, or how the inhabitants make it work.

When the Hachette family decided to move out of Windfall into the country, they chose a piece of land along a deserted road, tucked in between an old church with one wall caved in and the steeple canted at a dangerous angle, and a corn field that stretched off to a tree line in the distance. There were no other homes on that short stretch of road, though, despite its

privacy, less than half a mile away you could cut onto a county
road and be in Elizabeth City in less than twenty minutes, or
Old Mill in fifteen.

Their place was a four-bedroom, three-bath ranch, painted
North Carolina blue, and there was a ring of stones out front
with a flagpole embedded in cement where they flew Old Glory.
Despite the fact that maybe half a dozen vehicles would pass
their home in a month, and half of those would be tractors,
they had political signs in the yard supporting various local
candidates for sheriff or county commissioner. They owned
a truck, and a bigger truck, two ATVs, a bass boat (the ATVs
and boat were kept in the garage, the trucks, both with sizeable
monthly payments and year of debt remaining, sat outside in
the weather).

They had three hounds living in a long, clean, comfortable
run out back for hunting, and a boxer named Max who lived
inside and slept with their oldest son, Jeb—short for Jebadiah,
all of the children had good, biblical names—and watched
American Ninja Warrior with the family on the couch.

You could drive down a hundred country or urban roads,
in northeastern North Carolina and find families just like the
Hachettes. Old families with new brains, history with no anchor.
Living day to day, vaguely aware of the world around them and
beyond their social media feeds or the local tractor pull. There
is, in fact, no reason to write about this family, or their home,
except for that church.

Max knew. From the first day they moved in, he watched
out the back window, whining low in his throat. The family
joked about squirrels, or rabbits. They wondered if crows were
landing in the field separating them from the ruined house of
worship to taunt him. Then one night, when Max seemed to
lose his mind and nearly clawed his way through the back door,
they found one of the hounds dead in the yard. It wasn't in the
pen, though the door was closed. The other two dogs were hud-
dled in the back of their doghouse, wrapped so tightly around
one another that it was difficult to be certain they were not a
single, two-headed creature.

There were what looked vaguely like footprints in the yard.

Drag marks stretched from the kennel across the yard, ending at the lifeless body of the third hound. The dog's eyes were glazed, it's tongue lolled. Nothing seemed to be wrong with it—physically. More footprints led off toward the church.

Bobby Hachette phoned Cletus J. Diggs the morning after they found the hound... Bobby came from a different generation, where they'd been more focused on folksy, down-home names and less on the Good Book. He had known Cletus for most of his life—went to school with him in Old Mill, played football on the same team. The two hadn't spoken in ten years, but when something strange happened in or around Old Mill, Cletus was the man to call. The sheriff might or might not respond. The state police would definitely ignore anything off the grid. Cletus had a different reputation. Weird might as well have been his middle name.

Cletus didn't go straight to Bobby's place. He stopped next door at the ruined church, pulled just off the road, and sat, staring. The building was old, but not ancient. In a state that had actually had English governors during colonial times, it was fairly new, despite its ruined state. There was a plaque embedded in the dirt out front; Cletus had read it as young man. The building had been erected in 1911 by a Reverend William R. White. The ironic part of that was Reverend White had been a man of color. This church had been one of the first official places of worship for the freed slaves. Built by hand, one plank at a time, all the work and the materials donated by families so poor they probably went hungry for weeks at a time to make it happen.

Cletus knew his local history. At least, he knew parts of it that mattered. When he'd first read of this place at the library, he'd made the visit. He had not even told his friend Jasper, because, although Jasper had a good heart, he didn't have the sense God gave a screwdriver, and Cletus had known the place would not have the same effect on them both. He'd needed the experience for himself.

Despite the certificate hanging on his wall that designated Cletus as an ordained minister, he wasn't a big fan of organized religion. In his lifetime, churches had taken money from the poor, happiness from the free, and been responsible for more broken marriages, lost dreams, and misplaced honor than any other single source. It did not change the sacrifice that had gone into this building. Those men and women had wanted something—a place of their own—a connection to the unknown that they could count on. As such things so often did—it had ended badly.

For several years, the church had operated in peace. If anything, the local white congregations had reacted with relief. It was remote, far from the pews and sanctity of their own places of worship. It protected their ridiculous sense of privilege while relieving them of the guilt of exclusion by providing an alternative. Didn't matter that the alternative was rooted firmly in their cultural prejudice, only that it existed, and they could tell themselves they had done "the right thing". Until Tilly Nixon, who had wanted Billy Knight to escort her to cotillion, saw him staring at Irma Bowen and decided to accuse Jeb White, Reverend White's nephew, of following her and staring at her "lewdly".

It didn't matter that the accusation was petty, or untrue. A black man (or boy) attracted to a young white girl set off all the alarms. Most of the truly horrible things in those days had happened much farther south, but Old Mill, North Carolina, was not what you'd call progressive—not in the early 1900s, and not in the present. Tempers flared. Old hatreds rose and blossomed.

In 1923, on a cold October Sunday morning, the good congregation of the First Revival Church and Mission of Old Mill, North Carolina, had arrived to find the body of Jeb White swinging slowly from a branch of the old oak out front of the church. A burned cross smoldered several yards away.

Old Mill was a small, tight community. It was literally impossible to remove the Nixons, or the Knights, The Winslows or the Wootens from the mix. The sheriff had made a big show of investigating the murder. The congregations of all the local white churches had tutted and gotten teary-eyed and offered baked goods and prayers. The black community had protested and held vigils. They had been angry, and scared. Black men and women only appeared in public in groups, and only when absolutely necessary for school, or shopping, or church.

Except... they hadn't gone to church. No one could bring themselves to attend, with that tree right outside, with the memory so fresh.

There were other colored churches in the area, and slowly Reverend White's flock had dwindled, and then died away completely. Eventually, though he had burned candles and kept the doors opened every Sunday, the church had become a husk—a dead place where no one felt comfortable gathering, where the comfort of a loving God, tenuous at the best of times, seemed distant and cold.

Once every decade or so, some group of well-intentioned churchgoers ventured inside to check the lay of the land, or a team of ghost-busters ventured to spend the night. If the church was haunted, it was not the kind of haunting those people had sought. Everyone who entered grew more and more... uncomfortable. There was something "wrong" in the air, a discomfort that seeped through to the bone (or so the last paranormal "expert" to brave the abandoned building had claimed). Time had passed, the building had rotted, and the world moved on.

It was time for Cletus to move on, too.

"Damn it, Bobby," he said.

Then he climbed out of his truck and walked across the church grounds and into his old friend's yard. Out back, the remaining hounds bayed their welcome and warning, letting the family know someone was on the property. It was one of the reasons Cletus fished instead of hunting. The dogs drove him crazy. He had one—a mutt named "Dog," but Dog was quiet, laid in the corner when Cletus was home, and lived in his kennel outside the rest of the time. He didn't howl, and so far, he'd found no ghosts.

"You tellin' me we live next to a haunted church, Cletus?" Bobby said. "You don't really believe that? Do you?"

The thing was, he didn't. Cletus didn't say anything at first. He just stared out the window of Bobby's home toward the church. He knew the history... he knew that, if there was ever a place that ought to be haunted, that church was it. He knew something had killed the dog, but he didn't really believe it was a ghost. It was too much like a fairy tale, and though he'd seen and been involved in things that no sane person would believe, he couldn't really believe that a ghost was the culprit. It had given him a sort of sixth sense—the ability to pick up on a vibe that, in this case, did not feel right.

"No," he said at last. "I don't think a ghost killed your dog, Bobby. But I can't help thinking that there's something about that church and its history that's relevant. You live in the middle of nowhere. It's not likely someone came out here randomly just to scare you. You wouldn't know if anyone had a reason to be mad at you?"

Bobby looked lost in thought for a long moment, then shook his head. "I won't pretend there's no one out there that thinks I'm a butthead, Cletus, but no. No one in particular. I keep to myself, do my job... come home. I hunt and fish, but our family, we mostly keep to ourselves. I think I'd know if someone was mad enough to kill my dog..."

"Yeah, that's about what I thought," Cletus said. "I don't think it's about you. I don't know—yet—what it *is* about... but I'm going to do some digging. In the meantime, is there a place you could move your other dogs? The ones that don't live in the house?"

"No... boarding costs some serious bucks," Bobby said. "You think they might do it again?"

"Don't know," Cletus said. "Try to get out and check on them, if you can't move them. And if you let Max out, someone should go with him. Same with the kids. Let's play this safe until we figure out what's going on."

Bobby nodded. "I trust you, Cletus. We just want our lives back... We keep to ourselves. This is..."

"I know," Cletus said. "Believe me, if anyone in Old Mill understands how you feel, it's me. We'll figure it out. I'm going back into town to the library and do a little more digging. I know the history of that church, but it seems to me there's been some news about it that was more recent. I'll call you if I find anything."

Bobby rose and held out his hand.

"Thanks," he said. "I'm going to load those dogs up and

head over to Ed's place... Best idea I've heard since all of this started."

The front doors of the High Holy Evangelical Temple of the Sacred Light were closed, but light seeped under them from within and leaked onto the chipped paint of the front steps. It glinted at the edges of the partially boarded windows. Where the eaves met the roof, glowing streaks lined the weathered boards, striping mud dauber nests and flickering on tattered spider webs.

That light was unsteady. There was no electricity in the church. No phone or power lines dangling in from the dirt and gravel road. There was a cleared spot to the right of the building with a narrow patch you could drive over if you were careful. The ditch was easily five feet deep between the road and the raised area that held the church. There were no cars in the lot, and if there had been light to see, no recent tread marks or sign of passing feet would be found.

Behind the church, fields of soybeans stretched off to a distant tree line. There was a small yard in back of the building, the centerpiece of which was a graveyard with fewer than a dozen headstones. They were so old they were crumbling to dust, finally acknowledging the words of whatever long-dead preacher had offered their contents, ashes to ashes... dust to dust.

The wooden sign out front was warped and broken. The painted text was striped with age and faded by moss and weather. There had been no new announcement of a sermon or services in more than a decade. No one filled the pews or lit candles for the altar. Still, there was light within, and the structure—abandoned thought it might have been—was not empty.

A single soul still kept the watch. A lone believer knelt at the altar, once a night during the week and twice on Sunday. A moldy copy of the King James Version of the Bible lay open on the podium at the front of the room, it's pages tattered, damp and stuck to one another like fallen leaves after a rain. Scribbled notes filled the margins and several notebooks filled with tight, cramped script lay open beside it. They were newer, and in better repair.

The church was not deserted. Bedding was arranged neatly

on the front pew. The old fireplace smoldered where the previous night's fire had burned low. The insides of the front and
rear doors were locked tightly with an assortment of deadbolts
and chains.

The walls were covered in a wild montage of photos, newspaper clippings, photocopied sections of books. The stories
were linked by lines of colored yarn, hammered in place with
finishing nails. Unlike similar walls on TV cop shows, these
were all red lines, and they led in a steady progression from top
to bottom—from past to present. It was a linear and very literal
map of the sins of the fathers.

The first article was a photocopy... very old print. The head-
line read:

NEGRO ACCUSED OF LEWD BEHAVIOR FOUND HANGED

The article itself held little of value to history. It was what
one might expect, an attempt to make excuses for the crimes of
white men against black. A whitewash of the truth that would
leave all the holy people of Old Mill with some guilt, but not
enough to stick. It was mentioned that Jeb White was the son of
a local minister. It was mentioned that he was black and that he
had been accused of a crime. It was not mentioned—not a single
time—that there was no evidence the accusations were truthful.
There was no acknowledgment of Reverend White's loss, or his
pain.

The walls told a long, continuing story. Black man goes to
prison—no evidence, but, hey, he was black. Black teen accused
of rape... acquitted because he was not even in town, but then
beaten almost to death by unknown white men three nights
later. Police have suspect in... insert ten cases in a row in a single year... same lineup of suspects—all black—even in the case
of an ATM mugging where the victim was certain she'd been
attacked by a young white man in a pickup truck.

There were grainy photographs of men, women, children,
teenagers... girls who'd been attacked, or raped... boys who'd
been beaten, a few killed. Men run before the judge count-
less times without sufficient reason. As the years passed, the

number of deaths dropped but the number of cases increased and not all of them were black. There were Hispanics, Asians, even a couple of pale white girls, looking very out of place, their faces deeply shadowed and bruised, one of them with both eyes blackened so she could barely see.

The timeline was linear, and it began at the old church. It began at that hanging tree. It was a work drawn in bloodlines and scattered verses of scripture, linked by acts of violence and apathy. It was a portrait of an Old Mill, North Carolina, from a particularly bad angle. For Ezekiel White, it was a continuing spiral toward a very dark place.

He slipped in through the back door of the old church, another thin, elongated shadow scratching at the edges of the pews and trailing along the wall as he approached the remnant of the altar up front. He was getting old. It showed in the graying hairs over his ears, and the deepening lines of his features. Rail thin, prone to long bouts of fasting and prayer, he could have passed for a character in a modern zombie movie, except for his eyes.

They did not glow red, nor were they black, empty pits. Up close enough, they resembled the overly large, sad eyes from those Seventies black velvet paintings. Deep and brown, filled with pain. Most people who stopped long enough to meet that gaze were stunned or looked away in sudden shame. They were too deep, too real, and they seemed to cut straight through whatever mask a person wore to the core of who they truly were.

Ezekiel walked the length of his timeline, from the present to the past, trailing a finger slowly beneath the photos… touching one here or there, stopping to whisper words under his breath. He knew their stories, and he knew their lives. Each of those he'd immortalized on that wall he kept close to his heart. They were not all good people. Some of those, for instance, who were constantly in the police lineup were there because the odds were good they'd been involved. Some of those who had been arrested, and treated badly, had committed the crimes. They had killed, stolen, in some cases raped and mistreated women and children. The key—the thing that bound them one to another—was they circumstance surrounding their arrest, or the assumptions leading to their imprisonment or death. Or disappearance.

Ezekiel passed beyond the wall of photos and knelt at the altar. He lowered his eyes and whispered his prayers. They were not what one might expect from a preacher or a holy man. They were not, in fact, necessarily directed at the God of Sunday-go-to-meeting, thoughts, and prayers. They were directed at the victims, at their spirits, and their memory. They were directed at the dark underpinning of a single, Southern town on the outskirts of the Great Dismal Swamp.

The last photo in the long line had been printed down at the library off his phone. It was a shot of the Hachette home. The dog kennel was just visible out back. Bobby's pickup was in the drive. The old fence between the home and the church was broken and dangling from rusty wire. Face-out by the road, a political sign flashed blue with the smiling, puffy face of a white man in his sixties. It said, "Vote for Big Bill Nixon for Sheriff."

It wasn't the first time Nixon's name appeared. Not by a long shot. Most of the recent articles involving the rounding up of all-black lineups had happened on Nixon's watch. He'd been sheriff for nearly a decade. His days of running down "perps" were long past—a walk farther than from his desk to his pickup brought the risk of heart attack. He had to be prepped before talking to reporters, so he knew what cases were being investigated, and who was coming to trial. In other words, he was sheriff in name only, and had been for some time. It was not a name that did the county proud.

It was too much for Ezekiel. For that sign—that image—to be so close to the tree, for people who thought it was appropriate for a man of that ilk to enforce the law to have their kids, and their dogs, crossing through that broken fence without any concern over, or knowledge of, where they had chosen to put down roots. Too much. He would scare them off, make them move, if he could. If not... he would do what needed to be done.

There was no one else.

The light had begun to fade, but still he knelt. He didn't rise until the shadows were so deep he nearly disappeared into them and the images and pages lining the wall had melted into a single splotch. Then, silent and invisible, he slipped back out the back door and headed off into the fields.

"Cletus you have *got* to be kidding me..."

Jasper Winslow, sprawled back over Cletus' couch with a beer in one hand and the TV remote in the other, scowled. Cletus didn't even glance at his friend. His eyes were glued to the endless string of left-turning, multi-colored cars on the screen. They were three hundred laps in to a five-hundred-lap race, and it was starting to get interesting.

"You know me better than that, Jaz," he said. "Bobby is a friend, and I can't figure a better way to do this. You have a better idea shoot, otherwise, pass me another beer and watch the race."

It was a calculated play. Jasper might storm out and tell him to have sexual relations with himself. It had happened before. Cletus was counting on the greater part of a case of cold beer and two hundred more laps to win the day. Jasper might not be easy but he was predictable.

"It'll be fine," Cletus said. "It's not like we planned a fishing trip..."

Jasper snorted. In recent years, every time the two had tried to plan a quiet morning fishing, things had gotten weird. Weirder each time, in fact, and the only fish Cletus had eaten in a year had come from the Captain D's in Elizabeth City.

"It's one night," Cletus continued. "Two tops..."

"Two? Two nights alone... in a haunted church? Or, maybe not haunted, maybe it's just where some psycho with an electric machete hangs out between murders..."

"That's the dumbest thing I've ever heard, Jaz, and I've known you a long time, so..."

"What?" Jasper said." You said someone killed the dog... you said it was barkin' at that damned old tree..."

"An electric machete?" Cletus finally turned, grinning. "Tell me, Jaz, in that vacant space you call a brain, how exactly would that work? Also, nothing to worry about. Unless he has a big-ass battery, there's no power in the church."

"Yeah, that makes it a better idea," Jasper mumbled.

Just then the lead car hit some sort of soft patch, skewed left, then right, and skidded in a long 360 off the inside of the track. The other cars sped past as it spun to a stop.

"That ain't good," Jasper said.

"Nope," Cletus said, sipping his beer. Then, he said. "We'll settle in about eight o'clock. Give us time to eat and gather some supplies. Want to be inside and quiet before dark."

Jasper just shook his head and drained his beer.

Cletus had Bobby pick the two of them up in town. Jaz insisted on carrying in a cooler, and Cletus didn't ask what was in it. He knew, and he also knew it would piss him off. Jaz would drink beer in the face of a zombie apocalypse, and though it seemed like a damned fool idea, more often than not, it worked out. In any case, it wasn't worth arguing over, and without that cooler he doubted even his lifelong friendship would be enough to drag his buddy into a dark abandoned church with no cable TV.

"You sure about this, Cletus?" Bobby asked. "You going to be okay?"

"Yeah, we'll be fine," Cletus said. "We do this kind of thing all the time. We've got our hunting rifles, just in case. Don't expect to need them, but..."

Jasper glared at him but held his silence. Cletus rolled his eyes.

"Okay, not all the time, but it's not our first rodeo. Besides, as Jasper's Pap is always telling me, the boys in those NASCAR races just drive in circles. Missing a race is like not watching the clock spin around."

Jasper's brow furrowed, and Bobby laughed. "You two should be on TV," he said. "I just hope it's not a waste of time."

"Worst case, no one shows up," Cletus said. "Best case, we find out what happened to your dog... and we put an end to it."

Jasper could no longer maintain his silence.

"You know good and damn well that's not the worst case," he said. "And the best case is here in this cooler. I don't know how I let you drag me into these things..."

"It's my sparkling personality," Cletus said. "You can't help yourself."

"You bought the beer, didn't you?" Bobby asked.

Cletus laughed.

"I did not, but I didn't stop him."

Despite the beer and Jasper's grumbling, they settled in quickly, sending Bobby back home as soon as they could get him out.

"We don't know who we're dealing with," Cletus said. "We don't want to give ourselves away with too much activity. You go home, watch TV, and we'll keep watch here. Might not be anything to see, but after what happened with the dog, I don't think whoever it is is done."

"Be careful then," Bobby said. "And if you need me, make some noise."

"Will do," Cletus said.

As they watched him cross through the fence and head around the back of his house, Jasper shook his head.

"I will never understand," he said, "why I listen to you."

"I told you. It's my sparkling personality," Cletus repeated. His grin was wide, but Jasper didn't even turn to see it. He was already popping the top on his first beer.

They had a good view of Bobby's back yard. They could see the kennel out back where the dogs were settling in for the night, and they could see the front yard, the driveway, and the road beyond.

They settled in, Cletus taking up a position at the window, and Jasper leaning against a wall, sipping his beer. They didn't talk much, at first. The sun dropped slowly, and the shadows lengthened. The two had shared stakeouts before, and it almost always ended the same way: Cletus watching and Jasper drinking until he got sleepy. This night was no exception.

There was no sound, and the moon was obscured by silver-lined clouds. Nothing moved outside but the leaves of cornstalks in the fields, and the newer, smaller branches of the old tree.

Cletus paid attention to that tree. He could not help but think it had something to do with what was happening. In the history of the church, nothing was as life-changing and important as the hanging that had scattered a congregation—the hate that had ended a young man's life. He was surprised no one had chopped it down or burned it. He was almost as surprised that the church was still standing. Something had kept the wolves at bay… something had preserved that single site of bigotry like a monument. Was it possibly supernatural, or was there something he was missing?

Old Mill was like a magnet for weird. For all his grumbling, Jasper had stood by Cletus' side in the face of things that should have driven both men crazy. Despite the strange things they had endured and witnessed, it was no easier to consider the supernatural than it had been the first time it stared them in the face. The human brain, it seemed, had an incredible facility for ignoring the obvious in favor of the comfortable.

There was no movement anywhere in the yard. The corn in the fields waved gently in the wind. Clouds skipped across the moon. The dogs remained quiet and, after a time, the lights at Bobby's house flickered out one at a time until only the back porch was lit. Empty. Cletus' knees were sore from kneeling at the window to watch. He was about to ask Jasper to take a turn when a darker bit of shadow peeled free of the cornfield and moved slowly down the church side of the fence.

It was a man, moving quickly, but furtively. He squatted so that most of his body would be out of sight from Bobby's house. It wasn't good enough. The dogs barked, tentatively at first, and then louder.

The man stopped, dropped lower to the ground, and waited. Cletus held his breath. He knew the intruder couldn't hear him, but he couldn't help it. The dogs barked a couple more times, but then fell silent. Cletus watched, but no doors opened at Bobby's place. The family either didn't consider random barking a problem, even under the circumstances, or they were too spooked to check. Just when Cletus thought the stranger would either rise and continue whatever he had planned or retreat, the silence was broken. Twice.

Finally, too bored to sit still, Jasper downed the last of the beer he was holding, let out a loud, reverberating belch, and before Cletus could turn and try to stop him, he grabbed another beer and opened it with a loud, fizzing pop.

Things happened very quickly after that. The intruder leaped to his feet, spun toward the church, then took off around behind the building. The dogs erupted in a cacophony of sound, and the back door to Bobby's house opened, silhouetting the man with a shotgun cradled in his arms.

"Christ on a stick," Cletus muttered. He rose, turned, and ran out the front door of the church, heading for Bobby's yard with his hands raised. "It's me, Bobby. Don't shoot, for chrissake."

In the cornfield, there was a soft *WHOOF!* Cletus turned, as did Bobby. A cloud of smoke rose from the field.

"Hell, no," Cletus said. He turned and started running. He knew that while the corn was green, it could burn, and if it did, it was going to be bad, not just for the farmer, but for the surrounding fields, trees, and Bobby's house. He crashed into the corn and ran, stalks slapping him in the face as he passed through. It wasn't too far to where he'd seen the smoke, and he had an idea that if he got there quickly enough, he might be able to stop what had just started.

Bobby called out behind him, and moments later Cletus heard the crashing, cursing sounds of the other man in full pursuit. He hoped he'd dropped that shotgun along the way, because if he tripped, and it went off, it could get hairy.

Then, as quickly as his headlong rush had begun, it ended. He stopped short as he stumbled into a cleared spot. Smoke billowed from a hole in the ground, but none of the corn had caught. There were broken stalks where someone had passed quickly, but there was no sign of whoever had set the false blaze.

Bobby broke through seconds later, turning wildly and pointing the shotgun first one direction, then another. Cletus reached out and pressed down on the end of the barrel.

"He's gone, Bobby. Whoever did that is gone."

"But where..."

They both turned back toward the church, and the house.

"I'll be double-D Goddamned," Cletus growled.

The two took off again, making slightly better time over the ground they'd already cleared coming in. The dogs weren't barking, they were baying loudly. Crazed. Someone screamed. Cletus lowered his head and ran like he'd never run before, fighting against the thick, tripping stalks of corn trying to spring back upright. The moon shone down clear and bright, but they could not see more than the steeple of the old church, and suddenly they seemed miles away.

Ezekiel knew that his moment had come. There would be no second chance, and there would be no *first* chance if he hesitated. He had led the father and the other into the field—Diggs, he thought. Cletus Diggs. What was he doing here? Why would he protect them? It didn't matter. He knew what he had to do. The good book was not clear on many things, but "an eye for an eye" did not have gray areas. There was no statute of limitations on sin... or redemption.

He slipped from the field, moving quickly, and passed through the fence into the Hachettes' back yard. He ignored the dogs. He ignored everything. He had a single goal, and as he raced toward the back porch, he saw that—across the years and the pain, the darkness and the irreconcilable stain of that church, and that tree—the Lord had provided.

The back porch was lit brightly, and in the center of it, an old shotgun held in unsteady hands, a young man watched him approach. Ezekiel slowed... held up his hands... smiled. The boy hesitated.

"He nearly got away," Ezekiel said. "Your pa and Cletus are chasin' him down..."

The barrel of the shotgun dipped, and Ezekiel sprang. Before Jebediah Hachette could raise the gun again, Ezekiel slapped him hard across the face and the gun dropped to the ground. Ezekiel saw the silhouette of a woman appear in the doorway behind the boy, but he had no time for it. He reached down, scooped Jebediah up, and slung him over his shoulder. The woman came at him, and he lashed out without hesitation. His fist connected with her jaw and she staggered back and went down. Bearing his burden as if the boy were no more than a light sack of grain, Ezekiel turned and ran back for the church.

By the time Cletus and Bobby broke into the clear, the hounds were baying as if Satan himself were chasing them. The Hachette house was lit up as brightly as every lamp in the home could get it, and the church was equally shadowed. Bobby started for his house immediately and after only a moment's hesitation Cletus followed. He was worried about Jasper, but there were women and children, and it was not Jaz's first rodeo.

The racket the dogs created was jarring, and it erased any hope they might have had of hearing an attack or a retreat. They crashed through the hole in the fence and sprinted for the back porch. They saw Bobby's wife, Carrie, silhouetted, backlit by the brilliant illumination of every light in the house. Her arms were raised to the sky.

"What is it?" Bobby cried out. "What happened?"

"He took Jebediah," Carrie said. "He... took him."

"Where?"

Before she could answer, the two had turned. They knew. He would take the boy to the church. There was no other answer that made sense... not that this one did. But how far ahead was he? How long had he been gone? If he'd prepared ahead of time, how long would he need?

They ran, scanning the shadows for any sign of movement. Nothing moved. Nothing made a sound, except the baying hounds and Carrie's wails. If there was a sound, it could not be heard.

Ezekiel had been preparing for this moment for years. The tree... he'd climbed every branch of it that would hold his weight, had lain across the thickest branches, particularly the one he knew had supported the rope so long ago. He'd had no specific plan, before this moment, but he had always had the vague notion of how it would end—how it had to end. The Bible might be full of crap in a lot of ways, but that line about an eye for an eye? That was truth. That was the only answer that made sense or mattered.

So, he'd prepared. There was a thin nylon rope, very strong but looped and knotted in a traditional hangman's noose, on that branch. It had been wound tightly, the noose itself held to the top of the branch by a bit of duct tape. He had never been certain how he'd use it, or at least that was what he'd told himself.

Now he knew. Someone had to pay the price.

The boy over his shoulder kicked and scratched. He felt the first brush of teeth against his shoulder and took a jump, banging the boy's head against bone and stunning him momentarily.

There was an old stump beneath the tree, lying on its side. He'd left it there, knowing he might need it. He'd always told himself it would not come to that, that he'd find a way to explain how he felt, to bring some sense of *justice* for Reverend White, for Ezekiel's family. For the men lined up week after week to be stared at for crimes they did not commit. For the beatings and insults, the bitter hatred and the prejudice he'd chronicled year in and year out… For so many things that it made his head hurt to even think about it. Someone had to pay. Surely.

He reached the base of the tree and kicked the stump upright. It wobbled once and then stood precariously. With a quick shrug of his shoulders, he dropped Jebediah to the ground roughly and, using the stump as a step up, leaped to the branch, grabbed the rope, and yanked it free.

He was on his feet again in seconds. The boy had risen groggily and tried to crawl away, but Ezekiel grabbed him by the back of the neck with one hand and hauled him to his feet. He drew Jebediah back until his heel cracked into the stump and then he lifted. The boy had no choice but to take a step up and then he was on the stump, wobbling, depending on Ezekiel to hold him steady. There was no hesitation. Ezekiel grabbed the dangling noose and snaked it over Jebediah's head, tightening it deftly at his throat with a tug on the rope.

"It's not personal, boy," he said. "I don't know you. I don't know your daddy. I know he supports a man who thinks black men are not his equal, and I know the town—the world—has forgotten this tree. This place. What happened here. Do you know?"

Jebediah trembled violently and shook his head.

"N-no sir," he said. "Please…"

"Be quiet, boy. I'm going to tell you. A long time ago, an ancestor of mine, a preacher, watched over the congregation of this church. His son was hanged here, this very branch. You know why?"

Jebediah shook his head again.

"He was black." Ezekiel said. He tugged the noose again, tightening it around Jebediah's throat before the boy could speak. The sound of voices rose not far away.

"It's time," Ezekiel said. He lowered his eyes and began a soft, hurried prayer.

Jasper watched through the window. He was not good at being quiet or still. Out on a hunt, he was next to useless, scaring any deer or other game away before anyone could get off a decent shot, but this time he held his breath, moved slowly, and managed not to make a sound.

"Where the hell are you, Cletus?" he muttered.

He saw the man drop the noose over a boy's neck and knew he had to do something, but there was no way he could move his dead ass across that church lawn fast enough or quietly enough to stop what was about to happen.

He knelt, felt around by his feet, and found the butt of his rifle. He was a good shot, but not a great one, and he'd already had several beers, but he could not think of what else to do. He heard voices in the distance, and thought maybe the man would run, but instead, he hurried his movements, tightened the noose.

"Christ on a stick," Jasper said softly. He raised the rifle, flipped off the safety, and laid the barrel on the sill of the old broken window. He was afraid moonlight would glitter off of it, or he'd make a noise and give himself away, but he managed to sight in carefully. He held his breath.

The spot where the rope was tied around the branch was clearly lit by the moon and seemed to grow in his sight. He felt a sudden calm that was not only uncharacteristic, but damned spooky. He took another very deep, slow breath, and released it. As he did, he pulled steadily back on the trigger.

Several things happened at once. Cletus and Bobby broke through the fence from the back yard next door. The man spun toward them, the motion pushing the boy forward, off the log. He kicked it over and out of the way so that Jebediah could not swing back and save himself. The gun roared.

Jasper was not looking at the knot any longer, however. Nor was Cletus. Bobby ran toward Ezekiel and Jebediah, but he, too, stopped in his tracks. The rope parted. Jebediah dropped, and in doing so struck Ezekiel, who staggered and fell, facing up toward the branch above.

On that branch the dim figure of a young black man sat. His clothing was outdated, and his face was awash in sorrow. In his hands he held the two parted halves of the rope that had been tied to the branch. He opened his mouth and a single word washed over them all... it did not seem to be an actual sound, did not echo or reverberate, simply pressed in and through their minds.

"Enough."

Then he was gone. The branch was just a branch. Jebediah tried to rise, pulling at the rope around his neck. Bobby was at his side in seconds, loosening the knot and tossing the line aside.

Cletus dove on top of Ezekiel and held him down, though the man did not struggle. He simply stared up at the branch above him. Tears ran down his cheeks. A moment later, Jasper stumbled out of the barn to stand at their side.

"Did you see..." he said softly.

Cletus looked up at him, nodded, and then said, "Hell of a shot, Jaz. You saved him."

Jasper looked dubiously at the parted rope and down at the rifle in his hand. He dropped it and stood, staring dumbly up into the tree.

"Call Sheriff Bob," Cletus said softly. "Bobby, Jaz, and I will hold this guy here. You get Jeb home and into bed. Get him to his mother."

Bobby looked down at Ezekiel, his eyes dark and smoldering with anger, but he nodded. He rose, lifted Jebediah into his arms, and headed back through the fence.

"You saw that, Cletus," Jasper said. "I know you did."

"We all saw it, Jaz," Cletus said. "Don't mean anyone will believe it." He glanced down at Ezekiel, who had still not struggled or moved.

"Who are you?" Cletus asked. "Why?"

"Ezekiel. I'm Ezekiel White. "My great grandfather..."

The gears clicked and Cletus knew.

"Reverend White." He said. "He was the preacher here when..."

Ezekiel closed his eyes and nodded.

Cletus glanced up at the branch. Sirens rose in the distance, and for just a second he marveled that anyone in the local sheriff's department had reacted so quickly.

"No one remembers," Ezekiel said. "No one cares. They still line up every black man in Old Mill for any crime. They still shoot kids for pulling out cell phones and laugh over beers in private while they talk about us like we're some kind of lower life form. It hasn't changed."

"It's changed," Cletus said. "Just not enough. Killing that boy? That was never an answer. That eye-for-an-eye crap went out with the Old Testament if you're a believer. I'm not. I think men should be responsible for their own actions... their own lives."

"He stopped me," Ezekiel said. "Jebediah... he stopped me."

"Did you know?" Jasper asked, finally turning away from the branch to look down into Ezekiel's eyes.

"What?" Ezekiel asked.

"That the boy's name... was Jeb?"

Ezekiel's eyes widened. Then closed. The tears flowed again.

The sirens grew louder, and Cletus drew Ezekiel to his feet.

The moon slipped behind a cloud... and he pushed his captive toward the road in deepening shadow.

The wind picked up, just a bit. It sounded as if it whispered to him.

It repeated... "Enough"... and he felt the tears itching at the corners of his eyes.

"If there's a God," he said silently. "One day..."

IN THE HANDS OF AN ANGRY GOD

BY JOSEPH MULAK

There's just a few of us left now. As far as I know, anyway. We're so far away from civilization there could be millions of survivors still out there, but I doubt it. Things were bad when I left the city. I can't imagine they got any better.

There used to be eighteen of us. Just a collection of people who managed to stumble on the same remote cabin over the course of a few months. Seven of us have managed to stay alive up until now.

Bryce is still with us. Dammit. That self-absorbed pretty boy never ceases to aggravate me. Even now I can't look at him without feeling like I'm going to throw up. But he hasn't killed himself yet. I guess that's something I can say for him. I thought he would have now that he doesn't have his looks to get by anymore.

Even the women in our group, the ones that fawned over Bryce's handsome face and toned body, deny it now. They want to be seen as strong, independent, feminist women. In reality, they're the exact opposite of what they pretend to be.

Cass is the worst of them. If she could talk, nothing intelligent would come out of her mouth and I'm sure she'd use the word "like" more often than is necessary in every sentence. I've never been so grateful for the silence. I mean, she still draws her eyebrows on. Who's she trying to impress? Not Bryce. Not anymore.

Roxanne is the one person I can stand these days. Curtis used to be okay, but he's become paranoid since Brad committed suicide. I can't say I blame him. No one ever came out and said it, but I'm pretty sure they were a couple. Or at least sleeping together. I don't know that for sure, but the way they acted around each other, they just seemed close.

But Roxanne, now there's a woman with a good head on her shoulders. She can keep calm in any situation, and she didn't show the least bit of interest in pretty boy. Maybe that's why I like her so much. In a platonic way, mind you.

The cabin is large enough for all of us. It was cramped at first, but since the herd's been thinned out a bit, it's a lot better. There are three bedrooms. I share a room with Curtis. Roxanne and Cass have a room together, as do Camille and Autumn. Bryce is on the couch. Before, when we more than doubled our current population, people were sleeping in chairs, on the floor, wherever we could find the space. I wouldn't say I'm happy about the eleven people who killed themselves, but it *is* nice to sleep in a bed.

Curtis and I are in the living room. I have no idea where the others are. Maybe out for a walk in the woods. Maybe hunting for food. Maybe in another room in the house. Maybe dead. Who knows? I haven't seen any of them all day.

I'm reading. The cabin came stocked with lots of reading material, otherwise I would have gone nuts a long time ago and checked out like the others. Curtis is sitting in the chair across from me. When I look up, he's writing on his notepad. It's the little things I miss. Like the sound of a pencil scratching on the paper. You don't notice these things until they're gone. He tears out the sheet and hands it to me.

"Do you think this will ever end?" it asks me.

I shrug. No sense in writing something I can convey with a gesture. Paper is running low and I have no idea if we'll be getting more any time soon. I'm thinking at some point we'll have to find a way into town to get some supplies. Assuming there are any left. After a year, who knows how much has already been looted.

I hand the sheet back to Curtis and he starts writing something else on it before giving it back. "I miss Brad."

I write, "I know." And give it back.

"I miss the others too."

I nod. I get the impression Curtis is like me in that he has very little respect for those who are left. He spends a lot of time with Roxanne, but he tends to avoid the rest of them, like I do.

He doesn't write anything else, so I assume the conversation is over and go back to my book. The pickings are slim these days. I've already burned through the thrillers and mysteries and I'm reading the classics now. War and Peace. I figured it should last a while but I'm not enjoying it. It's dry and long-winded, but it's a time killer.

I can feel Curtis' eyes on me, and when I look up he's staring at me, pleading. I don't know what to do. He's upset, I can see that. He's alone and depressed and I have no way of comforting him. We're screwed. That's all there is to it.

But he won't stop looking at me and it's distracting. I have no idea what the hell he wants from me. Hell, I could use some comforting myself. Curtis isn't the only one who's lost people. I had a family once. Back before all this started. I had a wife and an unborn child.

Now they're gone and here I am with a bunch of strangers, most of whom I don't even like. Funny how things work out.

Camille and Autumn walk into the room, startling me. I don't hear their footsteps approaching. Of course I don't. I haven't heard anything in over a year. They're both crying and I know before they can show us. I know we lost someone else.

The girls lead us outside to the back of the cabin where Roxanne had found a shotgun and killed herself.

Dammit. I was hoping it was Bryce.

But I can't say I'm surprised. I can't blame her. I think about doing the same thing every minute of every day. I don't know what keeps me from going through with it.

I motion for the girls to go back into the house. Curtis and I grab shovels and start digging a hole. I can tell he doesn't want to. He's upset and shaking from holding back tears, but I don't want to do this alone. I'm holding back tears too, but I hide it better.

It's a difficult task. Not just the actual labour. But burying a body--a *human being*--never gets easier. I'm sure that someday

I'll be doing this for Curtis. And then I *will* cry.

We finish packing the dirt. I lean on my shovel and wipe the sweat from my forehead. I want to say something. Words of encouragement, my favourite memory of Roxanne. Something. But I can't. I can only think what I want to say. Writing it wouldn't have the same effect as if I'd said it out loud.

I go back into the house, but Curtis stays behind, staring at the spot where we buried our friend. I leave him to his grief.

The girls are in the living room, seated where Curtis and I had been earlier, both still crying.

Autumn takes out her notepad. Hers has a lot more blank pages than mine. She's not much of a talker.

"Why is He doing this to us?" she writes, and I shrug. I ask myself that same question every waking moment and I have yet to come up with an answer. I don't even have so much as a theory.

I wait for a follow-up question, but there isn't one. We already know *who* is doing this. We just don't know *why*.

I find an empty chair and sit. We all just stare at each other, trying to make sense of what our lives have become, why we choose to keep going on. But it's a useless endeavour.

We stay there until the sun goes down. Curtis hasn't returned and there's still no sign of Bryce. I think about going outside to look for Curtis but I'm afraid of what I might find. Maybe Roxanne's death was too much for him. The straw that broke the camel's back, so to speak. I can't take too much heart-ache in one day. If Curtis is dead, he can wait until morning.

I don't care where Bryce is. I don't want to see him, and I hope he's either dead or run away in search of something better. Maybe that makes me a bad person, but I don't care anymore. Think of me what you will. I am who I am.

I start to feel tired and leave the room. I go to my bed and lie down, since there's nothing else to do. I spend a lot of my time sleeping. Or, at least, lying in bed trying to sleep. With everything going on, it's hard. I toss and turn, unable to get comfortable.

Tonight is no different. I keep seeing Roxanne's lifeless eye staring at me. Just the one since half her face was missing from the scatter of the pellets. I can't get the image out of my head. I see it every time I close my eyes, so I keep them opened and I stare at the wall, hoping sleep will find me.

I feel someone in the room with me. I assume it's Curtis coming back, but when I prop myself up on my elbow to look, it's Autumn. She stands in the doorway for a few moments, as if trying to make a decision.

She walks over, slowly, and sits down on my bed, stroking my back.

I'm uncomfortable, but I can't say anything.

She kisses my neck several times and I remember the first time I made love to Amber after the world was taken over by the silence. I couldn't hear the sound of our bodies slamming together, her moans, her calling out my name.

It seemed empty.

I never touched her again after that.

When I found her dead in our basement, hanging from the ceiling, I thought it was my fault. I still do.

I can feel Autumn's touch as she places her hands under my shirt but can't hear the smack of her lips as she lifts it up and kisses my chest.

Maybe that's why I put my hands on her shoulders and push her away.

Or maybe it's because I still have the image of Roxanne stuck in my head and it dampens the mood.

Or even because I know she's looking for comfort and would seek it with any available man and I just happen to be there. But I know she would rather Bryce as he used to be, but she can't have that now. Not ever again.

Whatever the reason, I stop her. She looks at me for a long moment, confused, trying to figure out if I'm serious.

Even I'm surprised. I'd be lying if I said I never looked at her with lust, sneaking quick glances of her thin body when I thought she wasn't looking. Staring at her ass when she wore short shorts and the tight shirts that hugged her body and showed off her perfect breasts. I'd fantasized about this moment more often than I care to admit, but I just can't go through with it. I know it wouldn't be right.

She leaves the room and I'm left to wonder if it really happened or if I'd imagined the whole thing.

In the morning, when I see her, neither of us can look the other in the eye. I'm searching through the cupboards looking for something to eat. It's been a few days since I've had anything. I'll have to go hunting later since we're out of canned provisions. I don't think we're too far away from the nearest town. Maybe I can go for a walk later and find a store that hasn't been picked clean.

Autumn comes up behind me and sticks a note in my face.

"Did Curtis come back last night?"

I shake my head and write my own note. "If he did, he got up before me. He wasn't in his bed when I woke up."

She looks worried. She likes Curtis. We all do. There's a child-like innocence we found refreshing. I'm worried too.

"I'm sure he's fine," I write. "I'll go look for him in a bit."

She gives me a solemn nod and I can tell she's not comforted, but there's not much more I can do for her.

Bryce walks into the kitchen and I lose my appetite. That face. It makes me want to throw up every time I see it.

Autumn leaves as soon as he walks in and I see the hurt in his eyes. He knows it's because of him, but he has no control over it. I won't go so far as to say it's not his fault. It is. It was his own stupidity.

It was a few months back. There were more of us then. Fourteen, I think. One of our ranks was a fanatical religious woman. Nancy. An older lady. She was a little weird, but nice. The others made fun of her because she spent most of her time reading the Bible. Notes were passed between us, making fun of her and inquiring how she could still believe in God after what had happened. I tried not to make fun of her. I didn't see anything wrong with having faith in something that gives you hope. She wasn't hurting anybody by reading the Bible and praying. She was just trying to find some peace among the chaos, like the rest of us.

We were sitting in the cabin's living room. All of us. Passing notes back and forth, offering ideas as to what was going on. Nancy had dared to offer her opinion.

"God is punishing the world," she wrote. "Just as he had in

the days of Noah." The note was passed around. Most people glanced at it, realized it was just more of her religious gibberish and passed it along to the next person without giving it another thought.

Until the note reached Bryce.

He read it, the disdain showing on his face. He didn't pass the note. Instead, he stood up and walked out of the room, returning with a sheet of paper and a black marker. On it, he had written "FUCK GOD" and slammed the paper on the coffee table for everyone to see.

That's when Nancy ran out of the room.

We all assumed she was hurt by what Bryce did and needed a few moments to regain her composure, so we didn't think anything of it. I can't speak for anyone else, but I thought that Bryce had crossed a line and what he did was unnecessary and cruel. But he didn't deserve what he got.

What none of us had suspected was that Nancy had gone to the kitchen. Because of the silence, none of us could hear what she was doing.

She returned with a large knife and before any of us could react, she pounced on Bryce, slashing at him in anger. No thought behind it, just slashing blindly, hoping to hit something.

She got his face several times. He put his hands up to protect himself and got his arm sliced up pretty good.

It was the first time I'd seen someone in pain, screaming and begging for help without a sound. It was a surreal moment.

We rushed to his aid. If I'm being honest, I did it because I knew I would be judged afterward if I didn't at least pretend to help. We managed to pull her off, but not before the damage had been done. Bryce's face had been cut up beyond recognition.

Camille was a nurse. She grabbed the first aid kit and patched him up as best she could, but without the benefit of a hospital and the proper equipment, she was limited in what she could do.

Nancy continued to fight us, still trying to go after Bryce, which left us with the unpleasant task of figuring out what to do with her.

In the end, there was one option. We couldn't trust her. Kicking her out wasn't even viable since we had no idea if she might try to come back, this time wanting to kill more than just Bryce.

No. Death was the only way to ensure the safety of everyone else in the cabin. We hung her outside, behind the house. None of us knew how to tie a proper noose, so we stood there watching her struggle as she choked to death. It took a lot longer than I expected and I took no pleasure in watching her die. Hell, I wish she had finished the job on Bryce at least. But instead of killing him, she left him disfigured, the scars making his face look like ground beef. A fate worse than death, for Bryce and for us since we're the ones who have to look at him.

If he hadn't decided to be a jerk, he'd still have his looks and his pick of the women who are left. Poetic justice if you ask me. He insulted what she loves most, God, so she took away what *he* loves most, his looks.

So, Bryce hands me a note. "I found Curtis."

As difficult as it is, I look at his face, searching for some sign that it was good news. He shook his head.

Dammit. Another body to bury.

Five of us left now.

I scrawl a quick note and hand it to him. "Don't tell the girls about this." He nods and I run out the door to bury the body before anyone else can find it.

I realize how dumb this is before I even get there. There's no way I can bury Curtis that quick. Even with the two of us, it took over an hour to get Roxanne into the ground. By myself, it would take even longer.

I decide to drag Curtis into the woods and hide the body until everyone is asleep and I have more time.

I'm not going to tell you how he did it. It's too gruesome. It was almost as if he felt he needed to punish himself for something he had done and so made his own death as painful as possible.

I hide the body and hope no one asks me if I've seen Curtis. I don't want to lie but I'm doing my best to keep people alive.

I'm just not doing a very good job of it.

There's a river near the house where I clean up. My shirt is full of blood, so I take it off and leave it with Curtis' body. I managed to keep my pants clean, which is good. I can get away with going around with no shirt on. It would be embarrassing to have to explain why I'm walking around with no pants.

I go back to the house but I don't see anyone at first. It seems like everyone needs to be alone to mourn. I can't blame them. We all liked Roxanne. She had an upbeat personality that you couldn't help but like. It was going to take some time for all of us to recover.

I sit down on the couch in the living room. I don't bother trying to read. I know I won't be able to concentrate on a book right now. Instead, I just sit, trying to clear my mind of all the shit that's happened in the last little while and find some peace.

Of course, this doesn't happen. Trying to force it all out of my head just brings it back up and makes me think of it even more. God, too much has happened in such a short period of time. Less than a year and a half ago I was married, expecting my first child, had a great career. Now look at the way things are. The five of us could be the last people on Earth for all I know.

Autumn was the last person to arrive and she's been here for at least eight months.

I think.

It's hard to keep track of time these days, but I'm pretty sure it's been eight or nine months.

I don't know if that means anything, but the last time I was anywhere near civilization, it didn't look too hopeful.

When things went quiet, people panicked. Most of us thought we had gone deaf. It was like God had pointed a remote control at the world and hit the mute button.

It wasn't until we realized that everyone else was going through the same thing that we figured out we had it wrong. *We* didn't go deaf. *Everything else* went quiet. We had no idea why. Just one minute everything was fine. The next, no birds chirping, no scraping of shoes on the sidewalk, no wind rustling through the leaves, no dogs barking. Nothing.

So yeah, people panicked. But we got back into the groove. It was weird, but you know, if we, as a society, can band together, we can stick it out. After all, we still had electricity, running water. Even our cell phones still worked. We could text to communicate. We even had internet still, so email and instant messaging were great ways to keep communication alive too. We were set.

And it worked out great. That is, until the cell phones and the internet stopped working. That's when all hell broke loose. No one could stand to live in a world without electronic communication.

People turned feral, attacking others for no reason. People either committed suicide or were killed by some raving lunatic.

Weird that electronics were holding the fabric of society together. I mean, I always knew cell phones and social media were important to people, but this important? Not even I would have guessed it.

Amber and I hid in our home for as long as we could, but our supplies were low and I was going to have to go out in search of more soon. She begged me not to. She said she didn't know what she would do if anything happened to me.

I tried to be the voice of reason and told her that we would both die, not to mention our unborn child, if I didn't go. She gave up trying to convince me.

The next day I left. I was only gone a few hours. I had managed to grab a few things. Couple of days' worth of food, nothing much. Turns out it was all for nothing. When I got back, that's when I found her hanging in the basement. She had left a note saying she didn't want to raise our child in this world after what it had become.

After that, I didn't see the point in sticking around.

That's when I left and stumbled upon the cabin. There were already nine people there. Somehow we all happened to stumble upon it in the middle of nowhere. The rule of the house is that no one is turned away. Anyone who needs help, food, or shelter gets it. That's how we ended up with eighteen people under the roof at one time.

I see something moving off to the side. When I turn my head, I see Bryce entering the room. He's pale. He looks like he's about to throw up. Tears are welling up in his eyes.

My first thought is another suicide and I know my heart

can't take yet another. I just finished burying Curtis, I don't want to have to bury someone else so soon.

But then I notice the knife in his hand, fresh blood still dripping from the blade.

What did you do? I mouth the words slowly so he won't misunderstand. *What the hell did you do?*

He stares at me for a few seconds and I think he's formulating a response. But before I get one, he drops the knife and bolts for the door. Every instinct tells me to go after him and beat him until my knuckles bleed, but the knife and the blood worry me and I have to see what happened.

I check the bedrooms. Mine is empty, of course. I shared it with Curtis and he's gone now. When I check the next room, I find them. Camille, Cass, and Autumn. All dead, their throats slit. The kills are fresh. A few spurts of blood spew from Autumn's neck before stopping.

I can't believe it. As much as I hate Bryce, as selfish as he is, I never thought him capable of something like this. I'm sure the girls didn't see it coming either. Or heard it.

I drop to my knees, tears pouring from my eyes. I may not have liked them, but never would I have wished anything like this on any of them. But in a way, I envied them and the others that have gone before me. Their suffering is at an end while mine continues. I don't have the guts to end it like so many before me.

Maybe that's what Bryce was trying to do. End their suffering.

I think about going after him, but I have no idea which way he went. I have no wish to stumble around hoping to find him.

Instead, I stand up and go back to the living room. Back to the couch.

I don't know what to do. I am alone for the first time in over a year and I have no idea what to do or where to go.

Why? Why is this happening? I think. It's almost a prayer but not quite. I was never a spiritual person.

"You did this to yourselves."

It's a voice. An honest to god voice. I hear it. It's not my imagination.

I look around, trying to see whoever is speaking. But I'm alone.

I try to call out, hoping that the silence is gone, but nothing comes out. I try again, but get the same result.

"Don't bother. The silence has not been lifted. You can hear me because I am the cause of it and thus am outside of it."

Who are you? I figure if it heard my thoughts the first time, it could do it again. *God?*

"Some call me that, but I have many names."

Why are you doing this?

"As I said, this is your own doing. I didn't destroy you. You destroyed yourselves, as I knew you would."

But why? Why did you create the silence?

"What other choice did I have? Would anyone want to see their creation spew hatred from their mouths at every turn? You were not meant for this. I created you to be kind and loving toward one another. But you rejected that and you used words to hurt one another, to lie, to harm reputations, to bully, to cause others to take their own lives out of shame or because they could not take it anymore. I've watched this go on for centuries and I could bear it no more."

Oh my god, I'm going crazy. My mind has snapped, and I think God is talking to me.

"I had hoped that without communication, you would see the error of your ways, but in my heart, I knew it wouldn't change anything. I am sad to say I was right."

So what now?

"What now? Nothing. You will do whatever it is you decided to do. The human race will die out and there will be nothing left. As for me, I will go on existing as I always have."

You're not going to create a new race?"

"No. I have learned my lesson. I cannot create a race with freewill and expect them to love one another. It's not possible. And to create a race of mindless robots would be meaningless. Once all humanity is dead, your race will become extinct."

Am I the last?

"There are still many left, spread out across the Earth. I have been watching them as I have watched you. They're no better off. They will be dead soon as well."

I'm not convinced that extinction is inevitable. What if people have children? And those children learn to survive as well? We could start over."

"Maybe we will survive. Maybe we'll surprise you."

"I doubt that. I have been here since before the dawn of time. I created your race and have been watching it ever since. Nothing you do surprises me. You are predictable. You have a tendency toward violence that angers me, and I will ensure your destruction. There is nothing to be done about it. I should have seen this coming sooner."

I stand up. I'm not about to give up just because God tells me there's no hope. I know there are still people left. I just need to find them.

I start to search the cabin for supplies. There's nothing left for me at the cabin now. I need to move on.

When I find other survivors, we will work to rebuild our race and the humans will have dominion over the Earth once again.

Even though we are in the hands of an angry god, we will survive in defiance of the loving father who turned his back on us.

INTERCEPTING AISLE NINE

BY MATT HAYWARD

"What in the world is a *Squiggly* bar?"

Ronald glanced around the supermarket to make sure no one had heard his muttering. Seven or eight customers shuffled about the Supersave, each looking lost and sedated. A large man of undeterminable age waddled up the aisle with a basket in his hand.

"That the new Squiggly?" he asked.

Ronald placed the bar back on the shelf with the others and tried to look preoccupied with his search. "Fucked if I know."

Ronald didn't want to talk to anyone at three in the morning. God knows who they might be. Serial killers, junkies, weirdos, what other kind of person would be up shopping at this hour?

Me, Ronald thought. *I am.*

"Heard they're awesome." The large man scooped a bar from the shelf before wandering off with a smile.

Ronald watched him go before turning back to the Squigglys, squinting at their wrappers. He'd lied to the fat man. He *did* know the Squiggly to be a new product. Only he hadn't seen it advertised on a television commercial, in a magazine, or on the side of a bus. He'd seen it in a dream.

Ronald had woken at two-thirty, same as every night. He'd been asleep for less than twenty minutes, and even though every cell in his body had screamed for more rest, he'd known waiting for sleep would be a fool's errand. Insomnia was one hell of a curse.

So, instead, Ronald had crawled out of bed, slipped into a tracksuit, taken the elevator down to the first floor and gone across the street to the Supersave to shop—all on account of a phantom craving left lingering from a dream, one for a nougat filled chocolate bar called a Squiggly.

In his dream, short as it'd been, he'd been having dinner with Mary-Ann, his friend of five years from the apartment downstairs. The two had laughed and reconnected, having a very merry time while waiting for their meal in an upper-class restaurant. Beside their table stood a waiter with a pearly white, shit-eating grin and a face that demanded a punch.

Arms behind his back and in a voice perfect for radio, the waiter announced, "Don't let kids hog *all* the fun. Grown-ups can enjoy desserts, too!"

Then he ripped free his blazer to reveal a tie-dye T-shirt reading *SQUIGGLY!* across the chest.

"New from Carpco.," he continued. "A chocolate bar that's just *bursting* with soft and squishy nougat, the Squiggly!"

Silence followed while the waiter looked frozen in time. Mary-Ann lifted her knife and fork and cut into the chocolate bar on her plate as if nothing out of the ordinary had taken place. Ronald pushed himself from the table and smiled to the waiter. "Sounded like you were going to pee yourself you got so excited there, kid. You eat it. It looks like shit, anyway."

Then an ambulance had screamed by the apartment, bursting the bubble of the dream and leaving him confused and staring at the ceiling.

"Can I help you, sir?"

The question made Ronald jump. A friendly, square-faced man with a crop of curly brown hair approached. His nametag read "Pierce."

"Um, no thanks, that's okay. I'm not really sure what I'm looking for."

Pierce squinted. "Well, I believe it's a Squiggly you're after, right?" He plucked a bar from the shelf and presented it to Ronald in an open palm. Then his voice dropped in volume, his expression soured. "Only you're not so sure *why* you want it, am I correct?"

Ronald tried to speak but couldn't find his voice.

"Look, don't be so frightened," Pierce said, speaking from the side of his mouth. "This is all explainable, trust me. Will you follow me to the till and let me ring this up? I'll tell you more on the way. Just act natural. I'm Pierce, by the way. Pierce Tiernan."

Ronald said, "I'm still dreaming." But he followed the young man, all the same.

They passed an old woman with a basket full of shaving foam, a middle-aged businessman who looked out of place, a fat woman in running gear who stared at the baked goods, and a person whose gender was as confusing as what they wore.

"Here we are." Pierce got behind the checkout and beeped through the Squiggly. "That's fifty-eight cents, please."

Ronald handed over a Euro coin and took his change with a smile and a thank you, the everyday task still demanding a token of graciousness even though there were more important matters at hand. Confusing matters.

Ronald leaned into the checkout so as not to be overheard. "Look, Pierce, how in the world did I know about this... *thing*?" He waggled the bar like a flaccid penis. "I hate all chocolate to begin with, why would I... Why would I crave it and know it exists, all because of a... *dream*?"

Pierce gave a tight smile. "Marketing and advertising, my friend. The scum of the earth."

Someone in a far-off aisle sneezed. Ronald stared at the cashier; aware his mouth had dropped open. *Catching flies*, his father would have said.

"Ronald, don't be so surprised."

"How in the *world* do you know my name?"

Sighing, Pierce leaned forward, giving Ronald a whiff of his cologne. "*OneWave*. Ring a bell?"

"Certainly does."

Ronald had attended what the company OneWave called "Sleep Studies" for the past month, along with three or four other insomniacs. The position was sought after by many unemployed, sleepless citizens across Dublin city. Especially since Ireland's recession, when many folks were so worried that they couldn't sleep. Why not get paid for it?

"What have they done to me?" Ronald's voice shook.

Pierce indicated with his eyes as a hunched lady shuffled by. Once she passed, he spoke low. "oh, they're doing their studies, all right. Just not the type they're telling you. They're not trying to cure insomnia, Ronald. They're creating an algorithm to influence the subconscious mind."

Ronald wheezed a laugh. *It's a setup*, he thought. *Got to be.* "Look, Pierce, I don't know who's in on this or how you've done it, but that's amazing. Seriously. You would've had me if you didn't start sounding like Bill Hicks on crack."

Pierce's expression dulled. "Sure, okay. Hey, do me a favour. When you start having advertisements in your dreams for more products you've never heard of, come and see me, okay?"

Ronald's face fell.

"Listen. I'm an intern at OneWave. I've seen you come and go. I know you live around these parts. I *needed* to talk to you."

"What's in it for you to expose them?"

Pierce spoke through his teeth, "I just hate the bastards."

"Then why intern with them?"

"Look."

Pierce nodded to the side where a car turned in the carpark, its headlights briefly glaring off the front window in the SuperSave. Ronald watched until the vehicle indicated and left the lot.

"Was that a black SUV?"

"No." Ronald squinted out the glass, but the vehicle had already gone. "I think it was just a hatchback."

Pierce sighed, as if relieved. "Ron, they've got arms that reach far, know what I'm saying? If a black SUV came by, a Mercedes, a Land Rover, a *Pilote de Terre*, I'd be in trouble. Thank god."

Ronald had never heard of a *Pilote de Terre*, but he got the message. "Answer my question, Pierce. Why would you intern at OneWave, if they are, as you put it, the scum of the earth?"

"To be on the inside. Don't you get it? How else could I prove what they're doing? I needed definitive evidence, and I've got it now. The CCTV footage has all four of you insomniacs coming

in here at all hours of the night to grab a Squiggly, something you could *never* have possibly known about because there's been no advertising for the product. That's *proof.*"

"Couldn't it have been coincidence? Maybe the wrapping attracted us?"

"Oh, please. Look at this." Pierce grabbed the Squiggly from Ronald's hands and held it up in the light. "This is about as appealing as a brick. White packaging with one black word. Squiggly. That's *purposely* done, Ronald. They *made* it unattractive so that no one else would ever buy it within the first twenty-four hours of its release besides the insomniacs who were experimented on. And it's worked. You were the last one I was expecting to stop by."

"That big guy, the one who bought one just before me, he's...?"

"Another test subject? Bingo."

"Jesus."

Ronald pushed himself from the counter and rubbed at his forehead, the room seeming to spin. He'd suffered from insomnia as a young man, but the condition had slipped away over the years, only coming back full force when he'd been let go from his job as a bookkeeper for a law firm, a job he'd held down for almost thirty years. Then insomnia had moved back in like a headstrong ex-partner.

"Why would somebody do that to me? *How* would they do that?" Ronald asked.

The rate at which modern technology improved and advanced dumbfounded him almost daily. He remembered buying a bargain set of encyclopaedias back in the mid-eighties and had always enjoyed flicking through the pages to the amusement of his friends. Now his nephew could know the capital of Zimbabwe at the touch of a button. Ronald wasn't *completely* in the blue, though, in fact, he now even owned a smart phone, but getting used to the quick paced world still took time. As far as zapping advertisements directly to sleepers went, it didn't sound *completely* farfetched to him.

Pierce glanced around before speaking. "The Japanese set the foundation back in the early 2010s with that fMRI scanning.

It measured brain activity based on blood flow. The method, even back then, was able to produce recorded images of dreams with *fifty-percent* accuracy. Pretty cool, huh?"

Ronald nodded. "I agree, it is pretty interesting."

"They would wait until the sleeper reached REM inside the scanner, monitoring the EEG, then wake them and ask what they dreamt about. See, certain parts of the brain work while thinking about certain things, like cats, dogs, SUVs, whatever. It's all about patterns."

"So," Ronald said. "We're up to a point where we can translate a person's dreams onto a screen, like a TV show, right? What then?"

"Right. What always happens is *what then*. Some fat-cats wanted to know how they could capitalise on the technology. They patented part of the process and developed it further, learning how to *influence* those patterns."

"For the purpose of making money?"

"Of course? You'd hardly think they'd use it to cure nightmares or something, did you? They want it to make money to return their investment and start turning profit. And what's the easiest way to do that? Advertising. Always, advertising. Bid off to new companies seeking to broadcast their products and see who'll pay the most. Could you imagine having your product in a new market, one that isn't saturated with competitors? If it worked, your merchandise would be seen by every single person sleeping, all at the same time. How much would you pay for that slot? Makes something like an advert at the Superbowl in the US look like child's play. Am I right?"

A businessman approached the checkout and Ronald stepped back to allow him to pay. Pierce managed the transaction with a smile, but Ronald noticed the young man's hands shaking. Talking about OneWave really riled him up.

"Have a good night," Pierce shouted after the man, then turned back to Ronald. The smile slid from his face.

Ronald scooted closer. "Those *cunts*."

"Damn right, those cunts. But now I've got a case against them, I can try shut them down. But I don't know if it'll work."

"What do you mean?"

"These aren't the type of guys you'd like to go up against in a legal fight. They've got deep pockets. Every media outlet on earth is probably on their side with the advantage they'd get. You can only imagine the potential, and then you'll see why no one would want it stopped. At least, no one in the capital world."

"But you've got evidence now, right? And you'll have my testimony." Ronald's heart raced. "I'll stand up and say exactly what I can remember from the tests, with the CCTV footage of this place, they can't deny it, right?"

"Let's hope. It's the only reason I took this shitty job, so I could get that security footage. Send the intern, they thought... Little piece of advice, Ronald, never trust a smiling businessman."

The woman in the running gear approached with a three-cake pile in her arms. "Is this a get-together or is this a fucking shop?" she asked. "Move it, come on."

"Jesus, lady." Ronald turned back to Pierce. "I guess I'll let you get back to work."

"Right, no worries. Go home and get some sleep, Ronald. I'll be in touch tomorrow. I've got your number."

Get some sleep, sure. Like that's going to happen.

Ronald gave a quick smile. "Call me tomorrow. Please."

On his way back to the apartment, he realised he still held the Squiggly. Unwrapping it, he took a small nibble and rolled it about his tongue. The chocolate tasted like gooey wall-plaster, the nougat-like sadness.

This can't possibly sell well...

Unless, Ronald thought, you hi-jack people's dreams and implant an artificial craving. Jesus, soon enough the entire planet would all eat the same, dress the same, watch the same shows, have the same hopes and desires, all because it would be coming from an outside source. All because the entire population would be *told* what to like without even realising.

A thought came to Ronald then, and his stomach lurched: What if a politician paid for an advertising campaign that way? Manipulated the population into thinking he was *their guy*? Could that be allowed?

At a nearby rubbish bin, Ronald tossed the Squiggly and

wiped his hands on his jeans. He doubted even a rat would touch that crap.

"You're... You're just throwing it away?"

Ronald turned to the voice and jumped out of the way as a homeless man barged past. He dipped inside the bin, threw a used burger box, and came out clutching the candy like a Faberge egg.

"You know how hard it is for me to get one of these, mister?"

"I'm..." Ronald swallowed, his throat dry. "I'm sorry, I didn't think."

Wait, Ronald thought, *how would you know about the Squiggly?*

Before he could ask, the man shredded the wrapping and slammed the chocolate into his face with shaking hands. His neck bulged as he swallowed.

"You're wearing *those*?"

"Excuse me?"

Ronald followed the man's pointed finger to his black store-brand shoes.

"Why aren't you in line for a pair of CloudAirs?"

He sounded genuinely confused, as if Ronald had agreed upon an appointment and let him down.

"I don't know what you're..."

Ronald's brow creased as, over the hobo's shoulder, one man slammed another's head into the side of a building. The crack rang out.

"Jesus!"

Ronald took off, intent on breaking up the fight before the victim's head turned to pizza. Behind, the homeless man called out: "I don't think you'll get a pair, man, folks have been lining up all night!"

"Hey! Hey, stop that!"

Ronald reached the two just as the first man dropped the second like a bag of wet clothes. The aggressor panted and wiped his bloody hands on his jeans.

"Know how long I was waiting?" he asked, wheezing. Ronald shook his head.

"Two. Fucking. *Hours*." He punctuated each word with a

kick to the unconscious man's ribs. "And. This. Fucker. Wants. To. Skip. The... *Queue!*"

Something snapped and the victim groaned. Ronald backed off, his heart slamming—and banged into a couple cradling a box between them like a newborn.

The man snarled. "Fuck off, Grandpa! Want a pair then go get in line like the rest of 'em!"

Ronald stuttered for an answer, but the pair raced off. When they rounded a corner, he heard a hollow knock, and then the girl screamed. A crimson trail trickled into sight. Followed by a shirtless egg of a man dragging a baseball bat.

"Wha-what the hell?"

Ronald took off, his entire body shaking as his apartment complex bobbed into view. Behind, people screamed and yelled. A gunshot barked in the distance. He entered the passcode to the building and climbed the stairs, muffled voices booming from behind each closed door. A few words cut through: *"New shoes, Helen. Want me to be seen in these another fucking day?"* Then, *"Can't expect me to watch it without 3D, you cocksucker?"* And, *"If you don't move, I'll fucking* make *you move, Marty!"*

He unlocked his door, the key missing its target twice. Once inside, he slammed the door, double-checked the lock, and took a shuddering breath. The outside world had turned a dark and sinister place, with greed's teeth deep and empathy but a memory. Indoors, he could at least *pretend* all was okay. Until he slept, of course... Then he'd be invaded and violated against his will, just like the others.

But how? How did OneWave get to them all? Unless of course this wasn't their handiwork...

"A competitor?"

Despite the excitement of the night, Ronald's eyes stung with the need for sleep. He wanted to call the police, but of course, all lines would be clogged now. It'd been days since he'd slept for more than a three-hour stint, and his entire body hummed in a telltale way, making him head for bed. He'd hear all about the chaos in the morning. Hell, if the cops weren't quick, it might still be happening. Besides, being awake only meant stress with a topping of worry, both of which could lead to a heart attack at this stage in his life. He needed to take advantage of such depleted energy while the going was good.

After undressing, he eased into bed, the fresh sheets hugging him and sending a shiver of comfort through his body. The pillow sunk beneath his cheek, cool and soft. He drifted off almost instantly.

In his dream, a desert spread out before him in all directions. A high wind blew, making waves of the sand and rearranging the barren landscape. He stood on a dislocated highway, the tarmac beneath his feet fresh and dark. A road rarely travelled.

It's a lucid *dream,* Ronald thought. *I'm self-aware.*

Music suddenly boomed all around, coming from nowhere and everywhere all at once, like giant speakers built into the ground. A Western soundtrack played, Spanish guitars rhythmically picking a flamenco style. Ronald squinted to the horizon, where a watery heatwave danced and swayed.

Something approached, taking shape out there—a black dot in the barren wasteland. As it came closer, the purr of an engine increased. He made out the shape more clearly now. A black SUV.

A disembodied voice filled the air, the voice of a whiskey drinking, clichéd cowboy. *"Taking yourself where you need to be, isn't that what life is all about? Freedom. Living how you want to live. Going where you want to go. And it all starts by taking the road less travelled, partner. I've only got one question... Where will it take you?"*

The SUV broke to a smooth stop directly before him, forcing Ronald to guard his eyes against the sand. He flinched as light glared off the high-polished chrome hood-ornament, a symbol he didn't recognise: A horse on its hind legs with elegant text below. *Pilote de Terre.*

The driver's door opened with a satisfying pop and out stepped a man, dressed like a Spaghetti Western hero.

"Need an iron horse to take you where you need to be?"

Ronald recognised him instantly. Despite the large black Stetson perched on top of his head, his boyish features were too distinct. If the get-up was meant to make him more manly, it didn't work. It only gave the impression that Pierce Tiernan had dressed for a Halloween party.

"You son-of-a-bitch." Ronald gritted his teeth. "You're not trying to take these bastards down, you're *in* on it. People are *dying* because of this!"

Pierce continued his pitch as if Ronald's words blew through him. "*Pilote de Terre* would like to hand *you* the keys to the future. Take it. Fire up *your Iron Horse*."

Ronald swung a punch but the dream dissipated, puffing out of existence like an unplugged TV. He burst awake, caked in sweat and panting. The bedside clock read 4:30 a.m. He wiped at his face before scooping aside the bedcovers. Then he sat for a moment, head in his hands. Outside, sirens wailed.

Pierce's smug face floated about Ronald's third eye, mocking and laughing. "The bastard's a competitor…"

But if Pierce Tiernan was some kind of entrepreneur taking an internship at OneWave, how did he get in the door without them catching on? Unless he'd given them a false name. Unless he had the money and the means to fabricate a false background.

These people have deep pockets, Pierce had said. *These aren't the type of guys you'd like to go up against in a legal fight… Never trust a smiling businessman.*

But then why give his real name to Ronald? Why not develop the research in secret?

"Because the research is already complete and ready to go," Ronald said. The peach-fuzz on the back of his neck stood. "He was *gloating*. Because he knows he's sitting on gold and no one can take him down… He's untouchable. Robbed all he could from OneWave and started a rival business… And now… *That cunt!*"

Somewhere out in the city, a chainsaw roared to life. Ronald pounded the mattress with his fists. He had an idea to confirm his suspicions. His nostrils flared as he pulled his pyjamas on and scuttled to the living-room, firing up the laptop and taking a seat.

The only difference between OneWave and Pierce Tiernan,

Ronald knew, was that Pierce had finished his technology and OneWave were still plodding along in development. OneWave were still testing, and Ronald had seen not only Pierce's first official advertisement, but the power they could unleash, too. A flash image of a French SUV flashed before his eyes, followed by a flutter in his chest. A craving.

Pilote de Terre...

"It can't be true. It can't be."

After launching his browser, Ronald typed, *Pierce Tiernan Advertising* into his search engine.

The browser took a moment, then displayed the results. The first hit made his stomach drop.

"No," He moaned. "Don't let it be true."

He clicked the website and waited for the homepage to appear. Then he read the text.

Pierce Tiernan Inc. We make dreams a reality. Company website launching soon.

Screams filled the city.

INTRODUCTION TO "POLITICAL SCIENCE"

I'm sure there are those of you who will notice that my offering, "Political Science," is not written in the standard fiction format, and may be wondering what the hell a *play* is doing in this collection of stories. You deserve an explanation. I began this piece as a short story, but quickly realized that it would function better in dramatic form. An anthology like this is oriented toward activism, and it occurred to me that a truly active work would be one that can be not only read but performed as well.

In the past 12 years, I've written several plays, both short and long, most of which have been produced in one way or another, and I like working in the form. My goal here is to present it to you in both a readable and easily producible format, should you wish to take it to the streets or to your local stage venue.

Chet Williamson

POLITICAL SCIENCE

BY CHET WILLIAMSON

Lights up on generic living area: two chairs or perhaps a chair and a small couch, small side table with lamp. The two chairs are close together, angled to face both each other and downstage. In the stage left chair sits SUMMER, a woman in her mid to late 20s. Her face is illuminated by the laptop computer on her lap. She is looking at it intently, scrolling down. Her mouth stiffens in a line of anger, and she glares at what she sees on the screen. She mumbles something unintelligible, then crosses her arms, closes her eyes, and seems to concentrate. Her body tenses, and, after a few moments, she takes a sharp breath and opens her eyes. Her hands fall to her sides. She looks at the computer screen and smiles. She closes the laptop and sets it on the side table. She starts to walk toward the unseen kitchen off stage left when there is the sound of the doorbell. She stops, looks concerned for a moment, and then crosses stage right, stopping at the edge of the stage as though there is a door there. She looks through a peephole.

SUMMER. Hello? Who is it, please?

PHYLLIS. (*Offstage. Friendly, chirpy voice.*) Hi! My name is Phyllis Hansen?

SUMMER. Uh…yeah?

PHYLLIS. I'm your new neighbor!

SUMMER. (*Pause*) Okay.

PHYLLIS. I just moved in, and I wanted to say hello!

SUMMER. (*Pause. Flatly*) Hello.

PHYLLIS. Hello! (*Pause*) Neighbor!

SUMMER listens at the door until she realizes that PHYLLIS isn't going anywhere. She sighs.

SUMMER. Um, okay. Just a sec.

SUMMER mimes sliding off a chain bolt and opening another bolt, then turning a knob and opening the door. PHYLLIS enters. She is a middle-aged woman, well dressed in dark business attire, and is carrying a large attaché case. She is smiling and puts out her hand.

PHYLLIS. Hi! I'm Phyllis.

SUMMER. (*Tentatively taking her hand to shake*) Summer.

PHYLLIS. Nice to meet you, Summer. (*PHYLLIS continues to shake her hand.*) Now look, before I say another word, I just want you to promise me something.

SUMMER. (*Looks at her oddly as the handshake continues*) Ohhh-kay. What?

PHYLLIS. (*Very seriously, slowly, and clearly*) I want you to promise that you'll listen to what I have to say before you kill me. *If* you kill me.

SUMMER. (*Yanks her hand away*) I'm sorry, I don't…are you sure you have the right address?

PHYLLIS. Absolutely. You see, I wasn't telling you the truth. I'm not a new neighbor. (*She carefully sets down her attaché case, holds up her right hand, slowly reaches into a pocket and brings out a small ID holder, and shows it to SUMMER the way one would hold out a piece of raw meat to a lion. SUMMER takes it and looks at it carefully.*)

SUMMER. Aw geez.

PHYLLIS. Please don't overreact. I—*we*—don't mean you any harm. I'm just…the messenger.

SUMMER. (*Handing back ID*) Okay. (*Pause*) You know what I can do, right?

PHYLLIS. I *think* so. And that's why we have a great deal of respect for you. For your abilities. That's why we haven't sent a SWAT team in here. We thought a quiet approach would be better. You know, just a talk. Just between you and me. No one else. No one listening. Just us.

SUMMER. Are you mic'd?

PHYLLIS. No.

SUMMER. How do I know that?

PHYLLIS. You can pat me down if you like.

SUMMER. That would be silly. You guys have tiny mics and cameras that I could never find.

PHYLLIS. That's true. Can I just give you my word?

SUMMER. Since the first thing you said to me was a lie, sure, that'll work.

PHYLLIS. I'm sorry. Really. But I had to get in the door. For what it's worth, I *do* give you my word. No recording, no cameras. Just two women sitting and talking.

SUMMER. And after we're done talking, you arrest me?

PHYLLIS. I'm not going to arrest you.

SUMMER. Oh, you're going to give me your word on that too?

PHYLLIS. (*Pause*) Look, can we just talk?

SUMMER. Is it all on the record? Aren't you going to read me my Miranda rights?

PHYLLIS. No, I'm not.

SUMMER. You have to!

PHYLLIS. Not if I'm not arresting you. It's for your benefit. This way, if I tried to use anything you said in court, I couldn't.

SUMMER. (*Pause. SUMMER sighs.*) All right. Oh, all right, why not? I've never told anyone about this. Maybe it'll feel good to...unburden my soul. Whatever's left of it.

SUMMER gestures to the stage right chair. PHYLLIS sits in the chair, placing her attaché case on the floor by her side. SUMMER sits in the stage left chair, legs together, hands folded on her lap. Looking straight ahead.

SUMMER. But first, can you tell me how you found me?

PHYLLIS. It took us a few months. As you know, pretty much the whole world has been looking for you. But eventually one of our people figured out that you sent out an electromagnetic pulse, which was a big relief for those of us who don't believe in magic or...acts of God. I don't know how they did it, but somehow they were able to backtrack the pulse, if that's the right term. However it was done, they found the geographical coordinates of the source.

SUMMER. How could they do it that...precisely?

PHYLLIS. Drones? Google maps? I really have no idea. I'm a field agent, they tell me where to go and I go. To be honest, we weren't even sure it was you specifically, but your reaction pretty much... (*She shrugs.*)

SUMMER. I should've just played dumb, shouldn't I? Dammit.

PHYLLIS. Maybe. But you didn't. Water under the bridge, right? Now... (*Pause*) What interests me the most—

SUMMER. "Me?" Or "Us?"

PHYLLIS. Okay, *us*, but for the sake of...intimacy, let it just be me, because I personally have been...fascinated by this whole thing. And what I really want to know is how you did it—how you *do* it.

SUMMER. Well...it's just there. I mean, it's not one of those things that came on me slowly. It's not as though it's a—gradation—like one day I'm able to give people a headache, the next I'm capable of making their nose bleed, and eventually I can... (*She shrugs.*) I became aware of it all at once.

PHYLLIS. You mean with...the President.

SUMMER. Yeah. I was home from work sick that afternoon, and I had the TV on, and the President was on. He wasn't live, I mean he wasn't standing there in front of the press corps, but he was on a video screen next to the press secretary. (*She chuckles.*)

PHYLLIS. What?

SUMMER. Cracker Pudding. (*PHYLLIS looks at her oddly.*) That's my nickname for her -- the press secretary.

PHYLLIS. (*Chuckles*) Oh, that's mean.

SUMMER. Just you wait. (*Pause*) Anyway, my usual revulsion towards him—the President—came over me, and I just thought how interesting it would be if suddenly...his head exploded, just out of nowhere. No gun, no sledgehammer, no explosives, but something inside his head that just grew and grew until his skull couldn't hold it. (*Pause*) Oh my God, I can't believe I'm telling you this.

PHYLLIS. All you're revealing are the details at this point. Just pretend you're…consider me a friend. A confidante, that's all.

SUMMER. You can only hang me once, right?

PHYLLIS. No one's going to hang anybody, okay? Go on, please.

SUMMER. (*SUMMER sits back in a more relaxed position, closes her eyes, and continues.*) Okay, okay. So, I thought about seeing…all this happen, thought about it very intently. And it was funny—I felt this pressure inside my *own* head, as though my brain were a machine that was building up a head of steam, and I just felt that if it reached a certain level something would go click. (*She pauses.*)

PHYLLIS. Then what?

SUMMER. (*Opens her eyes*) I…let it go, I just relaxed and let that mental steam build up until the click happened, and on the TV screen I saw… nothing. (*PHYLLIS, who has been tensing, suddenly relaxes.*) It was kind of disappointing, you know? (*PHYLLIS gives a tentative nod.*) But then I realized that the appearance of the President on the video screens may have been prerecorded.

PHYLLIS. But you…you really thought it might happen?

SUMMER. I know, it seems absurd. Most people, including me, would just think of it as a wish-fulfillment fantasy, and when nothing happened, well, duh. But something inside me said there was more to it than that. So I sat back and watched the press briefing continue. The President finished making his stupid comments, and the video screens went black. Cracker Pudding opened the floor to questions, and a CNN reporter was talking, when that man went up to her and whispered something in her ear. Well, I'm sure you've seen the footage, how she reacted and cut off the briefing and ran out. And you know why. (*She pauses.*)

PHYLLIS. The President died.

SUMMER. And you know how.

PHYLLIS. His head came apart. Right in the oval office.

SUMMER. Mmm-hmm. And once the truth came out, a few days later, it appeared that his head had actually exploded from within.

PHYLLIS. And you really thought you were responsible for that? Right away?

SUMMER. I thought maybe I was, but he just could have died. It was when the news came out about *how* he'd died that I figured it was me.

PHYLLIS. You didn't think it might be a coincidence?

SUMMER. I supposed it could've been, but then when I started experimenting, I knew.

PHYLLIS. And that "experimenting"—that was...

SUMMER. The others. Yes. Only this time I wanted someone live, someone I could see, so there would be no mistake, so that I wasn't taking credit for something that someone else was doing.

PHYLLIS. So when the Vice President came on TV—

SUMMER. Live.

PHYLLIS. Yeah, live—you did it again. And you were watching when...

SUMMER. I was watching. So was the world.

PHYLLIS. And what did you think? When you saw it?

SUMMER. It was horrifying. But in a way, it was...rewarding. To see all that shining white hair replaced with, well, you saw, so you know. And that *sound*. Eww. But along with the horror and the shock, I felt justified. It was then that I was sure. And it was then that I started...making plans.

PHYLLIS. There were dozens after that.

SUMMER. Yes, but I tried to choose them carefully. I remember thinking that I didn't want to cause any wars. Not race wars, not civil wars inside this country, not wars abroad. But what I really wanted to do, and discovered that I could do, was just get rid of the people who were ruining the country. And maybe even the world, though I was more concerned about here than anywhere else.

PHYLLIS. That didn't stop you from...removing a few world leaders. Syria, North Korea, Russia. *That* nearly caused a war.

SUMMER. I know, I know. But I didn't want anyone over here getting the idea that a foreign power was taking out our leaders. I wanted to be an equal opportunity engine of destruction, to make sure that people knew it was a V for Vendetta kind of thing. Like a lone gunman, you know? Not some conspiracy by a shadow government. Or any government for that matter.

PHYLLIS. V for Vendetta. That's the one with the Anonymous mask?

SUMMER. The Guy Fawkes mask, right. One crazy person with a helluva lot of power. I couldn't come out with my own manifesto, since that could be traced back to me, so I had to make the attacks themselves a manifesto.

PHYLLIS. The general impression has always been that the person behind these acts has wanted to remove the more...reactionary elements from American life.

SUMMER. That's right.

PHYLLIS. So that would account for the Senate and House Majority Leaders, the presidential advisers, the head of the NRA, the right-wing radio and TV people—

SUMMER. That's right. I didn't want it to look like a complete *purge*. I just wanted a course correction. I wanted people to get the idea that if they actively opposed the progressive direction of the country, there would be consequences.

PHYLLIS. Their heads would explode.

SUMMER. Well, yeah. (*She laughs. After a moment, PHYLLIS laughs too, almost in spite of herself.*) It sounds awful, doesn't it?

PHYLLIS. Put like that, yes. (*Pause*) Actually, put in *any* way, yes.

SUMMER. I mean, to me the way people responded should have been a no-brainer... (*PHYLLIS flinches.*) Oh, I don't mean it like that. I mean, any *normal* person would say, "Okay, I'm a right-wing idiot troll, and I'm noticing that other people who do the things that I do and say the things that I say are having their heads explode. I think I'll stop doing and saying those things now and then my head *won't* explode." Am I right?

PHYLLIS. It certainly sounds logical to me.

SUMMER. And wouldn't that make you rethink your actions?

PHYLLIS. I'd rethink my actions, definitely. But it wouldn't make me rethink my positions, I'm afraid. It might make me cling to them all the more strongly if people like me are being... persecuted.

SUMMER. Well fine, fuck it, I don't care what people *think*, I care about what they do. If you want to be a racist, go ahead and be a racist all you want inside your head. But if you *do* something racist, you goddamned well better be afraid. If you want to think that industry should be able to dirty the air and water to the point where people die because of it, go ahead and think it. But if you want to help to do it, you'd better be afraid too. You hate LGBTQ people, feel free, but if you act on that hate, watch out. I'm only too happy to persecute assholes. (*Pause*) Sorry. I'm being preachy. And the thing is, I don't have to be preachy. All I have to do is... (*SUMMER mimes tossing something lightly in the air, and speaks softly.*) ...poof.

PHYLLIS. Did you ever consider nonviolence?

SUMMER. Well, that's all well and good until you realize what violence can do. Admit it, isn't life much nicer without those talk radio morons?

PHYLLIS. You've got me there.

SUMMER. (*Laughs*) You weren't listening when I got the big guy, were you?

PHYLLIS. No, but I heard the tapes later.

SUMMER. I liked my timing on that. I wanted to do it at a really good line? But since he'd been talking about me all the time that week, it wasn't very hard. I nailed him right as he was saying, "Liberty allows me to speak freely, and only death will..." And then you just hear him mumbling a little and then that sound. I repeat: "Eww." That's really quite a sound, isn't it?

PHYLLIS. I know I'll never be able to forget it. (*Pause*)

SUMMER. (*Clears her throat*) I'm talking too much. Getting dry. Would you like something to drink?

PHYLLIS. Um, maybe.

SUMMER. (*Laughs*) Don't worry, I'll bring you a sealed can. Coke? 7-Up?

PHYLLIS. Any diet?

SUMMER. You bet.

PHYLLIS. Diet 7-Up then, thanks. Um, you're not going to escape, are you?

SUMMER. No. (*Chuckles*) Actually, I'm enjoying this.

PHYLLIS. Strangely enough, so am I.

SUMMER *exits stage left to kitchen. While she is gone* PHYLLIS *pushes up her sleeve and adjusts what seems to be a wristwatch, glancing stage left frequently as she does so. She pulls her sleeve back down, and* SUMMER *returns, with two cans of Diet 7-Up. She hands one to* PHYLLIS, *then returns to her seat.*

PHYLLIS. Thanks.

SUMMER *pops the tab on her can first, and the sound makes* PHYLLIS *jump slightly.* PHYLLIS *smiles self-deprecatingly, and then pops her own tab. The can explodes, making 7-Up spray everywhere.* PHYLLIS *throws her free hand over her head, as if trying to prevent it from bursting apart, and closes her eyes. She freezes for a moment in that position, then slowly opens her eyes. Her body relaxes and she gives a huge sigh. All this time,* SUMMER *has been looking at her in amazement.*

PHYLLIS. Did you do that? With... (PHYLLIS *taps her head with her fingers.*)

SUMMER. No. I think I did it with... (*She mimes shaking a can vigorously.*) Not on purpose, though! I dropped the can in the kitchen. I'm so sorry! I mean, knowing what you know about me, that must've been...terrifying.

PHYLLIS. Only my drycleaner will know how much.

SUMMER. (*She laughs*) Thank God it wasn't orange soda— that stuff really stains.

PHYLLIS. You really didn't do it on purpose?

SUMMER. No! I swear! I did drop one of the cans but I didn't think that would be enough to, well...

PHYLLIS. It's okay. (*Pause as they both sip their sodas*) So. Now what?

SUMMER. I'm not sure. I guess that's up to you.

PHYLLIS. If it weren't. If I just walked out and left you alone, what would you do?

SUMMER. I guess...I guess I'd just keep doing what I've been doing.

PHYLLIS. Until?

SUMMER. Until... (*Long pause as* SUMMER *looks down, deep in thought*) I don't know.

PHYLLIS. Until the world is what you want it to be? Do you think that's likely to happen?

SUMMER. You sound like my mom. No, I don't think it's likely. But I do think I can make things better.

PHYLLIS. For how long? We found you, but we were just the first. Even if we let you go, it won't be long before others find you. Others who might not be as...sympathetic as we are.

SUMMER. Sympathetic?

PHYLLIS. If we weren't, I wouldn't be talking to you now. But you have to understand, you can't go on like this on your own. (*PHYLLIS pauses and takes a sip from her 7-Up*)

SUMMER. Wait a minute. Are you saying that...you're on *my* side?

PHYLLIS. No. What I'm saying is that at this particular time in this country *you* are on *our* side. It's been a long time since Mr. Hoover ran the show, but even he would have hated the position in which the powers that be have put the Bureau. Times have changed, and so has leadership. Or what passes for it these days.

SUMMER. (*Confused*) Well, I'm...glad I was able to help. I guess.

PHYLLIS. We appreciate it. Most of it. But the fact is, you've made some poor choices. Choices that, had you been given all the facts, you wouldn't have made.

SUMMER. Like?

PHYLLIS. Like the Irishman.

SUMMER. Seriously? Every fucking night, that asshole spewed his vile bullshit on radio and TV—he lied over and over just to support that treasonous son of a bitch in the White House, and you tell me—

PHYLLIS. He was one of ours.

SUMMER. What?

PHYLLIS. We turned him years ago. Didn't you ever notice that he was always the fool whose predictions never came true? He was our class clown, our poster boy for right-wing absurdities. A lot of crazies opened up to him, and that way they got on our radar a whole lot quicker than they would have otherwise.

SUMMER. Oh shit. I'm sorry, I had no idea...

PHYLLIS. Apology accepted. He played his part all too well. But you see, that makes my point. A loose cannon like you, working alone, is dangerous. (*Pause*) And frequently futile.

SUMMER. (*Slightly insulted*) Futile? What do you mean, futile?

PHYLLIS. The sexual harassment boys. The producer, the two directors, that actor—

SUMMER. But what they did was terrible! An example had to be made!

PHYLLIS. Examples had already been made. Their careers were over. They were humiliated, and they lost all power in the world that was so important to them. You were just adding insult to injury. (*She thinks for a moment.*) Or the other way around, really. It was…satisfying, but it was a waste of your talents.

SUMMER. So…what are you telling me? You haven't arrested me, you haven't tried to kill me—yet. We've just been two girls sitting around talking. About blowing people's heads apart. Where is this leading?

PHYLLIS. To a proposition. One in which we help each other. Right now, we're pretty much on the same page regarding who deserves your special…treatment. The problem is that you're limited to people you see on TV or read about in the news or online. What I'm saying is that we know a lot of people you've never even heard of. A lot of really bad people you don't even know exist. Not only here, but around the world.

SUMMER. (*Slowly*) Ohhh-kay, I get the picture. But how do you help me?

PHYLLIS. We protect you. We get you out of here because, like I said, it's only a matter of time before a foreign government tracks you down. That's dangerous to you, and it's dangerous to the country. If they've got bombs, and they learn that the pulse that killed their tinpot dictator came from the United States, those bombs might fly. You like traveling?

SUMMER. I don't know. I've never been out of the country. Well, except Canada when I was a kid. I liked Canada.

PHYLLIS. Well, you're about to see the world. We'll have you moving from country to country, city to city. Do a couple of jobs, move. A couple more, move again, always one or two steps ahead. You'll be living out of a suitcase, but the most deluxe suitcase you can imagine. We'll take good care of you. You'll even have your own staff.

SUMMER. (*She is up, walking back and forth, trying to encompass it all*) Okay, okay, that's, like, really weird. I don't know, I just don't know. I mean, what if I say no? What if I...I just don't want to live like that?

PHYLLIS. I'm afraid at this point that that isn't an option.

SUMMER. Huh?

PHYLLIS. I wasn't being totally honest with you. Now don't get upset and blow my head apart. Because right now there are several drones hovering over this building. Drones with missiles. And the people controlling those drones have been listening to everything that we've been saying. (*She shows SUMMER her watch.*) We want you to work with us, but if you refuse, we can't take the chance of your working with anyone else. Do you understand? I really hope you do, because once those missiles fire, we're both gone. Obliterated. And they've already got a perfect cover story for the explosion -- that old standby, the gas leak. It's amazing how often that gets used, and how easily people believe it. I won't touch gas, I've got all electric in my house.

SUMMER. (*SUMMER slowly sits down, looking up at the ceiling as if expecting a barrage.*) So what do I do?

PHYLLIS picks up her attaché case, puts it on her lap, and opens it. She removes a thick binder bound in black, and closes the attaché case, setting it back on the floor.

PHYLLIS. In this binder are names and photographs, as well as the locations if that's necessary for you, of people on whom we would like you to exercise your very special talents. You won't know who the vast majority of them are, but that's all right. We do. (*She stands up and takes the binder to SUMMER, who accepts it and places it on her lap.*) Now. I suggest that you pack whatever you can't live without, and when you're finished, you deal with the first three names in the book. After that, we'll start your exciting new journey.

SUMMER. (*Without opening it, SUMMER looks down at the*

book on her lap.) My God, it's so thick…so many names.

PHYLLIS. Oh, my dear…that's just the "A"s.

SUMMER slowly and dully looks up at PHYLLIS, who smiles down at her like a proud mother as the lights slowly fade to black.

END OF PLAY

GROUP OF THIRTY

BY JACK KETCHUM

When the phone rang just before lunchtime he was on the computer as he should have been, but he wasn't working, he wasn't writing. He wasn't even doing business via e-mail. He was reading the two weeks' worth of collected fan mail on his website and feeling more than ever like a fraud.

He didn't even have the will to answer these people.

Nor the phone either.

The message machine kicked in with the usual.

Then he heard *hello Mr. Daniels. Ah, you don't know me. My name's Will Harris and I'm calling for the Essex County Science Fiction Group out here in Livingston -- that's New Jersey. We were hoping you'd do us a favor. I...uh, a number of us have been reading you for a long time now and really like your work and we're wondering if you'd consider doing a talk at our monthly meeting. I'd have called sooner but I only just found that limited edition of THE NEIGHBORHOOD where Stephen King gives your real name and says that you live in Manhattan so I called Manhattan information and there you are, listed! I know you don't write much in the way of science fiction but that's fine because we're interested in fantasy and horror too and we thought, with Halloween coming up, it'd be awesome to have a horror writer this time. We'd pick up your expenses naturally and buy you dinner and...*

The machine cut him off. He considered the voice, waiting for the guy to call again. Young. *Awesome* gave that away.

Twenties, maybe thirties. White, middle-class. Used to working the telephone. But no expert at it. Not a broker.

Sales, maybe.

The phone rang again. The machine did its thing.

Then, *sorry about that, Mr. Daniels. Anyway, we'd pick up expenses and dinner and if you have any books you want to sign and sell here, you could bring them along. There'd be about thirty of us and we're all great readers. So, if you're interested and I hope you are, the date we have in mind is Saturday the 14th, though we could do it on the 21st if that's more convenient for you. Again, my name's Will Harris and you can reach me at 201-992-6709. That's 201-992-6709. Hope to hear from you soon. Thanks. 'Bye.*

He sat there staring at the computer, at the list of messages.

The people who read him. What did he owe these people? Anything? He felt he did. He'd reached out to the world with his books and the world—at least some small part of the world—was reaching back.

He didn't need it. It was not what he'd signed on for. But there it was.

At first it had been fun. Conventions, readings. Lines of kids twenty years younger than him waiting for his signature. For a word with him. Their hero. *The scary horror writer.* A lot of them wanted to be writers themselves. A lot of them women twenty years younger than him, some of whom were even willing to share his bed.

He collected the awards. Shook a lot of hands. Got used to the feel of hand sanitizer sticky and then smooth and learned how to apply it in the off-moments so as not to offend. Perfected the quick jagged pen-strokes of his pseudonym.

But he'd been doing this for over thirty years now.

Did he owe them still?

He felt he did.

And there he sat, doing nothing.

He supposed it was self-interest too on his part. Not the fame. Or in his case, minor notoriety. Not even the willing women. By answering the messages, by showing up at the conferences and signings and conventions he was cementing his connection to his readers. He was pitching them his legacy in hopes that they'd catch it on the fly and run with it after he was gone.

It was all about the books. His sole offspring.

And he wouldn't be here very much longer now to throw that pitch.

He might have years. But probably not all that many, considering.

He had emphysema. He had myelofibrosis. Neither of them acute just now. Both chronic. *Slow reveals.* Slowly draining him of energy. His lungs and his bone marrow in a competition to see who'd kill him first.

He still smoked a pack a day.

He thought the smart money was on the bones.

Though there was still the possibility of that other thing, doing something careless, drunk or sober, which could take him out yet.

You live well into your sixties. Half the time your back's out. Your skin's dry no matter how much you moisturize. You shrink. Your muscle tone goes all to hell.

As packages go you are severely damaged in shipping.

He closed out his message page and left the website in favor of saved e-mail. Scrolled down. Way down. This one was nearly eighteen months old now.

I wish with all my heart that we could do this, you and I. But we don't want the same things. I wish we did. You don't want kids, and I do. You want New York and I've had it with New York. I'm thirty-four. I've got to move on. I hate doing this via e-mail but I don't have the courage to talk to you right now. I'm sorry.

And then, *Love, Kate.*

Ridiculous, he thought, going back to this again. I should delete it. Wipe it out. Erase all trace of her.

But he'd kept *all* her e-mails. There were nights he'd be drinking too much again and the television wouldn't divert, the Netflix disc was the wrong fucking one for this particular fucking night, he'd chosen badly, and music was out of the question because music was essentially a happy thing even when trying its best to be a sad thing, music was optimism, the optimism of composing and then orchestration and performance, and as she'd *had it* with New York City he'd *had it* with optimism.

The joy of creation. The will to create. This past year he hadn't had much of either. His output had slowed to a trickle. Mornings he'd awaken to work-songs in his head reminding him. *SIXTEEN TONS. NINE TO FIVE. Hey Mr. Talley Man, tally me banana.*

Those bad nights he'd go back to the e-mails. Read through them one by one. There were dozens of them.

Pathetic, he thought. In Classical Greek the word *pathos* was the same for both *suffering* and *experience.* Those Greeks knew a good joke when they heard one.

For a small dinner party at a friend's house last month— a painter/designer who'd done good strong covers for his last three books—he'd gone to the liquor store shopping for single-malts. Bought a Glenmorangie for himself at forty bucks a fifth and a Glengoyne for the party at thirty-two. He'd never tried the Glengoyne before, but the price was right.

At the party he thought the Glengoyne clearly the better scotch and a few days later returned to the liquor store and bought two bottles. He took one in hand and with the other tucked under his arm walked down the winding narrow staircase to the checkout counter, aware that for some reason the upstairs seller was right behind him. The seller guided him to an open register. He paid the woman behind the register and went home and only then looked at his Visa receipt and learned he'd paid $119.99 for each bottle. With tax, $261.98. This was eighteen-year-old Highland Single-Malt Scotch Whiskey while what he'd previously bought was a mere ten-year. He now understood the teller's solicitude.

It took him all of thirty seconds' consideration to say to himself, fuck it, I'm drinking them.

They were very tasty. But for some reason he still preferred the ten.

Maybe it was the party, he thought. He knew most all of the people there and they were convivial people and he'd had a good time. Maybe the scotch had tasted better because of that.

He didn't get out much these days.

He looked at his calendar. He was free on the 14th.

He phoned Will Harris.

He'd been right. Sales.

Harris offered to drive the forty minutes into the city to pick him up and drive him back but that would mean he was Harris' captive for the duration and for all he knew he might not even like the guy. He told Harris he enjoyed the occasional opportunity to drive and asked if they'd spring for a rental and Harris said yes, they would.

Then he forgot all about the Essex County Science Fiction Group until the morning of the 11th when he received an e-mail from someone named Eleanor Bradley reminding him and sending him cheery directions to the venue and he checked his wall calendar and sure enough, his visit was three days away. He called Hertz and arranged for a rental.

The morning of the 14th he packed a dozen trade paperbacks into his travel bag and took a cab uptown and filled out the forms at the rental counter and by ten-thirty he was in the Lincoln Tunnel headed west. He hadn't been kidding Harris, he really did like to drive. And at this in-between hour traffic was fairly light. Jersey always got a bad rap. Once you left the Turnpike 280 was a breeze.

He got off at the South Livingston Avenue exit and spotted the Lutheran Church in no time. He was almost an hour early so he drove on by and found a little deli that served a nice fried-egg sandwich and decent coffee and sipped and ate them in the car.

The car afforded privacy. Every once in a while, he got recognized from his photo on a book jacket or his cameo in one of the movies. It happened rarely but it happened. He didn't want that now.

When he was finished he drove back through the sunny street and parked in the lot beside the church.

Will Harris was waiting for him at the side door. He wondered how long the guy had been standing out there in the cold. He had a big smile and a solid handshake. Hair cropped close to his head. Back straight as a pool cue. He was too small and slight to be ex-marine so maybe Navy.

He returned Harris' smile and told him to stop calling him Mr. Daniels. He was Jonathan, period.

Harris took his bag and led him down a flight of stairs. He heard the rattle of excited voices below.

"They use this room for Sunday School meetings," he said.

He knew about Sunday School meetings. As a kid he'd had to attend.

"I'll try not to pollute the air," he said.

He was happy that they didn't have to go through the actual church. The last time he'd been in one it had been for Bill Starr's funeral and he'd done so reluctantly. Starr wrote what those in the business called *quiet horror*, the equivalent of cozies in the world of mysteries. Strange, yes. Eerie, sure. But bloodless. A much gentler body of work than Daniels' own. Still it was a shock to find that Bill was Catholic. He guessed he'd thought that pretty much everybody who wrote this stuff was like him. Godless heathens. The service made him angry. It was all *Jesus this* and *Jesus that*. It pissed him off that they were using a good man's death to promote their fucking Lord.

Harris opened the door and there they were, standing between the rows of one-armed school desks, talking, drinking coffee out of paper cups and munching donuts.

"Guys? Mr. Jonathan Daniels, aka Ben Cassady."

Smiles. A round of applause. A plump, doughy little blonde of around fifty stepped forward and offered her hand. He noticed a slight limp.

"Mr. Daniels? I'm Eleanor. Eleanor Bradley. We e-mailed."

"Yes. Call me Jonathan."

"Jonathan. We're delighted to have you."

"Eleanor's our fearless leader," Harris said.

"Organizer, Will," she corrected.

There were further introductions. The crowd was mostly middle-aged or older, which disappointed him a bit. It was the young ones you were after. The ones with years of reading and book-buying ahead. He counted them. There were exactly thirty. Out of the thirty he would place only three of them as under the age of thirty. Two look-alike women who might have been sisters and a bearded burly young man.

He had to wonder how many guest speakers they'd had before him. Because he had the feeling they were looking at him as though he were some sort of exotic animal. Which perhaps in their world, he was.

He was offered coffee, which he declined and bottled water, which he accepted. He opened his bag and set his books out on the table in front of him. Six novels, two copies each.

Harris introduced him and they sat attentively at their desks as he launched into his talk. In her e-mail Eleanor Bradley had asked him to address the state of horror fiction today so, tired though that subject was, that was what he did, but began at the beginning, giving them a short primer, starting with some background on Poe and Lovecraft and Blackwood, ranging up from there to the forties and fifties with Bradbury, Bloch and Sturgeon and then to the bases of all modern horror, the blockbusters of the seventies, King and Straub and Blatty, V. C Andrews and all the rest, finally getting to his own stuff and that of his younger contemporaries.

He kept it light. Even got a laugh or two now and then. They seemed particularly to like Bradbury's statement about FAHRENHEIT 451. *I don't try to describe the future, I try to prevent it.* They were science fiction people, after all.

So it figured.

He finished by talking about the cross-pollination going on between horror and suspense, mystery, sci-fi and even teen romance and finally paraphrased King's famous line on Clive Barker. *I have seen the future of horror, and it's all over the place.* A little glib but what the hell.

Then he opened it up for questions.

He got the usual. *Where do you get your ideas? How long does it take you to write a novel? Why do you write the kinds of things you do?*

That last one, from Eleanor Bradley, seated with Will Harris up front, seemed to have a slight edge to it.

He gathered Ms. Bradley didn't entirely approve. He smiled.

"I try to fight the good fight while I entertain you. So that I tend to start with what pisses me off," he said. "Child abuse, animal abuse, thrill-killers, the legal system."

"Religion?" That from the young burly guy with the beard.

"That too. I took a swipe at it with INVASIVE EXOTIC. And again with THE ABORTION. True believers of any kind are pretty damn frightening to me."

"But aren't we all?" Harris said. "True believers, I mean. Aren't we all in one way or another? You believe in books, don't you?"

"Yes and no. You can recognize the power and value of books and still distrust the hell out of them. Look at MEIN KAMPF. Look at DIANETICS. There's one called RAGNAR'S BIG BOOK OF HOMEMADE WEAPONS AND IMPROVISED EXPLOSIVES. Very educational."

"But you believe in your own work, right?" said beard-guy.

"Sure. I write cautionary tales, mostly. I hope in some way they're useful. Though a lot of it's just for fun."

"*Fun?*"

It was one of the younger women he thought of as sisters. And she was scowling.

"You call the rape and torture of a young girl *fun*?"

She was referring to THE NEIGHBORHOOD.

"Of course not. That book was based on a series of true incidents, terrible crimes. There was nothing fun about it."

A balding man in back stood up and waved a manila folder at him.

"But you're on record as saying that it *was!*" he said.

He opened the folder and read.

"From an interview in *Cemetery Dance* #81. '*Some of these books are harder to write than others. Some, like CONCEALMENT, took a lot of research. I did background work on that for a year before even starting. Others come to you almost like dictation. Like they're full-blown in your head. WHITEY was like that, and THE NEIGHBORHOOD. Serious subjects, sure, but writing them wasn't like work at all. More like magic. It's wonderful!*'"

He closed the folder.

"Sounds like fun to me, sir."

Sir?

He was aware of a general muttering. The two young women had turned in their seats and were nodding at the guy.

"I was talking about the actual writing, the process. Not the subject. That's clear in the interview, isn't it?

"Is it? You were enjoying yourself imagining this...this degradation. You were having yourself a fine old time. At the expense of a young girl's pain and innocence!"

The guy was waving the folder again. The image of Joe McCarthy popped into his mind. He almost had to laugh. *I have here before me a list of names...*

This guy was seriously pissed.

"As I said on the phone, Mr. Daniels," Harris said, "we've read your work. Between us thirty, I'd say we know pretty much all of it. We've catalogued what you do to people. *Before* killing them. Eleanor?"

Ms. Bradley had a folder of her own. He hadn't noticed.

"Beating, whipping, burning, branding, cutting, rape, genital mutilation, castration, facial mutilation, starvation, biting—*a lot* of biting—incest, impalement with sharp objects..."

"I get it," he said. "There's a good bit of mayhem in my books, sure. So? You could say the same of any writer in the field."

"That doesn't make it right, though, does it? And we're not talking about *any writer in the field*. We're talking about you."

He was thinking, who the hell *are* these people? So he asked them.

"Who are you people? I don't get it. I don't understand what you expect me to say. You want me to defend myself? I'm not going to do that. Except to say that somewhere, somebody's actually *done* what I'm only writing about."

"Yes, they have," she said. "Our point exactly. You're aware of the Linda DeLuca murder?"

"Of course I am."

"Then you're aware that they copycatted THE NEIGHBORHOOD almost to a tee."

"That's not the book's fault or mine. A book's a book. You want to murder somebody, you'll find a way to do it. They could have used another book as a blueprint or no book at all. They chose mine. And mine was *based on a real case*, the Jackson murder. I assume you know that."

"Yes. So let's see. Exactly what have you done here? You've taken a real murder that not all that many people remember these days—it goes back to 1981, after all—and written a popular novel about it, which in turn inspires another murder. *You've perpetuated the first murder*, Mr. Daniels! Don't you see? But I'm sorry, I haven't answered your question, have I?"

"What? What question?"

"You wanted to know who we are."

He waited. She placed the file on her desk.

"I'm afraid we're guilty of a little deception here. We're not really a science fiction group, Mr. Daniels. Most of us couldn't care less about science fiction. And we're not really based in New Jersey. Most of us come from either upstate New York or Indiana. Because Elizabeth Jackson was murdered in Indianapolis and Linda DeLuca was killed in Peekskill. These were our neighborhoods! These were where these terrible things happened! We've corresponded for months now. The internet and *you* brought us together."

He'd gotten lazy in his old age, he thought. He should have vetted this bunch. *Time to get the hell out of here.* And it must have shown on his face because burly beard-guy got up and blocked the door, arms crossed in front of him. A tired, classic move. But effective.

"Any of you family?"

"No," she said. "We're concerned citizens."

Concerned citizens?

He sighed. "Okay, so what's the plan? What do you want from me?"

Harris stood up. Some of the others did too. The sisters. An old couple in back.

"*We want to hurt you, Mr. Daniels,*" Harris said. "Hurt you the way Elizabeth was hurt, the way Linda was hurt. Linda lived two blocks away from me. She could have been my little sister. She was a lovely, sweet young woman. And you helped kill her.

We're going to take you somewhere you won't like *and hurt you bad."*

He almost laughed. He *did* smile.

"Sorry. But you can't," he said.

"Of course we can. You can yell and scream all you want. There's nobody around to hear you. It's a Saturday. We've given the janitor a little something to take the day off."

"Fine. You still can't."

"You want to tell me why the hell not?"

"Sure. Congenital analgesia," he said. "You can hurt me, but you can't *hurt* me, if you know what I mean. I can't feel pain. Never have."

"That's ridiculous," said Evelyn Bradley. She was on her feet now too, glaring up into his face.

"You're right. It is. I used to worry that I'd bite my tongue off while I was eating. I'd take a fall and wonder if maybe I'd broken my leg."

"You're lying."

"No, I'm not. Look. Here."

He dug in his pocket and handed her his lighter. Held his left hand out to her palm-up.

"Light it and hold it under my hand. Let me know when you figure you've done enough damage. I'll wait."

It wouldn't be his first second-degree burn. He'd had to consider this problem all his life.

She hesitated. Then flicked the Bic.

Her hand trembled. His burned. He could smell it. Burning hair smelled little like rotten eggs, he thought. He couldn't feel a thing.

"Christ!" she said and slipped her thumb down off the lighter. She shook her head.

"I don't understand," she said. "If you can't feel pain, how can you possibly *write* pain?"

"Imagination," he said. "Something you people seem to lack. Plus I read up. Let me ask you something. Were you planning on killing me? Because if you were, you haven't thought this through. You kill me, all my books go back into print big-time. Including this one."

He held up a copy of THE NEIGHBORHOOD.

"Not to mention the probability of you getting caught."

"We won't get caught" said Harris. "All the arrangements have been anonymous. We've used fake names. Disposable phones. Temporary phone numbers." He sighed. "But that wasn't the plan, no. Our intent is to educate you, to make you *understand*. We're not murderers. We're...*Christians*! Well, except for Rothstein over there. We're..."

"You're ridiculous is what you are. Look, I'm sorry for what you consider your losses. But I had nothing to do with them."

He was being rough on them, he knew. If an entire room full of people could have a hangdog look, they did.

He walked to the door.

"Excuse me, son," he said.

Beard-guy stood his ground for a moment and then stepped aside.

In the car he realized he'd left his books and travel bag behind and thought fuck it, let them burn the books if they want. He'd give them that much. He also realized that he felt pretty damn good for the first time in months.

There was that woman at the last reading with the long dark hair. She'd seemed interested. He had her number.

He looked at his scorched left hand on the wheel. It was going to take a lot of bacitracin, a lot of bandages.

But he was going to write about this. He had to thank them.

He was back.

POSITIVELAND

BY JENNY OROSEL

Katie was startled awake by the door chime. Once again, she'd accidentally fallen asleep. Business had been at a near standstill for months. Without the subsidies she'd have had to shutter the doors long ago.

Bell. Door. That meant a customer! Someone wants music!

"Pleasant day, friend. Welcome to Positiveland Music and Record Center. How may I help you?"

He was a wisp of a man. Older, maybe 70s. Thin. Barely leaning on his cane. The few hairs left on his head were white. He looked around at the rows of CDs and thumb drives. The most popular approved musicians hung on the walls. Katie could tell that none of them interested him. She'd seen his type, many times. She could sense it in a moment.

"Hi, friend. Let me know if you need some help finding the proper music. I am here to be of assistance."

The little old man smiled then flipped through a stack of CDs. He said nothing, but browsed away. Having been through this a number of times, Katie wordlessly took her place behind the counter, ready to help with the special requests. In preparation she fired up the computer so she'd be able to check his credits when it came time. She went back to her Sudoku puzzle while it booted.

He flipped the name cards, walked each row with his slow, shuffling walk. Now and then he would backtrack like he thought he'd overlooked something very important. He never did, though, and kept on walking. Katie knew he'd never find what he was looking for in the aisles.

It wasn't until he'd browsed every row that he approached the counter. "Hello, friend. I'm looking for a song, but you don't appear to have it."

She set down her puzzle book. "Those are the free music. If it's a song you need credits for, I am required by law and the best interests of our nation to keep questionable music behind the counter pending approval. What is your credit account? I can bring up your totals then we can see what music is available at your level."

The man dug through his pocket and placed a well-worn card onto her counter. Katie immediately recognized it as one of the original printing.

"I haven't seen one of those in ages. You know there are replacements available for you at any time free of charge, right? You could have a nice, clean, smooth card."

"Oh, I'm well aware of that. This one works just fine, though. The number is there. It seems rather wasteful to replace it, doesn't it?"

The blinking yellow light on the man's watch caught Katie's attention. "Be careful, friend. Especially now, when you're looking to keep all your credits. Remember, more cards made means more people employed. More people employed is a good thing." Her own watch had a faint green glow. Subconsciously she breathed a little looser at the sight. "Besides, the newest cards are made from recycled materials, so by making new cards you're actually helping keep trash from the landfills!" Her glow was bright green and she heard that familiar ding as a new credit was added to her account.

"I suppose you're right. Better to keep people working and happy. That's the most important thing of all, isn't it? Keep them happy. Keep them occupied. Avoid unnecessary negativity." His own yellow glow started turning green.

"Speaking of happy, let's see what your account says and find you some music." Katie said through a smile, still happy to know she got another credit. There was an album she wanted to hear again. At this rate, it would only be a month more.

She rad his account and smiled. He'd be able to get almost

any song in her store. "Good news, friend. You've got 2,000 entertainment credits. That's quite a bit. Did you have something particular in mind?"

"An old one. 'Rainy Night in SoHo' by The Pogues. Do you have it?"

She knew that song. It had been her brother's favorite when they were teenagers. He'd played it so often she'd had to beg him to stop. Seemed impossible now but that's how it had been. She missed that. She missed him.

"If it's in the database, yes. We all have the same files available--no store is different than the others. It's better that way." She typed his request. An alert came onto the screen. Her heart sank, knowing what it took to get there.

"I'm sorry, friend. It says you've accessed that song too many times. That adds on a ten credit fee. You're almost there but you're short those ten credits."

The old man looked at his watch. It had the faintest yellow glow. Katie sensed those ten credits would take him longer than most. He continued staring at the watch as tears formed in his eyes. "I knew that was coming. I thought I had a few more listens, though."

"Don't worry, friend. Those ten credits can add up before you know it. In fact, I bet you can score those up by the end of the day. I believe in you." She gave him a well-rehearsed grin of encouragement.

He didn't see it because his eyes were still on the watch. "I'm not very good at this. My wife. She was the good one of us. I don't know why she put up with me as long as she did. She was a saint."

The yellow got a hint stronger.

"There are lots of good people in this world, friend. I'm sure she was as good as anyone else and no better than anyone either." Her green grew stronger.

His voice was barely over a whisper. The strain to contain his composure distorted his face and clenched his teeth. "That is bullshit. Some people are horrible. Allison wasn't. She was beautiful." Even spoken near silence, the watch picked up his words and glowed stronger, heading to the orange hue.

Katie felt desperate for the man. She thought of her brother. Music does things to people, especially those who were used to older ways.

"I have other songs here. Some of them don't cost a credit. I even have a few that can help you earn credits just by listening. Maybe we can sit and listen to a few of those. Not only will that help you get to ten, but it'll take your mind off the more negative thoughts."

"That was our song. It played at our wedding. That song was ours." The orange hue was getting dangerously close to red. She knew she had to do something before it was too late.

"Sir--friend, sorry, friend. Please, friend, think about what you are saying. Music belongs to everyone. Songs belong to no one. They belong to everybody. Let me play you some of the featured music. Please. It can help. Let me try. Please."

She wanted to reach out to him, put a hand on his shoulder. Calm him, tell him everything would be okay, but he would have to calm down. No touching the customers, though. That would be an automatic loss of a credit. That was not how people were encouraged to behave.

"I've tried that 'featured' music. It stinks. It all stinks." His watch was getting redder but it didn't faze him. "It doesn't do anything. It doesn't say anything. Even the lyrics don't say anything!"

Katie's hands were inches from touching the man's cheeks but she recoiled. "That is why some music is featured. It has important messages. Approved messages. Words can be dangerous. It only makes common sense that people would have to earn the privilege of subversive songs. Imagine what would happen if someone less…stable were to listen to unfiltered songs from the old days. Would you want to be responsible for that? I sure wouldn't."

The little old man wasn't even listening. "This was our song. We played it at our wedding. I used to hear it on the radio and be able to remember exactly what she looked like standing before me in her beautiful white dress. She is gone and all I have left are some faded pictures, some fading memories, and this song. Now I can't hear the song. She died ten years ago today and I'm not allowed to listen to one silly little song! I hate these new rules!"

The sharp alarm stunned him silent. His watch was flashing a bright red. Katie looked at her computer. Sure enough, he'd been penalized fifty credits for his unacceptable outburst. She looked at the old man. He knew. He knew what he'd done.

"It's my own fault and I know it."

She leaned down as close to him as she could get without actually touching him. "It's okay, friend. You can earn the credits back. You've earned them before, you can do it again."

"Fifty. Gone. That means I'm sixty behind. That means a minimum of six days, and that's if I'm good. If. I'm not good, though. And today was the anniversary. She died on this day ten years ago. In six days it's going to be gone. Just like her."

The man collapsed into the chair, face in his hands, sobbing uncontrollably. Every wail hit Katie's heart a little more. She knew what music could do to a person, to their memories. Her brother showed her what music meant. It's why she wanted a music store in the first place. The stricter the rules became, the less often she'd witnessed that kind of connection. It was less often, but she lived for when it happened.

She stared at the crumpled old man and realized, if she were careful, it could still happen.

She snuck off while he was lost in his own tears. She had to remember to not say a word for the watch to pick up, lest she lose any of her own credits. But she knew the song he requested. She remembered every word.

When the old man's sobs slowed enough that his breathing was regular again, Katie put a shushing finger to her lips. The old man looked at her with desperate eyes. Wordlessly she slid him the CD. She held eye contact with him, willing him to understand what she was saying.

He did. He understood perfectly.

He pressed the button on the side of his watch.

Within seconds police stormed the small music store. Katie was handcuffed. In the background an officer was reading her rights. She wasn't listening. Instead she listened to the old man talking to an officer, trying to make out as many words as she could through the confusion.

"was easier to tempt than others...will need some serious reeducation...it's like she wanted an excuse to break the rules..."

There were no more tears for the dead wife. There was no dead wife. And there would be no tears for Katie.

"I was just trying to be kind. I felt so bad for him!" she shouted for anyone who would listen.

The man who was putting the hand cuffs on her said, "You can be kind, or you can be fair. You can't be both and, by your age, you should know better. A few months to reeducate you on the way to be a proper member of society and maybe you can have your store back. After you learn to behave in the correct fashion."

As they led her off to the squad car, Katie had to wonder if she'd recognize herself once the corrections were made.

She glanced at the old man one last time. All traces of mourning were gone. Even with that she regretted nothing. At least, not yet.

MURDERERS

BY RICHARD CHRISTIAN MATHESON

People have no fucking idea.

Wish I could sleep like a goddamned baby like they do.

Wah-Wah. *Mommy-Mommy.*

Pricks. Whores.

Must be nice to have no worries.

Conscience? What fucking conscience.?

Must be nice.

Not my life.

Sweep. Clean. Repeat.

The cruel truth.

It's fucked-up. Fucked-down. Fucked sideways.

Who pays for that?

Me.

The Bible?

A stench of ugly stipulations.

Look in the mirror. Stare into your hollow idiocy. Your hypocrisy.

The disease in your eyes. Say hello.

Lies. Betrayal. Wars. Faceless, fat-assed corporate hogs; taking whatever the fuck they want. Bloated cannibals. Cities rotting. Guns strafing kids like stupid pigeons.

Pleas. Whimpers. Endless, poison waves, crashing on dying shore.

Murder.

All of it. Every fucking drop of blood.

Justice?

Fuck you.

Love?

Set the price.

What about you?

Did you ever hurt anyone? Did you ever say something cruel even though you say you didn't mean it?

Of course you fucking meant it.

Did you ever do something bad to someone that you claim to regret, even though you could give a flying fuck? *Did* you?

Did you ever tell a lie that got you what you wanted and when the person found out, after trusting you with everything they had, something inside them died?

Having a good time?

Ever take something from someone? A trust? A dream? A hope for something better? Did you ever betray someone? Fuck them over? Turn on them, without them knowing? Did you ever promise them something then take it away? Mock them behind their back? Did you ever do something fucking selfish and tell yourself it was all for the best? Did you ever take someone's belief in life, or in you, and strangle them with it? Take someone they loved from them? Did you ever burn down something they loved because there was nothing in it for you? Did you ever break their heart and sleep like a fucking baby?

Did you ever murder a piece of them?

You know you did.

Did you ever take something that's inside them that keeps them alive and believing life is fair and good until you crushed it because you were too fucking selfish to stop yourself? Have you ever wanted to be better than someone else? Judge them until it sickens them like ant poison and they can never feel right or good about who they are? Have you ever said such cruel things to them that they were never the same?

Look in the mirror. Stare into your empty, self-obsessed reflection. Eyes used to decipher the anxieties of others. False smiles that size-up weakness and vulnerability; calculate schemes, Find a way to take and never give.

Did you ever watch someone cry and suffer and didn't give a fuck?

People have no idea. You're one of them. You should rot. You already are.

Someone needs to save the helpless. The victims of the kind of hate you live for. Feeling superior. Better.

I save casualties from the tortures you inflict. Everything you've done to them. I give them the dignity you took from them like precious oxygen. I save them so they can have peace after you've reached-in and pulled-out their helpless, beating hearts because it served your greedy, empty, hateful, soulless fucking ends.

If it wasn't for self-rationalizing scumbags like you, people wouldn't need to escape from the suffering you cause.

I pay the price for your fucking sickness.

It's your fault. All of it.

I have to look into their souls, the way you can't look into your own because it's a vile contamination. And I have to face the truth of what corrodes them, hour by hour, minute by minute because of you. The ways you made them despise themselves and that feeling followed them through their whole life like an incurable disease and you gloated like the sick sadist you are. They way you infected them with doubt and fear and self-loathing and never looked back.

You did that. You took their hope. Their freedom. You took *everything.* You destroyed them. *Fuck* you.

Look at your reflection. Look into your eyes. Try to remember everyone you hurt and exploited. Every innocence you smothered. Every dream you stabbed to death.

Your despising vanity is my sanction; my invitation. I release them from their torture; the bondage and worthlessness you forced on them. I help them.

I soothe them as the blood runs. I hold their hand. Their skin gets cool.

Sweep. Clean.

I take their life.

But you fucking *murdered* them.

W.W.P.D.

BY PATRICIA LEE MACOMBER

The Bell Rang.

Changing of the guard.

Thirty children tried to cram themselves into the space of two as they escaped the classroom and ran autumn-breathed onto the playground. A quick tussle over swings and the yell of one disgruntled youngster and it was all over. Everyone settled into his or her rightful place on the equipment.

Franklin heard the bell and he wanted to return to the classroom. He wanted that more than anything, but he simply couldn't do it. At that particular moment, he was against the brick wall of the library, staring down the five-barreled shotgun of a fat kid's fist.

Next to him stood Freddy—short for Frederick—who was his best pal and the only kid in the school who was a bigger geek than himself.

Franklin turned his head to look at Freddy and he smiled. "WWPD?"

An unfortunate move, that. The fat kid with the dirty t-shirt and the food-spattered lips cocked that five-barrel shotgun and fired. Bone met bone met brick and the lights went out.

Frederick aka Freddy the Faggot held out another brick and smiled as the fat boy screamed. His buddy, the one who had landed the punch on Franklin, struggled beside him, his nose leaking blood on the food stains of his T-shirt. Freddy laughed and picked up another brick, tossing it in his hand as he watched Franklin set the previous brick in place.

Another brick and then another. The wall grew taller and the view of the fat bullies behind it grew smaller.

Fat Boy screamed as the shadows crept up his face and he realized that the air would last only a few hours.

"WWPD," Franklin laughed.

Freddy chuckled and handed him another brick.

"Yea, that's what Poe would do," Franklin coughed as light crept in around the rims of his swollen eyes.

The brick wall came slowly into focus, bringing with it a sting of pain and the realization that a shadow had fallen over him. At first he thought it might be Fat Boy. That's what Freddy and Franklin called them—Fat Boy and Spittle Man. His friend's sneakers told the truth. Gray and perennially untied, they could be none other than Freddy's.

Freddy held out his hand, somewhat spattered with blood and smeared with grime, and helped his pal up. "They only hate us because we're smart, you know."

Franklin pulled himself up and slowly dusted himself off, as though removing a bit of dirt could hide the beating from his mother's experienced eyes. He had a lot of experience getting beaten up and his mother had a lot of experience patching him up.

"They hate us because we're total dorks." He coughed and blood flew from his mouth. "Let's go home."

"It's the middle of the day. We can't just...leave." Freddy sounded as though the very idea were akin to murder.

"Can too. Your mom works all day and we can hide out there until time for me to go home. Maybe even clean up enough that they won't notice." He pushed the glasses back up on his nose and winced at the pain. No doubt, it was broken...again.

"I don't know about me, but your face is swollen enough that a blind man would notice."

Franklin thought for a moment, and then let a smile creep onto his face. "You could show me that new first edition Raven you got."

Freddy matched his smile and raised him a slight cock of the head. "Deal."

They stepped around the corner and headed off at a brisk pace. All of the library windows were on the other side of the building, so no one would see them leave. As long as they kept to the strip of lawns behind the houses, no one would ever see them, which was a good thing for two would-be punching bags.

Franklin searched the deep recesses of his pockets and came up with half a roll of Pep-o-mint Lifesavers. He popped one into his mouth, and then pressed loose another with his grimy thumb, holding it out to Freddy with a smile.

"It should be WWEAPD," Franklin announced around the candy. "What Would Edgar Allan Poe Do."

"WWPD," Freddy disagreed. "It's shorter, more succinct."

"But it sounds like the call letters for a radio station."

"Does not."

"Does so."

"Your way sounds like some stupid algebra equation." He stopped walking just shy of the Henderson's yard, in the little plain created by the meeting of the Henderson's and White's hedges and the parting of the fence. The two faced off.

"WWPD. What would Poe do? Adding in his whole name is superfluous."

"Kudos on the use of superfluous, but you're still wrong."

Franklin was about to disagree again when a shadow fell over the space between them. Twin mouths made twin "O's" and their eyes slowly traveled upward, squinting against the glaring sun until they spotted a dark object falling toward them.

The lights nearly went out for them both for the second time that day as a body hit the ground between them, bouncing twice and then lying still.

To their credit, less sturdy boys would have screamed and run. Whatever else might have been said about them, Freddy and Franklin had nerves of steel.

"Holy..."

"...shit!"

"Did you see that?" Freddy swallowed hard and looked briefly as though he might wet himself.

"No duh! Am I standing here?"

"I didn't hear any planes."

"No tall buildings around."

"How the heck does a body just fall out of the sky?"

"Out of nowhere." Franklin coughed and frowned and looked uncomfortably about him. "Crap!"

"Should we call someone? Do you think he's dead?"

"Again, I say...DUH! What's your IQ again? Two?"

"It's two-ten and you know it. But yea, I guess the dude's dead."

"What should we do?"

"You're asking me? Like dead bodies fall on me all the time? Sheesh!"

"Look at him. He hasn't been dead long, huh? I mean, like, maybe a few hours at best."

"At worst." They scratched their heads in unison, and then looked about some more.

"WWPD?"

Hands on their dirty jeans and heads tilted down, the two boys stared at the body as if it were a bug under a magnifying glass, about to explode. Together they nodded and with each nod their smiles grew wider.

"Ex-act-ly!"

Plans unspoken and ideas formed, Freddy moved around and took the man's feet while Franklin grabbed him under the armpits. Faces red and feet digging in, they tried to make off with the body. Several gasped breaths and a near-hernia later; they had progressed about five feet. They set the body down.

"We're never going to make it this way. We'll get caught." Franklin frowned at the man's body and at Freddy in turn.

Freddy snapped his fingers, legs gingerly carrying him behind the bushes. When he re-emerged, a wheelbarrow and a glowing smile preceded him. Together they hefted the body into the wheelbarrow and ran off toward home.

"He's God," Freddy announced suddenly, his breath coming in quick gasps and his legs beginning to ache.

"You're not a genius. You're a lunatic! God!" Franklin laughed as hard as he could without passing out from lack of oxygen.

"Think about it. He fell to earth and his body didn't shatter or splat or anything. There were no tall buildings, no planes, and no giant birds flying off to their nests. God died and he fell to earth at our feet."

"Yeah, right. There really is a God and he just now died. What exactly is it that kills Gods, anyway?"

"Lack of faith." A door slammed behind them. The boys ran a bit faster.

"If people stop believing in God, then he can't possibly exist. I realize that's a bit altruistic and perhaps a rather pedestrian view of the philosophical nature of…"

"Oh, three points for the use of altruistic. It's definitely not a seventh-grade word. And maybe I could buy into your theory if only I believed in God at all. Or, if I believed for a second that God wore a food-stained shirt and a pair of Air Jordans. But there is no God, ergo he could not have died and fallen at our feet."

"Not so, my friend. And an autopsy will prove it."

The idea, grotesque as it might be, intrigued both boys beyond measure and so they rounded the corner and sped for the unlocked back door of Freddy's house.

Franklin laughed into the crisp summer air and propped his feet up on the over-stuffed footstool that occupied the space before his chair. He tilted his head back and pushed up his bowler hat with the rim of his glass. A sip of Amontillado drew a sigh from his red lips.

Leaning back a bit more, he watched as black birds alit on Fat Boy's chest, pecking at his eyes to the sheer delight of Freddy the Faggot and Franklin the Frog. Fat Boy and Spittle Man screamed with each peck and thrashed about madly on the lawn as blood dripped into their ears and the birds drilled deeper into their eyes, exposing the gray matter of their brains.

"Nevermore!" Freddy chuckled as he and Franklin clinked their glasses.

"Have you ever done an autopsy before?" Franklin grunted as the boys lifted the man's body onto the rickety metal table in the basement.

"Now Freddy! Would I perform an autopsy and not let my best friend in on it?" Freddy laughed and dusted off his hands.

"Then how do we know how to proceed? And how in the world will we clean up the mess and dispose of the body?" Details always disturbed Franklin.

"We'll have to use the book I have on autopsies. It's a textbook from about thirty years ago but I doubt that much has changed. However, I propose that if we cut into the body, we shall find -- nothing..."

"...perhaps stars?" Franklin interrupted mockingly.

"We'll find nothing at all. Gods don't have organs or blood like mortals do. A quick clean slicing will prove once and for all that you are wrong, and I am right."

"You're sick. We're going to get busted. We'll go to some wretched mental hospital and—providing we ever get out—they will forever call us Fucked Up Freddy and Freaky Franklin."

"Well...then...WWPD?"

Franklin nodded slowly and pulled the chain on the bare bulb to light it. Freddy busied himself fetching the book as Franklin looked about for that one particular box he'd seen months before. Inside it were old wood-working tools, including an old whittling knife—sharp as any knife had ever been—and a large chair clamp.

Once he had laid hands on those items, he helped position the body. When all was ready, he let Freddy scan the book for a few moments before he started nagging at him to "hurry up already."

"Edgar would have loved this, you know."

"He would indeed."

Franklin leaned against the wall, elbows grinding against stone as he peered down at the man on the table. Whisk! The pendulum swung, the blade flickering with captured light as it reached its apex and started back the other way.

Whisk!

Another journey toward the opposite wall. Each swing brought it a fraction lower and made its swing seem more urgent. The man watched with keen interest, the eyes of God on the instrument of torture.

"WWPD," Franklin said as much to himself as to Freddy or the man.

Freddy's hand was amazingly steady, his vision amazingly clear. The whittling knife/scalpel pressed against the bared flesh of the body, his shirt pulled aside to reveal whiter skin. If they were right, there would be no blood. He pressed the scalpel down and watched the God's skin dimple. He drew it slowly across the flesh and watched for the chasing trail of blood.

No blood.

The pendulum made another trip across the large room before the boys, barely grazing the robes of the God beneath it.

Whisk!

A small trickle of blood ran from the bellies of Fat Boy and Spittle Man.

Whisk!

God looked up at the boys.

Whisk!

Fat Boy and Little Man screamed.

Whisk!

God died.

FAREWELL, FRANKENSTEIN!

(OR) THE POSTMODERN PROMETHEUS

BY ROBERT GUFFEY

"Farewell, Frankenstein! If thou wert yet alive and yet cherished a desire of revenge against me, it would be better satiated in my life than in my destruction. But it was not so; thou didst seek my extinction, that I might not cause greater wretchedness; and if yet, in some mode unknown to me, thou hadst not ceased to think and feel, thou wouldst not desire against me a vengeance greater than that which I feel. Blasted as thou wert, my agony was still superior to thine, for the bitter sting of remorse will not cease to rankle in my wounds until death shall close them forever."

--Mary Shelley, *Frankenstein*, 1818

Disclaimer: The following events are, to borrow a phrase coined by the late James W. Moseley, "shockingly close to the truth." Names and places have been changed to protect the guilty and innocent alike.

1.

On the first day of the Fall 2012 semester at CSU Sunken City, I told my English students they didn't need to buy any of the expensive, Department-approved textbooks listed on the syllabus. While they were still immersed in the ecstatic throes of my unexpected announcement, I leaned over the podium and said in a conspiratorial whisper, "But in exchange for this generous favor on my part, you must follow my instructions. Listen carefully: I've been told I cannot assign any form of fiction in this classroom. If anyone finds out I'm assigning fiction, I will be fired. A single sentence from any one of you will get me dismissed permanently from this campus. Do you understand what I'm saying? I'm giving you all a sacred task. I've been told that I cannot assign you the novel *Frankenstein* by Mary Shelley. By assigning you this novel, I'm putting my entire life on the line. There are certain entities now working in the English Department who wish to have me killed. I'm trusting all of you to work with me on this project. Despite numerous threats against my life, I have decided to forge ahead and assign *Frankenstein* anyway. I don't care what edition you get. Any edition is fine as long as it's unexpurgated. You can order it from online booksellers, used bookstores, wherever. Do not ask for it at the University Bookstore. If you do that, it could sink us all. All of you must cooperate with me and be smart. Do not attempt to buy *Frankenstein* through the bookstore. If anyone from the bookstore reports the fact that my students are inquiring about *Frankenstein*, that too could get me fired."

My students stared at me blankly.

2.

The attempt to drive *Frankenstein* into extinction began on April 20, 2012, Hitler's birthday. I tend to remember synchronicities like that.

Out of the blue, on the campus where I teach, a meeting was announced for that morning. All full-time faculty members were required to attend. I found myself sitting next to an aging radical who had served prison time in the '70s for the torture and imprisonment of two black women. Now he was in charge of the African-American studies department. He complained to me about the poor quality of the catered food. I agreed with him.

To my surprise, a middle-aged woman I had never seen before

abruptly announced herself as the head of the Composition Committee in the English Department, the committee that oversaw the day-to-day details regarding the numerous composition classes at CSU Sunken City.

Composition was a mandatory class for all incoming freshmen, so it provided jobs for a lot of English teachers, all of whom are responsible for roughly twenty-five students per class. Teaching Composition was never an easy task, but it's grown even more difficult during the past few years since many of these students are barely able to read or write.

Every teacher has a different style, of course, but I would assume that the main goal of any composition instructor is to make reading and writing fun for a group of young people who have never been awakened to the genuine magic that reading and writing can bring to a person's otherwise blighted life. The vast majority of these students have never had an aesthetic experience of any kind. This is not surprising, given how ineptly reading and writing is taught from kindergarten onward. When I was in high school, I often wondered if the teachers weren't going out of their way to *discourage* us from reading. In my freshman English class in high school, the teacher assigned us *Les Misérables* by Victor Hugo (a poor choice for high school students, freshmen or otherwise), and then compounded the problem by only requiring us to read random chapters. You couldn't even tell what the hell was going on in the narrative. It was like reading a cut-up novel by William S. Burroughs, except the cuts were being made by the teacher—seemingly with no rhyme or reason. When I began teaching composition, I swore I would do everything I could to instill in my students a love of the English language in general and literature in particular. This would seem to come with the territory, correct?

In the eyes of some people, apparently not. This mysterious woman, Dr. Karol Willeford, suddenly appeared in a puff of dark smoke in the middle of the composition meeting to announce that she and the Dean of the English Department, Dr. Simon Helfrick, had decided that literature could not be taught in the composition classes.

The composition instructors in the room stared at each other in disbelief. How could you teach a composition class effectively without teaching literature? Dr. Willeford explained: We could only use nonfiction essays from now on, and the essays had to come from a series of pre-approved textbooks that were all published by a single corporation based in Dallas, Texas. Helfrick and Willeford had entered into a dubious "arrangement" with this company, who had also catered the meeting. El Pollo Loco at eleven in the morning. Hardly anyone touched this food, of course. I don't know of anyone who wants to eat a room-temperature chicken enchilada at eleven in the morning. Oh, and the publisher also passed out complimentary bottles of Nestle bottled water. I never even opened mine. In fact, the bottle is still sitting on my office desk, slightly crumpled now, looking rather like an Academy Award statue made of plastic that melted slowly in the heat of the Southern California sun. If I stay in that office long enough, the bottle will melt away completely one day, wiping away my final reminder of that strange, fateful meeting.

Someone, I forget who, raised their hand and asked why this change had to be implemented.

Dr. Willeford had an answer: Apparently someone in the History Department had been complaining that too many of the composition instructors were using their position as English instructors to teach literature and not writing. Apparently, in the disordered brains of Willeford and Helfrick, there is a substantial difference between teaching literature and teaching writing (a difference the dynamic duo never bothered to explain). Let's be clear: This unnamed history instructor, the head of the entire History Department, had decided that too many English classes were being taught by English instructors. The history prof thought this situation should change and change quickly.

Keep in mind that all of this went down during a time when college professors were being let go left and right. The economy was in the tank and classes were being jettisoned by the dozens. Composition classes, however, are a constant. As I said, they're required for all incoming freshmen. No matter how bad the economy is, there's always a demand for composition instructors. So, the head of the History Department got it into her head that she could find work for all her laid off history profs if the history profs could be allowed to teach composition classes. But the only way to accomplish that would be to prove to the administration that the current English instructors were too incompetent to teach basic English.

It's all rather Machiavellian, I know, but the situation gets worse, folks… way worse….

3.

I was to learn later that the person who kicked off this campaign of oppression was none other than Yours Truly. The semester before, I had been assigned an English class that was "linked" to a class in the History Department. This was part of some experiment the college was pursuing to encourage interdepartmental cooperation or some sort of similar hippie crap. As a result, the twenty-five students in my composition class would leave my classroom and walk over to a different classroom for a history class taught by the aforementioned history prof. The students, of course, would chat among themselves about what they had just experienced in my class. For some reason, when this history prof heard I was teaching *Frankenstein* in my class, she went through the freakin' roof. I was told by reliable sources that simply hearing the word "Frankenstein" would send her into an inexplicable rage. She lodged a formal complaint with the college. (Why such a "complaint" wasn't immediately round filed, I had no idea… at least, not at that time.) The basis of the complaint was as follows: I, as an MFA graduate and creative writing instructor, was teaching literature in my composition classes in order to recruit students into the creative writing program.

This argument makes so little sense that I'm not even sure where to begin tearing it apart. Why would I care if these students entered the creative writing program? I usually try to dissuade potential writers from majoring in creative writing. I myself majored in creative writing and I'm not sure it helped me at all. And why would the teaching of literature in a composition class equate to the teaching of creative writing? I wasn't asking my students to write fan fiction about *Frankenstein*. I was asking them to write essays about *Frankenstein*, an acknowledged work of classic literature that ties into history, science, feminism, anarchy, bioengineering, and a thousand other topics facing human beings in the twenty-first century. There's more history in *Frankenstein* than in any class taught in the History Department. That should go without saying.

Now, there's a more sinister question involved in all this: How did this professor know I was an MFA graduate and a creative writing major in the first place? After all, I don't know shit about *her*. Even after I was told her name I didn't bother to look into her background. I'm too busy for such nonsense. But, apparently, *she* wasn't too busy to launch a private investigation into my educational background and the list of classes I've taught in the past. She then used this profile in her complaint. If she genuinely thought I was using my composition classes to recruit students into the creative writing program (again, why would I want *more* bad writers in the creative writing program, a program I'm only tangentially connected to since I'm allowed to teach creative writing classes only when a tenured professor is abruptly hit on the head by a falling meteorite and topples into a manhole or comes down with a debilitating case of the Zika virus?), why didn't this professor just *ask* me if that's what I was doing? If she was smart enough to figure out that I graduated from the MFA Program at CSU Sunken City, then she was probably smart enough to glance at the campus directory and discover my exact office number. This indicates she didn't believe I was actually guilty of the crimes of which she was accusing me. This was all a thinly veiled attempt to wrest the composition classes from the English Department in order to provide potential jobs for her unemployed history professors.

Or was it?

If the motivation behind all of this was as simple as that, why wouldn't the Dean of the English Department (a person who's supposed to be protecting people like me from baseless charges like this) simply tell this history prof to go take a flying fuck at the full moon? He didn't. Instead he capitulated to the complaint. In fact, he used the complaint as an excuse to do something he had been wanting to do for a very long time: remove all traces of literature and creative writing from the college's composition classes.

4.

"Wait a minute," you ask, "there are English professors who want to remove literature and creative writing from English classes? How is that possible? Why did these people become English professors in the first place if they despise all forms of literature and creativity?" Keep asking yourself that.

A flashback regarding the aforementioned Dr. Helfrick. I have a friend, an extremely talented writer with several fine poetry collections to his name, who also teaches composition at CSUSC. About a year before all this went down, my friend assigned a collection of poetry to his composition class. This particular collection was written by a man who used to go to school with Dr. Helfrick, a poet named Dietrich Volt who has become a well-renowned writer while Helfrick has become little more than a parasitic bureaucrat whose main goal in life is to make it almost impossible to teach students English. One night Helfrick was having dinner with his old college chum who mentioned *en passant* that one of Helfrick's faculty members had assigned Volt's latest poetry collection to a composition class at CSUSC. Now, understand, Volt wasn't bragging about this. It was a casual comment, nothing more.

Suddenly, as the flames were dying out on the cherries jubilee, Helfrick's face darkened to a deep, purplish red. He slammed his fist down on the white tablecloth and yelled, "He's not supposed to be doing that! No poetry in the composition classes! No literature! Just essays! Just nonfiction!" Helfrick became so enraged the waiter rushed over to ask if there was anything wrong with the meal. The good doctor had become unhinged.

Now, ask yourself: What was behind all of this? The sublimated, intense hatred of an insignificant little bureaucrat for an old school chum who had actually succeeded in pursuing a life of creativity? Perhaps. Or perhaps it was something even deeper....

When Helfrick said, "He's not supposed to be doing that," what did he mean? At that time there was no rule in the CSUSC English Department that prevented an English instructor from assigning poetry to a composition class. Why would there be? Who would even think that such a rule was either necessary or desirable? After that dinner, it's as if the frustrated rage of the slumbering bureaucrat had awakened. Realizing there was no such rule preventing literature from being taught in the composition classes, Helfrick decided to make one. How do you do that? Well, you need a complaint. But wait a minute, no one's complaining because there's no problem. So, let's create a program in the English Department in which certain classes are linked together. We'll say this is to promote cooperation between departments. We'll make sure a former MFA graduate is assigned to the English class that's linked to a class taught by a woman the bureaucrat just so happens to be casual friends with in the History Department. Perhaps there's an arrangement made beforehand between the bureaucrat and the history professor… or perhaps the bureaucrat simply knows the prejudices of the history professor and allows the chips to fall where they may.…

In either case, the story ends with all creativity being wiped out of the composition department. Consequently, Helfrick's old school chum will never be able to brag about his poetry collection being taught in a composition class in the CSUSC English Department while the fire is dying out on the cherries jubilee, by God.

(A brief sidenote: I've assigned a lot of peculiar authors in my composition classes, some that might elicit a complaint of two. I've assigned Charles Bukowski, Hunter S. Thompson, Philip K. Dick, Harlan Ellison, William S. Burroughs, Jack Womack, Rachel Pollack, Leigh Kennedy, Octavia Butler, even comic books by the likes of Will Eisner, Alan Moore, Chester Brown, and Daniel Clowes. And yet I never received a complaint from a student about any of these writers. During fifteen years of teaching, the only complaint I've received about the literature I was teaching came from a history professor who was apparently manipulated into doing so by the Dean of the very English

Department in which I work. That, kids, is called "irony," a concept that used to be taught in composition classes before such literary concepts were banned.)

5.

As you can imagine, this conspiratorial nonsense annoyed me. I went straight to the Chair of the English Department and demanded that something be done about this. She agreed the whole mess was nonsensical and confirmed that my "paranoid suspicions" were not paranoid at all. In fact, she told me (and this is a direct quote), "You are the target here, my friend, and you need to be careful."

"So what are we supposed to teach if we can't teach literature? How're we supposed to get these kids interested in *reading*?"

The Chair shrugged. "You have to do what you have to do. But whatever you do, make sure I don't know anything about it. And for God's sake don't include it on the syllabus!"

Of course, we were being told the only reading we could assign in these composition classes were nonfiction essays—but only the nonfiction essays included in the series of substandard text books for which Helfrick had been given baksheesh by the aforementioned publishing company in exchange for shoving this poorly written crap down the collective throats of every single incoming freshman whose deeply held prejudices against reading were just about to be confirmed. As far as I know, almost every teacher in the department immediately capitulated and did as they were told.

I went home, closed the curtains of my office, turned off all the lights, removed my magical apparatuses from inside my closet, and performed a complex ritual I had learned during my time with the Freemasons. (I'm a 32nd Degree Freemason... long story, best left for another time.)

Of course, as any practicing witch or warlock knows, black magic and curses inevitably swing back and hit the practitioner ten times worse than the target of the original curse, so it's important to be careful with these forces and not perform them when you're in a highly emotional state of mind. It's best to be as calm as possible. There are ways around the boomerang effect. You must never cast a curse, for example. Simply request the universe to do something positive for the people being oppressed by the bad guy in question. That's what I did.

The next day I arrived on campus and was told by my office mate that Helfrick had gotten into a serious car accident the previous day while riding his bicycle in traffic. The accident was so bad Helfrick ended up in the hospital. I'm not sure how this improved the situation on campus (perhaps it did in some way I'm not aware of), but it certainly did give me a chuckle. Never dismiss the healing effects of a good chuckle. Thanks, Universe.

6.

The next thing I did was to falsify all my syllabi. The reason for this was simple: Dr. Willeford had introduced a "new and better policy" that demanded all English Department faculty submit their syllabi in triplicate to her and her alone several days before the beginning of each semester. The amount of time it would take to scour through each syllabus is mindboggling. Was she really looking at every word of those syllabi? Or was it just the threat that she *might* look at them that was intended to be sufficient to keep everyone in line? Yes, English Department faculty were now like prisoners of war who never knew when the little rectangle in the metal door of their cell might slide aside, allowing the guard to peek through and see what they were up to in the darkness of their cramped hole. You better not be makin' an Iron Man suit in there, God damn it! And no books should appear on your syllabus that aren't published by this inept textbook company based out of Dallas, Texas. (Unbelievable sidenote: I checked into this company's pedigree and was amused/bemused to learn that the company's main office was based in the same Texas Book Depository Building where Lee Harvey Oswald supposedly took the fatal shot at JFK. Who could make this stuff up?)

7.

Of course, I don't think Willeford was actually reading those syllabi. Just certain ones, written by particular teachers. In fact, I began to notice a pattern. Only specific instructors would be harassed by Willeford, all of them relatively young males. No female teacher was ever chastised by Willeford. I even learned that some of the female teachers were slipping texts into their syllabi not published by the pre-approved Lee Harvey Oswald Publishing Company, and Willeford would do nothing about this. One poor guy I'm aware of was incessantly stalked by Willeford on Facebook. He mentioned in passing, in a very short post, that he had assigned his composition students an in-class writing assignment in which they were supposed to reimagine the text they were reading from their own unique perspective. Oh, dear. Willeford went through the stratosphere. She sent this guy a long screed via Facebook that was so brutal he had to crawl into a ball in the corner of his office and practice Primal Scream therapy just to get over the trauma of it all. Willeford was living up to her increasingly rancorous reputation.

8.

"I was required to exchange chimeras of boundless grandeur for realities of little worth."

--Mary Shelley, *Frankenstein*, 1818

To avoid any difficulty with Willeford, I wrote down a couple of approved texts on the syllabus, then on the first day I told the class, "Listen… see those required books listed on the syllabus here? Well, they're not required anymore. You don't have to buy them." I saw every student breathe a sigh of relief. Textbooks are already too expensive as it is. To complicate the situation by forcing them to buy overpriced, poorly written textbooks soaked in the blood of the 35th President of the United States is just too much to ask of any relatively innocent college student.

I then launched into the soliloquy I quoted in Chapter One of this saga.

9.

And that soliloquy wasn't an exaggeration. When I told my students I might be fired for teaching *Frankenstein*, something incredible happened right before the beginning of the Fall semester. Just before the start of each semester, professors generally order their books through the University Bookstore. A new program had been implemented that allowed us to place the orders through the Internet. In fact, we were not allowed to order the books in person or over the phone. It *had* to be done through the computer. To do this, you needed to log onto the University Bookstore website as an employee of the college. Just before the Fall semester began I did exactly this, following procedure (as I was told to do), and was surprised to discover—when I logged on—that I was able to view the book orders for every professor in the English Department. This should not have been the case. I should only have been able to view my *own* book orders. If I attempted to place an order (say, for *Frankenstein*), that order would be placed not just for my class but for every composition class in the department. I called the bookstore and asked them what the problem was. The bookstore employee seemed confused at first, then asked me if I was an "Administrator."

"Administrator?" I asked. "What do you mean?"

"You know... one of the heads of the composition committee."

"No, I'm not. I'm just a lecturer."

"Oh, I see. Someone mistakenly tagged you as an Administrator."

"Wait a minute... are you saying that whatever the English instructors order through their own private accounts can be tracked covertly by the composition committee?"

"Well... they're not private accounts. They're accounts assigned to you by the school."

I laughed. "But no one informed us that our online activity could be viewed by anyone other than ourselves."

"You shouldn't need to be informed about that," the bookstore employee said. "Shouldn't you *assume* you're being observed? Besides… do you have something you want to hide?"

"No, of course not," I said. "This was just a test to see how you would react to my questions. Your answers were acceptable. As you were, comrade. Be Seeing You." I then hung up and abandoned the idea of ordering copies of *Frankenstein* through the bookstore. The remarkable thing was that someone in charge must have gone out of their way to misidentify me as an "Administrator" so that I would be able to see what Willeford *herself* could see from her underground Batcave computer. This was no accident. This was a clever move on the part of an unknown ally within the System to let me know exactly what *not* to do. That may sound somewhat paranoid… but what kind of paranoid imagines that faceless entities are conspiring to *benefit* him rather than destroy him?

Who knows?

10.

So… back to the first day of class: "It's absolutely imperative that you listen to what I'm saying," I whispered harshly. "If even one of you makes the slightest misstep, we could all be in trouble. Now, let's put this to a vote. Those of you who would prefer to read the outrageously overpriced and exceedingly dull textbook from Dallas, Texas, please feel free to raise your hand." Nobody raised their hand. "I see. Who, instead, would prefer to read a fictional novel about a madman who resuscitates the dead, copies of which can be purchased online for roughly one dollar?" Everybody raised their hands. "Then it's settled. By agreeing to take part in this insidious conspiracy, you will be putting your lives in danger. But you're all adults, most of you have already broken any number of laws prohibiting a seemingly endless series of victimless crimes, and have no doubt lost your virginity several times over during the course of the past six years or so, so I think you're all capable of keeping a secret. Am I right?" Everyone nodded. "Excellent. Let's proceed."

11.

I made this same speech to five different composition classes that Fall. That's about 125 students. Any one of them could have ratted me out at any moment. No one ever did, not even the ones who received bad grades in the class or didn't particularly like me. On the very first day of class I placed a shiv in their fist and told them they were welcome to stick it in my back at any moment throughout the entire semester, and yet no one ever did. Why?

Each class would begin with me leaning over the podium and whispering, "Now remember, students, it's very important that you not tell anyone we're reading this book. It's wrong. What we're doing is just so wrong on so many levels I can't even begin to measure the depths of depravity to which we'll all sink before the semester's through. If anyone is unwilling to follow me on this voyage across the River Styx, feel free to transfer to another class where you can revel in the joys of analyzing expurgated *Reader's Digest* articles about the lives of Karl Marx, Gandhi, and Angela Davis. There's the door. You can use it at any time. No takers? Okay, then, let's get down to business."

12.

I never posted any assignments on SynchBoard, the omniscient campus-wide computer system that I now knew was constantly monitored by "Administrators." Occasionally I would post various innocuous assignments regarding the lives of Karl Marx, Gandhi, and Angela Davis just to throw the "administrators" off the scent, but I would never ask the students to read them. They would just float there permanently in cyberspace, unloved and unread, waiting fruitlessly for a student to interact with them. My SynchBoard was a false front city, like a western town on a movie lot lacking interiors.

I would give the students their assignments in sealed envelopes and ask them not to open them until they left campus for the day. Any questions regarding the essay assignments could be sent to my personal email address, not the school email address (which, as far as I knew, might also be visible to the omniscient "Administrators").

When they buckled down to write their papers about Mary Shelley or *Frankenstein*, I urged them not to include my name or the name of the class on the first page, just in case the paper got lost and was discovered by another professor (some of whom were rather toady-like in their eagerness to uncover the crimes of those who were not following the rules of Dr. Willeford).

13.

These cloak and dagger methods, when applied to teaching composition, had a curious and unexpected effect on the students. They seemed to enjoy reading a novel first published in 1818 more than any of them had a reason to. In previous semesters, I had had some limited success teaching *Frankenstein*. I had been warned by many colleagues not even to attempt it. "No eighteen-year-old in the twenty-first century is going to sit still for *Frankenstein*! They can barely handle *Harry Potter*!" I had been told the same thing about Alan Moore and David Lloyd's graphic novel *V for Vendetta*. I had been told that *V for Vendetta* would be way over the students' heads. They would never be able to comprehend it. They would be bored. They would hate it. They wouldn't know what order to read the panels in. These warnings went on and on. Finally, I just said, "Fuck it. Let's try it. Why not? What's the worst that could happen?" *V for Vendetta* turned out to be very popular with the students. Most of them had no problem following the various plot threads and multilayered themes that weave their way through the narrative. *Frankenstein*, being a prose novel and having been written almost two hundred years before they were born, was undoubtedly a greater risk. But, again, I decided to roll the dice and see what would happen.

The first semester I used *Frankenstein*, I was surprised at how successful it was. The students certainly did not reject it out of hand. After a while, once they got used to the antiquated prose, they even seemed to enjoy it. After reading their papers, and seeing how many students chose to write about the theme of alienation in the book, I suddenly realized that there was an almost subliminal and intangible connection between the teenage girl who wrote the novel in 1817 and the eighteen-year-olds who were now reading it in the twenty-first century. After all, *Frankenstein* is the only acknowledged classic of English literature written by a teenager. And though Mary Shelley's life was certainly not typical, not even for a teenager of the early nineteenth century (how many young girls of the early nineteenth century could say that William Blake was a regular visitor to her home?), nonetheless I think there's some sort of shared experience—having to do with the search for individual identity, the rejection of the father, and feeling like an outsider in a frequently harsh world that no one, aside from the most enthusiastic Buddhist, asks to be born into—that effectively bridges the vast cultural and temporal gap between Mary Shelley and today's teenagers. As long as we live in a world in which teenagers continue to be human beings, and not preprogrammed biological androids devoid of all emotion, *Frankenstein* will continue to have devoted readers.

14.

But now, during the Fall semester of 2012, the students were inexplicably even more enthusiastic about reading *Frankenstein*. Imagine how much this development would please Mary Shelley. Upon its initial publication, the novel was criticized as a work of blasphemy. The fact that it was still causing authoritarians to shit their pants one hundred and ninety-four years after its publication could only stoke a warm glow in Shelley's heart. How many works of classic literature still have this visceral effect on people? Do you ever hear about roving bands of bluenoses attempting to burn piles of *Robinson Crusoe*? *Treasure Island*? *Pride and Prejudice*? *The Jungle*? Banning *Frankenstein* was the best thing that ever happened to the book. The students couldn't get enough of it. Their essays that semester were the most creative and thoughtful I had ever read in a freshman composition class. What Edgar Allan Poe called the "Imp of the Perverse" could be blamed for this effect, but I didn't particularly care. All I knew was that my TV-numbed, computer-besotted, drug-addled students were clearly enjoying reading a complex novel composed in the early nineteenth century.

15.

One day after class, a student named Christina approached my desk and said, "Hey, I'm really enjoying *Frankenstein*. I didn't think I would… but after I got past the first couple of chapters I actually wanted to *keep* reading. I mean, y'know, it's actually kinda fun. It's cool knowin' where all this stuff comes from, all the horror crap you see in the movies…."

Christina was a Latina in her late teens or early twenties. Having read some of her essays during a previous semester, when she was enrolled in my remedial English class, I knew she had grown up in the darkest depths of Los Angeles. She had written in some detail about being trapped in a public school system she despised. Now she seemed almost embarrassed to be admitting that she was truly enjoying *Frankenstein*, a book assigned to her in a classroom.

Then the expression on her face changed. She almost appeared angry. "You know, I'm kinda pissed off," she said.

For a second I thought she meant she was pissed off at *me*… which didn't make any sense, since we had gotten along well before this moment.

Her right fist clenched at her side as she said, "You know what we were talkin' about today? All them books you mentioned?" Earlier, I had briefly discussed *Frankenstein*'s importance to the field of science fiction. I had brought up some titles I thought the students might have come across during high school. A couple of the students, who hailed from somewhat more affluent neighborhoods than Christina, knew exactly what I was talking about when I mentioned Huxley's *Brave New World*, Orwell's *1984*, Bradbury's *Fahrenheit 451*. Even if they hadn't read those novels, the more knowledgeable students at least knew the titles and understood the general subject matter of the books.

Christina now leaned close to me. Her voice lowered to a whisper as she said, "I feel *pissed off* that I don't know what they know. Those books you mentioned... man, I've never even *heard* of them. Not at all. Not until today. It... it kinda makes me mad... that they knew, and I didn't. My high school English teacher? Mr. Carroll? I mentioned him before in that essay I turned in at the end of last semester. Remember?" I nodded. "You know what he'd do every day? He'd stroll into class, put on a Snoopy video—the *same* Snoopy video—and then just leave the room. I mean, *every day*. Then he'd come back about five minutes before the end of class and shut the video off and tell us all to go home. This guy had *totally* given up on life."

I said, "So... what would all the students do while the Snoopy video was playing?"

Christina chuckled and said, "Same crap *I* was doin'. Laughin'. Talkin'. Some of them were gettin' high in the back. At the time I thought Mr. Carroll was the greatest teacher I'd ever had. I mean, at least he wasn't yellin' at me for shit I didn't do, y'know? But now that I'm here, and I'm listening to these other students the same age as me talk about books I ain't never even fuckin' heard of... well, I kinda wish Mr. Carroll had assigned me a book or two. I wouldn't feel so behind now."

"Wait," I said. "Just out of curiosity... how many novels do you think you were assigned during high school?" Christina just stared at me blankly. "You know, a rough estimate... you don't have to be exact."

Christina laughed and said, "Not even *one* book."

"In *all* of high school?"

Christina shook her head and chuckled once more. "No, no, I mean from kindergarten all the way up to the *end* of high school. No one ever asked us to read a book. I wish they had. The first time I ever read a novel cover to cover was when you assigned us *Slaughterhouse-Five* in that remedial class last semester. Anyway... I just wanted to thank you for making us read this crazy shit."

After she left the classroom that morning I sat at my desk for a while, just staring at the blank white wall on the other side of the room.

The next semester, Christina signed up for my Literature of Science Fiction class. Of all my students that semester, she seemed the most eager to learn.

16.

Meanwhile, Dr. Willeford's behavior continued to grow more and more bizarre. Any young male teacher ostensibly under her supervision who seemed to be disregarding her dictums would receive scathing rebukes at random moments—in the hallway, in an interdepartmental memo, via email, social media, text. One young teacher in his twenties, whose lifestyle certainly didn't depend on the five hundred bucks per month he was receiving from CSUSC for teaching a single English class, decided to assign Grant Morrison's recently published nonfiction analysis of the superhero genre, *Supergods*, in his composition class. After all, it wasn't a novel and seemed to be something that would generate interest in the students. He was right. It was an excellent choice. But Dr. Willeford didn't think so. You see, it wasn't on the prescribed list of textbooks produced by the Lee Harvey Oswald Publishing Company, thus cutting into the potential kickback money flowing into the deep pockets of Dr. Helfrick and the CSUSC English Department. Dr. Willeford sent this teacher the following email:

Dear Colleague:

I have just completed reviewing your wholly inadequate syllabi. Immediate compliance to the rules of the Composition Committee is hereby demanded. By assigning such non-approved texts as this Supergods nonsense, you belie your ignorance of the very basics of teaching composition. You must be made to realize that you are failing in your job to teach your students, per the previously stated guidelines prepared by the Composition Committee (see attached). If you are incapable of understanding the simplest rules of this

department—indeed, of this campus—you need not apply for another
English class next semester. I eagerly await your response.

   Sincerely,
Dr. Karol Willeford, Ph.D.

And here's how the teacher responded:

Dear Karol,

   I find it peculiar that I have, in your eyes, belied my woeful "igno-
rance" due to the simple fact that I dared to assign a nonfiction text
that might actually keep the students awake for more than a few sec-
onds at a time. The text in question has been successful in stimulating
the students' imaginations and critical thinking skills. Is this wrong? I
had been under the impression that the reading list you emailed to me
at the beginning of the semester was composed of recommended text-
books. It did not occur to me—nor was this revealed anywhere in the
accompanying directions—that these were the sole textbooks approved
by the Composition Committee. It was indeed clear that fiction was
not allowed (for reasons still not adequately explained to me), and as a
consequence I assigned a recent nonfiction text that might engage the
students in the same manner as a novel.

   I do apologize for engaging my students. I understand why this
might be distressing to you, and only to you, as this is clearly a feat
you have not accomplished during your entire career. As for securing
classes for next semester, please do not worry about that. I teach on
three other campuses. Feel free to take over the composition classes
at CSUSC yourself. It appears you're the only instructor in Southern
California capable of following the ridiculous guidelines concocted by
what you call the "Composition Committee" (i.e., you).

   With eternal love,

   ———————— ————————

The email Dr. Willeford sent in response was so deranged

that it almost made no sense whatsoever. As far I know, the teacher in question received no reprisals for this act of defiance, except for the obvious one (he wasn't rehired the following semester).

17.

"'Man,' I cried, 'how ignorant art thou in thy pride of wisdom! Cease; you know not what it is you say.'"

--Mary Shelley, *Frankenstein*, 1818

It was around this time that a colleague of mine ran into Dr. Willeford in the elevator. This colleague is not known for taking crap from anyone. Let's call her Jen. The second the elevator doors closed, Dr. Willeford turned toward Jen and said, "So... how are you adjusting to all the exciting new changes I've implemented in the English Department?" Without missing a beat, Jen responded, "To be honest with you, Karol, I just ignored everything you said. Have a nice day."

Karol seemed stunned. The doors opened, as if on cue, and Jen exited the elevator without looking back. The next morning, as I was leaving my office to go to class, Jen ran into me in the hallway and told me about this amusing encounter. About sixty seconds later I entered the elevator. Never before in my life have I shared an elevator ride with Dr. Willeford. So, who's in the elevator this morning? Dr. Willeford. The second the elevator doors closed, she turned toward me and said, "So... how are you adjusting to all the exciting new changes I've implemented in the English Department?" It was eerie. It was like walking into someone else's memory. I decided to evade the question rather than attack it head on. I effectively changed the subject. I said, "Have you ever been so confused that you almost don't even know who you are anymore?"

"Indeed, yes," she said, nodding with false sympathy. "I used to teach nine English classes in a single semester, driving from one campus to the next. So, I'm well familiar with the effects of exhaustion due to a heavy workload." I understood she was telling me this to try to convince me that she was a normal working stiff, just like me, just like everybody else in the English Department. By God, she had lived life in the trenches! She knew more than just a thing or two about teaching composition, yes sir. You ain't looking at any poser, mister man! I've lived the hard life. I can identify with your beaten down demeanor. I'm just like you. And you're just like me.

(It occurs to me, after writing the previous sentence, who Dr. Willeford most reminds me of. If you've ever seen the Harry Potter movie, *Harry Potter and the Order of the Phoenix*, you'll no doubt remember a character named Dolores Umbridge, the authoritarian professor who gets dragged off into the dark forest by angry centaurs in the third act; that character's condescending and falsely ingratiating tone exactly mirrors that of Dr. Willeford. Willeford, however, never wore Jackie-Kennedy-style pink dresses or pillbox hats. On the contrary, she wore only black and had several fresh tattoos prominently displayed on her forearms, as if to demonstrate to the young 'uns that she was on the cutting edge.

(Remember when the presence of a tattoo actually indicated certain character traits about an individual you could take to the bank? The current situation in regard to tattoos is rather like the 1950s when FBI narcs finally got the go ahead to start shooting up heroin and smoking dope on the job. Everything's up for grabs these days.)

I just nodded and said, "Well, I'm not confused because of *exhaustion*. No, the workload's fine. I'm referring to something a little more sinister. I'm talking about Weckmann Hall."

Weckmann Hall is the monolithic building located on lower campus where the President of the college and all her bureaucratic underlings have their offices. Whenever a teacher refers to "Weckmann Hall," they're referring to the *entire spider web system of unexplainable jabberwocky* that emerges from that building and the people/drones who inhabit it. The week before, Weckmann Hall had announced a new class schedule for the week preceding the Thanksgiving weekend. Instead of cancelling the Wednesday classes before Thanksgiving, which would be simple, they decided to move all the Thursday classes to Wednesday, then move the Wednesday classes to Tuesday. Huh? I still don't understand it. It so confused me that I told all my students not to come to class on Tuesday or Wednesday. Keeping track of everything I have to keep track of is hard enough as it is. Expecting me to teach my Tuesday/Thursday classes on a Wednesday and vice-versa would be enough to make my medulla oblongata melt.

Dr. Willeford smiled and said, "Yes, now that was ridiculous, wasn't it?"

I said, "It's almost like they were going out of their way to make it confusing for everyone."

The elevator doors opened and Dr. Willeford followed me out into the hall. It was at this point that Willeford said something that almost shattered my skull. She said, *with a completely straight face, with absolutely no hint of irony at all,* "It always frustrates me when bureaucrats like that have to make stupid changes just for the sake of making changes. It's as if they have nothing better to do than to control other people's lives."

I could only stare at her with stunned befuddlement. "Uh, yeah," I said, "I... know exactly what you mean. Uh... well, I need to go to class now."

"So do I. See you at the next composition meeting."

"Uh... yes... be seeing you."

I walked toward my class, still numb all over, trying to comprehend a brain that has absolutely no sense of self-awareness whatsoever.

18.

"In other studies you go as far as others have gone before you, and there is nothing more to know; but in a scientific pursuit there is a continual food for discovery and wonder."

--Mary Shelley, *Frankenstein*, 1818

Although I continued to do whatever the hell I wanted in my classroom, at the same time I wished to test the limits of what was acceptable to Willeford and Helfrick. Where was the limit? Why was fiction no longer considered acceptable in the context of English 100? We never received a direct answer to this question. During the two meetings at which both Dr. Helfrick and Dr. Willeford were present, the question was asked, "Why aren't novels acceptable any longer?" They both seemed affronted by the query, as if the answer should be obvious.

This is the closest we ever got to an answer. Dr. Willeford said, "Well, we're already forcing the students to buy a textbook." The "textbook" she was referring to, of course, was the cornucopia of poorly written polemics she and Helfrick were being paid to thrust down our collective throats. "To ask the students to buy a novel on top of that would not be fair to the student."

This explanation made so little sense on so many levels that I'm once again not sure where to begin deconstructing it. First of all, obviously, the only reason the student was having to shell out their hard-earned shekels on these horrendously overpriced textbooks was because *she and Dr. Helfrick were making us assign them.* So the main reason we couldn't assign novels was because of a problem the two of them had created. This was a classic case of applied Hegelian Dialectics: Create the problem, then offer a solution to the problem you manifested yourself. And the offered solution is never beneficial to anyone except the people who created the problem in the first place.

Here's another reason this explanation didn't make sense: I knew of plenty of female instructors—those who shared Willeford's firmly held political views—who asked for permission to assign a nonfiction text *besides the assigned textbook* and immediately received permission. Didn't that supplementary book cost extra money, the same amount of money a novel would cost?

Needless to say, there are plenty of novels—classic works of literature—that are now in the public domain and available legally online. The students are more than capable of downloading an entire novel, including *Frankenstein*, from the Internet. Since this would cost the student no extra money, does this mean it's acceptable to assign *Frankenstein* on top of the assigned textbook?

Answer: "No." Question: "Why?" Answer: "Fiction is not allowed to be taught in the composition classes anymore." Question: "Why?" Answer: "Well, we're already forcing the students to buy a textbook. To ask the students to buy a novel on top of that would not be fair to the student." Question: [Sound of my brain imploding.]

19.

Aside from Helfrick's deeply rooted personal problems with creative writing, which we've already touched upon and would no doubt require a highly trained psychiatrist and several doses of DMT to diagnose properly, there's a more troublesome aspect to this war against the imagination. The year this new policy was implemented corresponded with the introduction of the Obama administration's Common Core program that immediately began eating into the already decomposing flesh of the American education system like a rabid super-zombie created in a secret lab below the Pentagon. A lot of American children were being consumed by it. One of the main tenets of Common Core was the banning of almost all fiction from primary education, those crucial years when children will either learn to love reading or will be programmed to despise it.

Willeford and Helfrick were enthusiastic supporters of Common Core. Like good stormtrooper drones receiving commands from the High Executioner, they did everything they could with the limited resources at their disposal to impose the dictates of Common Core on the college level, on the freshmen who had just now managed to escape the destructive K-12 American educational system.

One can only speculate about the real agenda here.

As the great science fiction writer, Theodore Sturgeon, often liked to say, "Ask the next question." Who benefits from a nation of young adults completely unfamiliar with the mind-expanding world of literature, poetry, and fiction in general? Why train an entire nation of students to avoid fiction? Once the right question is asked, the answer is obvious. A nation unfamiliar with fiction will be unable to recognize fiction when it comes spewing out of the mouths of newscasters, teachers, composition instructors, college deans, Army recruiters, preachers, cult leaders, politicians, policemen, and the President of the United States himself. One need not bother attempting to expose the atrocities of a corrupt Presidential administration by comparing it to the horrors of George Orwell's *1984*. George Orwell? Who's that? 1984? What's the year 1984 have to do with anything? We're living in the twenty-first century. Don't you know that?

(By the way, I have one colleague who was expressly told by Willeford not to teach *1984* in his composition class. That title in particular was singled out in the discussion. The obvious symbolism of this should not be overlooked.)

We should also take into account Dr. Helfrick's personal ambition. I suspect that part of the covert purpose of all this posturing on Helfrick's part was to prove to Weckmann Hall that he could make bold changes when necessary. "Those idiots in the composition department, why, I can snap my fingers and watch 'em jump." (Oh, yes, indeed… but too bad about that bike accident, pal.)

Apparently, Dr. Helfrick succeeded in his goal. Within a few semesters after the banning of fiction from the composition department, he was promoted out of the Dean's chair and into Weckmann Hall. According to a reliable website that tracks such atrocities (<http://transparentcalifornia.com/agencies/salaries/school-districts/>), Dr. Helfrick now makes $206,710.33 per year. This was his reward for tearing fiction away from thousands of CSUSC students and implementing the strictures of Common Core on an entire college campus. Karl-Otto Koch got Buchenwald, Helfrick got an office in Weckmann Hall.

Times don't change but faces and names do.

20.

"'Begone, vile insect! Or rather, stay, that I may trample you to dust!'"

--Mary Shelley, *Frankenstein*, 1818

Ironically, Helfrick's abrupt promotion to Weckmann Hall soon led to a silent, unofficial disintegration of the fiction ban. The second Helfrick was awarded his fancy new office on lower campus, he allowed Willeford to swing in the wind. Without Helfrick's ham-fisted insistence on this fiction moratorium, more and more instructors simply began to ignore Willeford's authority. This led to an uncomfortable moment (described to me secondhand), when Dr. Willeford dragged herself into the Chair's office one day and cried into her tattooed forearms because (and this is a direct quote), *"No one around here respects my Ph.D.!"* A normal person, hearing themselves utter these dire words out loud without a trace of sarcasm or humor of any kind, would immediately realize that he or she is in desperate need of a vacation in the cackle factory. But not Dr. Willeford... she insisted on hanging in there for several more semesters, desperately attempting to force everyone to adopt her insistence that English 100 subject matter consist mainly of issues having to do with "social justice," an abstract phrase I still don't understand, for which Dr. Willeford offered no definition. Issues having to do with "social justice" were apparently those issues with which Dr. Willeford agreed personally. I suppose she thought no further definition was necessary.

As Dr. Willeford's sanity melted at an Arctic pace, like a Dali watch, I was doing my damnedest to chart out the cartography of this dark world that had taken root in the CSUSC English Department. The logic of the rules seemed to shift at random. All fiction was banned from the composition classes, correct? Correct. But when you asked Dr. Willeford if it was okay to require the students to write about a film—not a documentary, but a fictional movie like *Apocalypse Now*—Dr. Willeford would assure us that that was okay. Why? I still have no idea. No one did. One professor, who formerly used a whole variety of challenging and provocative works of literature in his class, began using nothing but movies... for the entire semester. They weren't even good movies. He'd have his students writing midterms on the themes of xenophobia in Finding Nemo. I was shocked to hear, during one particular composition meeting, that one of the required textbooks was a recently released primer entitled

Understanding Rhetoric by Jonathan Alexander, Elizabeth Losh, Kevin Cannon, and Zander Cannon. This was a composition textbook in graphic novel form illustrated by the same art team who had worked with Alan Moore on the critically acclaimed superhero comic book *Top Ten*. I was very familiar with the Cannons' artwork. At one time, only a few years earlier, I would have been laughed out of the English Department for suggesting we use a graphic novel as a textbook. Not only was Dr. Willeford advocating this, she was *forcing* everybody to use it. What was going on here? I decided to test the limits once more. While more and more English instructors were simply ignoring Dr. Willeford, I emailed her and asked her if it was okay for me to assign Alan Moore and David Lloyd's *V for Vendetta* to the class. Here's the exact email I sent her:

Dear Dr. Willeford:

I have a quick question. I've been mulling over the possibility of using Alan Moore and David Lloyd's graphic novel, V for Vendetta, as a required text this semester. Because I spend a lot of time in class analyzing media images, memes, and symbols of all sorts, I thought V for Vendetta might work well in that context (particularly since this graphic novel has been appropriated by the Occupy Wall Street movement as a major symbol of social justice). Also, I thought it might work well in conjunction with Understanding Rhetoric: A Graphic Guide to Writing. If this graphic novel sounds like it would be acceptable to use in an English 100 class, please let me know as soon as possible. My intention was to contact you about this matter several weeks ago, but I didn't receive my schedule of classes until earlier today. Thank you very much for your time, and I look forward to hearing from you.

Dr. Willeford wrote back, thanking me for "reaching out to her," then assured me that *V for Vendetta* sounded like a worthwhile exception to the fiction ban. So only fiction *in prose form* had been jettisoned from the curriculum?

Look, I'm a fan of comic books as much as the next guy and have been ever since I was about five years old, but the fact is that students don't need more visual media in their lives. *They absolutely need to read prose in order to fully grasp what would be expected of them in higher college classes.* When I had used graphic novels in previous classes, I soon discovered it was necessary to save the graphic novels for the end of the semester. If they started off with a graphic novel, they were often confused as to how to physically construct an essay. They didn't know that paragraphs needed to be indented. They didn't know that periods come at the end of a sentence. They didn't know that quotation marks indicate dialogue or quoted passages. They knew almost nothing about the basic conventions of essay writing because they had never been asked to read a book or write an essay during their entire K-12 experience. I found this to be the case not only with students from disenfranchised areas like Inglewood and Watts, but privileged students from Palos Verdes and Manhattan Beach as well. And yet despite this disturbing trend, Dr. Willeford and Dr. Helfrick—fueled by the insane Common Core initiatives implemented by the White House—were advocating a college level program that encouraged the students to do little else except study what they were already familiar with, i.e., TV shows, commercials, advertisements, movies, and Internet videos mixed in with the occasional "informational essay" trumpeting the causes of "social justice." Apparently, the tenets of "social justice" and "authoritarian censorship" aligned in the disordered brain or Dr. Willeford.

By and by, as more and more English instructors realized that Willeford was little more than a paper tiger without Helfrick's presence in the English Department, fewer and fewer people were paying attention to the "rules." An instructor who had fallen out of love with Willeford's heavy handed approach soon took over Willeford's position as head of the composition committee. A few weeks before the beginning of the 2015 Fall semester, I emailed the new composition head the following message:

Gwendolyn,

I'd like to think a message such as this is unnecessary, but I decided it would be wise to run this past you first, nonetheless. As a supplement to copious works of nonfiction, I intend to assign the novel Frankenstein by Mary Shelley for my Fall English 100 classes. In conjunction with Frankenstein, I plan to assign contemporary articles about genetic engineering, stem cell research, the origins of feminism, the origins of anarchism, etc. Is this subject matter now considered acceptable by the CSU Sunken City English Department? If this book sounds like it would be acceptable to use in an English 100 class, please let me know as soon as possible, as I'm preparing my syllabus now. Thank you very much for your time, and I look forward to hearing from you.

In her response, Gwendolyn told me I didn't even need to ask such a question anymore. Which is all well and good, except for the fact that no one on the composition committee bothered to announce that all the previous rules that had been so relentlessly pounded into our heads were no longer relevant. We could now assign novels and short stories and plays and poetry and any other form of literature that had been classically employed in English composition classes since their inception in Atlantis and Lemuria and earlier. As with most bureaucracies, however, no one wanted to officially admit they had been wrong. Therefore, no announcement. To this day, most of the members of the English Department are still under the delusion that fiction is forbidden in their classes.

I recall a psychology class I once took back at El Camino Community College in which Dr. McCrary, the head of the Psychology Department, told us a story about a horse that had been removed from a small field to a much, *much* larger field on a different farm. Surprisingly, the horse insisted on walking *the same small circle* to which it had been habituated, despite the fact that it now had access to so much more space and grass and air and freedom. It was as if the horse had never left the smaller farm in the first place.

There are three faculty members who now run the new composition committee. When I told one of them I was teaching *Frankenstein* again, he said, "Be careful no one finds out."

I told him the head of the committee herself had approved the use of *Frankenstein* as a required text.

"What? When did that rule change?" he asked. (Keep in mind that this was one of three teachers *who ran the committee.*)

I shrugged. "I'm not the person to ask," I said. "For me, it never changed."

But this conversation sparked an intriguing notion in my mind. Perhaps this fellow had the right idea. What if *Frankenstein* was *still* a banned text?

On the first day of the Fall semester, I whispered to my new batch of students that I had a special secret to share with them: "All fiction has been summarily banned on campus, you see. Though I have been told not to do so, I've decided to forge ahead and teach *Frankenstein* anyway...."

All of them leaned forward in their seats, eager to hear more.

"You will rejoice to hear that no disaster has accompanied the commencement of an enterprise which you have regarded with such evil forebodings."

--Mary Shelley, *Frankenstein*, 1818

QUARANTINE

BY NORMAN SPINRAD

If it wasn't the best of times, at least it wasn't the worst of times, or something like that, which is the opening line of a novel called A TALE OF TWO CITIES, and it seemed like this would be only a tale of one.

Back in the day before the Quarantine, Manhattan island was the heart and soul and pocketbook of New York City, to the extent that New York could have been said to have all three, Wall Street, Greenwich Village, Broadway and 42nd Street, and all that jazz. When you saw a movie or a TV show or an ad featuring New York, the Big Apple was Manhattan, not anything in what some visiting Californian must have dubbed the "Outer Boroughs," the moral equivalent of Anaheim or Eagle Rock as far as a Hollywood wise guy was concerned.

Not that I was a Hollywood wise guy just because my sales office happened to be located on the seventh floor of one of those unglamorous glass towers at the business end of the Sunset Strip. My enterprise was perfectly legal, or anyway imperfectly legal enough, to avoid unwanted government attention, and far from being any part of show business despite the glamor of the name of the real estate.

You could say I was a pharmboy from the sheep-pharm sticks making my way in the City of Klieg Lights. You could say I was a naive bumpkin or a sleazy operator and I wouldn't punch your nose, but call me a terrorist and I'll break your kneecap, those raghead camel-jockeys or whoever they were used me like only a pawn in their game.

Which was all I really was. A middleman, one of the unglamorous cogs in the machinery that keeps any economy running and pharmers feeding their sheep and pigs. I had grown up in the Pharm Country inland from the Californian coastal range and up country in the Central Valley between it and the Sierras.

My parents were third generation removed from their hippie ancestors and the Central Valley wasn't anything like Mendicino dope country or Big Sur artsy fartsy. They were second generation pharmers, and the Pharm Country looked no different from what it had long been until you descended to a molecular level.

There of course it was biomolecular Silicon Valley. My folks were no more than sheepherders, really, owning the flock whose milk produced the desired molecules inserted in their genomes ordered up by the clients from pharm labs with--and for sufficient extra payment black geneleggers without--pharmaceutical licenses .

So I grew up in the Pharm Country scene and knew enough to know that I didn't want to that I didn't want to spend the rest of my life smelling sheep shit long before I escaped from high school. And I had about as much talent for gene writing as I did for quantum physics, namely none at all, and even less interest in learning, seeing as how I knew first hand that those guys spent their working hours tediously bending their shoulders over nanoscopes and biosynthesizers, about as much fun as barrel of number crunchers.

But there *was* a place for me in the Pharming business, and having grown up in Pharm Country was a leg up. The geneleggers as persons, and even the presidents of legit corporate versions, were not exactly the sort of humans who interfaced well with the drug companies and drug lords who commissioned their products, and the Pharmers who grew and harvested the results from their sheep and pigs were not the sort of folks capable of or wanting to negotiate their own contracts.

So that's where I came it. That's what middlemen are for. The clients with the checkbooks give me the desired specs, I pharm out the work of turning them into insertable genes to a lab or legger, and make the manufacturing deal with the sheep herders, making my not unreasonable percentages along the flow. You don't have to torture your brain with any scientific detail or deal with stinky sheep.

A nice clean desk job in a nice clean office in a nice clean business.

Well okay, not squeaky clean all the time, maybe, but what business really is? Investment banking? Real estate? Accounting?

Gimme a break!

In the real world, the customer is always right as long as the checks don't bounce and you personally are not required to do anything illegal that you know of. Especially when you're working in a niche market where the customers are limited to drug companies whose number crunchers calculate that it's cheaper to farm out the synthesizing and production than to handle those ends themselves, purveyors of recreational drugs shall we say, and well-heeled nut cases think they can order up something to fix whatever might be ailing them and live forever.

You don't make a good living as a middleman by asking questions whose answers you don't want to hear or turning up you nose at sweetheart deals that maybe have a little odor of fish oil to them.

You would?

Oh no you wouldn't!

The clients is a blond surfer type in a slickly tailored suit I could never bring myself to afford, or that's the image he'd like to have, but beneath the dreads is the face of a shy little nerd who gets sand kicked in his face on Malibu each, and beneath the Eurotrash threads beats the heart of a geek.

When I Google him, he turns out to be head of technical development in a Silicon Valley company called Cyborg Services Incorporated that furnishes defense contractors with spook shop weapons control systems I don't even want to try to understand. His current bank balance is larger than his position would seem to warrant, but when I dig deeper, I see that it's recent, and beneath that there's something vague about a killing at an Indian Casino, before which it had been hovering about where it should belong..

When he tells me what he wants I just about shit.

Because that *is* what he wants.

"I want a virus that gives you diarrhea, man" tells me.

"You want *what*?"

"I mean, *them*, not you!"

"Them *who*?"

"Those CSI bastards who stole my patents!"

"Your company stole your patents?"

"Their lawyers did! You'd have to have an electron micro-scope to read the fine print."

A sad story, but an oft-told tale in Silicon Valley, and not exactly breaking news in Pharm Country either.

"It's got to be ambient," he tells me. "With as short an incu-bation period as possible. I want it to toss it into the air con-ditioning system and infect the whole damn building at once like Legionnaire's Disease. I want them all fighting for stalls in the toilet at the same time. They're so cheap there's only one a floor!"

I gotta laugh, wouldn't you?

"Will you send me the video?" I giggle.

"Send it to *you!* I'll put it on YouTube!"

"Sounds difficult but maybe doable," I tell him. This just sales pitch. Even I know that all that has to be done is lift a sequence from a dysentery bacterium or something like it and drop it in the right virus genome, a piece of cake, probably won't even have to be synthesized from the ground up, which is what I'm gonna tell the geneleggers I have low-bidding for the con-tract, blackleggers given the effect it calls for, of course.

"Uh, how long is the effect supposed to last? A self-destruct timer sequence is going to cost you a little extra."

But he's not interested in paying for bells and whistles.

"Who cares?" he tells me. "Let them shit in their pants until their assholes fall off!"

Okay, so in current retrospect, maybe I should've had the twinge of moral questionability in my gut, but my funny bone might be said to have been clouding my conscience, or maybe it was indeed the money. After all, this guy knew nothing about what the traffic should bear and I knew how much there was to lay my hands on.

On the other hand, you could say that I did, this seemed to be turning out to be the sweetest deal I ever made, so what the hell, I told myself, you can afford to be a sport and pay for the self-destruct timer sequence yourself, now can't you?

After I was through jacking the price for the virus, he handed me a further lollipop and then took it away when I asked him how much of the stuff he wanted the sheep to produce, figuring maybe I could toss the business to my own folks and do them their own inflated good turn of luck.

"All I need is a single spray-can sample I can blow through the air conditioning system on my way out the door," he tells me.

My stomach sank. This is a deal breaker. I make the lion's share of my commissions on ongoing production.

"I've never done a penny-ante deal like that," I tell him.

"Could you get it done?"

"Well yeah, but---"

"How much would you ask for two years' production at ten thousand doses per annum?"

I tell him. It's a lot of money. It's more than it should really cost. It's only a few thousand less than I know he has.

"It's a deal, I'll pay it all just for the sample. We don't want to give more than one building full of thieving bastards the terminal trots, now do we? It's just a practical joke, now isn't it?"

"Well, when you put it that way, you talked me into it…."

What do I care, you work with CSI and the spook shops and defense contractors who commission your brilliance, you get used to stuff like this. Don't ask, because we won't tell you, and if you persist, we might get pissed off, and pissing us off would not be good for CSI's business, which would not be good for retaining your position.

CSI stole my patents?

What an inside joke!

Anyone who worked in Cyber Control land knew that there were never any patents there to steal because what we so brilliantly invented to order was work for government hire that disappeared down the event horizon of security classification.

But that was the script I was handed, and I guess they were

right, whoever *they* were, it was good enough to get a Pharm Country businessman drooling for a deal where he would make out like a bandit and asking no questions that might get in the way.

Not that I wasn't making out like a bandit too, not that I was about to question what I was doing or why either, it was an offer from you have no need to know and one you do know it you would be real counterproductive to refuse.

Cloak and dagger stuff

I meet a woman in a casino who hands me a sack of chips worth half a million dollars, which I am to exchange for cash on the way out, and then deposit in my bank account. With this I am to buy the virus described in the genome specs she gives me with it.

"Hey, butter buns, wait a minute, what's in all this for me?"

Never fear, she tells me, once you hand over the virus package, the half mil will appear back in your bank account as the same gambling winnings, you walk away with them, and none of this ever happened.

Well, I had no self-interest in asking if this was an offer I couldn't refuse, because I sure didn't want to refuse. Half a million dollars! Who wanted to refuse this gift horse? Who was I to ask my unidentifiable benefactor why he, she, or it wanted a virus that delivered diarrhea?

I could see that if this wasn't classified secret it should be. Would I really want to know? Could it be anything worse than all the low toilet humor called up by even trying to not think about it?

You do get some weird orders in this end of the gene writing game, what the government licensed end pleases itself to call black genelegging. I mean, they work the high-end center, and we work the dodgy edge, so what can you expect?

So what ended up being called the Big D seemed like more of the same, and I wasn't going to have to deal with the usual sort of drug lord thugs who might ice you if something went wrong or stiff you on the payout if it didn't, this order came from a legit and legal agent.

He thought he was technically knowledgeable, but he really wasn't that up on the tech end, and the job was a lot easier than he thought it was, so I made out pretty well on the price.

We don't tell the middlemen, but those of us in this end of the trade have a whole library of cassette virus genomes that we share among ourselves, stripped-down chassis as it were, on which we can simply hang sequences to produce whatever molecule gets ordered up. Ambient spread sequences we've already got from pirated military genomes the military wouldn't dare to admit even exist, and self-destruct timers have long been worked out for the drug lords who don't want open-ended reproduction cycles to devalue their goods to zero by giving away permanent freebies. The first three weeks are free, kid, and then….

So the only original art really required was the diarrhea sequence. Why anyone would want that was not hard to imagine. Hey, there was a two-week cut-off sequence in the specs, wasn't there, so it's not like I was writing anything worse than a two-week dose of Montezuma's Revenge, and who but an angel didn't have someone he'd like to lay that on, and even then…

Dysentery was naturally the first thing to come to mind, but that's really a symptom, not a single disease, caused by whole clades of organisms even as complex as amoebas, and the cascades from cause to effect tend to get inelegantly complex.

I didn't have to do any real research to come up with cholera. Endemic in Third World environs, where it can even be fatal if untreated, but easily treated with IVs of doctored fluids in the developed world, and the neat thing about it is there's no complicated cascade.

The cholera bacterium produces a toxic molecule called CTX, or just "cholera toxin," which binds directly to the guts and causes the effect. No problemo! Just snip the sequence that codes for the toxin's production from a cholera genome, write it into your cassette virus genome, and run it through your DNA synthesizer. A schoolboy could do it in an afternoon, and given what some schoolboys are like, wouldn't surprise me if some of them had.

That's about how long it took me to do it, but of course you don't tell the customer that, we don't charge by the hour, but it still pays to sit on the product for a couple of weeks pissing and moaning about how difficult this order is to fulfill all the while to justify the price

Something like what experienced screenwriters do before they hand in the scripts they finished a couple weeks ago to their producers, or so I've been given to understand.

They never caught whoever delivered the stuff to New York or found out in the service of what cause this act of terrorism was committed, not for lack of the all the usual suspects, but because credit, if that is the word, for this outrageous outrage was claimed by every one of them.

In the living theater of terrorism, this was the mother of all custard pies that any race, creed, or religious nut cult of whatever size would want to take credit for throwing in the face of their own version of the Great Satan.

It wasn't even a suicide mission, just a free trip to the Big Apple for someone from somewhere who had only to spread the Big D virus around Manhattan with some kind of spray can for a few hours and leave before what was going to happen happened. He'd get it too, but he'd be outside with it long before the Quarantine wall went up.

Me, I wasn't so lucky. In fact my luck was so bad that it still has me wondering about things like karmic retribution, or when it *really* gets bad, uh, cosmic punishment for my, ah, sin.

Okay, after spending six months in the Quarantine Zone, I'm forced to admit that maybe procuring the Big D bug for a supposed nasty geekboy prank was maybe a bit greedily and deliberately naive, but hey, didn't his Google story more or less fit the cock and bull story he told me?

No one's ever pinned anything the client that ordered it up either, and no one ever will because I'm the only one who can finger him and if I do, I'm fingering myself.

Not that I don't give the *private* finger to myself for my innocent part in bringing Manhattan to its knees with its pants down.

When I think about it, and how can I not, there was a part

of me, a little cricket of conscience that might have taken temporary residence, and told me to hedge my retrospectively immoral bet by paying for a two week self-destruct sequence in the virus with some of my lavish and easily earned money.

Saving my own ass and the aching asses of all the survivors of the Manhattan Quarantine by doing at least a little bit of unwitting communal good just in case, as it turned out.

Or as cosmic justice or as Judge Doody might have it, let the punishment fit the crime with a bit shaved off for a little morally correct behavior. Maybe there ain't no justice in this world but the justice that you make, but that doesn't mean that you know you're making it at the time, and it doesn't mean you're gonna like it.

For instance, was it chance, fate, karma, or not at all divine retribution that I just *happened* to be in Manhattan when the Big D hit?

It seemed like a good idea at the time and even now I can almost convince myself that it was chance bad luck. What chance, or bad luck really is, though, is probably one of the top five unanswerable questions of human existence.

I was just another gawk-eyed tourist, that's all I was. I had made myself an easy major killing, and it seemed to me I had earned and could easy afford a quick vacation. I had never been in the Big Apple, though like everyone else in the known universe I had seen almost as much of it as TV and movie set as Los Angeles. And Los Angeles I knew in the real world, which was enough to convince me that the real New York was not going to be just the Disney version either.

So when I saw an ad for a three-day package, air fare included, with a single in the fabulous Grand Hyatt on 42nd Street and a fistful of discount coupons for trendy restaurants and fancy call girl services, I decided to blow some of my winnings on my virgin trip to the Big Apple. Cheaper and safer than to tempt mesmerized stupidity at the tables in Vegas again and probably a lot more entertaining than casino floor shows.

The Grand Hyatt was indeed on fabulous 42nd Street, but it was on *East* 42nd Street, above Grand Central Station, a huge subterranean metro and railroad hub. You didn't hear anything in your room, which was nothing to complain about, but the continual comings and goings of taxis and buses and cars and subway commuters clogging this stretch of 42nd Street was going to keep it from ever being more fabulous than what surrounds downtown major railway stations anywhere.

So after I had checked in, unpacked, and had a drink in the bar, I decided to walk west on 42nd Street to Times Square, which, from what I had seen on television, was like what downtown Tokyo also looked on the tube, architecture as hoardings for huge neon signs and huger video screens; a neon canyon of giant animated billboards and sci-fi magazine cover buildings, the hub of Broadway and 42nd Street, the belly button of the intersection of show business and Godzilla-scaled advertising.

I can't say I was disappointed by this architectural Vegas-on the Hudson spectacle, but I also can't deny that I *was* disappointed by the tourist trade that it drew, jamming the sidewalks and milling and baa-ing like confused corralled sheep in the intersections, made even the "family friendly" venues in Las Vegas seem like the back streets of Tijuana, tourists like you'd find in the malls around Anaheim Disneyland or suburban Orlando.

Time was, Broadway and 42nd Street had a juicy reputation for hookers and porn houses and interesting sleaze. I wasn't enough of a rube from Pharm Country to expect the X-rated to still be there, but I would have hoped that the tourist trade would be playing to its memory with at least little harmless R rated atmosphere.

But instead you had mom and pop and the kids from Pasadena, beered-out college kids in Bermuda shorts and unfunny T-shirts, wide-eyed rubes from Indiana and India, pink and green spandex tights over overweight asses, baseball caps for non-existent teams. Hordes of mall rats in a giant outdoor mall world, fast-food chain food restaurants replacing greasy spoons and bad-ass saloons, souvenir stands and trademarked sporting goods palaces for the Yankees and Mets replacing knock-offs of Fredericks of Hollywood and Virginia's Secret, first-run movie theaters replacing XXX with Parental Guidance Advised.

The Disney version, including musical shows produced by same dominating the Great White Way, for the middle everything tourist trade.

And what was I but another tourist out to gawk at the sights, and wondering why everything everywhere in the US of A was starting to look like everywhere else aside from the window-dressing? The same phony upscale ethnic fast food chain restaurants tarted up like the real things, the same department stores, the same chain drug stores, the same crowds of generic people.

Okay, maybe my sour mood as I stood there disappointed by the reality of a Times Square which was nothing like its fabled fantasy ghost might have been influenced by the growing realization that I had to take a crap.

And I had no sooner realized this than the situation started becoming urgent, like the results of eating off an outdoor taco stand in down and dirty Mexico, comes at you with a rush.

Could I make it to the hotel? It seemed less and less likely. Could I find a public toilet on 42nd Street or buy a toilet seat in a bar? Seemed easy enough, seemed like the logical thing to do, but I while I'm one of those guys who have no problem at crowded urinals, never in my life had I sat down behind a stall door and loosed a load or even imaged that I could bring myself to do it.

On the other hand, I had never crapped in my pants standing upright either, let alone while being jostled by the crowd of tourists on Times Square. If it had to be one thing or the other, I really had no choice.

So I trotted with the trots back towards the Grand Hyatt hoping against unrealistic hope that I could hold out till I got to my room, while more realistically and more and more frantically trying to find a less private refuge along the way.

I only half-noticed that I didn't seem to be alone in my urgency as I kneed-and elbowed through the crush of people shame-facedly averting their gazes from every one they could who had already lost control, more and more of them, screaming kids and cursing lager louts, old couples looking for holes to drop down into, men and women leaning against lamp-posts clutching their guts, even cops who had obviously lost it.

Until I saw that my chances of securing a toilet seat anywhere were slim and none. Similar cross sections of diarrheic
humanity were shoving and jostling and punching at each
other like rush hour crowds trying to fight their way through
the door to any establishment that looked like it might have a
crapper.

And lot of good it would have done me to fight my way
into a bar or restaurants. Looking through the windows, all you
could see were frantic mobs trying to push their way past the
crush at the rear by the toilets and hammering at the doors.

And then, at the intersection of 42nd and Madison, within
tantalizing sight of the Hyatt, I got caught by a traffic light
full of grid-locked vehicles on a sidewalk crammed with the
afflicted, and, no longer in motion, got a standing whiff of the
smell spreading like the mother of all class-room farts, and that
did it, I could no longer keep myself from adding my share to
the fecal stink.

And ended up slinking through the hotel lobby amidst
crowds of groaning and odorous fellow victims to my room,
where I had just enough time to strip and shower before I found
myself plunking down on the cold porcelain of the hungry john.

Between trips to the toilet and room service food and drink that
was later and later in coming and went right through me like
hot grease through a tin horn, I didn't even think about television through the sleepless night and way into the next morning.
I was too sick to think about anything until a desperate call
to housekeeping for more toilet paper was greeted by a coarse
distracted croak to the effect that every room in the hotel was
screaming for more toilet paper too and the staff itself was in
no condition to go far enough away from the nearest toilet to
provide it.

Then my illness reached my brain, and through it my conscience, and it penetrated my dysenteric torture that half the
people I had seen in the street were afflicted, and now the hotel,
and it didn't seem statistically likely that there was anything
that could have mobs of people inflicted at the same time other

than the virus I had procured for that guy who claimed he only wanted to use it on his bosses.

Let the punishment fit the crime?

My punishment *was* the crime.

I turned on the television to see how bad it was.

I had somehow hoped it would be nervous toilet humor titters, but if it had been, they were gone. What was genteelly being called the Big D after some kid had called it the Big Doody into an open mike was spreading from the general area of midtown Manhattan, the two main foci at Herald Square and Times Square having merged as the Big D rolled upward through Central Park and downward toward the Village, Tribeca, and Wall Street.

Homeland Security was closing all bridges and tunnels out of the island of Manhattan until further notice and the Center for Disease Control was reassuring the rest of the city that this Quarantine would allow whatever it was to be contained. That was the official line. The talking heads were paying little attention to it.

Most of the coverage was calling it a terrorist attack.

And it had to be. Somehow the virus I had given that cybergeek to take vengeance on his bosses with had fallen into terrorist hands.

Yeah, sure, more likely *I* had been in terrorist hands from the beginning, greed clouding my mind so that it had never occurred to me that I was being run through their scenario, that the fairy story I was happily swallowing was a threadbare cover.

Either way, there was nothing I could do about it now but sit on the toilet and groan. I couldn't go to the cops. I'd just get myself arrested. And what could I tell them that would do any good?

Well, I *could* let the public know that their intestinal torment and mine would be over two weeks after exposure, assuming that they survived that long. I could even take credit for it. I'd probably have to convince somebody. And to do that, I'd have to incriminate myself. If I told the true story, who would believe I had been such an innocent schmuck rather than a terrorist myself? The legal ire and public rage would be taken out on me. Big Time.

Still if I could email the CDC that the epidemic would be over in two weeks maybe *they* could calm the worst of the terror with the news....

But not from the hotel. It had to be anonymously from the nearest Internet cafe, and it was my moral duty to drag my aching and bleeding ass there. They were telling everyone now trapped in Manhattan to keep hydrated, how anyone else was trying to do that while seated on the john, I don't know, but it had been easy for me because I could reach the toilet sink faucet without getting up.

But everything I drank went right through me. At unpredictable intervals. TV witchdoctors were proclaiming that this was how dysentery and cholera and diarrhea in general were mass killers in third world countries, you dehydrated, toxified your kidneys, or even hemorrhaged to death through your asshole. In more advanced countries, you could ride it out by going to a hospital to be put on intravenous fluid feed.

Lotsa luck to the quarantined masses in Manhattan!

Lotsa luck to me, hero that I was, or call it shame-faced guilt, which was closer to the truth, I had to get to an Internet cafe, and if I had to piss uncontrollably through my rectum to do it, that's what I had to do too.

I made it down to the lobby with dry underwear and out onto 42nd Street, where I disgraced myself in public for the first time.

Nobody noticed.

Traffic had come to a standstill because no one caught in the cars or busses or taxis had what it took to drive. Crowds of tourists and commuters who couldn't get home were squatting right there on the sidewalk, clutching their aching guts, groaning, moaning, hopelessly wiping at their butts with shirttails and underwear, and cursing at whatever gods there be.

The streets were practically flooded with feces and vaguely brownish liquids, the stench had me retching, and I was far from the only one who would have been puking their guts out if they had anything left to puke.

My pants were soaking wet before I traversed the three blocks to the nearest Internet cafe, but I was no longer paying any attention to the state of my urinary dishabille, indeed there was a certain relief to surrendering to the freedom of a camel in the desert or a horse in Central Park....

The Mayor of New York was screaming from the Gracie Mansion toilet at Washington, Washington was screaming at us to come up with an antidote the day before yesterday, and as surely as the odorous symptom was known to always flow downhill, the suits above me at the Center for Disease Control were screaming downhill at me as the head of the research team to come up with the miracle at once or else.

But my white-coated boys and girls were already doing their usual crackerjack job. Volunteers in sealed environment suits had no trouble securing samples. Piles and pools of feces containing the D bug were everywhere. We had already sequenced the genome and knew what we were up against.

For all the good that that did.

There *could be* no magic ampules of antidote to *this*

The core was a simple cassette virus on whose genome you could hang a sequence for any molecule, we used it ourselves to deliver killed-virus vaccines, and so did commercial drug companies, everyone in the game who was anyone had the specs, for all practically purposes it was public domain.

But this thing had been devilishly tweaked. It had been made ambient. Its incubation time was speeded up to only six hours. After which, every ounce of fluid that a victim released, every breath, released more.

And a sequence had been coded into the genome for CTX, not a vaccine or a virus coat, but a simple molecule, the so-called cholera toxin that caused the symptoms, lifted from the cholera bacterium, for which there was no magic bullet antidote, the only treatment being IV infusions of hydrating fluid and salts until the toxin finally flushed out.

Worse still, even then no immunity was conferred, you could be reinfected endlessly. And everyone in Manhattan would be. Permanently infected and permanently infectious until...until...

The only upside was that Manhattan *was* an island, so the Quarantine could be easily maintained. For as long as it took. The administration was not amused when I told them that I had no idea how long that would be, but it would have been worse if I had told them the truth, namely that the Big D could not be expected to expire until everyone on Manhattan was dead.

And then I was handed an unsigned email which claimed that there was a two-week self-destruct sequence written into the virus genome.

Well, we were getting all sorts of crackpot quack advice, but this email claimed to be from the miscreant who had innocently commissioned its creation for a client who had convinced him he just wanted it for a disgusting schoolboy revenge against his bosses, which somehow gave it a certain credibility, at least enough for me to take a closer look at the genome.

Someone was going to pay dearly for missing it, because the self-destruct sequence was indeed there.

Or maybe not. After all I hadn't been paying attention to anything beside the toxin and the ambience and the incubation time sequences the first time around, so maybe it was forgivable, since I would also be forgiving myself.

Whoever had written the email seemed to believe he had solved our problem for us, that the timed autodestruct sequence he had paid his own money to insert in the virus genome would extinguish it in two weeks. It read like he expected the Nobel Prize.

But of course, he was wrong. The each individual virus would die off in two weeks within any given host, but each individual virus was reproducing and spreading its genome every six hours, previous infection did not confer immunity, each host could be reinfected indefinitely, and each of the hundreds of millions of copies spewed from every host's every orifice would have its own clock started at zero. The species itself would live as long as there were living hosts alive in the Quarantine zone.

That the D plague would only end when everyone quarantined on Manhattan Island had died, needless to say, was news I dared not kick upstairs until I had something positive to kick up with it.

Well, just as the bureaucratic frenzy roared downhill, I wasn't above channeling it likewise, and under this admittedly unjust pressure, one of my bright boys came up with a strategy.

Clever. Elegant. And retrospectively obvious.

The D bug had already been tweaked, or more likely synthesized, and of course we had the tech to do likewise and better. And we could take a tip from cutting edge insect extermination programs.

One of their promising techniques was to raise vast clouds of sterile clones of the target species more robust than the target species and therefore more successful at survival, thereby outcompeting it into local extinction, at least in circumscribed fields of test crops.

So we could clone the D virus, and snip out the sequence that coded for the cholera toxin, creating a version that would drive the original version to extinction by replacing it with its harmless self, since a parasite that doesn't kill or harm its host is going to outbreed one that does.

No sweat.

That was the good news.

How long would it take to render the original D bug extinct?

We ran it through the computer, the estimated current population of Manhattan, the two-week self-destruct, the six hour incubation period, and what it coughed out was the bad news.

It would take four to eight months.

Six months in the Quarantine zone, and I had sentenced myself to them, along with a two and a half million other people, the pre-die-off population, or so I was to learn later. At least it seemed that my email had gotten through to someone at the CDC, because they put out a press release that they had a means of salvation under development, so please be patient.

They didn't say how long it would take, but I knew because I had told them, and I alone knew they probably weren't really doing anything because *they* knew that in two weeks the D-bug would go extinct all by itself They were faking it, preparing to take the credit for the extinction of the Big D bug when it happened.

Meanwhile no one could leave Manhattan, but relief supplies and teams could get in, and at least as reported by what was left of TV coverage, the talking heads themselves speaking inside environmental isolation suits and croaking it out through respirator mikes, the National Guard, and the regular Army, and the Red Cross, and Medicines sans Frontiers were already active in Manhattan.

There was footage, all of it shot from high hovering helicopters through lenses as long as the proverbial ten-foot pole, of space-suited figures in white crossing the bridges in good formation, of the tents and field hospitals going up all over Central Park, Army trucks unloading crates of Meals Ready to Eat, the various government and relief agencies acting as if they were setting up a can-do American version of a Third World refugee camp.

At least this is what it looked like on television. My first actual contact with the relief forces was a knock on the door of my room by a space-suited soldier who handed me something that looked like a translucent enema bag filled with water. There was a hook at one end, and a syringe hanging at the other end from a yellow rubber hose.

This, I was informed in staccato military parrot-speak, was an SRU, a Self-Rehydration Unit, the use of which was demonstrated by hanging the bag on a doorknob, pushing me to the floor, and jabbing around painful in my elbow pit till he finally found a vein.

"The reservoir must always be positioned above the needle or gravity will not cause the solution to flow down the hose. Continue to drink copious amounts of water or other neutral fluids. The SRU solution will mitigate or even prevent dehydration symptoms other than the continued loss of fluids excreted by your anal orifice, but it is not at this time a cure for the viral-caused diarrhea. A third of a bagful should be infused every six hours, refills will be available as supply permits."

And out the door to the next room, and the next, and the next.

It seemed like a tranquilizer news story for those us of inside the Quarantine and window-dressing for the world outside.

Yes, it sort of worked, my trips to the toilet maybe lessened a bit, my flesh seemed to stop shrinking from my bones, and I was almost feeling human, at least for a couple of hours after that first dose.

But, I was a paying guest in the Grand Hyatt hotel, and there were at least two million people who weren't sealed inside Quarantine zone, clutching their guts in tenement and luxury tower apartments, holed up in fleabags, out there on the streets, out in the Central Park refugee camp tents, or wandering around looking for holes to stay sick in.

The SRUs seemed like military battlefield issue. How many of them could be immediately available? Certainly not two and a half million, the United States didn't even have that many combat troops. And even if the SRUs were instead meant and stockpiled for major Third World relief missions so that there *were* enough to go around, how long would it take to distribute them to two and a half million people?

They certainly couldn't do it in two weeks. They had to know that. Long before they could get the SRUs to more than a small fraction of the victims, it would all be over. They had to know that too, didn't they?

Or did they?

Maybe the CDC wasn't telling the relief authorities what I had told them. Or maybe Homeland Security had decreed that the troops would be better actors in this pacifying media show if they didn't know they were play-acting. Maybe the military figured it could use some good heroic civilian PR footage.

What was *really* going on out there?

Curiosity got the worse of me, or guilt got the better, or both, and I tanked up on a double dose of SRU elixir, and foolishly ventured to go outside for the first time in how many days I couldn't quite remember to have a look.

What assailed me was nothing like what I had been seeing on television.

The main entrance to Grand Central Station beneath the Grand Hyatt was like something out of Hieronymus Bosch or S. Clay Wilson, sheltering, if that is the word, a clogging encampment, if you could call it that, of the rotting dead and mewling dying, lying in a viscous pond of reeking brown liquid, with hardly an SRU in sight. Low-life pickpockets and drunk-rollers, many bent over in dehydrating agony themselves, retched their way through the dead and the barely still-living, squabbling among themselves for turf with bloody knives and the occasional brandished pistol.

Since they were occupied with easier carrion game like hyenas or vultures, I was mercifully ignored as I snake-danced through this horror show across 42nd Street, where a kind of rude field hospital had been set up inside a khaki tent, cordoned off by soldiers in full-battle gear to control the desperate hordes fighting, crawling, shoving, to get inside at what few SRUs there were before they were all gone, which looked like very soon.

I made my way west towards Bryant Park, stumbling through aisles of corpses and about to be corpses, the dead being picked over by pigeons and more crows than a city is supposed, even the marginally still living enveloped by clouds of less fastidious feasting flies.

Bryant Park was another refugee camp, but this one wasn't like the footage I had seen of the one in Central Park, not like anything that belonged anywhere in the United States, something more like Haiti after the great earthquake, only made much worse by sprawling behind the noble neo-Greek Classical architecture of the emphatically First World library building.

This obscene back yard was a lowland favela of packing crate huts and tents rudely fashioned from black plastic garbage bags, jammed, crawling, and overrun with stricken humanity and dead bodies no one had bothered to remove, stinking to the skies of feces and piss and liquefying flesh, with no cops or troops or relief workers in evidence. Here and there, the greasy smoke and sulfurish smoldering flames of garbage can fires perfected the hellish vision without doing anything to mask the stench of death and pestilence.

I turned my shamefully grateful back on the plight of the masses huddling in agony on the rim of the pit and retreated in dishonor back to the relative comfort of my swiftly degenerating four-star hotel.

By now, everyone knows all too well what happened after two weeks, namely nothing of salvational significance, not that this was probably much of a surprise to the remaining survivors, who no doubt now rationed their expectations to the hope of surviving another day.

Martial law was officially declared, there were now regular airdrops of MREs from the helicopters, and, so at least the news claimed, the crash production of SRUs, none of which had fallen from the heavens like mana as yet.

There was a limited supply of environmental isolation suits, no relief workers were allowed in or out without them, and so the field hospitals and forces of law and order were understaffed and overwhelmed well past the point of chaos.

I was probably the only person inside the Quarantine zone who was surprised and appalled by what had *not* happened.

What had gone wrong? Why hadn't the D-bug died off?

Well, of course, I know now. It took the powers that be another week to shower the zone with mist from helicopters and crop-dusters as if we were a herd of louse-infected sheep, while declaring that this would eventually vanquish the Big D.

It took another two weeks of aggressive investigative reporting and impolite grilling of the head of the Center for Disease Control to extract an unwillingly coherent explanation of what that mist was in terms the scientifically unwashed could understand.

We have created a harmless clone of the D-bug that will outbreed the variant that causes diarrhea into extinction, much as excessive use of antibiotics evolves microbes that are immune to them by process of natural selection. When that process is completed, the D-bug will be rendered permanently harmless, and the Quarantine will be lifted.

When anyone at the CDC was asked how long *that* would take, the reporter was referred to Homeland Security, from which the answer was always exactly the same:

"That information is classified."

No wonder it was classified! They really didn't *have* an answer, no one knew how long it would take for the benign D bug to breed its evil older brother into extinction, or really if it would even work, until it finally did, and the CDC got a collective Nobel Prize.

It finally took six agonizing months, and if they had even hinted at such an estimate, things would've gotten much worse inside the Quarantine zone even while they were getting better, in a way *because* they were getting better.

We were being dug in for a long haul, though we never knew it day by day.

Environment protection suits were few and far between, but there were plenty of us who would do a day's grim labor for the bags of SRU which were never really in adequate supply, and enough soldiers to keep control of what there was, and keep those who had gone feral at a distance.

I myself even removed rotting corpses from streets and apartments for my daily bag for a while, a disgusting enough job that had to done, but better than spending the same time moaning on a toilet seat.

Body counters accompanied us, and when the streets of Manhattan were cleared of dead bodies, and pieces of dead bodies, and puddles of decomposed protoplasm, the count was two hundred thousand, plus or minus a 20% margin of error, and something like 2 million survivors to be maintained until the Quarantine was lifted.

There had already been spontaneous tent villages and favela shacks springing up in the major parks, but then they sent in scores of thousands of collapsible cardboard shelters that became known as "rabbit hutches" coated with waterproof film and distributed them free, and orderly hives of them arose in every scrap of parkland or vacant lot.

Porta-potties were brought in. Well-guarded SRU supply depots were set up on major intersections. MREs were distributed daily at them too, and the bigger ones had field hospitals.

We were being taken care of, if not well, then adequately enough to keep the lid on, if not by all that much. Believe me, the Quarantine zone, far from the heroic images you see in the Hollywood versions now, was never exactly a selfless patriotic utopia where the lions laid down with the lambs for the greater good.

And there *were* people who smelled a perfumed sewer rat in the air, myself included, not that we could do anything about it. At the time, it pissed me off--the situation was being stabilized, *too* stabilized--but looking back from an informed and wiser perspective, it was better than telling us the truth.

Because chances are that had it been admitted from the beginning that the Nobel class genome-writing cure for our ills and key to our freedom from this cozy prison camp would take half a year to work, it probably would have ignited an enraged bloodbath.

Wouldn't you join in?

Facing months in this well-maintained American refugee camp on American soil for a crime you didn't commit without even knowing when you would be released, or even if?

Of course you would've.

Even I would've, even though I at least was being incarcerated for precisely the crime I *did* unknowingly commit.

But they handled it. They handled us professionally and adeptly for what turned out to be six months. A lot of us didn't like being handled like that at all, but in the end, I haven't heard anyone who had been there wish they hadn't done it, considering the alternatives. Like if mobs had rushed the bridges and the troops had to be ordered to fire. Like if anger turned to mindless self-destructive looting. Like any number of things to be glad of didn't happen.

Instead, things slowly got marginally better in the Zone. You could count on being clean and reinfected at unpredictable intervals, but as long as you had your daily bag, you could more or less function, and your health could be almost stable.

Everything was stable, or so it seemed. Food was free, and so was your rabbit hutch, SRUs required some labor, but there really wasn't much you had to do or could do. So you spent most of the time waiting. The incidence of diarrheic D reinfection was steadily waning, or so we were told, and it was easy enough to believe since I had fewer and further episodes of the trots myself.

Any day now....

Any week....

Any month...

Well we all know that even all bad things must come to an end, we do still believe that, don't we?

Don't we?

Won't they?

At the time, no one knew about the worse things coming when the Quarantine was finally lifted. The date and time were announced. Marines manned the bridge and tunnel entrances in their spiffy dress uniforms with battalions of press lined up behind them. On the Washington and Brooklyn bridges they even turned out brass bands and surviving glad-handing local politicians. A landing pad had been cleared of rabbit hutches on the Sheep Meadow in Central Park for the Presidential helicopter, otherwise jammed with the largest and certainly most welcoming crowd it had ever seen.

The President debarked in a white environmental suit with her seal emblazoned on the chest as her Marine band played "Hail to the Chief."

When she removed the helmet, took a deep breath, and waved her long blond hair as if she were still doing shampoo commercials, it was all over, and a great cheer went up.

It was all over except, that is, for the speechifying and the talk show blather and the back-slapping self-satisfied paens to the triumph of American scientific ingenuity and military professionalism over the forces of cunning and evil terrorism, which had not only destroyed the D-bug, but in the process had developed a viral counter-weapon that now would render any such attack powerless.

Right.

But out here in Pharm Country, we knew better, and if the likes of middle men like me didn't get it by ourselves, the cackling sort of leggers had already perversely and ghoulishly informed us that something like it, given the prevalence of even more ruthless and mercenary genewriters than themselves, was bound to happen again.

Every legger here, black or otherwise, had the specs of the original D-bug and its nemesis too. For most of the leggers this was sheer geeky curiosity, but inevitably there were those, some of whom were known by odorous reputation, to whom it would be just business.

And given the profusion of terrorist causes, given that it would be so easy to do that the black leggers unprincipled enough to take such contracts, never in short supply, would be competing to be the low bidder, they would not lack for clients.

"With these specs, it's a piece of devil's food cake," one of these bastards told me. "Write the sequences for ambient infection and speeded-up incubation period into the good old tried and true cassette virus core than everyone has the code for, and hang any cascade end-product toxin that does the dirty work you get paid for onto it, and hey presto, cut-rate cookbook chemistry bio-weapon for the terrorist masses. Cholera, Polio, Aids, whatever, name your poison, hah, hah, hah!"

This I was told before Orlando got hit with killer flu and Los Angeles with Ebola. Another of these ruthlessly mercenary black leggers did a masked TV interview pointing out that cloning and tweaking a benign version of each and every such virus would have to be done from scratch each time. And since there would not likely be a self-destruct sequence mercifully written into any new terrorist virus, breeding it out of existence or at least into harmlessness with Mr. Hyde's Dr. Jekyll brother would take years, not months, decades even, who knows, maybe forever.

"The offense will always have it over the defense."

And there you go.

And here we are.

Omaha. Denver. Austin.

The United States of America, the Great Satan, the Spider in the center of the web of global capitalism, the source of black helicopters, men in black, socialized medicine, secret alien conquest, choose your paranoid fantasy, and here we are in the cross-hairs of your viral gunsight.

Poughkeepsie. Madison. Memphis.

We're not in a *war* with anyone or anything.

We're just targets in a shooting gallery where anyone can play and anyone who wants to can afford it.

The United States of American, the Great Satan, the Spider

in the center of the web of global capitalism....

The city on the hill become like a Swiss cheese with new bubbles of pustulance popping up everywhere. There is no other honorable choice. Or for that matter even a dishonorable one.

Sooner or later, if we don't quarantine the whole country ourselves, the rest of the world will.

THE PRIME TIME OF SPENSER GOLDING

1

What the hell was he doing in Ala-fucking-bama?

The thought rattled along with Spenser Golding like a can tied to a back bumper, and it made him smile in spite of his situation. Not that it was so bad, but anytime he had an assignment that sent him too far off either coast, he felt ... what—uncomfortable?

Maybe.

Threatened? Not really.

But definitely out of his element.

He and most of his news colleagues at the Manhattan-based Digital News Network had plenty of pejoratives for what actually comprised *most* of the United States—"fly-over territory," "the red states" (a reference to the electoral college map that color-coded voters' preferences), "the mid-waste," and "the great American heartland" (which was always couched in sardonic tones and a knowing smile) were among the more frequently employed. Spenser knew and used them all. It wasn't that he didn't *like* the most of the states in the union, or even the people who lived in them; it was more accurate to say he just found them to be a bunch of selfish, insensitive, uneducated fools.

And he cut no slack for people like that.

Either they didn't understand, or they clearly disliked, the freedom of the press and the necessity of such groups as the ACLU and NOW and the NAACP and all the other entities which represented the *real* America. As opposed to all the gingham tablecloths and mincemeat pies and let's not forget the cornpone, no-sir-ree-bob!

And the South ... well that was all the red states' peculiarities and ills taken to a higher exponent. To Spenser, places like Mississippi and Alabama had only recently emerged from the Paleolithic and Okey-doke-la-homa could just as easily be on the dark side of the fucking moon. He honestly couldn't understand why anybody would ever want to visit places like that— much less deign *live* there.

But news did not constrain itself to the coastal cities of the Atlantic and the Pacific, which meant journalists from the biggest networks in the world would have to be sent into unfamiliar landscapes to get the real story. And that meant wherever the news was happening, DNN and Spenser Golding would be there.

He was driving a full-sized rental from the Huntsville International Airport, and he couldn't complain about that. You could always tell how far up the network food chain you were by the kind and size of rental car they approved for you. Spenser had been a news journalist with DNN for nine years now, and he was wheeling across rural Alabama in an Intrepid with power-everything, CD player, GPS navigational system, and leather seats.

Not so shabby.

And light years from the worlds of the subcompacts with the hard plastic interiors and a radio that *might* get you an FM station. Back when he was still learning his craft, he remembered getting keys to a lot of Chevy Geos and Ford Fiestas while he covered the train derailments and spring floods, which were the national equivalents to the local news channel's coverage of warehouse fires and the ubiquitous liquor store robberies.

Once he exit-ramped clear of the airport, Spenser grabbed his cell phone off the passenger seat, said a single word— "studio"—and it auto-dialed his office in New York.

"National desk," said a pleasant female voice.

"Hey, Cyndi, it's me."

"Spenser! Hey, what's it like down there in the bee-yew-tee-full South?"

"I just got out of Huntsville. I'm on the lookout for the signs for I-65. You hear anything on getting some video?"

"We've got Greg Oliveri driving up from Birmingham."

"I don't know him, do I?"

Cyndi paused, then: "Don't think so. But Larry says he's really good, so—"

"Yeah, sure," said Spenser, conjuring up an image of his boss, Larry Feldheimer, who had been out of the field for so long he had no *clue* which end of a digicam to look through, and there was no goddamned way he knew a good cameraman from a bad one.

"Anyway, you're supposed to meet him at the Motel 6 in a town called Blountsville. That's as close we can get you to the crash site, which is east of there."

"Right, place called Nectar Pond … I know, I know." Spenser reached out and punched on the GPS and map unit in the dash. "I'll find him. You got an ETA?"

"'Bout an hour and a half's the best I can figure."

"Okay, Kiddo, thanks," he said. "You give me a call if you find out anything I should know."

"There's one other thing," said Cyndi. "That lady from Jersey called—Estela Barboza."

Spenser sighed. *"Again?* Jesus, what'd you tell her?"

"I told her you were traveling on assignment. That you'd call her when you got back." Cyndi paused. "And she asked me if I thought you were really going to call her back, or if you were avoiding her."

"What'd you tell her?"

"I said you very busy, that *everybody* wants to talk to you about doing their story … and it just takes time."

"Good … good. That'll cool her down."

"Spenser, I don't think so. She says people are threatening to kill her."

He laughed. "Yeah, right! Attack of the Killer School Board! C'mon, Cyndi, you know I don't have time for crazies."

Cyndi didn't respond right away, then: "I don't know … she sounded scared … for-real scared."

"Well, just keep taking her numbers and putting her off. I'm gonna have to check her out a little bit more before I talk to her, okay?"

"Okay, Spenser, whatever you say."

"Gotta go," he said. "Call me later if you have anything I should know."

Clicking off the line, Spenser eyed the global positioning map, then punched out an expanded view. He was tooling down Alternate US-72, which should be intersecting with I-65 south any minute now. He'd always been terrible with sense of direction and finding his way around strange places. Sara-the-X, as he always referred to his former wife, had made a career out of ragging him about never getting good directions, refusing to look at the Rand McNally Travel Map book they kept in the seat storage pocket of the minivan, and *never* stopping to ask for help when he'd gotten them lost. Yeah, well fuck her and her Rand McNally. Man, he was glad he'd cut himself loose from her. There was nothing like being thirty-seven and single in the age of MTV.

Green signs announced the junction with I-65, and a glance at the GPS dash-map confirmed his position. Spenser loved that thing—his days of being a Wandering Jew were over, he thought with a smile. As he negotiated the ramps and merge lanes, he was directed over a bridge across Wheeler Lake, which—even though it was only late April—was already dotted with plenty of power and bass boats. Spenser grinned as he thought of all the cracker-dickwads out there with their Shakespeare rods and Zebco reels and their hats that said "Roll Tide Roll." How anybody could get any pleasure out of fishing was beyond him. *Hey, Sherm, pass me another nightcrawler, wouldja buddy?*

Yeah, that's me.

Spenser laughed out loud at his own *beau jest* as he cleared the bridge and guided the Intrepid south through the river valley of northern Alabama. Even though he didn't want to admit it, he found the countryside damned pretty, especially since all the blooms and blossoms and pale green leaves had already filled in. Spring came early to the South, in stark contrast to the bare-stick trees of Manhattan's Central Park.

But spring was never going to arrive for the 124 passengers of

Jet America Flight 223 out of Miami. The image kind of slipped in between the cracks of all his pleasant thoughts as Spenser reminded himself of why he was in Alabama in the first place. Information on the early-morning crash had been practically non-existent, which made everybody start to wonder if the FCC and the airline were keeping a deliberate lid on things. If this one had anything to do with terrorism, it would of course be even bigger and more dramatic than a "normal" plane crash, and that's why every media outlet had their people converging on the area faster than the Panzer divisions rolled into Poland.

His cell phone rang and he keyed the *talk* button. "You got Golding here."

"Spenser ... Cyndi. That cameraman, Oliveri, just checked in. He says he's running a little behind schedule, but he says he'll be there, okay?"

"Goddamn it, Cyndi! Who is this donkey? Does he know he's doing the video for *me?!*"

"Well, I assume—"

"Spenser Golding gets there *first*, goddam it! Spenser Golding *is* DNN, and I don't want this local-affiliate asshole screwing up my piece!"

"Hey, come on, Spenser ... try to cool down, okay?" said Cyndi, her New York accent creeping into her diction as she became more flustered. "Who you think you're talkin' to, here? It's not my fault, ya know."

"You got a cell number for this guy?"

"Sure," she said. "You want me to tell him anything he doesn't already know?"

Spenser could tell his production assistant was getting testy, and he knew he shouldn't push her too far because he needed her in his corner. Hurting her feelings or hassling her unfairly didn't really enter into it—he was far too utilitarian for that kind of crap-thinking.

"Well, I was thinking maybe *you* should talk to him instead of me, baby, 'cause you are just a nicer person that me, you know?" Spenser smiled at his application of the soapy charm. The chicks always fell for it—everybody except Sara-the-X and who cared about her?

"Okay ... and say what?"

"Something that will motivate him to get to that Motel 6 as fast as possible. That I usually get nominated for broadcast awards and if he's part of my team, it's going to make him look good when he wants to find that better job. You know the drill, baby. Make me look good and he's going to want to work hard for me." Spenser nodded to himself, agreeing with his own logic. "Besides, I'm too pissed off to talk to any camera-grunts right now, okay?"

There was a pause, which he knew was Cyndi just yanking his chain a little, then: "No problem, Spenser. I make things nice for you—but you owe me a drink at the Riga, okay?"

"Yeah, yeah. Count on it. Gotta go, baby. My exit's coming up. Give me a call if you hear anything about the crash. I assume all the 'alphabets' and Jet America are still on silent-running?"

"You'll be the first to know," said Cyndi. "Bye-bye."

Keying off the phone, Spenser returned full attention to the I-65 traffic, which had thinned out, other than the usual pha-lanx of trucks. He keyed in a larger map view to figure out his best way to gets to Blountsville.

He smiled as connected the dots on the colorful LCD screen. Looks like he had to take the exit for Route 69. *Oh yeah, I'll take that exit every time.* Head east to Hanceville, where he could take Route 91 north to the teeming hamlet of Center Hill, then a small, unnamed connecting road—probably dirt—into Blountsville.

Should be fairly painless, he thought as he watched the signs for any mention of Route 69. Besides, the closer he got to the crash site, he knew he'd be running into other advance teams from the local fire departments, maybe National Guard, or for-estry service—whoever was closest to the scene. And pretty soon after them would be the FAA guys, and if there was any-thing funny going down, you could count on ATF and FBI as well. That's why Spenser had to be one of the first journalists on the scene. Once it got too crowded, your chances of getting any scoops went down like a palooka in a fixed fight. Too bad the camera guy couldn't fly in on the local affiliate's traffic-cop-ter, but the FAA was very careful about who was flying where when a big jet went down like this.

That's okay, Digital News got lucky because they reached Spenser just as he was changing planes in Atlanta on his way home. The short hop to Huntsville had been the easiest and the fastest link to the general area where the jetliner went in. He was fairly certain none of the competition would be getting their people in place for *at least* an hour or two after him.

Of course, this Uncle Cornpone Cameraman could fuck that up real easy.

Better not to think the negative thoughts. Spenser had been seeing this kind of weird woman who worked for the William Morris Agency—*hey, how's that for some serious alliteration?!*—and she was always telling him about feng shui and negative energy and how to release all the "bad atoms" from his body and his thoughts. Hey, as long as she kept releasing her thong panties atoms from her *own* body, what did he care?

He was lifted from his thoughts by the sight of the exit for Route 69, which he took in a long decelerating curve. Then, just as he off-ramped onto the two-lane blacktop, it started to rain. But not just any ordinary rain—these drops were coming down like mortar shells in a barrage. Flipping his wipers up to full-tilt, he still couldn't see much of anything, and he had to creep along for a few miles while the storm passed over his position.

On his right, just outside of Hanceville, he passed a *huge* rambling one-story building that looked like a series of army barracks all hammered together. A garish sign announced the Pink Palace X-Rated Oasis. Videos, sex toys, and magazines! Biggest selection in the state! Spenser smiled. Where else but on Route 69, right?

Just beyond a grain and feed store in "downtown" Hanceville, he caught the junction with Route 91 north, and made the left turn. As he did this, the rain began to slack off as quickly as it had begun, but there were now patches of oddly heavy fog settling into the lower sections of country road the locals would call "hollers." *Weird*, he thought. *Never seen it like this before, right in the middle of the day.*

This made him drive more slowly than he'd wanted, but he didn't want to go sluicing off into some ditch, either. The fog continued intermittently all the way into Center Hill, no more than a crossroad with four buildings to mark it. He almost missed the sign for Mountain Grove Road and Blountsville, then eased the Intrepid onto the muddy, almost-single-lane road. Spenser wrestled with the steering wheel as the front end of the car settled into the dual track of tire ruts. Whether he liked it or not, the road was going to steer him along its path.

Leafy trees edged both shoulders, which combined with the gray storm-clouded sky to make things pretty dim. Headlights in the gray, soupy light were practically useless. All that, plus the mud and the fog, made this last leg of the journey insufferable; and once again he found himself in total disbelief he'd voluntarily taken himself into the heart of everything he'd come to loathe about rural America.

How much farther?

He checked the GPS display and was not at all surprised to see it had gone as dull and dim as the daylight beyond his windshield, giving him no clue as to where he might be. This was a brand-new car—that map-thing's not *that* cheesy, is it?

Pulling his attention from the LED screen, Spenser was just in time to see the muddy path dip into another hollow where a pseudopod-like extension of fog waited to close down on him. Easing up on the gas, he eased into the bank, thicker and whiter than anything he'd yet seen, and felt the front tires and the suspension chunk and jar and they gained purchase on something more solid than the muddy country road.

What the hell's going on?

2

And as if in answer, the hood of the Intrepid burst through the fog like the prow of a warship in heavy sea ... to reveal something that should not—make that *could not*—be there.

But it *was*.

Oh, Jeezuz H., what the fuck's goin' on here?

The sky. First thing was the sky. High, hard, brassy-red and angry with haze. And the landscape was suddenly flat and endless like a stretch of Arizona desert. No big mountains, but radiating a bleak, desperate heat and desolation.

But that was just nuts. No way …

Spenser had heard stories of weird weather patterns and inversions and even more esoteric meteorology like magnetic vortices and lenticular tunnels, but he'd never witnessed it first-hand like this.

Without realizing it, he'd accelerated and the sedan growled up to speed. Ahead on the pitted blacktop, on the right, a wood-pile in the shape of a slant-roofed building waited for him like some predator in search of a meal. Spenser's right foot eased off the pedal as he focused on what was the only significant object in this otherwise barren stretch of road that looked about as much like backwoods Alabama as the Guggenheim.

As he drew closer, more detail revealed itself. A dusty drive-way angled off the road, leading up to a long main building in the shape of an old Fifties diner, but made of sunbaked wood and paint so peeled and bleached, the color was somewhere and everywhere between red and brown and yellow. The roof sagged and the chimney leaned; the windowpanes were essen-tially opaque from dust, slime, and insect husks. Out in front a Sinclair gas pump with a flattened glass globe on top stood like a helmeted sentry, its crumbling rubber hose mute testament to the years since any fuel flowed. At the far end of the building was small garage, door ripped half-off its hinges.

Even though there was no good reason to stop here, Spenser slowed the Intrepid to a crawl. *You gotta be kidding me …*

The thought slipped through him like motor oil leaking from a crankcase as now he noticed other things: a sagging sign above the front door proclaiming *Joe's Gas & Gulp*, a water-well pump with its long handle cradled in rust, and down past the garage poked the snout of a cinder-blocked Chevy Bel Air. The old, Fifties dreadnought like the carcass of a once proud and powerful beast, its dull-black hide peeled and bleaching under a cruel sun.

Bleak. Desolate. Dead.

The words ate into him like battery acid, but they were not altogether true. As Spenser halted the rolling approach of his car just past the old Sinclair pump, he saw something move in the long shadows up by the entrance to the old building. How he'd not seen anything before unnerved him—because he was pretty damned sure nothing had been there at all.

But now, as he powered down the passenger-side window, and squinted through the haze, he saw an old black guy, dressed in a suit, wearing a cream-colored fedora, cocked at just the right angle. He was sitting in a white rocking chair. From the medium distance, Spenser couldn't assess any age to the guy, but he just had this feeling Cream Fedora was *old* ... really old.

For a minute or so, Spenser continued to lean slightly forward over the steering wheel staring at the old dude, who didn't move, other than an ever-so-slight oscillation of the chair ... back and forth ... as if in time to some ancient, geomantic rhythm.

"Howdy, mistah ..." the old guy finally said, and cracked a smile, which revealed a glinting gold incisor, visible even from the considerable yardage between them.

Unfolding slowly from the low-slung cockpit of the car, Spenser walked directly toward Cream Fedora, confirming his earlier supposition that the guy was older than the dirt that encrusted this shithole. The old man's face was like deeply grained mahogany and there was something funny about his eyes—kind of frosted over in that scary-blind way—that convinced you he shouldn't be able to see a damned thing.

But maybe he could ...

"Funny-lookin' car ya got there," he said. "Looks like a big bullet. Or maybe a big dick."

Spenser grinned.

"Better off bein' a bullet, I guess," the old guy continued. "Dick get ya in mo' trouble ..."

"How you doing?" said Spenser, noticing a cane next to the rocker with an ornate silver handle in the shape of a wolf's head.

"Doin' okay, pretty-might." The old guy reached into a vest pocket, produced a big pocket watch on a chain. He dropped his whole head to direct his gaze at the timepiece, then back up to regard the newcomer.

"I think I might be lost," said Spenser. "Is this the way to Blountsville?"

"Dis old turnpike'll git ya jes'about anywheres ya need da go."

Spenser digested the semi-cryptic answer. *Yeah, right.* "What I guess I meant is—where the hell am I? This doesn't look much like Alabama."

The old man smiled and the gold tooth took front and center again. "Now, come on, a-foe now, ya' ain't nevah been ta 'Bama … so how's ya know?"

The old guy was looking at Spenser, but it also felt like he was looking *through* him. Not a great feeling. But Spenser pushed on: "How'd you know that. How do you know I'm not an Auburn Tiger?"

"A-cuz you smells mo' like a New York Weasel!"

And with that the old man cranked back his head to unleash a cackling laugh half-emphysmatic and half-walpurgian.

"So what're you—a nightclub act? A little mentalist … a little stand-up? All you need's a little blues guitar?"

"Gave it up years ago." The man turned his head slowly toward Spenser. No smile this time—more serious shit running now. There was something cold and reptilian in the movement, which combined with those soul-boring eyes to make Spenser feel totally vulnerable.

A long silence rose up between them like a force field and Spenser considered just turning around and putting the Intrepid into *Drive.* Everything about this place, the gas pump, the old black dude, even the corpse of the Chevrolet with the web-cracked windshield … it was all *wrong,* totally out of whack.

Looking up over his shoulder, Spenser felt a flash of guilty relief to see his vehicle still crouched down, waiting for him. A part of him wouldn't have been surprised to discover it gone and him trapped in this impossible locale. Spenser knew places and situations like this didn't really exist, and he was either suddenly delusional, or had fallen asleep at the wheel and was either in a coma or was in some other way disconnected from everything—like being *dead* even.

Now that was a pleasant thought. Spending eternity with

Blind Lemon Jefferson, or whoever this guy was …

"Ya'ain't dead yet," he said in a velvety voice.

"Comforting," said Spenser. He absently fooled with the buttons of his *de rigueur* L. L. Bean khaki vest—the kind that made you look so dashing and outdoorsy on camera.

"Weren't men'da be. Jes' a fack, thass'all."

"So," said Spenser, thinking it might be a good idea to start over. "I'm sorry if I said anything to offend you. It's just that I'm a little rattled, you know … I mean, I have no idea where I am or how I got here."

"Yeah, I know. Dey all's say da same thing."

"All?" Spenser said with caution. "You mean—"

The old man chuckled. "Now, ya don' think you da onliest one ever show up 'round here, do ya?"

"Actually, well, no … I guess not. This looks like a jumpin' place. I don't know how you handle all the business."

Another dark chuckle. Gold tooth. A knee slap for effect. "Good. Ya'ain't loss ya sensa-yewmer. Dat's good."

"Why? Am I going to need it?"

"No, but I gots sumpin' ya mights ta need … soon-uh or late-uh."

Spenser watched him lift his splay-fingered hands off his knees, lean forward and reach for a beat-to-shit suitcase resting beneath his chair, between his legs, like a faithful hound. Its woven burlap and red leather, torn and scratched, spoke of hard travelin'—dusty bus stations, endless nights in Pullman cars.

Funny how Spenser couldn't remember seeing it there … 'til right now.

He watched the old man slide the suitcase out with great effort, slowly lift it to rest on his knees, where he slipped the spring-latches, carefully swung back the top like the lid of a casket. Spenser tilted his head to get a clear view of the interior, but the contents were half-shrouded in shadow.

"Less-see, here," said the old black dude, rummaging around with his right hand, all bony and thickly veined. "I knows I gots sumpin' in here foe-ya."

From where Spenser was standing, the suitcase looked like the open maw of the junk drawer we *all* have somewhere in our

Thomas F. Monteleone

house—the kitchen, the top pull of our dresser, a night stand, or the center slide of the desk. Filled with the usual assortment of scissors, paper clips, pens, pencils, pocket combs, film canisters, letter openers, shoelaces, Swiss Army knives, golf tees, cuff links, dead penlight batteries, tie-tacks, barrettes, loose coins, and …

… a pair of glasses.

"Yassuh, here we go, gotcha whats ya need right'chere." The old guy lifted the glasses from the midst of the oddments and held them up toward Spenser. They looked like an ordinary pair you could find on any optometrist's rack.

"Glasses?" he said. "What for?"

The old man's head tilted upward and the frosted-over eyes seemed to lock on like targeting radar. Spenser felt a coolness pass through him like his soul had been run through a strainer. "Ya'evah hear-a 'rose-colored glasses'?"

"Sure," said Spenser, looking at the spectacles cradled in the spidery, brown-skinned hand.

"Yeah, well deese ain't dem!" Another deep chuckle. The old guy sure knew how to amuse himself. "But … you mights wanna call'em 'no-colored glasses' … ! Yeah, dat mights be mo' like it."

"I'm afraid I don't get it." Spenser looked from the frosty eyes to the proffered glasses and back again.

"It usual-be like dat … come first … but time come when ya gonna dig it jes fine."

"I don't understand," said Spenser. "You want me to take these glasses and wear them?"

The old man nodded. His hand had been holding the glasses out like a display mannequin. "Dey like sunglasses, but better … hep ya see real good."

"Okay, what the hell—thanks." Spenser took the glasses, held them up in the brassy light. The frames felt light, yet substantial, well-tooled; the lenses clear with just the hint of topaz. He moved to put them in his shirt pocket and the old guy held up a long index finger.

"Naw … put'em on … gib'em a try."

Spenser paused, shrugged, and slipped on the glasses.

Instantly everything looked … *better,* like he said it would. Edges sharper, colors more saturated, and a clarity hard to articulate but sensed immediately. He'd never worn anything quite like them, and he'd dropped absurd amounts of money for all the designer styles over the years, having left pairs in the best restaurants in the country.

"Looks right nice," said the old man. "Dey suits ya jes' fine."

"So far so good. They seem to work great."

Adjusting his fedora, the man nodded, then slowly closed the lid of the old suitcase, padded the latches into place with his thumbs. After placing it carefully back under the chair between his legs, he checked the silver fob-watch, nodded slowly. "Time to get rollin' … 'less ya be late."

Spenser looked down at him, grinned. "How do you know where I have to be … or when?"

Old man shrugged. "Every man gots ta be somewheres … ya'ain't no different."

"Yeah, maybe I better be getting out of here." Spenser uncuffed his Movado to see the old man was right. That local cameraman would be hitting the Motel 6 any time now. "Which way to Blountsville?"

"Way you was headed … do jes' fine."

"Okay, well, thanks," said Spenser as a sudden awkwardness gripped him. He felt somehow silly and guilty for leaving the weird old black dude out here in the middle of—of wherever they were. After taking a few steps towards his car, he paused, turned back to look at old Cream Fedora, sitting all rigid and odd, with his big bony hands on his knees. "Hey, you know what? You never told me your name … or where the heck this place is."

His gold tooth transmitted a smile his way. "Divine," he said. "Dey calls me Johnny Divine. And dis here's da Turnpike. Da Brimstone Turnpike."

"Well, it was … uh, nice meeting you, Mister Divine. I guess I better be getting back to work."

"Nice ta meetin' ya as well, Mistah Goldin' … surely was."

The mention of his name stunned Spenser for an instant because he damned well couldn't remember telling the old bastard his name. But maybe he had.

Climbing in behind the wheel, he keyed the ignition and the big engine turned over right away. As he slipped it into gear, he thought about the guy's name and knew it had to be fake. A stage name. He was an old performer all right. No getting around it.

Spenser blinked his eyes and suddenly that fog was rolling in and up toward his car. He'd barely gotten into motion before the thick folds of whiteness began to curl over him. A quick look over his right shoulder at the Gas & Gulp revealed a fleeting ghost image of the pump and the bleached rocking chair—empty.

Before he could tap the brake pedal, Spenser felt the front-end dip and the tires sink into the soft mud. As the rear end repeated the move, the hood of the Intrepid had penetrated the fog to reveal the tree-lined road and the gray, wet sky. And even though he'd been expecting it, that didn't make it any less weird, and the hair on the back of his neck felt like the bristles on a wild fucking boar.

The rain had eased off, and the general visibility was improving, although that could have been chalked up to Mr. Divine and his glasses.

... so let's have a big round of applause, ladies and gentleman, for the entertainment stylings of Blind Johnny Divine! Let's hear it for Blind Johnny and his magic glasses! ... Thank-you-thank-you!

Spenser smiled at his cleverness in spite of a cloying sense of dread like cobwebs you can never really wipe free. A part of him wanted to dissect just exactly what had happened back there—as strongly as another part of him wanted to forget about it. Post it up to bad dreams and hallucinations and all that kind of dismissive rationality.

Only he knew he was just pulling his own crank on that score.

He sure as hell had met an old character who called himself Johnny Divine, and there was probably a citation on him somewhere on some Internet site celebrating old blues "legends."

But there was more to it than that, thought Spenser. Oh yeah, as if he figured he could slip that brimstone turnpike thing past him ... Oh right, yeah, *that's* a name you're going to find on all the maps, yessir!

Now let me see ... *brimstone* ... now, uh ... duh ... now wouldn't that be ... oh say, as in ... *Hell?*

And what a dead-on euphemism for the standard *Highway to*—?

Yeah, old Johnny Divine sure fooled me, he thought. *Dummy ole me.*

Spenser was feeling righteously indignant that the old guy could have tried to bullshit him like that as he nosed the car around a tree-lined bend to hit the town limits of Blountsville, defined by a roadhouse called the Belle Haven and an unfinished furniture outlet. Beyond these businesses a smallish Main Street took shape, leading down to an intersection where the Motel 6 sign dominated the "skyline."

Pulling into the parking lot, Spenser saw the minivan with the Channel 34 logo on the side. As he drifted to a stop beside it, he saw guy sitting behind the wheel wearing a Braves cap and a dark blue windbreaker. Spenser got out, waved, and the man wound down his window, greeted him with a smile. He had a young, earnest face.

"How's it going? Are you Mr. Golding?"

"Got here as soon as I could."

"Me, too!" He jumped down from the cab, came around the back of the car, and offered his hand. "Greg Oliveri. You ready to get some pictures?"

"Sure. How much farther to where it went down?"

"I spotted the sheriff when I first pulled in. He says Nectar Pond is about three miles northeast on a town-road. We've already got State Troopers and EMT vehicles on the scene. Federal boys still on the way."

"Are we the first news team?" Spenser checked his watch out of habit, ran a hand through his hair.

"You bet," said Oliveri. "That's great, isn't it?"

Spenser looked at his cameraman and recognized a younger version of himself. He remembered feeling the kind of pride and enthusiasm that jacked through this kid and he honestly missed those honest emotions. "Greg," he said softly. "Have you ever been to a crash like this? Like we're going to be seeing?"

"No, why?"

"Because it's going to be like nothing you can imagine. You're going to need a strong stomach."

3

The wreckage of Flight 223 peppered the meadow and thin forest beyond Nectar Pond with tens of thousands of still-smoldering pieces—of fuselage, luggage, seats, and bodies. As Oliveri panned the area, he knew his images would be heavily edited before they aired. In the midst of the blizzard of papers, briefcases, carry-ons and cell phones were lots of shoes, shreds of clothing and body parts. The kid was holding up pretty well until he panned across a pair of severed hands, still intertwined, holding each other beyond that final moment.

Spenser helped him through it by emphasizing the need to be professionals, and he urged Oliveri to shoot everything he could and worry about the editing later. Spenser helped him set up for the interview with the FAA reps, and later with the FBI field agent who indicated the Jet America 767 may have been brought down by terrorists. When Spenser asked the agent why there were such suspicions, the agent confirmed two passengers on the manifest had used falsified IDs purporting to be Americans—when in fact they were Saudi nationals. In addition, the preliminary analysis of debris believed to have been part of the luggage bay revealed possible residue from C4 explosives.

Before they packaged everything for uplink, Spenser told Oliveri he had one last thing he wanted to do, and if it worked, he wanted Greg to lens one final segment.

"What do you want me to shoot?" said Oliveri, who still appeared half-dazed from the shock of the crash scene.

"You'll see," said Spenser, who figured it was probably easier to just let the kid see the results rather than waste time with a lengthy build-up. One of the most important requirements to becoming a first-rate journalist was developing a reliable "hot-list"—a directory of confidants who worked in a variety of agencies and companies who could be counted on to provide inside poop nobody else could get.

Or, in plain language: sources for good leaks.

So Spenser called a friend who worked at the INS in Washington.

"Shelly, it's Spenser Golding. How's it going?"

"Spenser, you never call just to check on my welfare—what do you want?"

"The FBI just pulled the files on two Saudi nationals—I need their real names."

"Spenser, how do you know about that?"

"They just told me," he said quickly, and got her up to speed on his current assignment.

"I'll have to do a little snooping around," she said.

"I'll wait."

"Spenser, this might take some time."

"Bullshit, Shelly. You think I never heard of a computer? I'll wait."

Two minutes later she was back. "You were right. Here you go," and she spelled out the names of two men who had been on several agency's "watch lists".

"Thanks, baby," he said. "Next time I'm D.C., dinner at Dominique's."

Holding his notebook tightly in hand, he motioned to Greg Oliveri to follow him back toward the yellow tape, which marked off the outer boundary of the crash investigation field. While a swarm of emergency personnel textured the background scene, Spenser stared into the camera, adjusted his Blind Johnny sunglasses, and composed his scoop on the fly. "In addition, I've just been informed by reliable sources that the crash of Flight 223 was most likely the result of a terrorist bombing. Evidence indicates two passengers who boarded in Miami under false identities were actually Mustafa Azziz and Acmed Ibn Hakim. Although neither man has been yet linked to a known terrorist cell, it remains a distinct possibility their attempts to disguise their identities implicates them in the global Islamic jihad against Western civilization. This is Spenser Golding in Nectar Pond, Alabama, for the Digital News Network."

"That's a wrap," said Oliveri. "Nice work, man."

"Yeah, thanks. Let's uplink everything and go get a drink, whaddya say?"

Oliveri nodded and they headed back to finish up.

An hour later, they were sitting at the Belle Haven with mugs of Killian's, getting ready to tuck into a platter of baby-back ribs when Spenser's cell phone went off. Sometimes, its electronic chirp conveyed more than just a funny noise—and this was one of those times.

"Hmmm, that sounds like trouble," said Spenser as he reached for the Motorola in his vest pocket.

"How can you tell?" said Oliveri, who had shown himself to be really nice guy who liked to talk baseball and technology.

"Intuition," said Spenser, hitting the *talk* button. "Golding here."

"What in Jesus-fuck do you think you're goddamn doing with a piece like that!?" screamed the voice at the other end of the transmission. Spenser had heard the strident tone and word-choice before, and had no problem recognizing Lawrence G. Feldheimer in full-craze mode.

"Larry, calm the hell down," he said as softly as possible. Over the years, he'd learned it was the only way to deal with Feldheimer. The louder you yelled back at him, the louder *he* got, which did not make for good communicating. But if you spoke very softly, old fat Larry *had* to pipe down to hear what you were saying. "What exactly is the problem?"

"We had to edit the crap out of that wrap you did. "You can't piss off the Arab community like that! You know how it is—what's the matter with you?"

Now that was a good question. And until that very moment, Spenser hadn't really considered why he'd spoken so candidly about the connection to fanatical Islamic terrorists. He hadn't said anything untrue. "Why would we be pissing them off, Larry?"

"Because they don't like to be accused of terrorism any more than anybody else does!"

"Well, then, maybe they should start doing *less* of it." said Spenser. *Wow*, he thought. *Where did that come from?*

"You know, I know you've been under a lot of stress, Golding," said Larry Feldheimer. "I'm going to give you a pass on this one, okay. Just get back to the city by tomorrow. I'm sending the B-Team in to finish the on-scene stuff. I want to see you in my office, and Mr. Crossland wants to see *both* of us."

Spenser chuckled. "Oooh, I'm *sooo* scared."

"Not funny, Golding."

Spenser knew Feldheimer was terrified of Alex Crossland, VP in charge of Operations, but that didn't pertain to Spenser because he was one of the DNN's most popular on-air "personalities"—a term actually verboten in the rectories of the newsgathering high priests. You could *never* be heard admitting the presentation of The News was actually being done by people who could not only be recognized as personalities, but (worse) actual "stars." The whole notion that television journalism should wear the same shabby costume as regular entertainment TV was an anathema of the first mark.

"Oh, I wasn't trying to be funny, Larry." Spenser paused. "The simple truth is Crossland's a lot more hesitant to shit-can one of his stars than a skyscraper flunky like you. So don't try to threaten me, okay?"

"Golding, I—"

"Forget it, Larry. I didn't do anything wrong. I'll tell the same thing to Crossland tomorrow. See you on the seventieth Floor."

Folding the little Motorola and canceling the connection, Spenser looked across the table to see Oliveri smiling.

"Must be nice to talk to the boss like that."

"I don't make it a habit," said Spenser. "Pass the ribs, buddy."

4

The confrontation with Alex Crossland never took place and Spenser wasn't surprised. The only meeting to suffer engaged a heavily perspiring, amoeboid Larry Feldheimer.

"That just wasn't like you, Spenser," he said. "What were you thinking?"

"I don't know—the truth, maybe?"

"You were lucky, this time."

"Larry, the suits really didn't want to fuck with me. Better they just do what they did—which was chop up my video package and run with the message they wanted."

"It's more than that," said Feldheimer, mopping the sheen off his brow with a linen handkerchief. "You blurred the line, Spenser."

Checking his watch, Spenser half-turned to leave. "Let's stick a fork in this one, okay, Larry? I gotta get up to LaGuardia if I'm going to cover the Hatch Brothers."

"Yeah, just don't put me on the hot seat again, you hear me?"

Spenser smiled. "You and your hot seat were the last thing on my mind when I did that story. I guess I'm just sick of everybody making believe these terrorists aren't necessarily Islamic fanatics. Why the fuck are we afraid of 'offending' a bunch of people who openly admit they *hate* us and want to see us destroyed? Are we fucking nuts, or what?"

Feldheimer exhaled slowly. "I don't know … I just don't know."

"See ya, Larry." Spenser reached for the doorknob, paused and put on his sunglasses—the ones with no tint.

"Yeah, just be careful." Feldheimer paused, then: "Where'd you get those things?"

"You like 'em?"

"No. But they *do* make you look kind of smart."

That evening, Spenser was touching down at the Burbank Airport outside of L.A. It was one of those perks the masses didn't much know about. They all flew in and out of that absurd Mixmaster of planes and cars and ugly, phony people called LAX, while people who could afford the first-class tickets booked at the last minute could glide down into smaller, less-trafficked venues like Burbank. No crowds, no traffic, no stress.

He jumped the shuttle to the Preferred Customer pavilion where his Hertz rental awaited him. If DNN was pissed off, they had an odd way of showing it—the car was a sleek new Lexus. Spenser smiled as he keyed the ignition and headed for the courthouse in that part of the city where nobody ever claimed they went—downtown Los Angeles.

He arrived at his hotel in a neighborhood called Bunker Hill for reasons he'd never figured, and could see the lights of Chavez Ravine from his sixteenth-floor window. Despite the leather seat, the unlimited liquor, and the filet mignon, he was tired from his cross-country flight, and just wanted to surf through the cable channels for an hour or so before crashing. He thought about calling Robin, his lady-friend at William Morris, but wasn't all that in the mood to pretend he was interested in talking to her. He knew he should go over his notes on the Hatch Brothers case, but he wasn't up for that mess either.

And if he felt like being honest with himself, he'd have to admit he wasn't so sure of anything ever since he'd drifted into Joe's Gas & Gulp.

Funny, but he'd managed to keep most of that whole weird scene out of his conscious thoughts. Not that it bothered him, or any of that strange interlude he'd passed with old Mr. Divine, but there was this unarticulated sense that he'd be better off not dwelling on the encounter. And even funnier, the longer the time passed between him and odd Johnny, the more indistinct and less *real* it all was beginning to feel. Like rising up from an incredibly vivid dream, and then feeling it fade as the day and the world awake extended itself. Until finally stretched and distorted into little more than a bad memory, the dream retreats back to the bleak vortex of its birth. And is gone.

Is that what was happening to the Brimstone Turnpike?

Spenser smiled at the reconjuring of the name. Clever. Funny. Odd. All those things. And vanishing?

Maybe …

He shook his head slowly, remoted through the gamut of channels without allowing anything to catch his eye, then retrieved his laptop carry-on. Unzipping its document sleeve, Spenser pulled out a thick file on the Hatch Brothers case and forced himself to read it one more time. Better to be prepared when he reached the courtroom tomorrow.

The story of Melvin and Antuwan Hatch was repulsively enthralling. The two brothers were resident aliens from Jamaica, living in the Compton area of the city, were twenty-three and twenty-five when they embarked on their wild Tarantino-esque adventure of sex, drugs, and bullets. Even though Spenser had sifted through all the preliminary

material on their case, he could find no indication of what triggered the two young black men to go so totally berserk.

The Hatch brothers' previous entanglements with law and
order had been a few minor drug busts, a botched liquor store
job, and an assault charge in dance club. Not exactly an impres-
sive sheet, but they decided to change all that in a big way on an
early winter evening a year previously. They were driving their
Ford Explorer through Sherman Oaks when they rousted a man
named Gary Relling who had just used a Citibank ATM on Van
Nuys Boulevard. After forcing Relling at gunpoint to whack his
ATM card for the daily max in withdrawals of $2000.00, they
took him up to Mulholland, and threw him over the guardrail.
The victim survived a tumble down through the canyon brush
with a broken leg and a dislocated shoulder. He was the lucky
one.

Later that evening, the brothers pulled up behind a young
lady named Marybeth Cheever parking her car on Sunset and
Doheny. Melvin approached her as she was lifting a cello from
the trunk of her vehicle and fired a 9mm slug into her skull
from a distance of ten inches. For good measure, Antuwan
smashed the cello into firewood before he and his brother fled
into the darkness in their SUV. Around midnight, they showed
up at the Flintridge home of Drew and Joanne Havlicek, who
had the misfortune of having plenty of lights on while they
partied with two other couples. Like a beacon, the illuminated
house must have called to the Hatch Brothers, and they crashed
through some patio doors and took the six people hostage. One
of the men, a forty-year-old sitcom writer named Mark Cassutt,
tried to challenge them and received two Glock slugs through
his heart for effort. Then the Hatch Brothers decided it would be
fun to make all the remaining victims take off all their clothes
and run through a catalog of sex acts ranging from your basic
oral stuff up through the use of fruits, vegetables and some
vicious sado-sodomy deals. Ugly. Horrific. Real sick.

After that, they rounded everybody up into the Explorer for
a run to the ATMs. When all the victims had maxed their cards,
they found themselves on the fifty-yard-line of the Tujunga
High School football field—all naked, on their knees, and told

to expound on why each of them shouldn't be executed.

Apparently no one had come up with any convincing arguments because Melvin and Antuwan Hatch methodically put their Glock 9mm semi-automatics into the mouths of all five victims, obliterating the backs of their heads one by one. A man walking his dog witnessed the brutal, surreal killings, and was also shot by the fleeing brothers.

But he survived ...

... and became the material witness scheduled to testify tomorrow in what promised to be a ratings hit for Trial TV ... except that Trial TV wasn't having any part of it.

Tossing the file to the floor, Spenser wrapped himself in the bedsheets, and left the television on to lull him into a disquieting sleep.

And then morning light was attacking him with all the subtlety of a Malibu Real Estate agent. Spenser felt violated and dirty as he spilled from the bed and shambled into the shower. He couldn't remember anything of his dreams, but he suspected he'd been tangled in a grim rewinding of the L. A. Guignol according to the Brothers Hatch. It was difficult to immerse yourself in such a disturbing tale and not have it stain your every thought for a long time afterward.

And now he would be going to the District Courthouse to stare into the faces of evil in the flesh. Spenser knew it was one thing to simply read about monsters like these guys—but very different when you got a chance to stare the beast right in the eye. He didn't look forward to the experience, but he accepted it as part of the job.

Such were his thoughts as he donned his "blind-johnnies," and drove the Lexus east on Olympia Boulevard to the downtown municipal parking garage. Spenser wasn't sure why he was still wearing the minimally-tinted glasses, but he had convinced himself of experiencing enhanced acuity, softer polarization, and a lack of UV fatigue. Besides, he thought he looked pretty hip in them. Reaching his rendezvous with his cameraman from DNN's Los Angeles affiliate, a guy name Alejandro Reyes, he was ready to start working. They walked across the street to the huge, neo-classical courthouse building, and found their way through its marbled halls to the overflowing trial room.

The testimony of the chief witness in the case was Calvin Otansky, the manager of the Nite Rock Cafe in Tujunga. Just released from the hospital where he'd recovered from a near-fatal gunshot, Mr. Otansky looked frail and beaten, but remained undeterred by the glaring, threatening expressions of the Hatch Brothers and the abusive, near-slanderous cross-examination tactics of the impeccably-dressed Aldritch Taylor, a celebrity-type attorney hired for the Hatch brothers by the local chapter of the Multicultural Rights Coalition.

Spenser had not only seen Aldritch Taylor's Gospel-hour theatrics in previous, high-profile trials, but Spenser had also interviewed the man several times. Taylor had impressed him at those times as arrogant, self-aggrandizing, and less-erudite and educated than he'd like you to believe, but today, as Spenser watched the attorney's attempts to openly embarrass and discredit a man who could have easily become his clients' eighth murder victim of the evening, Spenser was impressed with Aldritch Taylor's utter lack of a moral center, of even the slightest whit of elemental, human decency. To watch Aldritch Taylor strut and pose and make light of Otansky's gut-wrenching depiction of the executions the man had witnessed, made Spenser physically ill.

But as the trial-day wore on, Spenser's queasiness was replaced by a gradual realization and a growing anger—not so much by what he did see as what he did *not*.

In fact, he felt surprised at his own personal revelations, and the urge to share them with his audience. That evening, when Al Reyes lined him up, with the obligatory architecture of the courthouse in background, Spenser prepared his special, on-the-scene, live report which would be broadcast in what was called "dialogue mode" with Scott Dennison, the DNN Prime Time News anchor, whose sonorous intro-voice boomed in Spenser's cosmetically-correct earphone.

"And now for an up-to-the-minute look at the Hatch Brothers trial in Los Angeles, let's talk to Spenser Golding on the scene."

"Good evening, Scott. Today, a grim recounting of the execution-style murders allegedly committed by Antuwan and Melvin Hatch of Los Angeles was delivered to a jury of six men and six women," said Spenser when he saw the red light flash on Reyes' camera. "The chief witness for the prosecution, Mr. Calvin Otansky of Tujunga, California, refused to be intimidated by the openly hostile and aggressive cross-examination of well-known attorney Aldritch Taylor."

"Spenser, do you really mean 'openly hostile'?" said Dennison, smiling a bit awkwardly on his side of the split-screen broadcast.

"I used the term only because it was appropriate, Scott. Aldritch Taylor tried to disparage Otansky's job—running a biker bar—as if this would make him a less credible witness or he did not have a high enough social standing to influence the fate of a couple of vicious Neanderthals like the defendants."

Scott Dennison's expression blanched for an instant as he chuckled inappropriately. "Uh, yes, Spenser … ah, any other details regarding Mr. Otansky's testimony we should know about?"

"Calvin Otansky remained calm and displayed uncanny powers of description. He was articulate and precise in what he saw, and later experienced firsthand," said Spenser. "But, I have to tell you, Scott, this trial has made me think of other issues that quite possibly are larger than the outcome of a single murder trial."

Scott Dennison's expression changed from wary to positively bright. His smile widened as he welcomed Spenser's comments: "Issues such as what, Spenser?"

"I've been reading the newspaper accounts of this case, both locally and nationally—although I have to be honest here and say there's been *very little* national attention accorded it—and I've listened to the commentary of many of my colleagues in the media … and practically everybody has been *very* careful to soft-pedal the racial aspects of this case."

Scott Dennison's expression closely approximated the well-known look of a deer in your headlights. His hesitation was obvious as he forced himself to do the required follow-up: "And just exactly what aspects might they be?"

"The defendants are black. The victims of their unrelentingly vicious crimes were all white. I see no distinction between the facts of this case—other than sheer numbers of victims—and that of the murder of Will Birdsong, who was dragged to death chained to the truck of two white men." Spenser paused for an instant as his anchor continued to grow paler, then continued: "But there is a difference, Scott—the death of Will Birdsong received major national media attention and was condemned as a horrific 'hate crime,' do you recall?"

Dennison cleared his throat feebly. "Ah, yes, I believe I do …"

"But this multiple-murder case is somehow perceived to *not be* a 'hate crime'. At least, no one has had the nerve to decry it as such, and after persistent questioning, I have discovered that the D. A. declined to try the case under any hate-crime statutes. But, I will submit to you and our audience that the brutal acts of the alleged murderers fall well within the media-accepted parameters of a hate crime."

"Well, hold on now," said Scott Dennison, attempting to regain his customary control. "You have no real evidence to suggest that—"

"Evidence? Let's hypothetically reverse the facts of this case, Scott. Suppose if you will the Hatch Brothers were *white* and their eight victims were black …" Spenser paused, shook his head, and stared into the camera. "Can you imagine how all the hate-crime enthusiasts and media darlings such as the Reverends Jackie Jession or Mal Dimton would be swarming into this city with their coalitions of protesters and strident muckrakers? I submit you could not *keep* them away from this case, and their cries of racism, skinheads, and white supremacists would drown out all other voices."

Spenser paused, again leaving Scott Dennison twisting in the broadcast wind. The anchor coughed nervously before trying devise an acceptable commentary. "Ah, I think you're not being fair when you choose to analyze this case along racial lines, Spenser—how can you presume what the defendants were *thinking?* What motivated them?"

"Isn't that what a hate-crime charge always does?" said Spenser. "Doesn't it *always* question motive as well as the act itself?"

"Well, if you put it that way ..." Dennison fumbled for a cogent response. "But, historically, hate-crime charges have been invoked when an atrocity has been committed upon *minorities* or what the conservatives call the 'protected classes'. Whites don't normally know the pain of racial injustice."

"Really? Well, gee, thanks for clearing things up for me, Scott. Too bad you can't explain it to the five white people who had their brains blown out on that football field." Spenser stared into the camera for an instant, and getting no further response from his anchor, said: "This is Spenser Golding reporting from the District Courthouse in Los Angeles. Good evening."

Reyes gave him a signal as the camera winked out. As the cameraman began packing up his gear, Spenser's earpiece exploded with the voice of Andy Hartenstein, the prime time news director.

"Golding! Are you fucking *crazy!?* What in hell do you—?"

Smiling, Spenser eased the mini-headset from his ear and disconnected the spiral cord from its power pack. He handed it and the mike to Al Reyes, who returned it to his aluminum carryall. Reyes hadn't said a word about the broadcast, but that wasn't unusual. In talking to hundreds of cameramen over the years, Spenser was no longer surprised to know most of them totally tuned out the words and substance of the talking heads they lensed. Just concentrate on the job and get it in the can— that's what most of them told you.

"Nice job, Al," he said. "Same time, same channel—tomorrow?"

Reyes gave him a thumbs up and headed back to the van.

As Spenser adjusted his glasses and looked up the steps of the courthouse, he watched the crowds of people descending. Some well-dressed, but most of them looking like slobs. It occurred to him that our culture was changing in so many ways, and in the main, for the worse. If you looked at the old newsreel footage of people in the streets or even at the baseball park, everyone looked *neater*, cleaner, more ... well dressed. Women wore more skirts and dresses; men wore white shirts, suits and jackets, hats that were somehow rakish and stylish. Now, most of us were content to wear jeans, baggy shorts, and the vulgarian raiment of choice—the T-shirt.

What was happening to us?

Spenser turned toward the parking garage just as his cellphone chirped. Smiling to himself, he reached into his pocket, knowing who wanted to reach him without checking the caller ID.

"Hello, Andy," he said softly. "Must have lost power back there."

"You goddamned moron! Spenser, what're you trying to do—get us *all* fired!!?" Hartenstein's breath was coming in labored gulps. He could barely get his words out. "You've created a *major* embarrassment!"

"What're you talking about?" said Spenser, walking along as he spoke, and realizing how silly he looked as he pressed the little device to his ear. Most people looked odd at best and usually ridiculous as they carried out involved and usually *loud* conversations while they invaded public space.

"Don't play dumb with me. Are you crazy?! Why did you bring up that hate-crime nonsense?"

"Because it's *not* nonsense when the blacks and the gays bring it up," said Spenser as he entered the garage. "So what exactly makes it 'nonsense' when regular old white people are the victims?"

Andy Hartenstein sputtered. "How dare you make this a racial issue! Who do you think you are?"

"I just thought it would be interesting to let people see things from a different perspective."

"Feldheimer is apoplectic," said Hartenstein.

"*Good* word," said Spenser. "You should think about getting back into journalism, Andy."

"Another thing—you *know* we don't call people 'black' on DNN!!! They're *African-Americans*!"

Spenser laughed. "Sorry, not *these* guys—they're from Jamaica."

Reaching his car, Spenser hit the little button on the keyless lockpad and opened the door.

"That doesn't matter!" Hartenstein was screaming now.

"You know what," said Spenser. "I've got to get behind the wheel, and I've heard it's very irresponsible to drive in L.A. while talking on a cell phone. So, tell Feldheimer I'll call him when I get back to the hotel. Bye-bye, Andy."

Spenser killed the power on the little phone and threw it on the passenger seat. Fuck him and the network he rode in on.

5

There was a recorded message on his cell from Cyndi, which paraphrased a call from that woman, Estela Barboza—a call which called him a hero and exactly the man who must listen to her story. But nothing from the guys on DNN's 70th floor. Apparently it was too late back east to get a call from Lawrence Feldheimer because he didn't call until the morning, and that had been after the competitive news networks and the early newspaper editions had had a chance to give their take on Spenser's coverage of the Hatch Brothers.

Other than a cogent, approving analysis on DNN's more popular competitor network, there was not *one* additional mention of anything he'd said. *New York Times, Washington Post, Los Angeles Times, USA Today, Good Morning America* … all silent.

It was like he'd never said a word.

Which is why Feldheimer had begun his conversation with a declaration that Spenser Golding was one lucky sonofabitch because nobody had decided to make a big deal out of his stupid remarks.

"Have you wondered *why* nobody wanted to take me on, Larry?"

"Because you were so wrong, so *god*damned stupid."

Spenser smiled, and looked at the screen of his laptop, moused in on a familiar site. "I think it's exactly the opposite of that," he said. "I think everybody knows I'm *right* and they don't want to mess with me."

"You arrogant bastard," said Feldheimer. He walked out

from behind his desk and began pacing and posturing. "I could destroy your career this very instant."

"It's your call, boss-man. I have a feeling there's another news network that'd be interested in seeing my résumé."

"I won't tolerate any more tricks out of you, Golding. Everything you do now will be put in the can for vetting first, before it gets on the air."

"No," said Spenser. "You do that, and I walk across the street to the competition, and I tell them *why*—that you guys wanted to sanitize my segments for the public's protection."

"You dare play brinkmanship with me!?"

"Think about it, Larry. In the meantime, chew on this. I just did a Lexis-Nexis search on how many pieces have been done on the Hatch trial ... as opposed to the Rhona Walker shoplifting trial."

Feldheimer chuckled. "What does *that* have to do with anything?"

"Well, let's see ..." said Spenser. "Only *everything*, I'd say. The media in general has offered the public it supposedly serves more than *five hundred* pieces on that vapid little actress's case— we got daily reports on what she wears to court, the names of her current films, all the usual Hollywood bullshit. But you, Larry, and your pals at most of the other stations and *all* the papers, have basically *buried* the Hatch Brothers' murder spree—eighteen articles, none of them Page One, and the only TV since the trial started has been *local* crap until yesterday—except for that 'other' news network that's beating the piss out of us in the ratings."

"What's your point?" said Feldheimer, but his heart clearly wasn't in it now. He had pulled out his monogrammed handkerchief, mopped his perspiring brow, and retreated to the bunker of his big, empty desk.

"Only this. You and all the other phonies who decide what is 'newsworthy' somehow reached the conclusion that the trial of a spoiled-brat bitch who never fails to embarrass herself on *Celebrity Jeopardy* was infinitely more important than a brutal massacre of eight people. That's not just shameful, Larry, it's disgusting."

"Are you finished?" said Feldheimer, after a brief silence.
"To tell you the truth, I think I'm just getting started."

6

But they didn't fire him.

Didn't even call him in on the carpet. When he returned to their eighty-two-story Manhattan fortress, he walked their plush halls with impunity. Nobody fucked with him. And they didn't try to edit his spots, either, which he continued to do with a suddenly keen sense of fairness.

After about a week of everybody giving him looks of questioning silence, something weird happened. He was walking to work one morning, along Sixth Avenue toward a klatch of vendors' carts on the corner of 49th Street when two black guys walked up on either side of him and began to match the pace and gait to his. Looking from one to the other, he noticed several things—they were both young, big, and well-dressed. But they still had the look of hired goons. Neither one said a word, but they crowded him from both sides, and for a second he though they were getting ready to do a snatch-and-run with the laptop computer he was carrying in a thing leather case over his shoulder. But they didn't try anything other than stay real close.

Spenser didn't like their attempt to be subtly intimidating, especially in the midst of all the pedestrian traffic of lunch-seeking office-types and the usual springtime tourists where they figured nobody would be paying attention. So when he reached the intersection and moved toward the row of vendors' carts, he turned to face his escorts. As he did this, he reached into the outer compartment of his laptop carryall, and pulled out his digital recorder.

Flipping it on, he held it up at them. They hadn't been prepared for this, and were stymied for an instant. Then, in purposely halting diction, intended to make the street argot sound as silly as possible, he said: "What's up ... dogs?"

The taller, more bull-necked of the two grinned. He looked like he should be playing strong safety for the Giants. "Very funny. You Mr. Spenser Golding, ain't you?"

"You know that I am."

"We got a message from our ... employer—the Reverend Malvin Dimton."

Spenser grinned. "I'm not surprised. Something spiritual and inspirational, no doubt ..."

"Not a-zackly. Reverend Dimton wants you to know he don't appreciate bein' made to look bad on the TV. So, he aksin' you to chill, brother. You gettin' the picture."

Spenser looked from Bull Neck to the other guy, shorter but wider. Your basic middle linebacker.

"Oh, yeah," he said, looking them up and down slowly. "I'm gettin' the picture. But it ain't *nothin'* like the picture Mal Dimton will get when I go on the air with my piece about *you* guys."

"What you talkin' about, man?" This was the taller one, the strong safety.

"Not much," said Spenser. "Why don't you two go find a corporation who doesn't have enough blacks on their board of directors—I hear they scare a lot better than guys like me?"

"What?" said Linebacker. "Listen, slim ... what you talkin' about?"

"Just tell the Right Reverend to be sure to catch my next broadcast."

They both looked at Spenser for an instant, then Strong Safety said: "Okay, but it better be good."

"I think we'll let your boss make that call. See ya, guys." He turned and walked away from the two of them, then punched up Robin's number on his cell.

When she finished her return-calls at William Morris, she met him for lunch, and he told her everything—from the strange Alabama fog to Joe's Gas & Gulp, Johnny Divine, and the Turnpike. And of course his "blind-johnnies." And he didn't play dumb about the effect they'd had on him.

Robin smiled over her Santa Fe salad. She was athletically lean with huge Mediterranean eyes, and a wide, interesting mouth. He liked her because she was attractive, but more so because she was smart.

"Spenser, puh-leeze. Do you expect me to believe all that?"

"Frankly, Scarlet ..."

"*Really?*" Robin tried to appear offended, but didn't quite pull it off. "Then why tell me at all."

Spenser leaned back in his chair, sipped his Pino Grigio. "Because it really happened. And because it's starting to feel less and less real. Saying it out loud kind of validates it, I guess."

"But you have proof," said Robin. "You have the glasses."

"So you *do* believe me."

"You couldn't fake it, Spenser. That man did something to you, it's obvious."

He shrugged. "Maybe I did it to myself."

"What do you mean?" She tossed a strand of her long dark hair from her angular face.

"Oh, come on, don't you see all the metaphorical stuff at work here?"

"Well, I guess I don't."

"The old guy, he called it the 'Brimstone Turnpike,' Robin. Now what does that sound like to you?"

She moved her fork absently through the salad, spearing nothing. "The good old 'Highway to Hell,' of course. It was a great song, remember?"

Spenser nodded. "Exactly. So let's extrapolate a bit. That's the route I was traveling. Despite all those bricks under my tires made at the Good Intentions Kiln and Foundry, right?"

Robin giggled in that small, sassy way he'd always found unavoidably sexy. "That's good, I like that one. Nice image."

"Yeah, sure, but am I right or wrong? *Was* my life going off track? Had I sold my soul to the Media Moloch?"

Robin's expression changed as she detected how serious he was. No fooling around now. "Yeah, you've probably cashed the down payment check—at least. But come on, Spenser, haven't we *all*?"

"That's a chilling thought."

She gestured around the restaurant with its trendy trappings and the tables full of stylishly dressed impression-makers. "I mean, look at this place—not exactly Wendy's, is it? And outside those doors, it's not Peoria."

Spenser smiled. "Maybe that's part of the problem. We've either forgotten how the people in Peoria really feel, or we just don't give a shit anymore. Either way, it's bad news."

"You know, I'm a good Italian, Catholic girl, but you're starting to sound like you've been Born Again, and even *we* don't
think that's such a great idea."

Spenser grinned, but his heart wasn't in it. He knew she was
just trying to lighten things up and meant nothing disparaging,
but he needed her for more than inside-joking, elbow-nudging
support. Reaching into his jacket, he pulled out the glasses, put
them on. The way the edges of everything assumed a suddenly
increased sharpness always jolted him for an instant. But he was
getting used to it. And he liked it.

"So what *are* these things?" he said softly. "Where'd they
come from? And *who* is Johnny Divine?"

"Does it matter?" said Robin. "Sounds to me like you met
your Guardian Angel, that's all."

"Oh, okay, whew ... I was worried there for a moment I'd
really had one of those life-changing experiences."

Robin shrugged, looking concerned, but still managing a bit
of exasperation. "Spenser, what do you want me to say? What do
you want me to do?"

"You really want to know?"

She nodded, blinked her big, dark eyes.

"Come with me. Back to Alabama. I want to find that place
again. I want you to meet that guy."

She obviously hadn't been ready for that one. "Spenser, are
you kidding? I don't need to see him for myself. I *believe* you.
Besides, I've seen your broadcasts—you couldn't be faking it. I
believe you. I think I know you pretty well, and I can *see* you're
different. Something obviously changed you."

"That's right." He stared at her for a moment. "Do you like
it?"

She reached across the table, took his hand in hers. "Let's just
say I'm really glad you trusted me enough to tell me about it."

"Yeah, I guess I did, didn't I?" He smiled. "But you didn't
answer my question—yes or no will do."

"Spenser, even you would have to admit you're sounding a
little reactionary."

"So you don't like it." That bothered him. He'd been thinking that what he really needed was a confidant, an ally in all this stuff. And she was backing away from him as if he might contaminate her with this new toxin he'd encountered.

"I didn't say that, but—"

"And the vacation to the Deep South?"

"Let me think about it, okay?"

"I'll take that as a *no*."

7

Robin's ambivalence bothered him more than he'd thought it would. The personal odyssey on which he currently labored seemed more daunting with the realization he probably didn't have anyone in his life he felt all that close to. Without articulating the desire even to himself, he'd been hoping Robin might want to volunteer for that mission.

For the first time in as long as he could remember, he felt very alone, and it was eating at him. Isolation. Alienation. All that *angst*-bullshit. Man, what was happening to him?

After leaving Robin at the restaurant, he walked slowly back to his office, where Cyndi greeted him with a stack of phone memos.

"Anything important?"

She projected her Smith College No. 3 Smile—the artful one that suggested insincerity without revealing it. "If they're for you, they're all important."

Spenser paused to rifle through, paused when he saw the familiar name. "Estela Barboza again?"

Cyndi's expression changed to something almost compassionate. "Oh, you probably didn't hear about it."

"Hear about what?" He felt an *absence* in his gut.

"Her car was bombed this morning."

"What?! Is she—?"

"She's fine. She called you right after it happened. She said to tell you she doesn't want to talk to anybody but you."

Spenser had the sensation of looking up to see a huge wave curling over him, or maybe the sun-blotting shape of a piano falling to the spot where he stood affixed. He felt sick and stupid and revealed. How could he have ignored this poor woman like he had? A fucking *car* bomb? Somebody was seriously pissed at her, and he'd treated her like some supermarket tabloid fan.

You know, Spence, sometimes you can be a real asshole.

As he drifted into his office, he began rearranging his priorities. Although Spenser had an interesting exchange on his digital recorder, and he wanted to invite his audience to listen in on how Reverend Dimton used his sparkling personality to influence people, he knew there was something more urgent at hand. He checked the latest off-the-wire services and the Internet. There wasn't much on the car bombing, but he noted the scant details and reached for the piece of paper with the callback number for Estela Barboza.

Dialing quickly, he was surprised to hear it answered on the first ring by a woman with an intriguing voice—firm, direct, silky but with a bit of an edge like fine bourbon. He identified himself and apologized for not getting back to her sooner.

"Oh, of course," she said. "I can understand you thinking I may not have been very newsworthy—till *now*."

"Ms. Barboza, it's not like you think. Believe me. I have been … kind of overwhelmed lately."

"I think I have you beat in that department," she said with no hint of humor.

"That's what I'd like to talk to you about," he said quickly. "Can you meet me at our studio?'

"When?"

"As soon as possible—but you tell me."

"I'm in Weehawken. It will take me about an hour."

Spenser confirmed the correct address and checked his watch. "I'll meet you in the lobby."

She was punctual and well-dressed in a subdued suit. Her jewelry was restricted to a delicate pearl-and-gold necklace and a Movado watch. She looked to be around thirty-five, and her rimless glasses gave her an air of sophistication and intelligence. He shook her hand and then they stood facing each other in a scene that could get awkward in a hurry.

"I'm glad you finally agreed to hear my story," she said,

looking warily around the reception area. Other visitors and staffers crisscrossed in and out of the elevators and doors to the street. No one appeared to give them any special notice.

"I'm embarrassed it took me so long." said Spenser. "You probably think the car bomb made me do it."

She gave him a very small sardonic grin. "You should stop now, Mr. Golding. Nothing will ever convince me otherwise. If I didn't think my story was too important to ignore, I would tell you to go to hell with the rest of your colleagues."

"I admire people who aren't afraid to speak their minds."

"Do you have a choice?"

"Don't want one. Come on, let's go to one of the studios. We can get some vending machine coffee, sit back, and you tell me what's going on."

He escorted her to the elevators, grabbed an open car, and punched up the right floor. Neither one spoke during that nether-time when they were forced to be close together in the small enclosure. Elevator interiors had a way of subduing people, he'd often noted.

"This way," he said as the doors slid apart.

"The only thing different about you," said Barboza. "Was that I never had a chance to tell you what I wanted."

"Different from what?"

"As soon as I told anybody who I was and what I wanted to talk about, they would start getting very distant, even openly disinterested."

"I'm going to assume you went to big networks first, right?"

"Yes."

"Big mistake."

"If you're wondering why I didn't call you first, I have to tell you I had no idea you'd be receptive. I have to be honest, Mr. Golding—I never liked your style very much … I never liked your attitude, I guess." She paused, obviously not comfortable being so openly critical. "So you were one of the *last* ones I tried to reach. But right after the first message I left with your office, a good friend of mine told me you'd been sounding different lately, quite a *bit* different."

"Yeah, well, thanks," he said. "That's good to know."

He smiled as they reached a glass-paneled door to an unused recording suite all done up in the latest designer patterns and color combinations. He invited her to take a seat in one of the chairs.

He pretty much agreed with her. On more than one occasion, even he himself had fought the urge to gag at some of his antics, and he told her so.

"You are very gracious," said Barboza.

"Nah, just realistic. Anyway, let's hear your story."

For the previous three years, Estela had been the vice president of the New Jersey chapter of the National Teachers Alliance, an extremely powerful union and political lobby. But she had been asked to step down by an ad hoc committee of "concerned" school administrators.

"And you did it?"

"Not officially, but I told them I would consider it."

"I assume that wasn't good enough," he said.

"No," she said. "I was acting sufficiently upset at the chance to lose my position in the organization. They wanted to punish me."

"And this committee—they're responsible for what happened to your car?"

"No, not exactly. But, I'm pretty sure I know who *is*."

"And they did it right in your driveway. They've gotta be crazy," said Spenser.

"Worse," said Barboza. "They are true believers, they are fanatics."

"Tell me about them."

"Three years ago I headed up a study sanctioned by the NTA to monitor the progress and the success of their dual-track bilingual classroom program in New Jersey."

"Dual-track?"

"Basically the program provides public education to Hispanic immigrants in Spanish."

"K through twelve?"

She nodded. "If they want it, yes."

Spenser had heard of these programs in other states like Florida and Colorado, but had never given it much thought.

"Okay, so what happened?"

"Essentially, the study showed the bilingual program to be a disaster. The kids who spent all those school years *not* learning English were several standard deviations *lower* in every kind of test you could imagine. They weren't succeeding in academics, in sports, in the job market, not *anywhere.* Not learning English put them at a terrible disadvantage in every possible way."

Spenser grinned. "And you needed a study to tell you that? Seems obvious, doesn't it?"

"You know," said Barboza. "I used to teach affirmative-action programs at the University of Arizona, and later at Berkeley, but I pulled out when the Chicano activists started demanding lower admission and graduation standards. And it got worse as the special interest groups on campus started getting funding to run programs that were nothing more than indoctrination organs to get people to hate 'Anglos'."

"Chicanos and Anglos," said Spenser. "You don't hear those terms out east all that much."

"That doesn't make them any less offensive to me." Barboza flushed as she spoke and her breathing had increased as she spoke of something of obvious importance to her. Spenser identified with her passion and her sincerity—if for no other reason than he had recently uncovered some of his own.

"So, anyway, you were saying—you know who bombed your car."

"Yes, I think so. When I compiled the results of the bilingual study and submitted my report to the NTA, some of them *refused* to even read it. And the few that did—they went absolutely crazy! Not only were they unhappy with the pitiful outcomes of their precious program, but they wanted me to suppress the data and rewrite my conclusions and recommendations."

"Which were—?"

"To *stop* the program, of course! I strongly suggested getting all the Hispanic children into mainstream classrooms where they could start learning English as *fast* as possible."

"They hated that idea," said Spenser.

"Oh, yes, of course. And when I refused to compromise my

study or lie about my conclusions and recommendations, they asked me to resign."

"And put a bomb in your car?" Spenser couldn't connect the dots.

"Not right away. But I went public with the story—even though I didn't get much coverage, I was also trying to organize a referendum for the next election to see if the electorate would vote down the bilingual program." Ms. Barboza paused to sip from her water-cooler cup, then exhaled slowly. The details of her story, though intimately familiar to her, still had the power to upset her. "And that's when things started to get personal."

"How?"

"I was getting threatening calls and letters. The activists feel I am a traitor to their cause. They think I'm a 'turncoat,' and they want to destroy me." She pushed her dark hair away from her cheek. She had a wide, expressive mouth. Huge eyes.

"I don't get it," said Spenser. "Why would the leaders of the Hispanic community and the NTA not want the kids to learn English?"

"You know, I had trouble with that one, too. I couldn't figure it out. I mean, my parents came to the United States from Argentina when I was six—I couldn't speak a *word* of English. They put me into the first grade, and guess what? I not only learned to speak and read, I was an A-student by the end of the year. That's what happens when you immerse the kids in all-English classrooms—they *learn*."

"I still don't see what the NTA would be—"

"Think about it!" said Barboza with deeply sincere emotion. "My experience was not unique. If Hispanics can succeed in this country the same way all the other immigrants have done it—by learning English and moving up the economic and job ladders— then all then all the hustlers will be out of jobs."

"The 'hustlers'?" Spenser said.

She looked at him with an expression of haughty disdain. "Yes, you know the types—Linda Chavez called them 'the ethnic hustlers in the perpetual grievance industry'—and she's so dead-on right. I can't stand those *bastards!*"

"'The perpetual grievance industry', I like that." said Spenser.

"They wouldn't like you."

"They sound dangerous," he said.

"Yes, what they had done to my car was supposed to intimidate me, but I don't scare very well anymore, Mr. Golding. I am sick of these two-faced people who claim they care about children and education when all they want to do is preserve their unions and their jobs and their abilities to do inferior work and get away with it. And then claim they were victims! That something *else*—never themselves—caused all the problems."

Spenser was impressed. He liked her story, and he liked her presence and passion in telling it. He asked her if she could stay in the building for a taping and she agreed.

8

The day after his show on Estela Barboza aired, DNN received thousands of phone calls and emails. They were fairly evenly divided between viewers who agreed with her position, admiring her courage, and those who believed she was not only wrong, but was also a truly evil woman. Spenser spent a few hours looking through the feedback and he noted one very disturbing aspect to a significant sampling of the negative correspondence—a lot of it read as if it had been composed by the same person. The dreary redundancy of the words like "traitor" and "heretic" and "whore" were not only absurd, but scary.

The essential message of the hate-mail, as well as the message to be read between the lines, echoed through his thoughts as he cabbed home to his small brownstone off Central Park West. It was a warm, early-summer night in Manhattan, and Spenser was feeling dog-tired. But it was a fatigue borne of satisfying labor, and he liked that feeling. His bosses had stopped bugging him because the latest ratings analyses had been posted and—surprise!—his numbers had been on a sharp incline ... *up*.

So even if Feldheimer *hated* him and what he was saying (and he did), it was ultimately *okay* because people were watching. And that was the *real* reality TV—getting people to keep their lunch-hooks off their remotes. And that meant Hartenstein and Crossland could only complain *so* much before they had to back off and genuflect to the altar of the Great God Nielsen.

Such were his thoughts as the cab drifted to a stop outside his house on West 79th. Jumping out, Spenser passed through a small wrought-iron gate, and took a few steps up his short walk before he noticed it.

And it stopped him in tracks.

On the landing of his front steps, under the sill of his front door, sat a small package wrapped in brown paper.

Oh shit ... that does not *look like something from L. L. Bean.*

Taking a step closer, Spenser studied the rectangular thing in the ambient light of streetlamps and scattered porch lights. Tied with standard twine, it had a white label with his name block-printed in fine, Unabomber-style.

Oh yeah, I'm picking that up and yanking off the strings ... you just bet I am, he thought as he pulled his cellphone from his pocket and hit his pre-assigned button for nine-one-one.

"What happens if it goes off when the robot picks it up?" said Spenser. His voice sounded amplified in the small confines of the NYPD van, which had been placed at an angle to block traffic from entering his street at the corner of 79th and Central Park West.

Sergeant Morris Schaller of the Metro Bomb Squad had been looking over the shoulder of a young policeman working a console with a joystick and an LCD screen. Schaller's thin, angular face seemed dominated by his salt-and-pepper mustache, even though it was trimmed Errol Flynn-neat. He turned to address the question with a wry grin.

"You ever heard the expression 'blow your doors off'?"

"That's my point," said Spenser. "How much damage could it cause?"

Schaller shrugged. "Hard to say. The X-rays didn't show very much dense material. If it's C-4, it could take out your front rooms and a couple of the neighbors'. If it's regular TNT, it might be a fizzle."

"I'm ready with the extensors, Sarge," said the young operator.

"Do you watch *BattleBots*?" said Spenser.

"Yeah," said the younger cop, smiling. "How'd you know?"

"Just a guess …"

"Okay," Sergeant Schaller nodded. "Give it a shot …"

The operator nodded and began to move the joystick, but he'd barely touched it when the LCD screen whited-out and the van was rocked by the sound and shockwave of an explosion.

"Aw fuck," the sergeant. "Let's go …"

Reluctant to see what was left of his house, Spenser was the last to clamber down from the van's rear door. Beyond the twisting yellow tape and sawhorse barriers, he strained to see through the still-unfolding clouds of smoke and powdered debris. All around him, he could feel and hear the collective responses of his neighbors—some shock, but mostly outrage. The assembled firefighters were already moving in with their hoses and axes.

"What happened?" said Spenser, knowing he sounded incredibly stupid. "Can you see how bad it is?"

"Take it easy," said Sergeant Schaller, controlling their advance with outstretched arms. "Doesn't look too bad."

Easy for him to say. The front door, foyer, and the bay window to the dining room were simply *gone*. Damage to the flanking homes was surprisingly minimal, but that was not Spenser's big concern at that point. He didn't really even care about his own place—that's why you bought insurance. No, it was a lot more than that. This was the first time he'd felt the violence and the misguided loathing of somebody else this close up. All the years of seeing it happen to the Other People, and it had finally come home to roost.

How do you like them apples? He could hear the familiar, archaic phrase from his childhood, and he was thinking he didn't like these apples even a little bit. As the cops and firefighters pooled and eddied around him, Spenser felt himself suddenly yanked back to his days as a nine-year-old boy in Chevy Chase, Maryland, right near the border of D. C. where his father worked as a lawyer for the FCC. He remembered growing up hearing all the wonderful stories about JFK and RFK and how wonderful it was the Jews were prospering in Israel. He also recalled visiting his cousins, Ira and Sam, who lived in nearby Baltimore, in a beautiful neighborhood of oak-shaded streets called Forest Park. Back then, he found it strange that one day his uncle announced the family was moving to the suburbs, to a town called Pikesville in the county, because of "blockbusting."

It was a term he'd never heard before and his mother had politely explained that blockbusting occurred when someone in the neighborhood sold their house to a "Negro."

And what exactly was wrong with that? he'd asked, as his mother drove him to his Cub Scout meeting at Temple Oheb Shalom. She'd looked at him sweetly and smiled when she explained: now that a Negro would be moving into Forest Park, *everyone* would have to move.

Another *why?* brought another piece of the answer: because even though Negroes were just like everybody else, *nobody* really wanted them living *right next door.*

Yeah, he thought, things seemed so simple, so long ago …

The minutes warped past him in a weirdly inverted view of how things worked. It was the first time he'd been on the victim side of the microphones and lenses; the first time seeing his colleagues for the parasitic, insensitive leeches they needed to be. The "journalists" had descended on him with a growing locust-frenzy, especially after his identity was verified. Spenser recognized many of the eager faces behind the mikes and the cameras, and he was surprised to see how they all pretended to not know him at all.

Initially, he tried to accommodate them with answers to questions so inane, so callous, so off-the-fucking wall …

Were you upset when the bomb went off?

Did you ever think you'd be the victim of terrorism?

Do you think it was a random attack or because you're a celebrity?

Will you try to reach out to your attackers?

There were lots more, some dumber than others, but all of them fell somewhere into the general category of intrusive. And after about an hour of trying to be civil to people who'd forgotten the meaning of the word, Spenser stopped it.

Not by making any declaration or trying to create a memorable scene or anything overt. He simply stopped talking and walked away. He didn't know where he was going, but he needed to get away for a while. Maybe a bar, maybe a phone booth where he could call his insurance people, maybe just a walk down Fifth Avenue.

But he didn't get very far along Central Park West before he heard his name being called. The rumble and hum of the traffic had masked the sound, but somebody was calling after him and he spun abruptly around to confront the persistent jerk, whomever it might be.

"Now look—" he started to say, his jaw muscles tight and angry.

But he stopped when he saw her.

"I'm sorry," said Estela Barboza. "I didn't mean to scare you."

She was standing about ten feet away. Dark hair loose and whipped by a soft evening breeze, she wore a classy spring outfit in muted pastels. Thin, understated gold necklace. She looked like a commercial for any number of expensive women's products.

"No, no," he said. "*I'm* sorry. I thought you were one of the wolfpack back there."

"I had tried to get here as soon as I could. I was so shocked when I heard about it on the news and they mentioned your name." Estela moved closer to him. "I feel so bad! I feel so—"

She was close enough so he could smell some kind delicate perfume. Ultra feminine. Very nice. He was surprising himself to realize he was so glad to see her.

"It's okay. Not here … you don't have to—"

"But that's why I rushed over here. I want to talk to you."

"I … I was just going to go hide for a while," he said. "But I think I could use the company."

They went to a small bistro on 56th between Fifth and Sixth, where he commandeered a table for them—just cocktails. Funny thing, but he wasn't feeling very hungry.

"You know why they did that, don't you?" she said.

"Are we both in agreement we're dealing with some very pissed-off teachers?" He grinned without humor, sipped off the initial layer of his Glenlivet.

"I'm in shock," said Estela. "Nobody is that much of a fanatic, are they? To kill the messenger?"

"Messengers get killed all the time. Don't you ever watch the History Channel?"

"I feel responsible. Your house is ruined. You could have been killed," she said. "I am so sorry."

"It's not your fault," he said, pausing to sip his single malt. In fact, once he'd been able to get away from the mob scene at his house, his subconscious had been working things out, and now things were beginning to bubble up to the surface. "And you know what—in one sense, I'm almost glad it happened."

"What? Why?"

"Because it tells me that I did something that made people react. Maybe not *think*, but at least I *reached* them. And if I reached some of the bad guys … well, maybe I reached some of the good guys, too."

Estela looked at him with an expression of concern and some puzzlement. "But isn't that what you always do?"

He sighed, smiled at the irony of what she was asking him. "Always? Well, lately, I'm not so sure. I spent a lot of years believing I had everything figured out, had the world by the horns, and was exactly the right person who should be telling everybody else how to think. And now, I'm almost forty years old and I'm wondering what the hell I've been doing with my career."

"And now, what? This bombing makes you think twice about—?"

"No, not at all. The bomb doesn't have a lot to do with it. There's something else …"

Looking across the table, Spenser sorted through a wave of thoughts crashing over him. Despite being deeply interested in talking to this woman, it was gradually occurring to him that *none* of his friends had done so much as she had in coming to check on him. No work-buddies, colleagues, bosses, relatives … your basic *nobody* had even tried to call him on his stupid little cellphone … and they all had the number. So what were the odds of *none* of them seeing the news or hearing about it through the jungle telegraph?

Bad odds, my friend.

And speaking of friends, what about Robin? If she cared so much about him, believed in him so much, then where the hell was she?

"Ah ... Mr. Golding?" said Estela.

"I'm sorry," he said. "I was just thinking about something. Didn't mean to get lost ... and please, don't call me that. Just Spenser, okay?"

She smiled, sipped her Merlot. "Of course. I'd be glad to."

"I guess I'm a little more distracted than I thought. What was I saying?" He didn't usually lose focus like that. Must have been a combination of the stress and the fact he was starting to feel a real attraction to this lady.

"You were saying there was something else ... but I'm not sure what you meant."

"Oh, yeah, that's right," he said, and at that moment, he knew he could trust her. Reaching into his jacket, he pulled out his Blind Johnny glasses.

"... so," he said several minutes and several stories later. "Do you believe me?"

"The best lies are the ones kept simple," said Estela. "Something as complicated as your story can *only* be true."

"Funny thing is," said Spenser. "I haven't felt the need to wear them as much lately."

"What do you think that means?"

He shrugged. "At this point, either I don't know ... or I don't *want* to know."

"I've felt like that." She paused, then pushed on. "I must tell you I am somewhat surprised by your story—not so much by the content, but what it says about you."

"What do you mean?"

"You told me a tale quite familiar in both South American literature and folklore: the encounter with the Mysterious Stranger. It is so widespread, I have often thought it must surely be based in truth."

"And that's why you believe me?"

She smiled, held her wineglass, but did not drink. "No, not at all. I believe you because of what you told me of yourself, of the changes you feel have happened to you. Nobody bothers to go into the heart when they need the stuff of lies."

"That's an interesting way of putting it." He paused, looked into her eyes. She did not look away. That was nice. "I can tell you—nobody's ever listened to me that carefully."

She smiled. "Maybe you never had anything that important to say before now."

Sharp. Funny. He definitely was liking her. When he had tape-interviewed her story, he'd picked up on her obvious character pluses of courage and a belief that suggested great passion. But he was learning even more now and it was intoxicating.

"That's probably true," he said, holding the no-colored spectacles in front of the table candle as though inspecting them. "But I have a lot more that needs to be said."

"To me or your audience?"

"Both ..." He reached into another pocket for his digital recorder, pausing to smile at how dependent we'd become on witchcraft-like technologies. "Listen ..."

After hearing the exchange with Reverend Dimton's "associates," her expression changed subtly. "Don't do it, Spenser."

It was the first time she'd called him by his first name since they'd been sitting there, and there was a familiarity, an intimacy that seemed far more natural than he could have hoped for. "Why not?"

"Because they don't sound like nice people."

"It seems like we both have a knack for attracting those types." Besides, it's about time somebody stood up to that guy. He gets a free pass every time he gets in front of a camera. He can say any outrageous crap he wants and nobody ever calls him on it."

"Is that what you want to do?"

"After the audience hears how his goons tried to scare me, I'll invite him on the air to give his side of the story. He'll hang himself."

"How do you know he won't do something dangerous?"

Spenser shrugged. He had no answer for that one. "Well, let's just say I'm hoping he's not that stupid."

"All indications suggest that he *is*," said Estela. Her features were sternly fixed. No hint of trying to be clever. The noise level in the cafe seemed to be increasing; more people were coming in for late dinners or early drinks.

"Well, I guess what I'm saying is that I don't believe I can turn back now." He cleared his throat, knocked back the rest of his scotch. Holding up the "blind-johnnies," he continued. "Something's changed in me."

"Have you thought about getting some help?"

"You mean like the police?" Spenser smiled. "I'm not sure they like to hear stories of raw paranoia."

"I can vouch for that. They hadn't done much for me until my car was blown to pieces."

"Forensics are getting to be incredibly good," he said. "If they get a little lucky, too, they might get some good evidence from my house."

Estela sipped from her wineglass, spoke softly. "Speaking of your house, where are you going to go tonight?"

Shaking his head slowly, he tried to suppress an embarrassed grin. "You know, I hadn't given it a thought. I guess I should call the fire department guys and the police ... God, I feel like an idiot. I just walked away from the place. I didn't say anything to anybody."

"Spenser, I don't want you to take this the wrong way, so I'll just spell everything out, okay?" Her eyes were bright and fixed sharply on him.

"Sure, go ahead."

"You are welcome to stay at my place in Jersey—it's right across the river. I have an extra bedroom with its own bath. You can use the phone and the computer. But please understand: I'm not coming on to you, okay?" She sat up straighter in her chair, adjusted her hair and necklace, as if that could make her look any more dignified or more classy. "I like you, I think you're a good person, but that's not what this is all about. You helped me; I just want to return the favor."

"That sounds great, thanks," he said.

"Really? You're okay with that?"

Spenser smiled. "Believe me, no offense taken. None at all! In all honesty, it's completely refreshing. Estela, you've got a lot going on, and I have an idea it would take a lot of time to get to know you."

"Finish your cocktail. We have a lot of work to do."

9

The next day grew more complicated because of his unwillingness to speculate and talk to the media-types who bugged and cajoled and badgered him for the whole story of the bomb-attack. Feldheimer tried to push him as well, but Spenser was more interested in producing his piece on the Reverend Mal Dimton and his "emissaries" of goodwill and brotherhood.

Spenser didn't pull any punches as he exposed the mob-tactics of the well-dressed preacher, who spent far more time at demonstrations and in front of cameras than he did in any churches. Over the years, he had become a media-favorite as a spokesman for any minority cause. How he had achieved this anointed status was a mystery to anyone who bothered to look into his questionable past. Maybe all the journalists were afraid to take him on, fearing tar from his racist-brush, but Spenser was pissed, and it was about time Reverend Dimton was revealed to be the crook and charlatan he was.

When the piece was finally in the can, it was after seven in the evening, but he could still get it on the late-night block. It was tight and polished and held back nothing.

Which is precisely why Larry Feldheimer *hated* it.

"No fucking way!" he yelled. "You want all those guys down there with Dimton telling the world DNN's a racist corporation?!"

Spenser was seated at the console of an editing suite. Several monitors sat behind him with stopped frames of his face in them—leftovers from his editing. "That's always the problem, isn't it? Somewhere along the line, we all started to believe it was worse than being called a murderer or a child molester."

"Spenser, you can't—"

"All I want to do is tell people if their champion *looks* like a thug and *quacks* like a thug ... so maybe he *is* a fucking thug." Spenser turned and touched a panel on the board and the DVD with segment slid silently out in its drive-tray. He lifted it carefully, dropped it into a jewel case.

"No way I can let you on the air," said Feldheimer.

Spenser held up the disc like a Eucharist offering. "No problem, Larry, I'll take this across the street to NewsFax. Something tells me they won't turn it down."

Feldheimer's plump features grew pinched, his complexion flush, and he looked like he might burst in one final hypertensive aneurysm. "You can't take that anywhere! That's company property!"

Placing the disc in his jacket pocket, Spenser smiled. "I'm willing to let the lawyers sort that one out."

"Give that to me!" said Feldheimer, as he lurched forward, grasping for Spenser's pocket.

Without thinking, Spenser grabbed Larry's $200.00 Paolo Zileri silk tie and yanked downward. Hard. The slow, overweight man dropped toward the floor as if poleaxed, and his chin chunked into the carpet like the business end of a hammer. And he lay there stunned for a moment, as if deciding whether or not to lapse into unconsciousness.

Wow, thought Spenser. *That was incredible. I couldn't have done it better if I practiced it.*

"Get up, Larry. I've got work to do."

Slowly, Feldheimer rolled over, pushed himself up to a sitting position. His breathing was erratic and it was hard to tell if he was more scared or angry. "Golding, I'm going to sue your ass—!"

"Sorry, sir, but you don't have any witnesses ..."

"I can't believe this! What's happened to you?"

"Larry, you can write up a disclaimer. Saying you had nothing to do with the Dimton piece. You can swear you never knew anything about and I'll sign off on it—I don't give a shit."

Wiping some perspiration from his eyes with the back of his hand, Feldheimer squinted. "What?"

"You heard me. I don't want you to lose your job, and I don't care about mine. What's so hard to understand?"

Feldheimer haunched up onto his knees, tried to pull himself up on the edge of the editing suite console. It was hard but he made it, plopped into a chair. He looked beaten, broken. "I don't get it ... I don't get *you*, Golding."

Spenser nodded. "I don't expect you to, Larry. For most of my life, I don't think I was getting *myself*."

Feldheimer stared at him, but said nothing.

Spenser continued: "Just don't try and stop my broadcast. I've already couriered a copy of my piece over to NewsFax. They'll run it if they get a call from me."

"You bastard—you're lying!"

Spenser shrugged. "You want to take a chance, go ahead."

"Traitor!"

"All depends on which side of the fence you're on—you know that."

"Golding—!"

"See you later, Larry. If you have anything you want me to sign, leave it on my desk."

"Wait!"

But Spenser was already out the door and heading down to Traffic, where they would cue up his segment for the late-nite edition. Nobody would say a word; nobody questioned a "celebrity" like Spenser Golding.

And they didn't.

Five hours later, Spenser was in the living room of Estela's loft in Weehawken. They were seated on a couch in muted floral patterns. Original paintings and lithographs hung on the walls where there weren't bookcases brimming over with hardcovers and paperbacks. There was a smallish LCD screen on the coffee table and it was flashing and melting from the DNN logo to a commercial.

"That was incredible!" she said with a smile she didn't bother to hide. "Talk about stirring up a hornet's nest."

"Thanks. It was a little tough to do on the fly, but we've got so much file-copy on Dimton, I didn't have any trouble finding what I needed. And my stuff with his goons came through great, didn't it? I even did the type-over transcription myself, just to make sure nobody missed a word."

Estela poured some Merlot into two goblets, offered him one. They clinked, then she said: "To your courage!"

"Let's not get carried away," he said. "Nobody in here but us chickens—you being the exclusion."

For the next hour or so, they sipped wine and exchanged *bon mots*, getting all warm and fuzzy, and really enjoying each other's company. Spenser sensed something special in her that women like Robin and the others lacked. Estela had intellect and wit, but she had a warmth and a sincerity he didn't see much in his business. Most people had this image they needed to project all the time, and she just refused to do it. She was very real—in a way Spenser could only pray to ever be.

He liked her.

Which meant he didn't plan to reprise any of his old lines or moves. The only way things would ever work with Estela was simple evolution. If there was anything going on between them, let it develop without any clumsy intervention by him. He felt very fortunate to have a nice place to stay while the arson and forensic teams finished up at his brownstone. And wasn't it interesting how all his "friends" and colleagues didn't exactly fight it out amongst themselves for the honor of offering him any help.

Such were his thoughts as he lay in the dark, feeling the warm afterglow of the red wine. He couldn't wait 'til morning, when he could get a solid read on the reaction to his piece on the underbelly of the Reverend Mal Dimton.

As it turned out, he didn't have to wait that long.

"What?" he said groggily into the darkness. Someone had called his name softly. He must have drifted off into a pleasant, wine-buzz sleep and now he heard Estela's voice in the night. Did this mean she—?

"Spenser!" she said in an urgent whisper. "There's a call for you!"

"A call?" Now he was awake. "How? Who even knows I'm here?"

"You'd better take it," she said.

Placing the portable receiver to his ear, he said: "Yeah?"

Spenser Goldin'?

"You got'im. Who is this?" He added the question, but he had a very distinct idea who it was from the street cadence and inflection in the male voice.

Jes' somebody ain' too happy wif yo' shit on the reverend.

A coldness passed through him. He didn't like the idea of someone who sounded like this not being "happy wif his shit." But he couldn't let him know that.

"Gee, what a surprise," he said.

Listen up, dawg. You in the muthah-fuckin' jackpot, now.

"We'll see about that." Spenser tried to work up some real anger, but it wasn't coming through.

Soft laughter. *Only if you around to see ...*

Instead of concentrating on the voice, Spenser's thoughts pushed through to another level. These guys might want to make themselves *sound* like hip-hop street punks, but if they had been sharp enough to locate him, and now knew where he was for *certain*, wouldn't it be a great idea to keep him on the phone and distracted long enough for ... ?

"Hey, can you hold on a sec? My other line's ringing."

Lissen-up, chump! You—

Hitting the call-waiting button, Spenser threw the receiver across the bed, and jumped up to pull on some clothes. A digital alarm clock glowed redly—4:35 a.m. Estela was looking at him with obvious distress.

"What's wrong?"

"Get dressed. We've got to get out of here—right *now*."

10

In less than three minutes, they were out the rear entrance, around the side alley, and up to Estela's new Honda. The neighborhood streets were dark and empty. Spenser made her stand off by the edge of the alley while he slipped in behind the wheel. If anybody had been here already to rig a charge under the chassis, he didn't want her going with him.

Keying the ignition, he pinched his eyes shut ... and *nothing* happened other than the sound of the engine kicking in. Estela jumped into the passenger seat and they were off the curb in a squeal of tires. She directed him through a cross-hatching of intersections, then so many lefts and rights he had no idea where he was until she got them onto Route 3 West. There were several sets of headlights far behind them, but the way he was feeling, any other vehicle that appeared had to be viewed as a possible threat. He pushed the Accord as fast as he dared until he saw signs for the Turnpike and yanked the wheel in the direction of the southern access ramp. As he drifted through the automated Stop-Get-Ticket booths to get his personal toll card for the trip, he spotted the flash of headlights in the rearview.

Closing *fast*.

Already? It was possible. He and Estela hadn't said much during the mad sprint through the neighborhoods; they both knew they could be in very big trouble. How could he have been so damned arrogant, so stupid? Didn't he think those assholes might try something like this?

Good question, that.

"Hang on," he said punching the gas, and pointing the hood toward towards the on-ramp. The Accord responded with authority, surging away from the ticket machine and up the on-ramp. A quick assessment of their position on the Turnpike gave him a list of options—they could just burn it up and head south for the next couple hours till they reached Delaware, or they could drive until the first exit where the State Police had a barracks (but where the hell was *that?*), or they could try something more quickly to evade any pursuit.

As they reached the merge-point, Spenser veered into the rightmost lane. At this hour, the traffic was thin other than the omnipresent trucks running at middle-of-the-night highball-speeds. He maneuvered to reach the outermost speed-lane as Estela craned her head around to look through the rear window.

"The car behind us didn't stop for a ticket." her voice was

even and controlled. She could have been describing a match of lawn croquet. "It's moving really fast."

"Okay, that might be who we've been worried about," he said. Without hesitation, he leaned into the accelerator and the Honda ticked through the rpms toward the redline. He was doing around a hundred and the front-end suspension was holding true. This was some car …

"They're falling back a little," said Estela. "Now picking up …"

"The road's pretty straight! I'm going to jack it some more."

Huge columns of tractor-trailers began whipping past them, their dark hulks like slow, ponderous beasts. Spenser slowed only enough to weave in and out of the trucks, to see if the headlights in his mirror followed his mad path through the tunnel of night.

And they always did.

"Okay, that's our crew," he said. "Definitely not out for a family drive."

He pushed the car to its limits and they were rocking at one hundred and ten. If he topped this speed, he had no idea whether he could keep it under control or if the car's engineering would hold up. If the Turnpike were not so perfectly straight, he'd never have gotten this far.

"They're going to catch up," said Estela.

"No, they won't." But Spenser wasn't sure he even believed himself.

Looking to the signs along the rightmost lane, he saw they were approaching a service-road exit for maintenance vehicles. If he remembered correctly, from all the times of driving past it, the road also ran through the marshy meadowlands near North Arlington. You could always see the landfills being constantly groomed there.

The headlights had drifted into the far-left lane, closing slowly like a predatory bird who knew it had plenty of time to swoop down on its slower, clumsier prey. Spenser, hurtling down the center-lane, was just clearing a long line of 18-wheelers.

Without thinking about it in advance, trusting instinct rather than rational deduction, he tugged the wheel to the right just enough at that high speed to make their vehicle *leap* across the right lane, in front of the line of trucks.

Then, hoping the long column of trailers would form a barrier, Spenser continued to angle to the right, shooting the off-ramp to the service road. For an instant, the Honda's tires screamed like they were going to give up their traction, but then suddenly held as he braked down, oversteering onto the ramp and doing a rapid deceleration toward a sharp right turn dead ahead.

He felt himself letting go of a breath he must have been holding and his chest burned for an instant as he sucked in new air.

If he'd done it right, the trucks would have blocked his pursuit like big lineman pulling out on a power-sweep. Best of all would be if the bad guys hadn't even been able to *see* him take the service road. But even if they had, they couldn't do anything about it until they reached the next exit.

Unless, of course, they were crazy enough to drive *backward* up the shoulder.

"Wow ..." he said. "I think that worked!"

"I'm glad you didn't tell me what you were planning ahead of time," said Estela. "I would have said no way."

"Are you kidding? If I had even *thought* about it, hell, I would have said no!"

They both laughed small and nervously as he yanked the car through a hard right and headed across a narrow stretch of two-lane asphalt, which bisected a huge, swampy meadow. The sky was beginning to get paler behind them. Soon it would be dawn.

"Where does this go?"

"There's mountains of landfills out here, and then local roads beyond them. If we can get through before they see us again, we might be able to lose them."

"At least for now," she said in her rock-steady voice. Estela unhooked the seatbelt, turned fully in her seat to scan the road behind them.

Spenser had slowed down as he cruised through the barren landscape. In the pale ghostlight of pre-dawn, he could have been streaking across the face of some distant world, as cruel and bleak as their future might be. He pressed the accelerator and edged up his speed on the patched and broken roadway. The shocks got a good workout as he approached seventy and he figured it might be too much for the conditions. Better to back off a bit and keep it—

"Oh, *no!*" Estela's tone did not belie her fear. "Headlights ... way back by the ramp."

"Big or small? Fast or slow?" he said, concentrating on the road ahead, which was beginning to wind and thread its way through the dumps like a meandering river.

"They're low to the ground and coming on fast."

"Then we can rule out a truck," he said. "Sounds like trouble."

"What're we going to do?"

"We're going to try outrun them. Nothing else we can do." Spenser tried to sound resolute and confident, but wasn't fooling anybody. How the hell had he gotten himself into a mess like this? And he felt worse that he'd dragged this poor, courageous woman into it with him.

"The lights are getting closer. They are really going fast!" she said.

The first woman he met, probably in his whole life, who seemed really *right* for him, and he was working up a good case for getting her killed. *Nice job, Spence ...*

"Hang on."

He pushed the accelerator to the floor and leaned back in his seat, straightening his arms to the wheel to keep it steady under the bad-road pounding.

The sun was coming up at their backs and the glare of the pursuing high-beams was getting washed out. He couldn't judge distance very well in the changing patterns of light and shadow. As he braked for a slight, but unbanked, curve to the right, he saw some sort of white barrier ahead. From this mileage, it looked like somebody had stretched a banner or a sheet across the road.

But as he drew down on it, backing off down to an eighty-five that felt like they were *crawling*, he suddenly saw what it was.

When he'd been about four years old, he stuck a fork into a wall receptacle. The sparks had been nothing compared to the *jolt!* that shot through him, and that's what seeing that fog bank did to him all over again. He actually felt a fucking jolt.

Because it was impossible. Just totally impossible.

But that's what it was—the yellowish, rolling Alabama fog he'd seen only once before.

And now, they were almost on top of it. Fifty yards, and it looked as thick and impenetrable as concrete.

Turning around, Estela saw it, too. "My god, what's that?"

Behind them, the headlights grew as large as moons, closing in, less than a couple hundred yards.

"I'm not sure," he said.

But he *was* sure ... and he felt himself beginning to smile as their car punched through the fog like a cruise missile ...

... to emerge in a place where the sun always beat down so hard as to give everything a beat and bronzed look. That heavy, reddish-planet Mars haze was suddenly all over everything and Spenser's hands were shaking as he tried to hold onto the wheel.

"Madre de Dios!" Estela whispered as she leaned forward in her seat. She also *knew* what was happening here.

The dead-black highway stretched off to a vanishing point and Spenser backed off on the gas, tapping the breaks to get control on the new surface. Up ahead on the right, just as he remembered it, was paint-blistered, falling-down complex known as Joe's Gas & Gulp. The lines of sway-backed roof and glass-domed pumps stood out against the smeary sky. And for some reason, Spenser felt like he was home.

"Can you believe this?" said Spenser. He was slowing down, drifting off into the driveway and lot, looking for someone.

But the bleached-white rocker was empty.

"This is impossible!" said Estela in a harsh whisper. "It can't be—"

"But you know it is," he said as he jerked the car to a halt by the pumps. He popped opened his door and threw out a leg. "Hurry up! Let's go!"

"Where're we going?"

"We've got to find him." Spenser said. "We got to—"

Just at that instant, they heard the high-rev scream of a car engine, and turning back toward the road, Spenser saw a low-slung, black Mercedes leap from the fog like a panther. It skidded and fishtailed even though its driver hit the anti-locks, shocked by the sudden change of venue. After the Mercedes came to a stop, then it began to creep carefully up the hot strip of asphalt, then it accelerated as it locked in on their position.

Spenser grabbed Estela's hand yanking her to the left toward the collapsed garage and the rusting corpse of the blocked Chevy. There might be some tools for weapons, or at least a place to hide.

Behind them, the Mercedes did a power-slide into the parking lot, sending up huge plumes of dust and gravel. Before it even came to rest, all four doors had sprung open and wide bodies were levering themselves out.

Looking back, Spenser saw them all hunched and running with their hooded sweats and dangling arms ending in polished 9mm semi-autos.

As Spenser ran, tugging on Estela to keep up, he expected to feel the hot, stinging *slap!* of a slug taking out the back of his head at any second. But he also found a part of himself oddly detached from the turmoil, and that part was wondering how he'd come to this bizarre point in his life. A life that until recently had been mainly concerned with stuff like business-class upgrades, the best places to get your shirts done, and the biggest Sunday morning brunches on the Upper West Side. A life that had changed and now might abruptly end.

As they neared the edge of the garage, the windshield of the old, black Bel Air exploded into snowflakes of safety-glass.

"Right there, Jack!" yelled one of their pursuers.

And Spenser stopped. Not because he was scared. Because he knew it was *okay*.

"Shoot 'em! Shoot these muthah-fuckahs *dead!*" said one of the four goons.

"Oh, I don' think so," said a raspy, *basso profundo* voice.

A familiar voice. And one that carried on the dead air of the place despite being barely more than a whisper.

The four thugs, dressed almost identically in the gray, baggy rap-sweats, turned as though choreographed to see its source. Mr. Johnny Divine stood just off the front stoop of the diner, leaning on his silver-headed cane, but looking somehow strong. With his fedora cocked at rakish angle, and his cold pearlescent, pupil-less eyes burning out of his dark face, he looked formidable indeed.

"What you boys want here?" said Johnny.

"We got bidness wif these two," said the guy in front, who'd been pointing his stainless at the center of Spenser's face.

"Who da'*fuck* are you, ole man?" said the next one in the group. "Yo bettah keep yo ass outta this or yo be nex!"

"Well, I kinda run things hereabout," said Johnny.

One of the other hoppers looked around, as if noticing more of the details of the place for the first time. "Well ... you ain' be runnin' *this*. Now jus' step back, Ole Tom!"

Three of the hoppers laughed.

But the fourth, the leader with the shiny Glock, spoke to Spenser, but with no street-ligations this time: "My boss says you've committed a sin of biblical proportions, and he's anointed us to be the instruments of your punishment."

"What happened to the ebonics patois?" said Spenser.

The thug smiled. Big teeth. Wide and white. "That's just for effect. I get tired of it sometimes."

"Oh, I don't know," said Spenser. "I think it kind of ennobles you."

"You would do well to shut the fuck up," said the leader.

"Don't you think it's going to look pretty bad for Dimton if I turn up dead?" said Spenser. "Right after I did the character assassination piece on him?"

The leader smiled. "First off, who says you're even going 'turn up'? And second, why don't you just let the reverend worry about that?"

Estela glared at him with wide eyes. There was a passion in her, radiating off in hot waves of anger, and if she were in any way afraid, these guys would never know it.

"Get back in your car. We're going to be taking you for a little ride," said the leader, and directed his troops with a discreet nod of the head.

"Jes' a second now ..." said Johnny Divine. "Seems like you boys wasn't ta lis'nen'."

One of the thugs turned, held his handgun in his outstretched hand, and pointed it point blank in Johnny's face. "We be listnen' jus' fine. Now stay outta this foe I cap yo ass!"

Johnny smiled and slowly raised his hand, extending a long index finger to touch the business end of the gun. Everybody seemed transfixed by his slow, deliberate movement, and no one moved until Johnny touched the gun's snout.

In an instant, the weapon was glowing a deep, cherry red, then shifted for a moment from blue to white before *disintegrating* in brilliant burst like a magnesium flare.

The thug, at this point, was screaming as the sleeve of his sweatshirt went suddenly limp. As it fell to his side, what had once been his arm sluiced out of the smoldering cloth in a hot rush of white ashes. He continued to wail in orchestrated agony as he began to whirl and convulse.

Everyone backed away from him as smoke continued to seep from the seams of his clothes, soon replaced by tongues of white-hot flame, as the righteous, cleansing fire spread through him. And then, as if reaching some sort of critical mass, he was suddenly consumed in a final burst of blue-white energy. His skeleton burst from his clothes like a blackened scarecrow for an instant before imploding into the purest of white ash.

Estela was crying, as were the thugs, who were now backing away from Johnny, who had remained leaning on his cane, calmly admiring his pyrotechnics.

"All right, gen-a-mens ... who's next?"

"What the *fuck's* going on, here?" said the leader, who had dropped his stainless steel Glock, and was holding his hands up in front of his waist. "Where the hell are we, old man!?"

"I was wondering when you might notice," said Spenser.

"Tell'im, Mistah Goldin'," said Johnny.

"Welcome to the Brimstone Turnpike," Spenser said, then reached out and drew Estela close to him. She melted into him and it felt just right.

"What's that?" said the leader.

"Oh, you be ta knowin' soons enough." Johnny smiled,

gesturing at his surroundings. "I could always use a little he'p 'round here ..."

The three thugs crowded together, started backing off. "Man, what you talkin' about!"

Johnny Divine looked *through* them with his translucent eyes, and they broke into a run toward the Mercedes. They jumped in and fired it up as Johnny, Spenser, and Estela watched. In a furious spinning of tires, the car ripped from the lot, throwing up a rooster tail of dirt and stone, and shot through the gears down the Turnpike.

"You're letting them go?" asked Estela.

Johnny shook his head, pursed his lips. "Naw. Dey be back real soon. Dey be supprized ta turn the nex' turn ... and see it brings 'em right back here ta ole Johnny ..."

He chuckled at this, then turned and walked slowly back to his rocking chair. Estela and Spenser followed, noticing the beat-up old suitcase lodged safely between its runners. Johnny sat down, began to rock, as he looked at Spenser with an avuncular smile.

"You done good," said Johnny. "Some don't do like you, but *you* ... you done real good."

"Thanks, but it would've never happened without you."

Johnny smiled. "Maybe. Maybe not ..."

"I was going to come lookin' for you, you know."

"I know."

"In Alabama ..." said Spenser. "I had no *clue* I'd find you up here."

"Well, Sonny," said Johnny. "Dis here Turnpike ... it's a mighty long road ... and y'all can pick it up jes' about anywheres."

"Thank you," said Estela, putting out a hand to him.

"Yes, ma'am, you surely welcome, you is ..." Johnny pulled out his pocket watch, stared obliquely at it. "Time fo you two ta be gettin' on with ya lives ... besides, I be expectin' some comp'ny any minute, now."

"Yeah, I guess you're right," said Spenser. They turned toward the car, and Spenser paused, turned back. "Oh, I almost forgot."

"Wha'ssat?"

Reaching into his shirt pocket, Spenser pulled out his "no-colored" glasses, his "blind-johnnies," and handed them to the old man. "I honestly don't think I'll be needing these any more."

Johnny Divine smiled, accepted them. "I think you right."

They shook hands, and Spenser leaned down to give him a hug. He felt old-man frail under the loose-fitting clothes. "You *are* an angel, aren't you?"

Johnny smiled. "Sumpin' like dat."

11

When they were back in Estela's car, and had passed through the fog, the sun was burning off the morning Jersey mist. Neither one of them, for the moment, could speak about what had happened, or where they would now go, or what they would do with the rest of their lives.

But Spenser Golding was smiling ... because he *knew* they'd think of something.

ABOUT THE AUTHORS

ROBERT GUFFEY

Robert Guffey is a lecturer in the Department of English at California State University – Long Beach. His most recent books are *Bela Lugosi and the Monogram Nine*, coauthored with Gary D. Rhodes (BearManor Media, 2019) and *Until the Last Dog Dies* (Night Shade/Skyhorse, 2017), a darkly satirical novel about a young stand-up comedian who must adapt as best he can to an apocalyptic virus that destroys only the humor centers of the brain. Forthcoming is a collection of four novellas entitled *Widow of the Amputation and Other Weird Crimes* (Eraserhead Press, 2020). Guffey's previous books include the journalistic memoir *Chameleo: A Strange but True Story of Invisible Spies, Heroin Addiction, and Homeland Security* (OR Books, 2015), which *Flavorwire* called, "By many miles, the weirdest and funniest book of 2015." A graduate of the famed Clarion Writers Workshop in Seattle, he has also written a collection of novellas entitled *Spies & Saucers* (PS Publishing, 2014). His first book of nonfiction, *Cryptoscatology: Conspiracy Theory as Art Form*, was published in 2012. He's written stories and articles for numerous magazines and anthologies, among them *The Believer*, *Black Cat Mystery Magazine*, *Black Dandy*, *Catastrophia*, *The Chiron Review*, *Hypnos*, *The Los Angeles Review of Books*, *The Mailer Review*, *New Reader Magazine*, *Pearl*, *The Pedestal*, *Phantom Drift*, *Postscripts*, *Selene Quarterly Magazine*, *The Temz Review*, *The Third Alternative*, and *TOR.com*.

JESSICA MCHUGH

Jessica McHugh is a novelist and internationally produced playwright running amok in the fields of horror, sci-fi, young adult, and wherever else her peculiar mind leads. She's had twenty-three books published in ten years, including her bizarro romp, *The Green Kangaroos*, her Post Mortem Press bestseller, *Rabbits in the Garden*, and her YA series, *The Darla Decker Diaries*. More information on her published and forthcoming fiction can be found at JessicaMcHughBooks.com.

JACK KETCHUM

Jack Ketchum is the pseudonym for a former actor, singer, teacher, literary agent, lumber salesman and soda jerk – a former flower child and baby boomer who figures that in 1956 Elvis, dinosaurs, and horror probably saved his life. His first novel, *Off Season*, prompted the Village Voice to publicly scold its publisher of violent pornography. He personally disagrees but is perfectly happy to let you decide for yourself. He has won multiple Stoker Awards, and has written over twenty novels and novellas – including several with film director Lucky McKee. Five of his books have been filmed to date. His novella *The Crossings* was cited by Stephen King in his speech at the 2003 National Book Awards. Dallas Mayr – Jack Ketchum – passed away on January 24, 2018.

CHET WILLIAMSON

Chet Williamson has written in the field of horror, science fiction, and suspense since 1981. Among his many novels are *Second Chance, Hunters, Defenders of the Faith, Ash Wednesday, Reign,* and *Dreamthorp*. His most recent publications are *The Night Listener and Others* (PS Publishing), and *Psycho: Sanitarium*, an authorized sequel to Robert Bloch's classic *Psycho* (St. Martin's Press).

Over a hundred of his short stories have appeared in such

magazines as *The New Yorker, Playboy, Esquire, The Magazine of Fantasy and Science Fiction*, and many other magazines and anthologies. He has won the International Horror Guild Award, and has been shortlisted for the World Fantasy Award, the HWA's Stoker Award, and the MWA's Edgar Award. Nearly all of his works are available in ebook format at the Kindle and Nook Stores.

A stage and film actor, he has recorded over 50 unabridged audiobooks, both of his own work and that of many other writers, available at www.audible.com. Follow him on Twitter (@chetwill) or at www.chetwilliamson.com.

JENNY OROSEL

Jenny Orosel has appeared in various anthologies, including books published by Cemetery Dance and Bloodshot Books. Her nonfiction has been published by Cinema Knife Fight, Insidious Reflections, and others. She currently lives in Texas with her husband Bill, their daughter Coraline, and various four legged family members (one of which is trying to climb up her as she types this).

ELIZABETH MASSIE

Elizabeth Massie is a two-time Bram Stoker Award-winning and Scribe Award-winning author of novels, short fiction, and media-tie ins. She is the creator of the middle grade series of spooky novels, Ameri-Scares (Crossroad Press.) Her novels and collections for adults include *Sineater, Hell Gate, Desper Hollow, Wire Mesh Mothers, Homeplace, Naked On the Edge, Afraid, The Fear Report, Dark Shadows: Dreams of the Dark* (co-authored with Stephen Mark Rainey), *Buffy the Vampire Slayer: Power of Persuasion, It – Watching*, and more. In addition to her commercial work, she also writes for educational publishers including Scott-Foresman, National Geographic, Zaner-Bloser, and Mason Crest. Massie is currently at work on a new Ameri-Scares novel, and an historical horror novel, *The House at Wyndham Strand*.

A ninth generation Virginian, Massie lives in the Shenandoah Valley with her husband, illustrator and theramin-player Cortney Skinner.

MATT HAYWARD

Matt Hayward is a Bram Stoker Award-nominated author and musician from Wicklow, Ireland. His books include *Brain Dead Blues, What Do Monsters Fear?, Practitioners* (with Patrick Lacey), *The Faithful,* and *A Penny For Your Thoughts* (with Robert Ford). He compiled the award-winning anthology *Welcome To The Show,* and wrote the comic book *This Is How It Ends* (now a music video) for the band Walking Papers. In 2017, Matt received a nomination for Irish Short Story of the Year from Penguin Books. He is represented by Lane Heymont of the Tobias Literary Agency, and can be found on Twitter @MattHaywardIRE or at his website www.sundancecrow.com

THOMAS F. MONTELEONE

Tom Monteleone has published more than 100 short stories in numerous magazines and anthologies—they have been nominated for many awards, and have appeared in lots of best-of-the-year compilations. His notorious column of opinion and entertainment, *The Mothers And Fathers Italian Association,* currently appears in *Cemetery Dance* magazine. He is the editor of eight anthologies, including the highly acclaimed *Borderlands* series edited with his wife, Elizabeth, of which, *Borderlands 5* and *Borderlands 6* won *Bram Stoker Awards.* He has been an Instructor at the *Borderlands Press Writers Boot Camp* since its inception fifteen years ago, and witnessed more than 80 graduates of the program see their books published.

He has written for the stage and television, having scripts produced for *American Playhouse* (which won him the *Bronze Award* at the International TV and Film Festival of New York and the *Gabriel Award*), George Romero's *Tales from the Darkside,*

Sony's *The Unkown,* and an execrable series on Fox TV entitled *Night Visions.* He has written many feature-length screenplays, none of which have been produced, but have made him plenty of money anyway.

Of his forty-plus books, his *NY Times* bestselling novel, *The Blood of the Lamb* received the *1993 Bram Stoker Award,* and *The New York Times Notable Book of the Year Award.* His five collections of selected short fiction are *Dark Stars and Other Illuminations* (1981), *Rough Beasts and Other Mutations* (2003), *The Little Brown Book of Bizarre Stories* (2004), *Fearful Symmetries* (2004),which won the *2004 Bram Stoker Award,* and *Dark Arts* (2017). His novels, *The Resurrectionist* and *Night of Broken Souls,* global thrillers from Warner Books, received rave reviews and have been optioned for films. *The Reckoning* (2000), a sequel to *The Blood of the Lamb, and The Eyes of the Virgin* (2002) have been published by Forge. His omnibus volume of essays about the book and film industries entitled *The Mothers And Fathers Italian Association* was published by Borderlands Press (www.borderlandspress. com) and won the *2003 Bram Stoker Award* for Non-Fiction. He is also the author of the bestseller, *The Complete Idiot's Guide to Writing a Novel* (2004, 2010), and recently turned in his latest latest novel, a thriller entitled *Submerged* (2017). His books and stories have been translated into fourteen foreign languages. He's a writer—please don't call him an "author." Writers *write.* Authors merely "auth." In 2017, the Horror Writers Association honored him with their Lifetime Achievement Award.

He likes the Baltimore Ravens and Orioles, computers, sour mash whiskey, fine red wines, comics, tons of books to read, movies, all kinds of music (except the stuff sung by people wearing big hats or pants down to their knees), and teaching his daughter how to be an independent thinker. He has been married to Elizabeth for a long time and loves her dearly. He also likes to talk to big crowds of people and read his stories to them. Despite being dragged kicking and screaming into his seventies (and losing his hair), he still thinks he is dashingly handsome—humor him.

GEORGIA R. BUNS

Georgia R Buns is a creature of mystery, and prefers to remain that way. Blank is based on a real life paranormal experience.

JOSEPH MULAK

Joseph Mulak is the author of Little Angels, Ashes to Ashes, and the short story collection Haunted Whispers, as well as close to twenty short stories published in various anthologies. He lives in North Bay, Ontario with his wife, Alicia. He has five children. You can buy his books, find out more about him, or just stalk him at www.josephmulak.com. He loves stalkers. They make him feel important.

PATRICIA LEE MACOMBER

Patricia Lee Macomber is the former editor-in-chief of *ChiZine*. She has been published in "Cemetery Dance" magazine and such anthologies as "Shadows Over Baker Street," "Little Red Riding Hood In the Big Bad City," and "Dark Arts."

Her novels include the Jason Callahan Psychic Detective Series, *Zombie: A Love Story, Casual Casualties, Love Lost, Stargate Atlantis: Brimstone & Remember Bowling Green – The Adventures of Frederick Douglass – Time Traveler* (With David Niall Wilson), and her newest novel *Star Quest: The Journey Begins*.

Currently, she lives in North Carolina with her husband, David, and their daughter Katie.

DAVID NIALL WILSON

David Niall Wilson has been writing and publishing horror, dark fantasy, and science fiction since the mid-eighties. An ordained minister, once President of the Horror Writers Association and multiple recipient of the Bram Stoker Award, his novels include *Maelstrom, The Mote in Andrea's Eye, Deep*

Blue, the Grails Covenant Trilogy, *Star Trek Voyager: Chrysalis, Except You Go Through Shadow, This is My Blood, Ancient Eyes, On the Third Day, The Orffyreus Wheel*, The DeChance Chronicles, including *Heart of a Dragon, Vintage Soul, My Soul to Keep, Kali's Tale, A Midnight Dreary* and the stand-alone spinoff *Nevermore – A Novel of Love, Loss & Edgar Allan Poe.* His novels in the O.C.L.T. series include *The Parting, Crockatiel,* and the novella *The Temple of Camazotz* He is also the author of the memoir / cookbook *American Pies: Baking with Dave the Pie Guy.* David can be found at www.davidniallwilson.com and can be reached by e-mail at david@davidniallwilson.com.

David lives in North Carolina with his wife, Patricia, their daughter Katie, and an ever-changing assortment of pets including (at least) five cats, a dog a chinchilla, a canary and a three-legged turtle.

RICHARD CHRISTIAN MATHESON

RC Matheson is a #1 bestselling author and screenwriter/producer *The New York Times* calls *"...a great horror writer."* He has created, written and produced acclaimed television series, films and mini-series, including his adaptation of Stephen King's *"BATTLEGROUND"* which won two Emmys. Matheson has had fifteen movies produced, including cult favorite *"Three O'Clock High"* and has worked with Steven Spielberg, Dean Koontz, Roger Corman, Tobe Hooper, Nicholas Pileggi, Stephen King and many others. Recently released is *"Nightmare Cinema"'s "MIRARI"* directed by Joe Dante. Matheson's dark, psychological stories appear in his three, critically-hailed collections *"SCARS And Other Distinguishing Marks", "Zoopraxis",* #1 Bestseller *"Dystopia"* and over 150 major anthologies, including many *"YEARS BEST"* volumes. He is the author of the highly-praised suspense novels, *"CREATED BY"* and *"The Ritual of Illusion."* Matheson is a professional drummer and studied privately with CREAM's Ginger Baker He is the president of MATHESON ENTERTAINMENT.

NORMAN SPINRAD

Norman Spinrad's multi-faceted career has spanned over fifty years as a legendary American speculative fiction author, essayist and critic, as well as an accomplished journalist, public speaker, songwriter, and radio show host. His fiction has won the Prix Apollo and the Utopial's LifeTime Achievement Award, and he has been nominated for the Hugo Award, multiple Nebula Awards, and numerous other awards. His books includes modern classics like *Bug Jack Barron, Agent of Chaos, The Star Spangled Future, He Walked Among Us, Pictures at 11,The People's Police, Osama,The Gun,* and many others.

Spinrad is also a screenwriter for feature film and television, and some consider his Star Trek episode, "Doom's Day Machine", to be one of the very best of the original series.

Spinrad's book *The Iron Dream* (1972) was described by Harlan Ellison as "disturbingly fascinating..."; his work has been described as "depraved, cynical, utterly repulsive" (Donald Wollheim), "delightfully bonkers" (Thomas M. Disch, and "extraordinary" (Ursula Le Guin).

Spinrad lives in Paris, France, and continues to write and publish internationally. He is also teaching himself to play keyboards.

MICHAEL PICCO

Michael Picco conjures his tales in his dimly lit, cozy studio in the high country of the Colorado Rockies. When he's not bathed in the glow of his computer monitor, he's out wandering through the forests, where you'll find him snapping photos or running from a bear. Michael loves collecting odd clichés, making people laugh, and strong, freshly-brewed coffee. He received his B.A. in writing from Western State College in Colorado. Michael's most recent release is *Scenes From The Carnival Lounge, A Collection of Odd Tales.* He was inspired to write *Hey Nonny Ding Dong...* after a conversation he had with a homeless man who claimed to be a retired Army sniper.

Curious about other Crossroad Press books?
Stop by our site:
http://store.crossroadpress.com
We offer quality writing
in digital, audio, and print formats.